SEVEN DREAMS

THE LOKANT LIBRARIES: 1

CHARLOTTE E. ENGLISH

1

Few aristocrats across the Seven Realms could match the importance of The Extremely Honourable Lady Fenella Chartre. She was the highest of the high; she knew it, and everybody else knew it too. Few would dare to compete with her for the first place at table, at even the most prestigious of dinner parties. No one would attempt to precede her out of a room. She secured the attentions of the most prominent gentleman present at any event, and without even trying. Her importance gathered around her like a cloak; it was evident in her every movement and gesture, every stitch of clothing that she wore, and every coil of her smooth blonde hair.

Equal in consequence was her brother, The Remarkably Honourable Edlen, Lord Bastavere. Fortunately, his height was a perfect match to his consequence, and permitted him to look down his long nose at the lesser persons around him without much straining his lordship. They made a handsome pair, everybody agreed, and had been enjoying the very best of society for some years.

Today, they had ventured beyond the borders of Irbel and explored into Nimdre. Their extremely large, thoroughly imposing and almost impossibly shiny carriage was making its way, at approximately half past seven in the evening, along a quiet but reassuringly well-kept road in northern Nimdre. It was drawn, of course, by a team of four high-stepping, perfectly-matched nivvens, their pale grey scales gleaming in the dying light. The destination of the noble pair was the grand country home of Dame Halavere Morann, a lady of lesser importance (naturally) but sufficient consequence to attract the interest of their lady-and-lordships. Lady Fenella reclined at her ease, gazing idly out at the darkening countryside as she reflected with satisfaction upon the delights of prestige, importance and superiority which she would enjoy at the Dame's autumn ball. Her brother wore the faintest hint of a scowl upon his noble features; he had, perhaps, been obliged to forego some more eligible plan in favour of this evening's entertainment.

'What a delight it shall be, I am sure!' said Lady Fenella, in the peachiest of plummy accents.

'A dead bore, I should think,' muttered his lordship in reply.

'Pish,' said Lady Fenella. 'You will be able to ignore at least half of the young ladies, and break the hearts of all the rest. You always enjoy that.'

Lord Bastavere ventured no response, and silence fell. Her ladyship resumed her lazy scrutiny of the countryside, and her dark eyes began to drift shut.

In the ordinary way of things, nobody would be so foolish nor so bold as to interfere with their lord-and-ladyship in any way whatsoever. Such a grand, large carriage may, in the course of ordinary logic, appear as a superb prize to adventurers, low-lifes and other such persons as that, but such had never been the experience of this noble pair. Their vehicles, their beasts, their garments and of course they themselves radiated such imperturbability, such an inflexible determination to carry all before them, that no one had dared cross them in the smallest respect.

Until today. Lady Fenella's reverie was rudely interrupted by a sudden lurch of the carriage as it swerved to one side, two of its wheels leaving the road altogether. After that it came to an abrupt stop, and the sounds of some loud altercation split the evening air.

Lady Fenella thumped her hand upon the roof of the carriage and called, 'Wendle! What has occurred?'

Receiving no response, and finding that the shouting continued unabated, her ladyship stuck her head out of the window of the carriage. She observed immediately that a desperate figure stood in the road not far away. The man was wearing the customary uniform of general depravity: dark colours, generally black, and a hooded cloak which admirably shrouded his features. His attire may, perhaps, be a little shabby, which suggested to her ladyship's keen eye that he was not the most successful of footpads. This impression was borne out by the disreputable condition of the rapier he wielded, though she could not deny that he wielded it with apparent skill. Her poor coachman, Wendle, was held at bay by the vicious weavings of this weapon as its wielder whipped it about in a tolerably threatening manner. Her footman stood at a little distance, obviously preparing to rush the swordsman in an attempt to disarm him.

'What is it?' said Lord Bastavere in a bored tone.

'Why, it is a hold-up!' replied his sister in accents of pure delight. 'A real one! Though I think it sadly disappointing. There is not even a pistol, only the shabbiest of rapiers.' She opened the door as she spoke and jumped lightly down into the road, taking all due care to hold the hem of her cerulean silk skirt out of the mud. 'Hallo!' she called, with a cheery smile. 'Goodness, I have never seen a real highwayman before! How very obliging of you to choose our carriage for your exciting adventure.'

The hood-shrouded head turned swiftly in her direction, and the highwayman's movements faltered in an instant of confusion. 'Stay back!' he shouted hoarsely, and in heavily accented Nimdren. 'I will kill your coachmen if anyone approaches me!'

'Of course, of course,' said Lady Fenella soothingly. 'It is our valuables you want, I suppose? Shall you be absolutely obliged to take my gown? It is undoubtedly fine, and would fetch a great price I am sure, but I am so very fond of it.' She stroked the beautiful silk as she spoke, heaved a long sigh and began to unlace the bodice.

This gambit confused her assailant very much, for he stammered one or two unintelligible things and blurted something wholly incomprehensible. This proved opportunity enough; Lord Bastavere, who had crept up upon the hapless highwayman unseen, grabbed him in a rough bearhug and shook him until he dropped his weapon. Wendle hastily retrieved it and took it well out of reach.

'Thank you, my dear,' said Lady Fenella, with the warmest of smiles for her brother. 'I would have been very sorry to part with my gown, I admit. Though to save all of our lives, I would have done it!' This last was added in laudably tragic tones, paired with a brave smile which quivered only the slightest bit.

Lord Bastavere made no reply, busying himself with securing the hands of the highwayman behind him. This appeared to cost him more effort than might be expected, given the tall and powerful frame his lordship enjoyed, and the shorter and undeniably thinner physique of the other. A wrestling match occurred, which Lord Bastavere appeared, incredibly, to be losing.

The reason for this soon became clear. The highwayman's body began to warp in the oddest way, shimmering and flickering in an alarming fashion. His strength appeared to grow by the second, and soon he threw off Lord Bastavere altogether and ran some few steps away.

Moments later, there stood not a man at all but a draykon. The beast was very large indeed, and appeared all the larger when he reared up upon his hind legs, flexing his vast, webbed wings and roaring a challenge at the carriage and all associated with it. His scales were a dark amber colour, a hue which her ladyship could not help finding utterly charming. He bore besides a long snout, vicious-looking teeth and wickedly curved, opalescent claws.

'A shapeshifter!' cried Lady Fenella delightedly. 'My word! Some say one meets with them everywhere these days, but I did not previously believe it to be true.'

The draykon roared again, and showed himself to be tiresomely determined to charge the carriage. This notion did not appeal very much to her ladyship. With a short sigh, she removed a compact voice-box from a pocket of her voluminous gown and spoke into it.

'Teyo, we're going to need you,' she said crisply in the Irbellian tongue. 'Be suitably terrifying.'

She put the voice-box away once more, and smiled calmly at the draykon. The creature was certainly enjoying his triumph: he amused himself with a bit more thrashing and roaring, flapping his sail-like wings in a manner he no doubt considered to be extremely alarming. In fact, it *was* rather alarming. If he chose to attack the carriage, considerable damage would no doubt follow. But he did not, which both relieved and puzzled her ladyship.

Lady Fenella and her brother stood side-by-side, watching.

After perhaps a minute, Lady Fenella removed an attractive, bejewelled timepiece from another pocket and glanced at it.

'What could possibly be keeping him?' she murmured.

'There he is,' replied his lordship, with a nod at the road behind them.

Another draykon came soaring down it, wings spread wide and mouth open in a shattering roar. This beast was considerably larger than the first, his scales gorgeously carmine in hue and his teeth and claws so very impressive, Fenella always felt agreeably faint on beholding them. The second draykon landed near to the first, the ground shaking with the impact, and screamed so violently at his smaller counterpart that the amber-coloured creature shuddered and transformed at once back into a man.

'I tried,' the man muttered as he held up his hands.

'Thank you, Teyo darling,' said Fenella, with a sweet smile.

The carmine draykon took off once more and soon disappeared into the encroaching darkness, tipping his wings to Fenella as he went.

'How very exciting!' Fenella said, approaching the hapless highwayman with a conciliating smile. 'Poor soul, am I right in thinking that you are sadly short of employment opportunities? I may be able to help you there!'

'Rena!' hissed his lordship incomprehensibly. 'We do *not* need another one!'

Lady Fenella ignored this magnificently, too occupied in shepherding her fine skirts over the muddy road to pay attention to her brother. 'I cannot stay for the present — a *most* pressing appointment to attend to, I'm sure you understand — but if you can contrive to remain here for an hour or two, we shall return for you with all possible haste.'

Her quarry merely stared blankly at her, his mouth hanging open a little.

'Quickly, quickly,' said her ladyship, just a little testily. 'I *did* say I have an appointment, did I not? And you have already sadly delayed us.'

'What kind of opportunity?' said the highwayman at last.

'One which would make the utmost use of your unusual talents,' she replied with a smile. 'Oh, I can always find a use for another shapeshifter. There can be no question about that! It would be of the utmost usefulness. And then there is your talent for disguise. I have seldom seen a woman masquerade more

5

successfully as a man.'

'Wha…' spluttered the dark figure. There was neither hoarseness nor gruffness in that single syllable; it was spoken instead in the unmistakeable high, clear tones of a woman. A fairly young one, most likely. 'How did you know?'

'My dear,' said Lady Fenella grandly, 'You are speaking to an expert.' Her voice, too, had changed; all of its exaggerated plumminess had disappeared, and a mild Irbellian accent had emerged. She made a curtsey of exquisite gracefulness, a single dimple appearing in one cheek with her mischievous smile, and straightened. 'We'll return,' she said. 'I would take you along in the carriage, only I would find that a trifle difficult to explain. The needs of the masquerade must always come first, as I'm sure you know.'

With this pronouncement, her ladyship got back into her spectacular carriage — the paint of which, upon closer inspection, might appear to be a little *too* shiny, and perhaps rather too new — and waited while her brother regained his seat beside her. She thumped twice upon the roof with a suitably commanding air, and the carriage drove off once more.

'Serena,' said Lord Bastavere. 'What was that about?'

Miss Serena Carterett shrugged. 'I never pass up the chance to recruit, Fabe. Good people are awfully difficult to find when you want them.'

Her brother, Mr. Fabian Carterett, merely sighed and flopped back into his seat. 'Whatever you say,' he replied.

Serena smiled.

They arrived at the ball later than planned, but since that only emphasised their importance, neither one of the siblings considered it at all to be regretted. In fact, many others had had the same happy thought, and their carriage was obliged to wait in line for some minutes before they could be gracefully ejected from it and welcomed into the house.

Dame Halavere's abode was sumptuous indeed. It bore a suitably symmetrical facade, was several storeys high, and constructed from an excessively attractive (and expensive) silvery-coloured stone. It was sizeable enough to contain twenty bedrooms at the least, and the grounds — though little of them could be seen in the darkness — were extensive. Serena gazed at the whole picture with undisguised covetousness for some moments before she ventured up the several steps to the entrance, her brother solicitously holding her arm.

Dame Halavere herself was stationed near the front of her grand hall, still poised to welcome her guests. She was aged somewhere in her thirties, Serena judged, with handsome features and the pure, snow-white hair that proclaimed her Lokant heritage. She wore it so proudly, in fact, that she had single-handedly overcome some of the wariness — nay, even prejudice — that had greeted the Lokants upon their coming to prominence within the Seven Realms. They were not native to Serena's world, and wielded strange and powerful abilities which bore little resemblance to the sorcerous magics which were familiar, and trusted, within the Seven. The draykoni, likewise, were but newly restored, though they had become steadily more prominent during the last two years. It fell to individuals such as Dame Halavere to overcome the natural cautions of an alarmed people, and since she wielded such fearsome weapons as a beautiful smile, an undeniably handsome cleavage and all the most desirable trappings of wealth, culture and sophistication, she was doing an admirable job of it.

Serena eyed her with some misgivings, watching closely as her hostess greeted those ahead with perfect graciousness and civility. Halavere was a high-ranking member of a new Lokant organisation. Its inevitably wordy name — the Lokant Heritage Investigation and Training Bureau — was typically shorted to the LHITB, or just the LHB. Dame Halavere had received significant training; Serena's sources reported that she was a strong medic, but showed little talent at the art of dominating the minds of others. This latter, of course, was responsible for much of the distrust aimed at the Lokants and their part-blood descendants in the Seven. Indeed, if Dame Halavere were skilled at such an art, she could force Serena to see whatever she wished her to see, concealing truths behind a species of illusion. Then, of course, it would be virtually impossible for Serena to discover anything at all about the questionable activities she strongly suspected Dame Halavere of indulging in.

Serena did not entirely trust her sources. If Halavere had concealed her talents in this area, it was better by far that she should never have reason to distrust Serena and Fabian.

Hence the masquerade. Serena gathered the silly, self-important and vivacious persona of Lady Fenella Chartre around herself, drew herself up to her full (albeit not especially impressive) height and stepped forward in her turn.

'Dame Halavere! Such a delightful ball! I am enjoying myself immensely and I have but just stepped through your doorway.' Serena curtseyed and simpered, as Fabian made his bow.

'Ah, the sumptuous siblings,' said Halavere, with an arch look at Fabian. He did make a very handsome lord, Serena had to admit, especially with that gorgeous blond wig. Ever quick to use every possible advantage, Fabian bestowed upon his hostess a silky smile in response, and held her hand just a little too long.

'You are most welcome, and I hope you will enjoy yourselves,' continued Halavere. With that they were dismissed; Halavere turned to greet the next guests in the line, and Serena and Fabian were free to wander into the rest of the house.

The ballroom was gloriously lit up with floating lanterns, and decked with wondrous flowers in hues of indigo, cream and gold. Strains of beautiful music drifted forth, and the air was filled with the delicious fragrances of flowers and edible delicacies. Serena could not repress her delighted smile as they entered, her gaze wandering from the many guests whirling about the floor, to the stunningly decorated walls and the vast bowls full of colourful punch standing on tables along one side of the room.

'Remember, we are *not* here to dance,' whispered Fabian, her delight evincing only a disapproving frown in response.

'But we must dance a little!' she whispered back. 'How very odd it will appear for us to attend a ball without dancing! We do have parts to play.'

'One dance, and you may dance with me,' Fabian conceded, and immediately led her onto the floor. The orchestra was playing a mellifluous waltz at that moment, which suited Serena perfectly. Her natural tastes for music, light, colour and liveliness led her to exult in all events of this kind, and ensured that Lady Fenella Chartre was one of her favourites of all the roles she played in the course of her duties.

She was, in truth, an agent of an investigative bureau in Irbel. Their organisation bore strong links to the government of her home realm, but was largely independent and funded by private individuals. Their acknowledged purpose was to oppose crime in all its forms, but its focus was upon organised crime, and upon one group in particular: the largest, most extensive and most ruthless of all the criminal organisations of the Seven.

They called themselves the Yllandu, which meant "Unspoken" in Ullarni. Serena supposed it was intended as a reference to the extreme secrecy of the organisation itself, and all of its activities. The name sounded absurd to her; she and her band tended to call them the Unspeakables instead, which amused them all greatly. But the Yllandu were no laughing matter. The organisation was vast, spanning all of the Realms except for desolate Orlind, and there was no low to which they would not stoop.

More worryingly, they had adopted the new Lokant and draykoni descendants with enthusiasm and had been attempting to recruit all of those who showed even the least skill in any related area. It had been whispered that they had even attempted to sway the founder of the LHB, Lady Evastany Glostrum herself, though of course her ladyship had proved impervious.

Dame Halavere probably had not. Her name had come up repeatedly in connection with several recent crimes, and though they were but rumours, Serena's superiors had judged it best to investigate. Word had reached them of a meeting that was to take place tonight, under cover of Halavere's grand ball. The topic under discussion was to be a new job — and not just any job. *This* job was extremely important, enormously lucrative, and to be entrusted only to the most talented, most loyal, and most reliable of the Unspeakables.

Unfortunately, nobody had any idea what the job *was*. It fell to Serena and Fabian to keep Halavere under close observation tonight, and attempt to overhear whatever was said at that meeting. There were only a few obstacles in their way: namely the presence of approximately two hundred other guests, the necessity of concealing themselves and their true purpose from their hostess, and the minor complication that they had no idea who Halavere might be meeting. Or whether she would even risk attending that meeting in person.

Fortunately, the Carteretts had one or two other colleagues stationed around the house tonight.

2

In the cloakroom of Dame Halavere's country mansion, two temporary members of staff were hard at work accepting the many cloaks, coats, mantles, hoods and scarves of their employer's guests, and assisting them in changing their outdoor shoes into dancing slippers. Teyodin Bambre was a little too tall to be strictly nondescript, but he had covered his shaggy, dark brown hair with a neat wig of an indeterminate hue and had adopted besides a bland expression perfectly suited to his role for the evening. A man of early middle years, he wore his age well, though there were a few tell-tale lines around his eyes and mouth. He attended to the gentleman guests with gracious solicitude; a worthy servant, but never so helpful as to excite comment, or to encourage anyone to remember him.

His colleague, Egg (or Egrenne, though she hated to be addressed by that name) performed the same service for the ladies. She was ten years younger than her associate, in truth, though she could have passed for a few years younger still. Her skin was also a few shades lighter than his darkish brown, though neither could be called pale. Her dark red hair was concealed beneath a black wig, she had bound almost flat the feminine assets which could not help but attract attention, and she was attired in the uniform livery of the Morann family. Teyo did not even glance at her as he went about his business, nor she at him; they were too well practiced at this art to betray any acquaintance with one another.

As Teyo worked, he set about committing to memory every face that appeared before him, together with any memorable details about that person and, if he could contrive it, their name. He also kept his ears open for any snatches of overheard conversation that might help him to determine who among Dame Halavere's guests was her appointed contact.

They had been assisting the guests for an hour already, and the task seemed endless. Just as the flow of ball attendees seemed to finally be slowing down, a fresh flood of them would burst through the doors, setting Egg and Teyo bustling once more. Teyo's memory was excellent, but even he was beginning to lose track of the many faces that had passed before his eyes. Most of the conversation he heard, moreover, was vacuous in the extreme and of neither use nor interest to him.

...delightful party... Dame Halavere so beautiful... goodness, but these shoes do pinch! I hope I shall be able to dance in them... careful with that, man, it is the finest silk! Who can that lovely young woman be, there in the violet gown? ...heard about Miss Galler? Cannot countenance how she can show her face... shabbiest of refreshments at Sir Tatton's last week, do hope Dame Halavere's will be better...

In addition to all of this, Teyo was also obliged to keep track of his companion, friend and co-spy, Jisp. The creature was tiny, lithe and orange-scaled, with a blunt snout and lively black eyes. The sticky yellow pads to her toes allowed her to climb anywhere and everywhere, and he had frequently found this to be a useful talent.

He had discovered his draykon heritage a year ago, and very suddenly. He had been wandering across a field, deep in thought, and abruptly he had not been human anymore at all. He did not know how his sudden transformation had come about — certainly through no will of his own — but he understood it to be an increasingly common occurrence these days.

He had received training since, and one of the best perks of his unexpected heritage was his ability to bond and communicate with animals. He and Jisp had formed a strong friendship soon afterwards, and they were greatly attached to one another.

Not much happening down here, she reported from somewhere beneath a pile of shoes. *These things stink.*

Okay, switch to the pockets, he instructed her. He could not, as a servant, risk going through the guests' pockets himself; if caught, he would be instantly dismissed and his part in the evening's job would be over. Jisp, however, was perfect for the task. She instantly busied herself with climbing the ranks of coats and cloaks which hung on racks behind him, and nosing her way into all the nooks and crannies they contained. She transmitted to him a series of mental pictures of everything that she found within: handkerchiefs, snuffboxes, an occasional pipe or pot of rouge. Nothing of interest.

And then: a note! Jisp painstakingly nosed her way over the scrawled words as Teyo fought to focus both on that and the shoes of the gentleman before him. *Midnight by the fountain,* it said. Teyo's heart beat a little faster. *Do not wear your...* oh. The next word was a vulgar term for women's undergarments.

Teyo muttered something under his breath as he hung up the next cloak. He was disappointed, though he couldn't help feeling a flicker of appalled fascination as well. Did the high-and-mighty truly attend grand society events without their underwear, and engage in scandalous trysts in their hosts' gardens? So much for all their vaunted propriety.

Jisp continued with her explorations without any further excitement. The flow of guests was at last beginning to wane, and Teyo was prepared to give up, when he noticed that Egg was trying to attract his attention. She made a surreptitious signal, which he translated as: Kitchens, half an hour.

Jisp had completed her survey of the pockets of Dame Halavere's guests, but she was so well entertained that Teyo left her to rummage as she wished. There was little danger of her being discovered, in spite of her bright colours; she had an unerring nose for danger and a remarkable talent for disappearing at a second's notice. He passed the appointed half-hour in the scrupulous performance of his duties, a footman to the core, and by the time it was over new guests had ceased to arrive, and Teyo was free to depart. He did so speedily, lest his temporary superior, the butler, appear at an inopportune moment and order him elsewhere.

The kitchens were in chaos, of course. A banquet for hundreds of people had to be prepared, and everything *must* be perfect. Regaled with the sights and aromas of myriad glorious dishes, Teyo was briefly sorry that it would not be possible for him to partake of it. But he was able to palm a tiny fruit tart on his way through, together with a second one for Egg. They were warm in his hand as he slipped through the rear door into the pantries, and down a flight of steps at the back.

He and Egg had explored the house earlier that day, and agreed upon a meeting point. A disused storeroom lay behind a broken door in the cellar. Egg had left the leaning door open several inches, and Teyo slipped inside.

It was almost fully dark. Egg had a tiny glow-lamp for purposes such as these, and she had muted its already subtle light by covering it with a lightweight cloth. Fine cambric, he judged, with a pretty lace border. She had filched a handkerchief from one of the lady guests.

'Resourceful,' he murmured, indicating the handkerchief with a nod.

Egg flashed her wide, mischievous grin. 'I am. Thank you. Find anything much?'

'A very, *very* steamy love-note,' Teyo replied, widening his eyes.

Egg coughed. 'Anything relevant?'

'About eighty snuffboxes and a truly appalling number of handkerchiefs. Oh, and Mr. Archiban Binker is to wed Miss Tia Wennan after all, though it was not thought that he would come up to the mark.'

Egg nodded wisely. 'Wonderful news. I was wondering when those two would get together. Meanwhile, I have been hugely successful.'

'In that case, you win food.' Teyo handed her a fruit tart, and devoured his own in one bite.

'Thanks,' Egg said, her mouth already full of pastry. 'Do I win two?'

Teyo shook his head. 'The degree of your brilliance has yet to be demonstrated. It is not yet certain that you merit two.'

'You merited one without doing anything at all!' Egg protested.

'That's different. I was the thief of this operation: I get spoils.' Teyo folded his arms.

Eg sighed. 'Fine. Come with me.'

This, Teyo had not expected. He followed her out of the pantry, keeping a cautious eye out for passing staff. Egg led him to the other side of the spacious cellar, and Teyo became gradually aware of a faint sound: the sound, perhaps, of somebody writhing about and trying, mostly unsuccessfully, to shout around some kind of obstruction in the mouth. Egg threw open the door to one of the liquor rooms and whipped the handkerchief off her light-globe as she did so, allowing its light to blaze much brighter.

The room beyond was full of fat wooden barrels, probably containing brandy. It also had an occupant. A man in groom's attire was lying face-first over one of the barrels, his legs and arms trussed up with something that looked suspiciously like stockings. Teyo raised an eyebrow at Egg, who shrugged.

'What the—' she said loudly as she stepped forward. 'Oh, my giddy goodness! Are you all right?' She had developed the broad vowels and drawling intonation of a local country lass, and when she ran forward to assist the captive, her demeanour was of shock and charmingly dim-witted concern. She soon managed to untangle the stocking which bound up the man's hands, while Teyo ripped away his gag and the bindings on his legs. He got a good look at the captive's face in the process, and understood at once why Egg had stuffed him in the brandy cellar.

'Of course I'm all right!' spat the man, and shoved past Egg without another word. He vanished through the door, leaving Egg to waggle her eyebrows at Teyo in an intolerably smug fashion.

Because Teyo had seen the man before, of course. His younger years had been neither as productive nor as respectable as he might have liked; he had, to his regret, been a member of the Yllandu. It was never easy to extricate oneself from such an outfit, but Teyo had managed it at last. He had offered himself to the Torwyne Agency of Irbel, and been accepted. For the past four years he had been working with Serena, Fabian and Egrenne to oppose everything the Unspeakables attempted to do in Irbel or Nimdre.

Egg's captive was Yllandu. He had joined the organisation just as Teyo was leaving, and the two had never been acquainted. He had a distinctive face, however: pale and violently freckled, with a nose that veered sharply to the left.

'And now we follow,' Egg said proudly, and darted after the escapee. Teyo wandered after, pausing only briefly when the returning Jisp opted to scarper up his trouser-leg.

Serena had danced once with Fabian, once with the lively and *very* handsome Lord Darnwell, and once each with Mr. Rostover and Mr. Brackly. 'Both *so* eligible,' she breathlessly confided to Fabian a little later, as she downed a glass of punch.

'Can you not stop dancing for five minutes?' he returned in a disapproving tone. His eyes scanned the crowd as he spoke, ostensibly gazing with suitably admiring intensity at all the prettiest young ladies present. Serena knew that he was actually keeping an eye on Dame Halavere.

'It must be my gown,' she said modestly, lightly touching the silk. 'It puts the gentlemen in such a *fever* of admiration, how can I be expected to resist?' She smiled winningly.

'We have work to do,' he reminded her in a low voice.

'I am working.'

'You're flirting.'

'That can be work.' Serena finished her punch, set down her glass and swapped with Fabian. It was his turn to busy himself about the punch-bowl, and hers to maintain a surreptitious scrutiny of Dame Halavere's movements, together with those of any other guest who might be behaving in unexpected ways. She noticed one gentleman — Trimble, his name was; an incorrigible libertine — slipping out of the rear door with Mrs. Vasher. Both were notoriously free with their favours, and Mrs. Vasher was doing far too much giggling for Serena's taste.

'Probably she is not even wearing underwear,' Serena muttered under her breath.

'What was that?' whispered Fabian around his punch-glass.

'Nothing.'

Nothing else untoward occurred. Dame Halavere was dancing with Sir Kunley Prosh, a gentleman of advancing years who Serena instantly dismissed as a candidate for intrigue. He was far too simple-minded. He danced rather poorly — only his great wealth made him tolerable either as a ball-guest or a partner, she suspected — and smiled at his pretty partner in such a fatuous way that Serena felt reassured: nothing of the remotest interest could be going on inside *that* head.

When the dance came to an end, Halavere rejected the invitation of the next gentleman to approach her and made her way towards the garden doors.

Two men came towards Serena at the same moment, their intentions writ large upon their amiable faces, and she made a noise of frustration. 'I should have brought Teyo into the ballroom,' she hissed at Fabian.

'What?' he blinked. 'Why?'

'Because then we could have pretended to escape into the garden for a daring tryst, and I would not be stuck with these people.'

'Would it have been pretend?' Fabian asked with interest.

'Naturally.'

'Probably?'

'We're going to have to do it the other way,' she sighed.

'Oh, no,' Fabian muttered. 'Please don't do that again—'

His entreaties went unheeded. Just as her first would-be dance partner arrived with proffered hand, Serena began to sway slightly on her feet, her hand lifting to her forehead with an intriguing little fluttering motion. 'Oh,' she whispered faintly, 'I do feel so very…'

She was not, in her weakness, able to utter another syllable before she sank into an elegant swoon. For a second, she thought that Fabian was not going to catch her after all. She shot him a glare from under her eyelids and, with a sigh, he broke her fall with every appearance of solicitude. Gone was Fabian Carterett, replaced by the perpetual boredom and faint, spoiled sneer of Lord Bastavere.

'Oh, no, is it the vapours again?' he murmured with becoming concern. 'My poor, dear sister. What could be causing these repeated fits? I do hope it is not anything fatal.'

Serena was too artfully unconscious to be able to attempt any reply, though she made a mental note to smack him for it later. A little crowd had gathered around her, thrusting several bottles of smelling-salts under her nose at once. The aroma made her cough, her eyes watered, and she was obliged to recover.

The operation proceeded with well-practiced ease from there. In a trice, Fabian had explained to the company with brotherly concern that his sister required a little air; he had elbowed away the solicitous advances of the gentlemen and fended off the (largely feigned) concern of the ladies. He gently shepherded Serena out into the gardens, reassuringly unaccompanied, and there she underwent an instant and miraculous recovery.

'You are so very *good* at that,' she said, beaming.

'I've had a lot of practice,' he said dryly, offering her his arm. 'I begin to think ballrooms are hazardous to your health. You cannot enter one without falling into a swoon.'

'Quite right. I will have to give up the dancing and the flirting, and leave them both to Egg.' She took his arm and they promenaded serenely through the darkened gardens, their path lit by way of dozens of light-globes floating just overhead.

It did not prove difficult to locate Dame Halavere. She had left a trail of heavy perfume, so powerful as to outdo even the exotic flowers for dominance. Serena followed her nose.

The garden was laid out in an ornamental arrangement, framed by tall hedges which divided it up into sections. Halavere's trail led through a corridor of red-blooming vines and past a grand marble fountain. Serena thought she could hear giggling coming from behind one of the hedges. Fabian tried to turn towards it, but Serena pulled him back, shaking her head.

'*Not* Halavere,' she muttered, with an expressive roll of her eyes.

Fabian snorted. 'I like this party.'

'I can't tell you how uninterested I am in hearing about that. Come on, this way.'

The soft scrunch of feminine footsteps on gravel sounded from somewhere ahead, and Serena and Fabian came to a halt. Peeping around a hedge, Serena observed Dame Halavere, but dimly visible in the moonlit darkness, lingering in a corner of the hedge.

'She's skulking,' she reported in a faint whisper.

'It's always so promising when they skulk,' Fabian replied with approval. He peered around Serena's shoulder and added, 'This is an especially promising skulk. She is certainly waiting for someone.'

'Undoubtedly,' Serena murmured. 'Perhaps we could talk about it later?'

Fabian gave one of his soft snorts, and subsided. They waited in silence, until Serena's straining ears caught the sounds of another set of approaching footsteps: heavier, probably male. The newcomer came into view moments later, and Serena could not repress a smile of mingled satisfaction and amusement. He was dressed as a groom, though his disguise was mediocre at best. He had none of the air of a man of the stables; he displayed the peculiar combination of swagger and furtiveness that marked out all the most desperate characters, and even the once-broken nose of a born brawler. It could virtually be considered a uniform among the Unspeakables. Why could criminals never display any imagination?

She waited in breathless anticipation, but to her disappointment, neither party spoke. The Desperate Character merely glanced about into the shadows in a disappointingly cursory fashion, and then handed something to Dame Halavere. What it was Serena could not, in the darkness, determine, but it seemed to satisfy the lady; she nodded, tucked the thing into a pocket of her gown without looking at it, and immediately withdrew. Serena feared for an instant that she would pass by them on her way back to the house, but she disappeared into the darkness on the other side of the hedge. The Desperate Character returned the way he had come, leaving Serena and Fabian alone.

Fabian stuck his hands into his pockets and stood for a moment in thought. 'Worth pursuing?' he eventually enquired.

Serena shrugged. 'Could've been anything.'

'A grocery list,' Fabian agreed.

'A recipe for hair pomade.'

'The name of his tailor.'

'A love note.'

'Mm,' Fabian said appreciatively. 'Scandalous.'

'We had better find out,' Serena decided. 'All that skulking has to indicate *something* juicy.'

'Has to.'

'But how to retrieve it? The pockets of a lady's ball gown are closely guarded.'

'Egg could do it,' Fabian suggested. 'Or Jispie.'

'True, but where are they? I don't want Halavere to have time to use or destroy whatever it is, before we can get to it.'

A hint of wariness crept into Fabian's tone. 'What exactly do you have in mind?'

Serena directed at him her most winning smile. 'Dearest Fabe, seeing as you are quite the handsomest of brothers—'

'Oh, no,' he said firmly, cutting her off. 'I am not seducing a woman again just so you can go rummaging in her pockets.'

'Actually, I thought that you would do the pocket-rummaging.' She paused. 'That came out a little wrong.'

Fabian gave one of his snorts of laughter, but he still shook his head. 'Absolutely not. Besides, if we don't have time to find Egg, what makes you think we have time for that?'

'All you have to do is dance with her. Come on!'

18

Fabian began to say something else, but Serena had already darted away in the direction Halavere had taken. She had learned the trick long ago of moving quickly and quietly on any terrain, gravel included, and she soon caught up with Halavere. Their hostess appeared to be making her way back to the ballroom, but slowly, and by a circuitous route. Serena and Fabian followed a cautious distance behind, keeping a close eye on her, but she met no one else nor did her hand ever stray to the pocket in which she'd secreted whatever her associate had given her. At last she disappeared back into the swelling music and welcoming lights of the ballroom.

'Go!' Serena hissed.

'Egg's probably already on it,' he protested.

'Egg could be doing a million other things right now.'

Fabian thought about that for a second. 'I don't really think that's possible, no.'

Serena gave him an inelegant shove in the direction of the ballroom. He gave a deep, long-suffering sigh, but he went. Serena trailed inside soon afterwards and observed, to her satisfaction, that Fabian had succeeded in securing Dame Halavere for a dance, and was whirling her around the floor. He was clearly exerting all his considerable powers to please, and not without success, for the lady's attention was fully focused upon him.

Serena drifted back to the punch bowls. She could rely on Fabe to get the goods; though he was not nearly so talented a pickpocket as Egg, he was certainly equal to this challenge. She was soon solicited for a dance herself, an invitation which she accepted, and a pleasant half-hour or so passed happily away. Fabian danced all the while with Halavere.

They met by the buffet table soon afterwards, and under cover of handing her a laden plate with all possible brotherly solicitude, Fabian hissed, 'Piece of paper. Blank.'

Serena almost dropped the plate. 'What?'

'Nothing on it,' he clarified.

Serena suppressed a sigh. 'I know what blank means. How can it be blank? Surely it is some kind of invisible message.'

'It's blank,' Fabian repeated.

Serena drooped over her plate of sweets, disappointed and puzzled. Had Halavere's contact deceived her somehow? Or did she know, or suspect, that she was under observation and had acted out the whole charade in order to deceive? Perhaps the real meeting was taking place somewhere else, or perhaps it was already over. What if she knew *who* was here to watch her? Serena thought not, but couldn't be sure.

'I think we'd better behave ourselves for the next while,' Serena said sadly.

Fabian sighed. 'How boring.'

On the other side of the garden, Teyo and Egg were particularly well-concealed. Teyo's draykon heritage granted him more than passable skill at sorcery, arts which had long been familiar and widely practiced across the Seven — even if their source had only recently come to be understood. He had cloaked them both in a patch of shadow, making them indistinguishable from the darkness around them. As such, it had been possible for them to creep up very close to Halavere and her contact without being seen.

They watched the exchange in silence, and a touch of disappointment. Halavere didn't even look at the piece of paper; she merely stuffed it into her pocket and walked off. Teyo had been hoping to see some kind of altercation, which might have revealed more about the purpose of the meeting and the extent of Halavere's involvement in Unspeakable business. He was obliged to content himself with the knowledge that her evening would grow somewhat complicated as soon as she realised the paper was blank.

'I'm going to follow him,' Teyo whispered to Egg, who agreed with a silent nod. They tailed the Unspeakable Gentleman all the way around the edges of the extensive gardens and up to the edge of the wide lawn that surrounded the house. It would be much harder to follow him across all that, and he suspected there would be little point; the man's purpose had apparently been fulfilled, he had no one further to meet and no other tasks to accomplish, and he was leaving. Teyo thought he could be left to return to whichever rat-hole he was crouching in tonight, and turned back to Egg.

'Thoughts?' she said.

'Think anything else is likely to happen tonight?'

'Her Dameship is due to throw a fit at some point, but I'm not sure we'll be able to catch that show.' This last was spoken with some regret.

Teyo nodded. 'We've got what we came for. Let's find Rena and Fabe and get out of here.'

Their associates were summoned by the simple means of sending Jisp into the ball room and up the legs of either Serena or Fabian, whichever she encountered first. This errand complete, Teyo and Egg retired to the gates to await the arrival of the stupendous Chartre/Bastavere carriage, which soon drew up. They piled inside, and Teyo sank gratefully down onto the seat opposite Serena.

'I had no idea the life of a footman was so exhausting,' he muttered, sagging. 'Two hundred cloaks later, and my arms hurt like—'

'Whiner,' muttered Egg.

'Only tell me you have something fabulous to report, and it will all be worth it,' Serena said. 'Fabe and I failed. We saw Halavere meet someone, but he apparently gave her a blank piece of paper. Maybe a decoy?'

Egg rolled her eyes and groaned. 'We've been working together how long? Four years, isn't it?'

Serena turned a hopeful gaze upon Egg. 'You found something?'

Egg gave a snort. 'What do you think I was doing while you were tearing up the ballroom? Knitting?'

Teyo gave her a reproachful glance, and she patted his knee in brief apology. 'Sorry, Teyo. I don't mean to imply that knitting isn't an exceptionally worthy pastime.'

Teyo nodded cool acceptance of this concession.

'You switched the paper!' Serena guessed.

'Of *course* I switched the paper,' Egg uttered with infinite weariness. She took the real paper out of her pocket and thrust it at Fabian, who was sitting opposite. Serena immediately craned her neck to look at it too.

'I caught Halavere's contact before the meeting ever took place,' Egg continued. 'He stuck out like a sore thumb, did you notice? Anyway, I got the paper off him after I tied him up and chucked him over a brandy barrel.'

Serena and Fabian were too busy consulting over the contents of the note to pay any heed to Egg's announcement, and she turned a piteous stare upon Teyo.

'There, there,' he said soothingly. 'I know you were brilliant.'

'I need a pay rise,' Egg muttered.

'So, this place,' Serena said. 'You two know who it belongs to, right?' She displayed the note, upon which was written the name Bellaster Park.

Teyo and Egg both shook their heads. 'High society is your field,' Egg said tartly.

'It belongs,' said Serena with a great sigh, 'to Baron Anserval.'

'Who?' said Teyo.

'Baron Farran Anserval!' Serena elaborated in a grand voice. 'The King of Pomposity! He's fabulously wealthy. He purchased his barony a few years ago and settled down in southern Irbel, at the incredibly ostentatious Bellaster Park. Since then he's devoted himself to buying basically everything of any value that comes in his way. The house is stuffed with rubbish by now.'

'What does Halavere want with any of that?' Teyo enquired.

'I don't know,' Serena said with a small frown. 'I might guess that he is an associate of the Unspeakables as well, but probably not? It looks more like he's a target. In which case, perhaps he's acquired something that Halavere wants — and, perhaps, that the Unspeakables want too.'

'A robbery!' said Egg in delight.

'Maybe.'

Teyo frowned. 'Private houses are difficult to infiltrate, especially these grand places. Any chance he'll be giving a ball soon?'

Serena said nothing, only sighed. Fabian answered instead, with a particularly fiendish grin.

'That won't be a problem,' he said.

Egg kicked him in the shins. 'Don't be mysterious. Tell us why it won't be a problem.'

'Because,' he said with relish, 'The good Baron Anserval happens to be horribly in love with Serena.'

'He is *not*,' protested Serena, sitting abruptly upright with bristling indignation. 'He is in love with Lady Fenella.'

'You're right,' Fabian apologised. 'A most vital distinction.'

Serena nodded gravely. 'I can't deny that it is a useful happenstance, but it is *most* tiresome. He really is the most dreadful bore.'

Fabian made a soothing noise. 'Perhaps Oliver won't wish us to pursue it.'

Teyo raised his brows. Oliver Tullen, their boss, was typically in favour of their pursuing everything that came up in connection with the Unspeakables; he would certainly send them after this little mystery. Serena knew it, too, for she turned upon Fabian a withering look and made no reply.

'Yes, I suppose you're right,' Fabian said, nodding wisely. 'You'll just have to steel yourself, sis, and put up with an hour or two of fervent admiration.'

'*Which* hour or two?' Egg demanded. 'We have only a place. No date or time, or anything to tell us what's happening there or when. And we haven't got much time to figure it out. Switching the paper won't slow Halavere down for long. She'll wring the information out of somebody soon enough.'

'Stake-out,' said Teyo.

Egg sighed. 'I suppose.'

'No matter,' said Serena with a brilliant smile. 'There are more of us, now, after all! Many hands make light work, and all that.'

Teyo blinked. 'What?'

Serena beamed at him. 'It's time to go and pick up our new recruit.'

3

When the carriage arrived at the site of the ill-fated holdup, Wendle slowed it to a near-crawl, as per Serena's instructions. She waited expectantly, but nobody hailed the carriage, and it did not stop to collect anybody. She unfastened the window and stuck out her head, hoping to catch sight of a dark figure lurking in the moonlight.

The road was empty.

'Has he fled?' said Fabian, with too evident satisfaction.

'She,' Serena corrected. 'And yes, it looks like she did.' She sat back, disappointed.

'You mean we're not getting an inept highway robber on the team?' Egg said, with awful sarcasm. 'How shall I bear my disappointment?'

'We're not getting a second shapeshifter on the team,' Serena corrected.

Egg shrugged. 'We have Teyo.'

'Who may appreciate some help in that area, from time to time.'

'So? Ask Oliver to find us someone. You can't just pick people up off the road.'

'I really don't see why not,' Serena murmured. She glanced at Teyo, hoping for some support, but he only gazed back at her thoughtfully, and said nothing.

Fabian thumped the roof of the carriage in the signal to drive on, but at that moment something caught Serena's eye outside the window, and she threw open the door. 'Wait!' she called, though whether to Wendle or to her new recruit, she couldn't say.

Both obeyed her. Wendle drew the carriage to a complete stop, and Serena jumped down to find a slight, dark figure a few feet away. The person in question looked Serena's way, hesitated, and then turned and ran.

Serena swore. She couldn't give chase, not in her voluminous ball gown.

'I'll get her,' said Teyo behind her. Serena heard the thump of his feet as he jumped out of the carriage and he passed her, running at full tilt. He soon caught up to the fugitive. Serena watched with a little anxiety; she had seen that Teyo's quarry could use a blade. Would she attack him? She couldn't tell, in the darkness, whether the girl had tried, but Teyo soon reappeared, leading the girl with her hands secured behind her back.

'Don't take it amiss,' he was saying in his low, calming voice. 'No one's going to hurt you.'

'Oh? Then why am I restrained?' growled the girl, though she made no attempt to escape. 'Doesn't look like I have any choice here.'

'You do,' Teyo replied. 'Hear the lady out. If you want no part of it after, then off you go.'

The girl squinted suspiciously at Serena, who smiled reassuringly. 'Come into the carriage,' she said, 'and I'll tell you what this is about.'

'Oh, no,' said the girl, shaking her head. 'You're not getting me in there.'

'Then we'll talk out here,' said Serena easily. She found a light-globe in one of her pockets and let it go. It immediately floated up a couple of feet and began to shine nicely, allowing the girl to see Serena's face. And vice versa, she'd hoped, but the girl still wore a mask and a hood.

'You waited for us,' Serena said. 'Why?'

'I need work,' the girl replied bluntly. 'But when I seen that carriage again, I changed my mind. What do the likes of the aristocracy want with me? Nothing good, can't be.'

'We aren't aristocrats,' Serena said. 'It's just an act. We were out on a job tonight, and it was a useful cover.'

'What job?'

'Espionage,' Serena said with a broad smile.

'You aren't spies,' said the girl. 'That's ridiculous.'

'No, true. We aren't, precisely,' Serena agreed. 'We do espionage sometimes. We also do breaking and entering; retrieval of valuable objects (which some lesser-minded persons sometimes call "theft"); interception and restraint of dangerous persons (which is sometimes known as "abduction"); and, umm… there's more.'

'Thrilling heroics,' said Teyo.

'Oh, yes! Plenty of that.'

'So you're crooks,' said the girl.

'No!' said Serena with a laugh. 'Goodness, no. Or… I mean, some of our methods aren't always wholly *legal*, but we aren't crooks. We *catch* the crooks.' This pronouncement produced an immediate increase of alarm in her reluctant audience, and Serena added hastily, 'We aren't the authorities either! We help them. Sort of.'

'You're making a complete mull of this, Ren,' came Egg's voice from inside the carriage.

Serena sighed. 'It's always so hard to explain.'

'Well, you've caught me,' sighed the girl, sagging in Teyo's grip. 'What happens now?'

'We weren't trying to catch you,' Serena hastened to clarify. 'We're trying to recruit you.'

'*You're* trying to recruit her,' muttered Egg. 'Or him, or whatever.'

'Fine. I'm trying to recruit you,' said Serena. 'You've got some skills we can use.'

'Yeah? And my current occupation as a robbing thief doesn't bother you?'

'Half of us have similar backgrounds.'

'You?' said the girl with obvious scepticism.

'No, not me. Some of the others.'

The girl twisted her head to regard Teyo with what was probably a questioning look. He remained impassive, however, and said nothing. Teyo wouldn't readily talk about his past even with his friends, let alone a stranger.

'Will there be food?' the girl said abruptly.

Serena blinked. 'Why, yes. Yes, of course we'll feed you.'

'Every day?'

'Three times a day. More, if you like.'

The girl considered this. 'Somewhere to sleep?' she added.

'Somewhere to sleep. Your own room, most of the time. Food, shelter, clothes. Pay.'

The girl's eyes widened at this. 'All that *and* you're going to pay me?'

Serena frowned. 'Of course. That's how employment works.'

The girl muttered something incomprehensible, then shrugged. 'Okay, I accept.'

'That's great!' enthused Serena.

'Why?' said Teyo softly.

The girl shrugged. 'Sounds too good to be true, but whatever? I got few choices.'

Teyo said nothing, but let the silence stretch.

'I was part of a gang,' muttered the girl. 'Back in Irbel. We weren't much, but we did all right. Then I Changed, for the first time. I couldn't help it! I didn't even know I could. They were afraid, and they kicked me out.' Her voice held bitterness and weariness, and for the first time Serena realised that she might be very young indeed. 'I tried to manage on my own, but they spread the word around and nobody would help me. So I've been on the road ever since.'

Serena sighed inwardly. The arrival of draykoni shapeshifters hadn't pleased everyone. Some welcomed them with interest, fascination and awe, and openly cultivated their powers. Others viewed them with extreme distrust and, in some cases, open fear. A small but lethal band of disgruntled draykoni had launched a war against the realm of Glinnery two years ago, and though they had been defeated, the damage they had wrought had been considerable. Not everyone forgave that, or forgot.

Serena didn't think this girl was dangerous, however; she had quickly capitulated to Teyo's superior strength, even in draykon form.

'To us, your draykoni heritage is an asset,' she said with a smile. 'As you might guess from Teyo, here.'

'You're Teyo?' the girl said over her shoulder, and the big man murmured assent. 'Okay. So it's nice to meet another draykon, *and* some people who aren't going to try to kill me for it, but do you think you could let go of my hands? You're hurting.'

Teyo stepped back at once. Serena waited, momentarily afraid that the girl might take flight. She did not, however. She stood there, rubbing her wrists in silent thought for several moments. Then she dragged off the dark hood that covered her hair, and pulled away the mask. Serena studied her face with interest. She was very young; perhaps only seventeen, or even less. But she was tall, and fairly well-grown, which accounted for her ability to pass as a man — though where she had learned to mimic the movements, speech and mannerisms of a young male, Serena would be intrigued to discover. She had spoken of Irbel, but her colouring suggested strong Nimdren heritage: she bore paler skin than was common in the Daylands realms, and her grimy, wind-tossed hair looked very pale in the darkness.

'I'm getting in the carriage now,' the girl announced. 'It's cold out here.'

Serena grinned and stepped back, holding the door for her new colleague. 'Welcome to our little team,' she said. 'May we know your name?'

The girl hopped nimbly inside and grabbed a seat in the corner, as far away from the others as possible. 'Anders,' she said.

Serena frowned. 'That's your name when you're being a man, isn't it? What about your real name?'

There was silence for a while, and Serena thought she wouldn't answer at all. At last, though, she said in a whisper, 'Iyamar.'

It had probably been a long time since she had used the name, Serena guessed. Left alone and fending for herself at such a young age, she had probably found it safest to maintain her masculine masquerade at all times.

Teyo and Serena piled back into the carriage, and it proceeded on its way once more. Introductions were made all around. Egg had grown a little more gracious since hearing Iyamar's story, though she obviously still harboured some distrust. Serena expected indifference from Fabian, but to her relief he was coolly friendly to his new colleague.

'What if she's Yllandu?' Egg whispered to Serena, while Teyo engaged Iyamar in conversation. 'She could be a plant.'

'I don't think so,' Serena whispered back.

'But what if she is?'

'Then Oliver will soon find out.'

The Torwyne Agency owned numerous properties across Irbel

28

which were available for the use of their employees; Serena's team rarely had to travel far to reach one. At present they were based just over the Nimdren-Irbellian border in a town called Vallune, and thither they retreated with all possible speed. It was always a disconcerting experience, crossing from Nimdre into Irbel at night. Irbel was a Dayland realm, which meant that a permanent cloak of daylight was maintained during the night-time hours. It never grew dark in Serena's home realm, only dimmer. Nimdre, however, had no such magical constructs, choosing to maintain a traditional day-night cycle. Serena and her team passed from deep darkness into the soft, golden glow of Irbel's Day Cloak in an instant, and all were obliged to shut and shade their eyes for a few moments until they grew used to the sudden influx of light. Serena welcomed it, once her eyes had adjusted; she had grown up in permanent sunglow, and sometimes found it hard to cope with the velvet darkness of Nimdren night.

The Daycloak had been created many generations ago. Its purpose was to provide an ideal habitat for specific, and numerous, plants and animals which originated from the Upper Realms (or, as the draykoni were now calling it, Iskyr). This place existed outside the Seven Realms, on another plane entirely — though it was adjacent to, and accessible from, any place within the Seven by way of gates which sometimes opened up. There were multiple suns up there, and as such, darkness never fell; its native flora and fauna were dependent upon the strong sunlight, and quickly withered away without it.

The realm could be dangerous, and it had long ago been decided that it was far more expedient to bring the vital, medicinal plants and most useful (or desirable) animals down to the Seven, rather than sending regular expeditions up to gather them. And so, the Day Cloak had come into being, along with the Night Cloak, in other parts of the world, for there was a mirror realm known as the Lowers in which there was no sun at all.

The draykoni had now settled in both places, and were, by all accounts, rapidly taming those realms. People spoke of imminent trade agreements between the different worlds, which may someday render the Day and Night Cloaks unnecessary. For the time being, however, they remained in place, and Irbel knew nothing of darkness.

Most of Serena's team were Daylanders like herself, and used to the eternal light. Teyo was the only exception, hailing originally from Nimdre. It had taken him years to get used to sleeping in full light, and he still wore a dark sleep mask sometimes.

Vallune was a pretty, rural place, and Serena had been pleased to choose it as their headquarters for the present mission. It was within reasonably easy reach of Iving, Irbel's capital city where Oliver Tullen was based, and also within reach of Dame Halavere's country estate. They were staying in a small, unassuming little house on the edge of town. The house was narrow, but three storeys high, with a timber frame and white-washed walls. The streets around it were charmingly cobbled, and behind it there was nothing but serene fields. It possessed an air of quiet, comfort and peace which Serena found soothing to return to.

Iyamar stared at the house for some moments before she went inside, her expression unreadable. Serena wondered how long it had been since she had slept in a house, and in a proper bed. It gave her some pleasure to assign the girl her own room, a neatly-kept chamber with fresh bedding and a basin of clear water for washing.

The rest of the team retired to their assigned chambers with obvious relief. It was past three in the morning, the job had been a long one, and Serena's detour regarding Iyamar had delayed them still further. She could not regret it, in spite of the delay. She understood Egg's concerns, but her gut feeling told her that Iyamar was a valuable find. She only hoped that Oliver would agree.

The last thing she saw before she fell into her own bed was Teyo, wandering down the hallway with his sleep mask in one hand and a bundle of knitting in the other. He gave her a tiny, lopsided smile on his way past, in which she read a mixture of amusement and resignation. Did that mean he approved of Iyamar, or not? Teyo was so hard to read.

Serena shut her door on him, and went to bed.

Serena dragged herself out of bed early the next morning, though she would have delighted in a longer rest. Her team had been extremely busy of late; she had been playing three different roles regularly, and there had been little opportunity to rest.

Perhaps, she thought with faint hope, the matter of Halavere Morann would soon be resolved and she could apply for a bit of leave.

Everyone else was sluggish as well, apparently, for she wandered downstairs to find a deserted ground floor. They were still sleeping, most likely, except for Teyo. His history with the Unspeakables was a source of eternal regret to him, but it did furnish them with one advantage: he had retained one or two contacts within the organisation, and once in a while they were willing to take the risk of sharing information with him. The current job could scarcely be completed without more details, and Teyo would have left before dawn in an attempt to secure it. She quickly crossed her fingers, wishing him success.

She took a cup of tea and a bread roll through to her favourite window seat, and discovered Iyamar huddled behind the curtain. The girl was fast asleep, and in repose she looked so very young that Serena began, for the first time, to doubt her judgement in hiring her. Was it work she needed, or something else? Care, perhaps? A foster family?

No, perhaps not. Even in sleep, there was a mulish set to Iyamar's pointed chin. She wanted work, and she wouldn't readily accept anything else, Serena guessed. Certainly nothing that would threaten her independence.

Still, she was young. She proved to be almost as pale-skinned as a Darklander, which was rare in Irbel; perhaps she had mixed heritage. Her hair was very pale, too; not the pure, Lokant-white one sometimes saw, but pale blonde. Her features were curiously neutral, neither pretty nor plain. A blessing, Serena knew, if one wished to pass for a man. Serena's own features were too decidedly feminine to permit such a masquerade easily.

She sat quietly, drinking tea and savouring her breakfast, until she heard Teyo's soft footsteps behind her. She turned with a smile, and a finger to her lips. His brows rose at the caution, but when he saw Iyamar curled up in the corner of the window, he nodded and gestured Serena into the kitchen.

'Did you learn anything?' Serena asked, keeping her voice down.

'Bits and pieces,' Teyo rumbled in reply. 'Most of it useless, except maybe for one thing: there's a rumour that Halavere's after some kind of key.'

'Oh? A key to what?'

Teyo shrugged. 'Nobody knows. She used Pietre Grine — that's the "stablehand" we saw last night — to track it down, and apparently he succeeded.'

Serena nodded slowly. 'Baron Anserval's got this key, then, whatever it is. We'd better try to warn him.' She heaved a great sigh as she said it: there was little chance that the Baron would see it as anything but unwelcome interference, so it would be an unpleasant task. She felt an obligation to try, not least because it might make her job easier later. Whatever this key was, Halavere couldn't be permitted to walk off with it.

'I wanted to see Oliver today, but that won't work,' she sighed. 'We need to get a watch on Anserval's house immediately. She won't delay long before she goes after this key.'

Teyo nodded, saying nothing. He looked as tired as she felt, Serena thought, surveying him with some concern. He was taller than she, a large man with broad shoulders and a big, brawny build that would soon turn to fat, if he weren't so active. Those shoulders were a little slumped this morning, however. His shaggy brown hair was more disordered even than usual, and the shadows beneath his eyes were deep and dark. At better times, Teyo bore a youthful vigour which belied his forty-something years, but today he looked every one of them.

All her team needed a break, she knew, but there was little chance of that for a while. She wanted to speak of it, but Teyo didn't welcome that kind of solicitude, so she merely said: 'Have you eaten? There's tea as well.'

Teyo accepted these offers with quiet gratitude, and Serena silenced one or two of her worries by ensuring that he was, at least, decently fed. Jisp clambered onto the table top as well and partook of a sumptuous meal of fruit, enjoying an occasional caress from Teyo as she did so. Serena smiled to see it, knowing that the two of them were probably conversing about something or other within their own minds. It made her a little bit envious, sometimes, for she had no special or magical abilities of her own. It reassured her to know that Teyo had that kind of companionship. He was a quiet man and somewhat withdrawn; always friendly and obliging, but close to no one.

She drank a second cup of tea, sitting at the table in silence with Teyo as she turned over the upcoming task in her mind. She could take on the duty of warning the Baron herself, though she would not be able to do so in the role of Lady Fenella, and it would be advantageous for her to appear in that character. Egg and Teyo would have to take that duty, then, and afterwards infiltrate the house in the guise of servants, or something else. She would leave that to them.

Fabian would accompany Serena herself, which left Iyamar unaccounted for. It was far too soon to take her out on a job, but what else could be done with her? Serena dared not leave her behind, not least because she was afraid that the girl would not be there when they returned. Her doubts of last night had not been wholly assuaged by the explanations and stories she'd been given. Besides, Iyamar needed help. Serena couldn't guess at the whole of her story, but she sensed that there was more, and her newest recruit obviously was not in the best shape.

Could she entrust her to Teyo? As a fellow shapeshifter, he seemed to be the obvious choice. But he had frightened Iyamar in his draykon shape — indeed, that had been the whole point — and Serena had noticed that the girl had kept as much distance as possible between herself and Teyo last night.

Egg was a brilliant woman, extremely talented at her job and wholly reliable, but patience was not her strongest point. Nor was Fabian likely to be the most understanding of companions for Iyamar; he could be hasty, even rash, sometimes, and though he was not insensitive, he would forget that Iyamar might need support.

That left Serena herself. She sighed inwardly, puzzling over the question of how to keep Iyamar with her without breaking character as Lady Fenella. She could be dressed up as a footman, probably, for she would easily pass as a boy. That would have to do. Wendle could keep an eye on her while Serena was in the house with the Baron.

Teyo finished his repast and sat back in his chair. Serena realised he was watching her with one of his impassive expressions, totally unreadable. She lifted a brow at him.

'Figured everything out?' he enquired.

Serena nodded, and sipped her tea. 'I think so.'

'Of course you have,' he said, with a hint of a smile. Then, with a tired sigh, he levered himself up from the table. 'I'll be ready to leave in twenty minutes,' he said. 'I'll get the others up.'

Serena smiled her thanks and left the table. She poured the remains of her tea away with some regret, wishing she could linger over it, but it couldn't be helped. Time to rally the team and go.

4

Baron Anserval was sitting at his ease in a particularly fine wing-back chair, his attention wholly occupied by the delicate antique book he was cradling upon a pillow on his lap. He was surrounded by antiques, in fact; the chair in which he reclined was a velvet-upholstered fancy, more than two hundred years old and displaying an excessively fine claret colour. A matching chair and divan stood nearby, standing at elegant angles to a pleasingly elderly carpet of lively hues. The walls of his study were lined with expensive bookcases, each shelf well-filled with agreeably faded and crumbling tomes, and his cabinets bristled with rare and fine ornaments. It gave him the greatest satisfaction to sit and admire his collection, and also furnished him with a pleasing sense of superiority towards those who had not the fortune to be so well-provided with antiquities as himself.

He gently turned the pages of the book upon his lap, his newest acquisition. The brittle parchment was protected from his hands by way of the thin, white cotton gloves he conscientiously wore; after all, if one was to accept the stewardship of such a broad collection, one must likewise accept the responsibility of caring for them suitably. The Baron took all such obligations very seriously indeed. He was also ready, at a moment's notice, to regale any interested parties with a detailed history of every item in his study; indeed, in his entire collection.

And everyone, he had long since concluded, felt an interest in antiquities, for his lectures had always been greeted with very flattering attention. It behoved the privileged to share their rarefied knowledge with the improperly educated, and the Baron took this obligation very seriously as well.

Not, of course, that he had any intention of reading this book, or any other that presently stood upon his bookshelves. Though he naturally possessed the keenest interest in the refined and scholarly pursuit of reading, not for the world would he subject his precious and fragile tomes to the punishing interference of page-turning. At present, he was cheerfully engaged in viewing some one or two of the illustrations that graced the pages of his newest prize, before he returned it to its proper station upon the shelf, behind its protective glass covering.

He had not yet completed this task when his butler arrived at the door to his study, which was standing ajar, and knocked delicately upon it. He looked up with a faint frown, surveying his employee over the top of the professorial glasses he had elected to wear.

'A lady and a gentleman to see you, my lord,' said that worthy person.

'But what are their names, Barrage?' said the Baron testily. 'I trust I am acquainted with these people?'

The butler gave a slight cough. 'I believe not, my lord. They are emissaries from the Bureau, so I understand.'

The Baron's frown grew deeper. 'Oh! The Bureau. You misled me when you termed them a *lady* and a *gentleman*. One does not expect agents of the *Bureau* to bear any proper eminence at all. What is their business?'

'They chose not to divulge that to me, my lord,' said the butler with an apologetic bow. 'The matter is, I gather, somewhat urgent.'

The Baron gave the weariest of sighs and carefully closed his treasured book. 'Let them come in,' he instructed, and his butler discreetly withdrew.

He had no notion at all what the Lokant Heritage Bureau might want with him, but it did not take him long to venture a guess. Perhaps he had inadvertently acquired something which was of interest to the Bureau, or possibly even of use. He could not consider selling any piece of his collection, of course, but it would be amusing to field — and summarily reject — a flattering offer. He waited in pleasant anticipation of such a treat, and soon enough he heard heavy footsteps approaching.

No refinement at all, he thought with pleasant satisfaction. Only the very common walked with such a laboured tread. The two agents presented themselves at his door an instant later, and he took a few moments to observe them at his leisure.

The first to enter was a female. She was of barely moderate height, with a thin, wiry frame. Her drab brown hair was cut unappealingly short, which he hated to see in women, and her features were unremarkable. She was clothed in the nearest thing the Bureau had to a uniform, namely a dark blue tunic and matching trousers, with a plain white shirt underneath, and black boots. She bowed to him with neither expression nor air, and stood with her hands behind her back.

Her associate proved to be male, and much taller — taller even than the Baron himself, which he did not view with much favour. This fellow had a little more countenance, he thought. The man's face was expressive, though his dark eyes bore the same bland expression as his colleague. He was a partial Lokant, judging from the pure white hair which crowned his head; though undoubtedly over forty, he was by no means old enough to have acquired such a colour by natural means.

Overall, the Baron was not impressed. Such a colourless pair he had rarely seen, even among the Bureau. They scarcely possessed a memorable feature between them. He smiled upon them with gracious condescension, aware that to find themselves in such surroundings must feature as a high treat with them.

'It is always a pleasure to welcome our excellent friends from the Bureau,' he said mendaciously as he rose from his chair, setting his precious book carefully aside. 'What is the nature of your business here?'

The female was casting surreptitious looks around his study, he observed. He was pleased to note such an apparent interest in his treasures, though she could not be expected to know anything about them. 'We come bearing a warning,' she said, focusing her attention upon him. 'We have received information that something among your recent acquisitions has attracted the attention of a Lokant of known criminal connections, and we believe that your house may stand at risk of a robbery.'

This confident pronouncement somewhat took the Baron

aback, especially since it was delivered without an ounce of the deference which ought to be due to his position. His brows snapped together, but before he could speak the woman's associate stepped in.

'Your house is very well secured, my lord, we can see that at a glance. Our superiors, however, judged it best to ensure you were aware of the increased risk, in case you would wish to make further arrangements.'

This speech was much more satisfactory, and uttered together with a pleasing little bow. But the man's superiority of manner did little to convince the Baron. 'My good man, do you have the smallest idea how many objects of value are housed here?' he demanded. 'The combined worth of all my treasures would buy your life many times over, I make no doubt. It would not be the first time my beauties have drawn the avarice of low persons, and I have spared neither effort nor expense in protecting them. What, I ask you, do you imagine there is left to do?'

'An upgrade to your security arrangements, perhaps,' ventured the male one. 'Alarms, locks, everything. Lokant technology can be difficult to defend against, and—'

Here the Baron felt obliged to cut the man short. 'My systems are upgraded every six months,' he said with a dismissive wave of one manicured hand. 'I employ the very best locksmiths, engineers and sorcerers, naturally. There is no more to be done *there.*'

'Increased personnel,' said the female. 'Lokants are extremely adept at infiltration through arts we cannot match, and it's hard to catch them—'

'I have plenty of personnel,' said the Baron.

'The Bureau would be more than happy to assign some of its best security operatives to this case,' said the man. 'They would be at your disposal upon indefinite secondment, and they are well trained in countering Lokant arts—'

'Out of the question,' said the Baron crisply. 'I employ a great many security personnel, all of whom are chosen individually by my chief of security. I cannot countenance the admission of strangers into my private household, no matter who vouches for them. I am surprised it could be suggested.'

He trusted that such a decided statement would silence their impertinent suggestions, but it did not! They had more to advance. The Baron became engrossed in the examination of his perfect fingernails and heard very little, until the word "key" caught his attention.

'I possess no keys,' said the Baron promptly. 'Except those which open my own doors, of course, all of which are perfectly plain and ordinary.'

His visitors exchanged an indecipherable look; protested; asked further questions, and made more suggestions. He had borne enough, he felt, with rising irritation, and he put a stop to any further communications with a few brusque words.

He thanked the well-meaning persons civilly enough. He was a man of breeding, and would expect nothing less of himself. They were wise enough not to press the issue, and they took their leave soon after. The female one did not make him a bow even upon leaving, which deepened his displeasure considerably. He made a mental note to send a letter of complaint to Lady Glostrum at his earliest opportunity. She was a sensible woman, and if he just gave her a hint, he had no doubt she would act upon it at once.

Teyo took off the white wig as soon as he had got beyond Baron Anserval's spacious grounds. It made for a risky masquerade, as it did not take much for a true Lokant (or even a partial, sometimes) to realise that the white-haired pretender before them possessed no actual Lokant abilities. Besides, it made him feel conspicuous, and he had never appreciated that feeling.

Egg stalked beside him, rigid with irritation. She had no patience for foolishness, and was easily riled when faced with such fatuousness as the Baron had displayed. But Teyo found it more amusing than annoying. Such incredible self-satisfaction was usually the product of a remarkable degree of ignorance, and he couldn't help but marvel at it. At least the Baron seemed to be enjoying himself.

Serena had been right to despair of the success of their errand, but she had also been right to insist upon it. The fool had been warned; if he chose to do nothing with their information, he could have no grounds to complain once he had lost the sought-after, if mysterious, artefact.

And lose it he would. Serena was determined to prevent Halavere's acquiring the key, whatever it was, but she had no interest in leaving it in the Baron's possession either. She meant for the team to secure it themselves, and Teyo fully agreed with her. Whatever this key may be, and whatever it proposed to open, if it was of interest to the Unspeakables then it was of interest to them.

The Baron's emphatic declaration that he possessed no such key gave him pause. It had not appeared to him that Anserval was dissembling. Probably he was telling the truth, which mean that either he had lost touch with some parts of his collection, and had forgotten about a key; or that the key did not especially resemble a key, and might be mistaken for something else.

Or that his information was incorrect, he thought sourly. His contacts were not always reliable. They meant well, or so he believed, but they could be mistaken. Or, perhaps, this key they spoke of was part of some other operation, and nothing at all to do with Dame Halavere.

No matter. They had to proceed with the information at hand, and hope for the best. The fact that even the Baron had no idea which object Halavere might be after was a problem, though. Anserval's house was stuffed to the rafters with trinkets; how could they possibly expect to identify which was the one Halavere wanted?

'Pompous idiot,' muttered Egg. Teyo grunted a wordless agreement.

A carriage stood waiting for them in a side road just out of sight of Anserval's imposing manor. Unlike Serena's ladyship-coach, as she called it, this one was plain black and unmarked, and drawn by a plain, unremarkable pair of nivvens. Wendle sat comfortably sprawled upon the box, the reins held idly in one hand. He tipped his hat to Teyo and Egg as they got inside and shut the door behind them. Teyo realised belatedly that the footman perched unobtrusively at the back was their new teammate, Iyamar. He would have sworn that the footman was indeed a man, in spite of his prior knowledge; nothing at all would betray her true identity otherwise, save perhaps for the curious look she had given Teyo and Egg as they disappeared inside the carriage.

This coach was roomy inside, though never quite roomy enough for their purposes. Teyo swapped his white wig for a plain, straw-blonde one he dug out of one of the boxes stashed between the carriage's seats. His Bureau tunic and trousers came off, to be stuffed hastily inside the costume box. He donned in their place the unobtrusive, neat browns of a gardener. It would be better to pose as a footman for this task, but Anserval was one of those who insisted on purchasing a special, highly distinctive uniform for his indoor staff, and they hadn't had time to have a copy made.

'Prosing prat,' continued Egg, as she rapidly swapped her own costume for the whites of a housemaid, exchanged her wig for a brown one with a neat chignon, and dusted a blush of pink onto her cheeks. By the time she was finished, her whole demeanour had changed – everything from her posture to her movements, gestures, accent. Everything. Teyo always marvelled at her remarkable ability to turn into someone else entirely at a moment's notice, a talent she shared with Serena and Fabian. She even seemed to be taller than she had a few moments ago. His own abilities in that direction were much more limited. He was never fully able to hide such distinctive features as his height and broad shoulders, and even his shaggy hair resented its orders to disappear properly beneath a wig.

It was fortunate that he possessed other talents.

Once they were ready, Teyo thumped on the roof of the carriage. Wendle, ever reliable, moved off at once, and within minutes they had arrived near the rear of the manor. Egg exited the carriage first, Teyo following behind.

They were obliged to walk a little way to reach the house. Egg led the way, routing them behind a tall hedge. Teyo did his best to keep his head down, though he was uncertain of his success. Baron Anserval's country mansion was almost as impressive from the rear as it was from the front. If anything it looked even larger without the complementary setting of ornamental gardens. Little decoration adorned the back; this space was taken up mostly with the stables, workshops, brewery, buttery, dairy and other outbuildings. The house itself was built from a luxurious golden stone, but the outbuildings were made from a mere grey substance which Teyo found most unattractive. It was of a piece with the Baron's general character, he reflected; the man cared mostly for show.

Teyo stood watch as Egg made her way into the house. She nimbly avoided the notice of those few staff who occasionally strayed into the rear courtyard. Her objective was to locate the Baron's library, study and gallery and divide her attention between them. She would acquire the accoutrements of a

41

housemaid's trade on her way and devote herself to dusting, most assiduously, every item of the Baron's collection she could reach. If she found the supposed key, she would secure it and leave.

Teyo's task was a little different. He took Jisp out of his pocket and laid her gently onto the floor. Then, taking a deep, slow, breath, he assembled in his mind a vision of a similar creature, albeit of more modest colours. His version of Jisp sported dark, woody brown scales with subtle bronze highlights to its tail, and a cream underbelly. He satisfied himself about the colours before he proceeded any further, for it would not do to wander the corridors of a fine house in a suit of clashing colours. When he was satisfied, he focused his thoughts upon his vision and allowed his body to change.

As a shapeshifter, he was not limited to either his human or his draykon forms. He could shift into virtually any shape he pleased, provided that it was a living being. It was an ability his team had long found useful, and as such, he was not surprised that Serena had leapt to recruit Iyamar when she'd had the chance. To have one shapeshifter on the team was an advantage; to have *two* would be an asset indeed. He suspected, however, that she would encounter some trouble there.

It was not something to ponder over now, he cautioned himself. Focus on the job at hand. His large human form rapidly diminished, changing as it did into the skinny, four-legged, scaled and nimble shape he had chosen for himself. When he was finished, he eyed Jisp from his new vantage with some interest. They were approximately the same size, now, and he noticed myriad shades and hues among her orange-and-yellow hide that he could not see with his human eyes. She really was a most attractive young beastie, he thought with some discomfort. It was always disconcerting to take this shape.

Off we go, he told her. *Be careful.*

She returned only a profound sense of deepest derision to this last, and scampered off. He followed at a cautious distance, watching to see that she was not observed. She was not, of course. By this time, Jisp was almost as well-trained and practiced as the human members of their team. She had long since mastered the demands of sneaking, and had even learned to alter the colours of her hide on occasion, if she wished to blend in. She did that now, muting the violent orange hue of her scales to a drab brown that barely stood out against the stone-paved courtyard.

Soon they reached the house, and split up. Their joint task was one of reconnaissance. They would endeavour to visit every room in the house by some means or another, and they would cover walls, floors, ceilings, shelves, windows and everything else in their attempts to locate either the key which Halavere sought, or any sign of imminent intrusion by the same lady — or anybody else, for that matter. Teyo scurried through the kitchens, dodging the feet of the slaving kitchen staff, and up the stairs into the hall as Jisp dashed her way towards the grand stairway and the first floor. If he didn't miss his guess, it was just about time for Serena and Fabian to arrive, and he was relying upon them to keep the Baron busy.

Serena donned the role of Lady Fenella Chartre with pleasure as she was helped down from the ladyship-coach by a liveried footman. But her good feelings soon began to give way to exasperation as she observed the footman's uniform. The poor man was dressed in a crimson jacket and trousers with gold ornaments, gold braid, gold embroidery and even polished gold leather boots! Nothing could exceed the pure ostentation of such a uniform for a mere footman, and she knew that the majority of the Baron's numerous staff wore similar attire. Combined with the overly imposing frontage of the golden mansion which towered above her and the plethora of gold-leaved shrubs, hedges and trees with which the Baron had decorated his garden, the effect was almost prostrating. Serena eyed it with vast distaste, but as the Baron himself stepped out of the front door at that moment and came hastening towards her, she was obliged to conceal her disapprobation behind Lady Fenella's bright smile and enthusiastic manner.

'My lord!' she gushed with suitable rapture, 'I declare, the gardens are more beautiful every time I come here! How do you contrive it?'

The Baron, revolting man, caught hold of her hands and kissed them both, leaving Serena to conceal a faint shudder of distaste. It was not that he wasn't handsome; though rather older than her twenty-nine years, he was in excellent shape, and though he was only of moderate height he displayed a fine figure. His hair and moustache may be greying, but his features were handsome, and his green eyes were decidedly fine.

It was his manner which revolted, together with his taste. Both were inferior and encroaching. She was glad of Fabian's presence as he stepped down from the carriage behind her. The Baron may view Lord Bastavere's appearance with poorly concealed impatience, but Serena had insisted on his accompanying her. As committed as she was to the job, nothing could persuade her to undertake her distasteful role as the Baron's entertainment without support. He had a detestable way of getting her alone at every opportunity, and his behaviour when he succeeded was not such as to inspire Serena with confidence. She had a secret hope that today, just for once, she might contrive to escape from the Baron's clutches without having to field another proposal of marriage.

A faint hope, she realised with an inward sigh, as she observed the twinkle in his eye which he no doubt considered roguish. Still, she had Fabian to play the desirable role of fifth wheel, and as long as the Baron was focused upon her, he would not notice the extra housemaid who was wandering the halls of his house, or the pair of suspiciously lively lizards currently sticking their sticky feet all over his walls. She hoped that her team had managed to infiltrate the house without any problems, and also that Iyamar, left with the costume coach, was getting along suitably with Wendle.

Their primary objective was to find the key, or whatever it was, before Halavere arrived to claim it. She had some hopes that Egg, with her natural inquisitiveness and her eye for the unusual, might manage to identify it. Failing that, perhaps Teyo's unusual draykon senses might reveal it, should the thing prove to be unremarkable to the eye. Either way, they would need time. The house was enormous, of course, and much of it was littered with collectibles.

She exchanged some lively nothings with the Baron for a few minutes, allowing herself to be conducted over the gardens. Fabian said nothing at all as Serena exclaimed rapturously over every single violently golden bush or tree or flower which her tiresome companion chose to show her; he merely followed in silence. It was part of his role, of course. Lord Bastavere was snobbish in the extreme, and not at all shy of showing his contempt. She might wish, though, that he would talk a little, and share the burden of entertaining the Baron, even if he could only be rude. Were some of these bushes *painted* gold? They were. They absolutely were. Serena averted her gaze with a strong shudder, and plastered back on her smile.

She kept the whole party out in the gardens for as long as she could, aware that she was giving her team plenty of time to scout the interior. At length, however, the Baron would not be dissuaded from leading her inside. The autumnal weather was just too chilly, alas, for her to propose tea in the gardens, and she was obliged to allow herself to be led into a drawing-room on the first floor. This, too, was appallingly golden, and she seated herself in a gold-upholstered chair with a sigh, arranging her fine lavender velvet skirts around herself with ostentatious fastidiousness.

This sigh of hers had been audible, she realised with dismay, as the Baron turned a questioning look upon her. 'Never say that my fair Fenella finds something amiss!' he cried, with lively dismay. 'If one single thing in my humble house is not to her taste, she must say so at once, and it shall be rectified *instantly.*'

A man who referred to a lady of his interest in the third person ought to be shot, Serena thought savagely. She yawned theatrically and sagged back into her seat, disclaiming, 'Oh! No, my lord, how could I possibly object to such charming arrangements? In truth, I am a little tired. I attended a party yesterday eve, and I was coaxed into remaining later than was strictly wise.'

'I am overcome with regret!' he declared extravagantly. 'I should have been present to attend you, Fenella. Under my guidance, you could not have overstrained yourself.'

Fabian's lip curled visibly, and Serena hurriedly exclaimed, 'How *good* you are! But I can take care of myself, you know.'

'Evidently not!' returned the Baron with a fatuous smile. 'For here before me is the proof, in the shape of a wilting damsel.'

Serena's increasingly murderous reflections were mercifully interrupted at this moment, by the entrance of a blindingly red-and-gold clad employee bearing a golden tray of cakes which he laid upon the tea table. Another followed and set beside it a second golden tray full of sandwiches, and yet another set an (inevitably) golden teapot in the centre, together with matching cups. Serena took advantage of the Baron's momentary distraction to gaze around herself, taking note of the number of cabinets that lined the walls. They were all filled with assorted objects, and she hoped that Egg, Teyo or Jisp had managed to examine this room before their party had occupied it.

No, she realised a moment later, for surely that was the lively little person of Jisp darting along the skirting-board. Or perhaps it was Teyo. The lizard, whichever it was, scrambled up the wall and disappeared over the top of the nearest cabinet. Serena, heart thumping a little at this audaciousness, hoped fervently that the Baron had not noticed.

He was too busy pouring tea. Serena was appalled to observe that even the steaming beverage which splashed fragrantly into the dainty cups was gold. He was definitely getting worse. She would have to throw that golden silk ball gown away, she thought regretfully; it was something of a favourite, but after today she would never be able to look a golden object in the face again.

She was further alarmed to note that the Baron's attention had turned to his antiques, and that the notion of showing them to his guests had entered his head. A moment ago she might have been delighted at so perfect an opportunity to hunt for the key herself. Now that they had a lizardly visitor, she wasn't so sure.

Fabian had not observed their tiny guest, she swiftly concluded, for he accepted the Baron's offer with alacrity, casting a swift, meaningful look in her direction. As Lord Bastavere, he was at his stateliest, and she felt that even the egotistical Baron Anserval was a little bit impressed by his lordship's demeanour. Not that he required very much encouragement. Scarcely giving his guests time to finish their tea, he was up and offering Lady Fenella his arm.

A thought occurred to Serena; a ploy which, if she could pull it off, might both salvage the situation and secure them a considerable advantage. She smiled her charming best at the Baron, accepted his arm with every apparent pleasure, and proclaimed, 'How discerning a collector you are, my lord! Truly, I have never seen so fine an array as is displayed in this room.'

The Baron, caught between a swelling satisfaction and a lowering chagrin, made a comical picture. Gratified he could not help being at this high praise, but nor could he resist pointing out: 'In this room! My dear lady, you must be aware that this is but a fraction of the whole.'

'Oh!' she replied, blinking. 'To be sure. Now that you put me in mind of it, I do recall some one or two things in the hall, and perhaps the library.'

'Mere nothings! Trifles! My exhibits run the length and breadth of this humble house, in point of fact, though I need not scruple to entrust *you,* Lady Fenella, with the truth. I do not keep my finest pieces on public display. How could I? They must be constantly guarded from the predations of the greedy and envious.' He lowered his voice to a conspiratorial whisper and added, 'What would you say if I told you that there are secret rooms in this house?'

Serena regretted, for a brief, sharp instant, that the only way to handle such an ignorant fool as the Baron was to pretend to even greater vacuity. It grew wearing. She composed her face into an expression of suitable surprise, and exclaimed.

The Baron was satisfied. 'Very cunning, is it not? My acquisitions come under constant scrutiny, and if I did not take all possible pains to protect my treasures, I daresay I should lose them all. The very best and rarest are safely tucked away, and so I have no apprehensions.' His chest swelled with satisfaction as he made these fine pronouncements, and he nodded his own approval to himself. 'I daresay your lord and ladyship would like to see them?' he added.

Finally. Serena, relieved that she would not have to coquette her way into these "secret" rooms, smiled her perfect approbation of this plan. 'What a great treat!' she declared. 'How I long to see these rarest of treasures.'

'Are they so very fine?' said Lord Bastavere, with a harsh laugh. 'They cannot rival the collections of, say, the Iving Gallery, or the Irbel National Museum?'

The Baron, bridling, returned that it most certainly *could,* and Serena blessed her brother in her heart. Nothing would now stop the Baron from showing them every part of his vaunted collections, and though the prospect was a stultifying one, she felt some hope that they would be able to locate the key before Halavere showed up.

The problem of Jisp — or Teyo — had slipped her mind in the midst of these manoeuvrings, but before they had reached the door she was horrified to observe a tiny, lithe form scurrying beneath her skirt. Moments later she felt the dubious and unsettling sensation of many sticky toes and a scaled little body worming its way up her ankle. The creature clung to her leg and remained there as she walked with the Baron and Fabian through the wide hallways of the house. She *hoped* it was Jisp under there.

Blessing the lucky chance which had led her to don particularly voluminous drawers that morning, Serena tried to ignore the clinging pressure about her lower leg and chattered in the liveliest fashion all the way through the house to the centre, near the main staircase. Here they paused, and the Baron, with an expression of enormous pride, activated some mechanism that lay concealed behind a revolting painting of pink-faced infants that adorned a secluded corner of the hallway. A previously hidden door swung smoothly open. Behind it, Serena observed a staircase leading down into the depths beneath the house.

The Baron advanced to the top of the stairs and clapped his hands loudly three times. Lights instantly began to flicker to life below, revealing the considerable extent of the stairs. Serena was impressed in spite of herself. The Baron certainly spared no expense, either in hiding his treasures or in impressing his guests. That light set-up alone must have cost a fortune. She allowed herself to be conducted down the stairs on her host's arm, leaving Lord Bastavere to wander along behind.

At the bottom, a long corridor stretched away with several doors set into it. Serena stared at them in some dismay. Surely they did not *all* lead to galleries full of antiques? Her comfortable notion that they might secure the key before Halavere even arrived began to fade, and doubts returned.

The Baron was already opening the first door, and she was soon called to precede him inside. She noticed, with further astonishment, that he did not use a key to access this room. The locking mechanism was altogether different, and involved the pressing of a series of buttons in some kind of sequence. It was not at all reminiscent of anything she had seen before, which raised interesting, and not wholly encouraging, possibilities. Exchanging a brief glance with her brother as she went inside, she concluded that he was as mystified by it as she. She made a mental note to pursue this subject later, for before her stretched a vast hallway well-lit by hundreds of floating light-globes. The walls were lined with cabinet after cabinet, and long glass-topped display cases occupied the centre of the room. A swift glance revealed all manner of curiosities stashed behind those glass panes, from statuettes and books to hair ornaments, tea cups and jewellery.

There must be many hundreds of objects down here, she realised with a sinking heart. Maybe thousands. And if every other room in the Baron's cellar contained a similar quantity of goods, how in the world could they identify which one was of interest to Halavere? Even if the thing was so obliging as to resemble a classic key in shape and structure, it could take forever to find it among all this nonsense.

But she had Fabian to help her — and Jisp, or possibly Teyo. Her passenger clambered back down her leg as she formed this thought and slipped away. Serena caught a glimpse of a tiny scaly body scuttling speedily away, and hastily averted her gaze in case her host happened to look.

The Baron began his tour near the door, and Serena quickly realised that he intended to recount the full history of each cabinet. Worse, he did so with an air of decided pedantry, one hand clutched possessively over hers as it rested upon his arm. Despairing, she tried once or twice to hurry the tour along a little more quickly, or at least to interrupt the lengthy flow he was working himself into, but with little success. Lord Bastavere, with typical arrogance, rolled his eyes and wandered off. The Baron paid little notice.

Serena was not left to agonise for long in this state of wretched frustration. Her irksome guide had just launched with gusto into an account of the provenance of a tiny painting featuring two nymphs portrayed in spectacularly lurid colours, when a short gust of wind sent her skirts billowing. With this unexpected sensation came the sound of somebody jumping softly down onto the floor from a height of, perhaps, two or three feet. Startled — for nothing her brother could possibly be doing would explain either the wind or the noise — she turned.

A stranger stood in the middle of the room, directly between a long case displaying tarnished timepieces and an even larger case bearing a heavy load of old coins. The woman was tall, with statuesque posture and dark eyes. She wore close-fitting green trousers, a plain cream cotton shirt, thick leather gloves and a purposeful expression. Her pure-white hair was bound up in a style of severe practicality, ruthlessly pinned down and wholly unadorned. She was not at all old, judging from the smoothness of her skin, so she must be of Lokant heritage.

But she was *not* Dame Halavere.

'What's this?' demanded the Baron. 'I sincerely hope this woman is an acquaintance of yours, Fenella!'

'I have never seen her before,' Serena replied tightly. 'Unless I am much mistaken, she is looking for something in particular.' She realised, belatedly, that her role had slipped during this speech, but the Baron didn't appear to notice. He strode off in the direction of the intruder, shouting imperatives and threats, all of which she ignored. Instead of *ceasing her disgraceful intrusion* and *removing herself from this vicinity at once*, or even of *explaining instantly how she came to gain access to this place*, the woman walked briskly to the other side of the room. Without pausing, she drew back her arm and delivered a swift, brutal punch to the glass front of one of the cabinets. The glass shattered, the woman reached forth and grabbed a single object — and vanished.

Fabian, dashing towards her with deadly purpose, was left standing stupidly on the spot she had so recently occupied. The Baron was shocked into silence, though alas, only briefly. He then responded with still greater vituperation, cursing all and sundry and demanding explanations of nobody in particular.

Serena merely stood, thinking. The woman was no Partial Lokant, that much was clear. She was a full blood, and powerful indeed. It was known that the pure Lokants — and, very occasionally, one or two of the part-bloods — could transport themselves over long distances in the blink of an eye, but it was not thought to be a flexible ability. It required major preparation beforehand in order to do it, and something like a waypoint had to be laid down by somebody; one did not simply transport oneself through doors, or past walls, or to any spot which had not been previously selected and (in some unfathomable way) prepared for the purpose. This much she understood.

But this woman had appeared in a very specific place, somewhere very private and virtually inaccessible. Could it be that somebody had placed a waypoint here, in this room? How had that been accomplished, and why? Somebody among the Lokants must already have known, some time since, that the Baron's collection was likely to be of interest. But how had they marked the place, and how had the woman known exactly which cabinet to look in?

Most likely the Baron's staff were not as supremely loyal as he thought; the woman must have had help from someone employed at the house. Damn, they had worked fast. Serena choked on a feeling of deep chagrin, for the job had failed utterly. If there were full Lokants involved, and such powerful ones as their erstwhile visitor, the job had never had any hope of success. All the efforts of the day and half the preceding night had been wasted.

Or perhaps not, entirely. She had not been close enough to see precisely what it was that the Lokant had taken from the cabinet, but Fabian probably had. She hoped that this one small thing, at the least, could be salvaged from an operation otherwise doomed to failure from the start.

There was nothing to be gained from remaining any longer. The Baron was no longer of any interest, and she was heartily tired of playing Lady Fenella. She swept from the room with Fabian close behind her, leaving the Baron loudly proclaiming his determination to register a formal complaint with the LHITB.

5

Oliver Tullen's offices were situated near the centre of Irbel's capital city, Iving. It was a long way to go from the realm's southern border with Nimdre, but Serena felt the importance of consulting him at once. She required his approval and advice regarding Iyamar, as soon as possible. Moreover, their surveillance of Halavere had ended in failure, and she was unsure how to proceed. The key, if it was a key, was probably stashed away in some far-off Lokant Library by now. It was impossible to follow; there were many Libraries, as far as anybody in the Seven knew, and they were situated way off-world. Nobody save another Lokant could hope to follow them there. A report would have to be submitted to the LHITB, and beyond that, Serena and her team were at a loose end.

She couldn't even be certain that Halavere had had anything to do with the theft, in the end. True, she had met with a known Unspeakable and Baron Anserval's address had changed hands, but there was no indication that she had been involved with the rest. Serena suspected that the Dame might have contacts with one or more Lokant Libraries. Perhaps they had used her — and, through her, the Unspeakables — to find the supposed key, and Halavere had merely passed on the information. Any such connection had to be reported, of course, and Halavere would have to be monitored. She hoped that Oliver would have more interesting work for Serena's team.

She set out for Oliver's office early in the morning, leaving Egg and Fabian behind. Iyamar had to be presented immediately, and she wanted Teyo's company too. Since he was most likely to be volunteered for the task of training their new recruit's draykon abilities, she wanted him to be present to discuss it with their boss.

They were only obliged to travel by nivven as far as the city of Trayce in south-eastern Irbel. From there, the overland railcar conveyed the three of them into Iving. It was a relatively new piece of infrastructure, of which Serena heartily approved. Not of an engineering turn of mind herself, she did not properly understand by what means the long metal carriages were conveyed along the rails that had been laid between Iving and Trayce — and other cities — less than ten years ago, but the speed they achieved far outstripped the capacity of even the liveliest nivven steed. Better still, their interiors were luxuriously equipped with well-padded chairs, allowing her to relax at her ease as she sped on her way to the capital.

Iyamar had clearly never experienced this mode of transport before. Her young face was touchingly filled with a mixture of awe and fascination, though she strove to hide it whenever she noticed Serena looking. She was far more interested in the workings of it than Serena, too, and peppered Teyo with questions, all of which he answered with his customary patience.

At length Iyamar fell silent, absorbed by the rapid passage of fields and hills outside the window as they sped along. Serena took the opportunity to ask Teyo a question she'd been postponing since the day before.

'Yesterday,' she murmured to him, keeping her voice low. 'Tell me that was Jisp.'

He grinned at once, dashing Serena's hopes, though he had the grace to look a little sheepish. 'Erm, 'fraid not,' he said, with a trace at least of apology.

'No!' said Serena, aghast. 'Teyo. *What* possessed you to run up my skirt?!'

'I couldn't let you all run off to the secret and interesting places without me!'

'But my *skirt*, Teyo? *Up* my skirt?'

'It was the only thing I could think of at the time.'

Serena sighed. 'You, um. You didn't… *see* anything while you were under there, did you?'

'Your ankle,' Teyo returned promptly.

'My ankle.'

'Yes.'

Serena thought about that. 'Only my ankle?'

'There was a lot of fabric going on down there,' Teyo said apologetically. 'But,' he offered, brightening, 'It *was* a very shapely ankle.'

Serena eyed him.

'Though now that I think of it, it looked more like a tree trunk to me at the time.'

Serena's eyes opened wide. 'My ankles are not of such stupendous proportions as all that, Mr. Bambre.'

'My perspective was a little disordered.'

Serena sighed. If anybody had to be dashing up her skirt in the guise of a lizard, she'd rather it was Teyo than anyone else. He was trustworthy, unthreatening and, she was sure, quite uninterested in her in *that* kind of way. Still, to have one's friends rummaging around among one's undergarments was a disconcerting experience for any woman, and Serena could only gather her tattered dignity around her, lift her chin, and stare frostily out of the window.

'I really didn't see anything,' Teyo muttered.

Serena ignored that.

Oliver Tullen's eyes were pale blue, and piercingly intent. He studied Serena's little group expressionlessly as they were admitted to his office. As ever, Serena had no way of knowing what he was thinking.

They never travelled to Oliver's openly, without disguise. One never knew who might be watching, after all. Serena had cast the three of them as a well-to-do city family returning from a visit to the country. They were dressed with neatness and propriety, though not ostentatiously; the goal here was to blend in. Oliver's gaze slid from her to Teyo without comment, which meant, to her relief, that their efforts had passed inspection.

He looked at Iyamar for rather longer.

'Miss Carterett,' he said in his soft voice. 'Mr. Bambre. What can I do for you?' He gestured to the chairs that were arrayed before his desk.

Serena took one gratefully. The shoes she'd chosen were but newly added to her wardrobe of costumes, and they were pinching a little. 'We need to report,' she replied, 'and I'm seeking approval for a new recruit.'

Oliver's eyes flicked back to Iyamar. 'I see.' He was a slight man in his sixties, or thereabouts, with dark grey hair beginning to turn white. He always wore the same thing: a dark blue shirt and deep brown trousers and boots, with, as appropriate, a heavy black cloak. He never wore jewellery. He was the uncontested master of all things disguise; no one could best him. He had once turned up at his own office in the guise of a lift engineer, and though he had been Serena's teacher and mentor for years, even she had not recognised him.

'Begin with the young lady,' he said.

Serena grinned. She had cast Iyamar as her young brother in today's masquerade, interested to test, and possibly improve, her new team member's skills in masking her gender. And she *was* good. Once her wig, make-up and clothes were in place, Iyamar had slipped effortlessly into the role. So convincing was her every movement and gesture, even Serena was hard-pressed to remember that she wasn't really male.

But nothing got past Oliver.

Iyamar glanced at Serena, uncertain. 'My name's Anders Gollon,' she said in her boy's voice. 'I'm here to —'

'This isn't an audition,' Oliver interrupted.

Iyamar blinked. 'It isn't?' she said in her normal voice. 'I thought —' She stopped herself, and nodded. 'Right. Iyamar Hale. These people picked me up the other night and told me there was a job in it.'

'And are you interested in this job?'

Iyamar shrugged. 'I said yes, but I don't know. Yesterday was about the most boring day of my life.'

Serena winced. 'I was obliged to leave her with Wendle,' she apologised. 'There was, ah, not much going on out there.'

'I missed *all* the good stuff,' Iyamar sighed, slumping.

Oliver looked her up and down. 'Do you imagine that the "good stuff" is allocated to raw recruits?' he said coolly.

Iyamar blinked. 'Well… no. I suppose not.'

'No. Train hard, do well, and you'll get to do the exciting things. Serena here was kept on surveillance for two years before I let her play a role.'

Serena grinned and nodded. Goodness, but she'd been bored! So many hours spent crouched outside somebody's house, or hovering at the back of bars, waiting for something interesting to happen. Very little ever did.

Iyamar's expression turned a little sullen, and Serena was afraid she might revolt. But then the girl apparently made some kind of decision, for she sat up straighter and nodded. 'That'd be fair enough. I want this job.'

Oliver's gaze returned to Serena. 'Where did you say you found her?'

Serena related the whole history of her encounter with Iyamar, ignoring the girl's obvious discomfort. She didn't try to soften any of it; there would have been no point. Oliver could practically smell a lie, no matter how small.

'I didn't want to do it!' Iyamar burst out, when Serena had finished recounting her failed attempt at robbing their carriage. 'I was desperate.'

Serena expected another stinging retort from Oliver, but he surprised her. 'That sometimes happens,' he informed Iyamar. 'You showed initiative, at any rate.'

Iyamar appeared to be as surprised as Serena, for she opened her mouth, managed to say nothing at all, and closed it again abruptly.

'You also showed ineptitude,' he continued. 'Clumsiness, rashness and a deplorable lack of control. You will need a great deal of training.' He looked at Teyo as he spoke, who grinned ruefully.

'I'll train her,' he rumbled.

Iyamar began to look mutinous again, for no reason Serena could understand. But she swallowed whatever objection she might have been thinking of, and nodded once.

'Good. It is always an advantage to have another shapeshifter on our books,' Oliver said, with a trace of a smile for Serena. 'Get her registered on your way out.'

Serena nodded, pleased and a little relieved. If Oliver had refused to take her, she had no idea what else she might have done with Iyamar.

'Now the report,' Oliver said.

Serena recounted the events of the past two days. She thought she detected a flicker of annoyance in Oliver's eyes as she reached the part where the key had been taken from right under their noses, but he said nothing. She ended by taking out the sketch Fabian had made of the missing object, and handed it over. 'We've never seen anything like this before,' she said.

The sketch portrayed a little curled-up round object resembling a sea shell, though it was not precisely like that at all. The thing had been made from some kind of stone, Fabian said; whatever it was looked like ordinary granite, save for the tinge of green in its make-up and an odd silvery sheen.

Oliver looked at the sketch without comment, and finally laid it down upon his desk. 'Halavere will be kept under watch,' he said.

Serena nodded. That was the end of the interview, she knew; she didn't expect Oliver to share any of the things that might be passing through his mind. 'What do wish us to do now?' she asked.

'Train your new recruit,' he replied.

Serena blinked. 'That's it? No new jobs?'

Oliver watched her in silence for some moments. She couldn't tell whether he was thinking, or merely waiting. At length he said: 'Unless I miss my guess, this isn't the last we will see of this affair of the key. When it comes up again — and I do not think it will be a long wait before it does — I'll want you free to take it up.'

He must know something else about it, Serena thought with a little thrill of excitement. If only he would share his knowledge, rather than dropping cryptic hints and dismissing them! She knew better than to ask. She got up to leave, Teyo and Iyamar immediately following her lead.

'Stay in Iving,' Oliver added just as she reached the door. 'You can take apartment 43, Allerside.'

'And Halavere?' she said, turning around.

'Not your concern at the moment.'

Serena dipped him a curtsey befitting a housemaid to her employer, her lips curving in a roguish smile. She won a tiny answering smile from him, which gave her great satisfaction.

'Time for paperwork,' she said to Iyamar as she ushered the girl out of the office.

Iyamar frowned, hesitated, and finally said: 'But I can't write.'

Serena stopped dead in the corridor. 'You... what?' she said faintly.

Iyamar hung her head. 'Nobody ever learned me,' she apologised.

'Taught,' Serena corrected. 'Nobody ever taught you. But

we'll change that, post-haste.' She spoke briskly, but with a sinking heart. Good gracious. She'd realised there would be a lot of work to be done with Iyamar, but even her wildest estimates appeared to fall short of the truth.

Never mind, it was hardly the girl's fault. She exchanged a look with Teyo, reassuring herself that he was still in favour of the project. Of course he was; nothing exceeded Teyo's patience or good nature. She had never seen him upset, or even a little bit ruffled.

'I'll do the writing for you,' she said to Iyamar. 'But later, we'll start lessons.'

Iyamar nodded.

'Can you read?' Serena thought to ask.

'Nope.'

Serena sighed.

6

Serena was concerned that her team would be bored over the coming weeks, with no assigned tasks to work on. She found herself mistaken. Not only did the lull in activity grant them all time for some much-needed rest, but she swiftly found that everybody had something to teach Iyamar, and everybody was very willing to participate, to her pleasure and relief.

Egg — seeing, perhaps, some vision of her former self in the much younger Iyamar — swiftly carted her off for lessons in her particular talents of lock-picking and pick-pocketing. Also, more peculiarly, wig-making. Egg was the artist behind most of their hair options; it was something of a hobby with her. She claimed to find it relaxing, and undertook it in the same spirit as Teyo's knitting. Why she felt it necessary to impart any of this ability to Iyamar was less obvious to Serena, but she chose not to interfere. Anything that would help her friends and colleagues bond with her new recruit was to be encouraged.

Serena and Fabian began teaching Iyamar what Serena thought of as the "Basic Skills", those being the elegant arts of dissembling, disguise and character acting. Iyamar excelled at the latter, having gained some degree of practice already during her time on the streets. There was rather more to be desired with the others, but the girl threw herself into the pursuits with laudable enthusiasm, and Serena was pleased with her progress. She sent regular reports to Oliver, and since she heard nothing from him in response, she was able to assume that he was as pleased as she was.

Teyo, meanwhile, began the task of teaching her to read and write. For the present, he left her shapeshifter abilities alone; she had more than enough to occupy her time and her mind, and he could not persuade her to focus on her draykoni talents.

This did not worry Serena overmuch. All in good time, thought she, and Iyamar's zeal for learning could not possibly be faulted anywhere else.

In some ways, perhaps, she was a little bit too zealous. Taciturn at first, Iyamar swiftly conquered her shyness under the friendly encouragement of her new colleagues and began to ask a great many questions. She wanted to know about everything. Every job they had ever undertaken, and why; every opponent they had conquered, or failed to subdue; how they had learned all of their various arts and skills; how they had come to work for Oliver Tullen and the Agency; and so on.

These last bothered Serena just a little. There came a quiet afternoon about two weeks after their meeting with Oliver, when Serena and Iyamar were engaged in an elocution lesson — or Serena's version thereof.

'You said Teyo used to work for the Unspeakables?' said Iyamar, having rapidly picked up the jargon of Serena's team.

'I did,' Serena replied guardedly. She felt a faint stab of guilt for having imparted something so personal about Teyo's past. Perhaps she should not have, though she had meant it for the best. She'd wanted Iyamar to realise that her background was by no means unusual in her new line of work.

'And Egg?' continued Iyamar.

Serena shook her head. 'Egg's never been Unspeakable. Just a thief, for some years. Remember your accent, Iya. Today you're a farmer from southern Irbel, remember.'

Iyamar paused to think for a moment before venturing her next question. 'Well'n, ma'am. Wharbeit thous't be a roguish snabble-catcher?'

'A snabble-catcher?' Serena said, laughing. 'Did you make that up?'

Iyamar grinned. 'Happen I might've.'

'It is an excellent word.'

'You're avoiding the question,' Iyamar observed.

Serena surveyed her new charge thoughtfully. She was

avoiding the question, as it happened, though she might wish Iyamar to be a little less aware of it.

'You said you don't share that background,' Iyamar prompted helpfully.

Serena shook her head slowly. 'No, that's true. Fabian and I are... well, we have reasons for doing this.'

Iyamar said nothing, only stared at her new mentor with a hopeful shine in her icy-blue eyes which sent Serena's heart sinking into her boots. 'I'll tell you some other time,' she said.

Iyamar sat back, arms folded, and surveyed Serena intently. 'Is it a dark secret?'

'Not really.'

'Not really dark, or not really a secret?'

'You're very persistent,' Serena said, eyeing her with some displeasure.

'I don't see how I'm meant to get information out of people if I'm not,' said Iyamar reasonably.

Serena folded her own arms, and stared back. 'I'm not a fit subject for interrogation.'

'Why not?'

'Because I'm your boss.'

Iyamar pouted. 'I'll get it out of you eventually.'

Serena rolled her eyes. 'Oh, probably. But for the time being, back to your brogue.'

Iyamar shook her head, and effected one of her lightning-swift subject changes. 'I want my rapier back.'

'What?'

'My rapier. I might need it.'

'Not on my team, you won't.'

'What? Why not?'

'We don't do violence,' Serena said firmly. 'Ever. And we *certainly* don't do killing.'

'But you're crookish.'

Serena eyed her with grave displeasure. 'We're not crookish! We've been over that. Even if we were, we still wouldn't do violence.'

'Why not?'

'I'll tell you another time.'

'Tell me now,' Iyamar said stubbornly. 'I can't be a team member if you won't tell me anything.'

The girl had a point, Serena thought with an inward sigh.

'Because we've all lost people, that's why.'

'You mean you all have people who were deaded?'

'Right. Deaded.'

'Who?'

Serena narrowed her eyes. 'People.'

'Tell me this one thing and then we can go on with the lesson.' Iyamar smiled hopefully and added, 'Please?' in a wheedling tone.

'Teyo's parents were killed when their house was robbed,' Serena said rapidly. 'Egg lost most of her family, though she still won't talk about how it happened. And Fabe and me, we lost our father when he... well, he killed himself.'

Iyamar blinked. 'Oh.'

'Right, so. Nobody wants to do any of that... that violence stuff.'

Iyamar thought about that for a while, and finally nodded. 'Okay. You can keep the rapier.'

'That's lucky,' said Serena with a crooked smile, 'because I already threw it away.'

Iyamar glared at her. 'You had no right to do that!'

'Nope,' Serena agreed, 'but I didn't want it in the house.'

'Meh.'

'What was that?'

'I said, "Meh."'

'Lovely. Can we get on with the lesson now?'

'Woar, me-lady, to be sure'n we can.'

Iyamar's queries put Serena in mind of a duty she had been postponing. That evening, she detoured past Fabian's room on her way to rest and knocked. Receiving a grunt of invitation (or she hoped that was what the ungracious sound meant), she went in.

Fabian was lying sprawled upon his bed, still fully dressed. He looked truly like himself, which was a rare event these days, for he delighted in his characters even more than Serena did. She sometimes wondered whether he took pleasure in being someone else because he found it difficult to be himself.

He did not look best pleased to be interrupted, and she realised with dismay that he was having one of his difficult days. He gazed at her out of shadowed dark eyes, his near-black hair hanging in a tousled and unwashed mass down to his jaw. 'What is it?' he muttered.

Serena stepped quickly inside and shut the door behind her. 'How bad is it?' she said quietly.

He shrugged. 'I've had worse.'

She nodded, studying him for signs of trouble. After a few seconds of this scrutiny, he snorted with annoyance and threw a pillow at her. 'Stop it,' he growled. 'It won't kill me.'

She returned only a crooked smile to this sally, and sat down gingerly on the end of the bed. 'I was thinking… we ought to pay a visit, tomorrow. If you think you're going to be up to it?'

Fabian considered that in silence, and finally shrugged. 'I don't know. I'll try.'

Serena nodded once and got up. Fabian hated to be cosseted, no matter how bad he felt. Privately, she thought that company was good for him on his dark days; the way that he pushed people away only worried her more. But to linger when he clearly wanted solitude would only irritate him, so she made her way briskly to the door. 'You know where I am if you need me,' she said on her way out. Fabian sighed heavily, and said nothing.

She knew that his ungraciousness betokened frustration with himself, not with her, though it still disheartened her sometimes. Fabian had been prone since childhood to dark, dark days, and this tendency had only grown worse since… well, several years ago. At such times, he said, he would awake to a mire of self-hatred and despair, and nothing helped except to wait for it to pass. He despised it as a weakness; feared, sometimes, that even his friends would imagine he was being self-indulgent and feeble. Serena knew better, and so did Egg and Teyo. Nothing could exceed Fabian's own hatred and resentment of this aspect of his character. If he could change it, he would.

She only wished there was more she could do for him. There was nothing, save to go to bed and hope that, in the morning, he would be restored to his livelier self. But she left her door slightly ajar when she retired, just in case.

They left the apartment before dawn on the following morning, moving as quietly as they could to avoid waking the others. The Day Cloak still blanketed the city of Iving in the gentler, soothing glow Serena liked so much. Sometimes, when she was not too busy or too tired, she stayed awake well into the

Evenglow hours just to savour the ambience. She took little pleasure in it today, however. Her errand was not a happy one, and though Fabian assured her he was up to making the visit, Serena was not so sure. There was still that shadow behind his eyes, and he spoke very little as they rode the railcar across the city.

Their destination was a tall building on the outskirts of Iving. It was not quite a hospital, but not quite a home either, though it was well-kept and pleasant enough inside. Serena and Fabian climbed the stairs up to the fourth floor and made their way to a room with the number eighteen set into the door. Serena knocked, and a cheery female voice bade her enter.

She did. The speaker was a uniform-clad carer of middle years, her chestnut hair bound up into a neat bun. She made an admirable picture of efficiency, but Serena loved her for her smile and welcoming manner.

'Good to see you!' she said, her hands full of blankets. 'She's on the balcony. Here, why don't you take her these?' She offered the blankets to Serena, but Fabian stepped forward and claimed them with a nod of thanks. The carer — her name was Ferna, though they had never learned her surname — smiled upon them both and quietly left the room, closing the door discreetly behind her.

Serena made for the narrow door that led to the balcony, frowning slightly. The weather was too cold for sitting out there, surely? But then, the blankets. Ferna knew best, of course, but still, the wind was chill indeed.

A forlorn figure sat huddled in a rocking chair just outside the door. She was wrapped up to her chin in a huge woollen shawl which she clutched tightly to herself, as much for security as for warmth, Serena guessed. Her grey hair was tousled from the wind, and hung loose; she had not permitted Ferna to braid it today, apparently. She looked up as Serena arrived, and stared at her for several agonising seconds without a trace of recognition in her eyes.

'Good morning, Ma,' said Serena with her warmest smile.

Serena and Fabian were both undisguised today; they never pretended, when they came here. It only confused and frightened their mother, who struggled to recognise them even without the complications of wiggery and make-up. It was one of the things that saddened Serena the most, for she had once

64

delighted in their playacting. Now, Serena even tried to keep her curly, dark brown hair in the same simple hairstyle when she visited, afraid that even the smallest alteration might be enough to hopelessly befuddle her mother.

Fabian devoted himself to spreading Ferna's blankets over Theresa Carterett's knees and tucking them in. He was always so gentle with her, even though it terrified him to see her. He feared that, someday, whatever it was that afflicted him with dark moods and self-destructive thoughts would turn into whatever it was that robbed their mother of her memory and her personality. Nobody, least of all Serena, could truly reassure him, for nobody knew if the two things were connected.

Theresa turned her eyes away from Serena's face without seeming to know her, and watched Fabian's endeavours with dreamy detachment. Disappointed, Serena pulled up a chair and sat nearby, drawing her own coat closer around herself. The view was appealing from up here, she could not deny. A little of the city was visible to the left of the little balcony, and to the right were spread an array of fields interspersed with hedgerows and little copses, their leaves burning golden in the rising sun.

'Are you warm enough?' Fabian murmured, and was rewarded with a sudden, glowing smile.

'Why, yes, dear,' she said, and Serena's heart leapt. She knew him! 'Thank you,' continued her mother. 'What a kind man. You remind me of my son.'

There was silence for a moment, and then Fabian smiled awkwardly and touched her hair, very gently. 'I'm sure he's a fine fellow,' he said.

Their mother nodded her agreement and began to reminisce in a low voice. All of her memories of Fabian were from his childhood; she seemed to recall nothing at all from the many years that had since passed. But a smile often touched her face as she recounted his adventures and escapades, and then she began to talk of Serena, too, in similar style. Neither interrupted her, choosing to allow her to enjoy her memories as she chose.

At length, she fell silent. She had grown tired, Serena judged, for she was drooping into her shawl. Serena rose to leave, bestowing an affectionate embrace upon her mother. It made her happy, even if Theresa didn't realise from whom it came.

But as she straightened, her mother's eyes fixed upon her face with an expression of startled recognition. 'Serena?' she whispered.

Serena's heart leapt. 'Yes!' she said, smiling. 'It's me, Ma. And Fabian, too. We're here.'

Theresa stared unseeingly at Serena, and then at Fabian, her mouth slightly open. Then she said: 'Where is your father?'

Serena bit her lip. 'He's dead, Ma,' she said, as gently as she could.

Theresa's face crumpled, and she began to cry. 'Why won't he come back?' she sobbed.

Serena exchanged an agonised look with Fabian. Theresa persisted in the belief that her husband had left her, and would someday return; she could not be persuaded that he was gone forever. There was nothing to be done but comfort her as best they could.

When Serena and Fabian finally took their leave, it was in silence and with subdued spirits. They wandered down two streets, despondent and dismayed, before Serena finally spoke.

'I need ice cream,' she said.

Fabian nodded. 'Lots of it, and quickly.'

7

Two days later, Serena took her usual walk into the centre of Iving to peruse the news. A set of large bulletin boards occupied one side of the central city square, displaying all of the latest headlines, and towards these Serena directed her steps. The boards were fashioned via a mixture of Irbellian engineering (unrivalled across the Seven, naturally) and the more ethereal talents of their sorcerers. The ones in the city square were, of course, the very latest example and very impressive indeed. They were enormous, and the quality of the pictures they displayed was remarkable. Serena paid a visit every day, if she possibly could, to keep abreast of the latest news.

Usually there was little of any particular interest, but today swiftly proved to be different. She perused three of the four boards rapidly, finding nothing remarkable, but the fourth... it was devoted entirely to a single story, which was unusual. The bottom two-thirds was given over to a cycling display of pictures, bright and vivid, and the headlines screamed in huge letters across the top.

Ancient Site Discovered at Balbater!

The report, though brief, was packed with information. Serena read it quickly. A new archaeological dig had opened up near the town of Balbater in southern Irbel, and it was proving to be extremely interesting to academics across the realm. More than that; they were fevered with excitement, babbling about the site's total dissimilarity to anything that had been discovered before. The pictures showed what appeared to be an underground cavern, but curiously it was filled with what appeared to be living vegetation, and of a kind Serena had never seen before. Looping vines of a curious, vivid aquamarine hung down from a rocky ceiling, decked with blue-and-purple leaves and golden flowers. Trees and bushes of myriad shapes and sizes clustered in groups, their foliage dazzling in cerulean and hyacinthine hues. The floor was carpeted in a strange kind of grass, much of it jade or teal in colour. There was even a river running through some part of it, the water black and darkly sparkling.

Serena was entranced. She sometimes thought that, had things turned out differently, she might have applied to the University of Iving's archaeology programme and taken up the life of an explorer and academic. She suffered more than a little envy of the people who were, even now, exploring this miraculous site, learning about it and preparing their reports for the elucidation of the world. Too bad that she had no reason whatsoever to go.

The picture of the black river popped up again, and Serena froze. Something had caught her eye, so tiny an image that she had missed it before. She darted closer to the board, scrutinising the image as closely as she could. No, she had not been mistaken.

A fierce excitement blazed in her heart, and she stepped back with a huge smile. Taking her voice-box out of her pocket, she switched it on and waited. When it lit up, she spoke.

'Fabe?'

'Yeah?'

'Get everyone ready. I'm going to see Oliver, and then I think we'll all be taking a little trip south.'

Wisely, Oliver did not attempt to interfere with Serena's plans. It might have been the shine of enthusiasm in her eyes, or possibly the way she threatened to pelt him with custard if he refused; either way, he took her ideas seriously and made no opposition to her going. He did note, in a dry tone, that one or two obstacles stood in her way.

'It'll be swamped,' he observed. 'You'll never get in as you are.'

Serena merely nodded. She'd already anticipated as much, and had relayed instructions to Fabian accordingly.

And he had done an admirable job of preparing her team, she found on her return to their apartment. She arrived to find that Teyo and Egg had donned their LHB uniforms once more and bore convincing-looking credentials. Fabian and Iyamar had taken the guise of a pair of university academics from, they informed her, the history faculty of a tiny university in far eastern Nimdre which nobody had ever heard of. Their identification documents looked real enough, though; Fabian had dashed them off in record time, but he had done a typically excellent job on them nonetheless. They had prepared a matching costume for Serena, who donned it hastily but with care. When she was finished, Serena Carterett had disappeared in favour of a slightly dumpy Nimdren woman approaching middle years, her light brown hair untidily drawn up into a bun, her clothes simple and serviceable.

'Very good work, Mr. Trall,' Serena said to Fabian, practicing her Nimdren elocution.

He bowed with the stiff, somewhat imperfect grace of a stuffy older man, his brittle grey-locked hair flopping slightly into his eyes. 'You are too kind, Miss Huandre.'

'Mrs,' Serena corrected.

Fabian coughed. 'Forgive me.'

She gave him a regal nod of forgiveness, the majesty of the gesture mildly belied by the twinkle in her eyes, and hefted her pack full of Emergency Things. 'Off we go!'

They took the railcar southwards, and within a few hours they disembarked on the outskirts of Balbater, prepared to walk the rest of the way. Though as it happened, they weren't obliged to. News of the site had spread fast, and, as Oliver had predicted, there was a great deal of traffic on its way from Balbater to the site, which lay a mile or two to the west of the town. Some enterprising souls, particularly quick off the mark, had set up a nivven-and-cart relay service from the town to the dig, and Serena found two waiting. She sent Egg and Teyo on ahead in the first cart, and followed a couple of minutes later in the second with Fabian and Iyamar.

They were both excited by the prospect of the site, she judged, though Fabian hid it well. Iyamar really did not, though Serena was too touched by the girl's enthusiasm to correct her demeanour. It was Iya's first real mission, even if there was little for her to do but show up. Serena remembered all too well how she had felt on her first expedition, several years ago now, and took more than a little pleasure in the sparkle in Iya's eyes as the younger girl took in the countryside.

Soon, the fields gave way to jagged hills and the road narrowed. Serena sat with barely concealed impatience as their driver was obliged to slow for the passage of other carts trundling back and forth. Then, as they approached the site itself, they had to crawl their way through crowds of people. Serena cursed the boards just a little. If they hadn't made such an event of it, most of these people — bored bystanders, for the most part — wouldn't be here. Then she remembered that she wouldn't have known about the site either, and swallowed her irritation.

At last, they were set down near the base of a rocky hill that rose abruptly away to the west. Serena paid their driver while Fabian collected her bag. Iyamar, dressed once again as a boy, jumped down with alacrity and stood staring around herself in high anticipation. She was playing the student to Serena's professor, so her eagerness was not at all out of place.

Serena looked around for Teyo and Egg, but couldn't see them. She hoped they had already gained access to the site. She couldn't see the entrance to the dig itself amidst the throng of people, and it took some minutes before Fabian discovered it and led Serena and Iyamar there.

Two LHB agents stood guard over it on high alert, their eyes ceaselessly scanning the crowds. As she watched, two daring enthusiasts approached the guards, talking animatedly, but they were briskly turned away.

'I didn't expect the LHB,' Serena muttered to Fabian. 'Do you think Egg and Teyo made it through?'

Fabian gave a minute shrug. 'Couldn't say. Let's try our luck.'

Serena let Fabian take the lead, following closely behind him with Iyamar. He addressed the nearest LHB agent in his thick Nimdren accent, and waved his fake identification documents. There followed a conversation which Serena couldn't hear over the tumult of the crowd, but it appeared to be successful, for Fabian gave her a nod and gestured forward. Serena allowed the agent to glance at her and Iya's documents, which he did with gratifying brevity, and they were through.

The dig site was situated underneath the rocky hill, Serena surmised, for the entrance was a jagged crack in the side of the hill. She wondered, briefly, how the crack had come to be there; it must, surely, be newly-made if the site had been but just discovered. She expected to find some kind of natural passage on the other side, but instead, and to her great surprise, she found a staircase of stone blocks, neatly made and showing no signs of wear at all. What was this place, that someone had taken the trouble to build stairs but few people had ever used them?

Fabian led the way down, and Serena motioned Iyamar to go ahead of her. She brought up the rear, pausing occasionally to examine her surroundings. The staircase wound around and steadily downwards; someone had scattered light-globes all the way down, so the stairs and walls were properly illuminated. At the top, the rock appeared natural enough in its dark grey hue and blocky appearance. But as she climbed down, she noticed that the appearance of the surrounding walls — and the stairs beneath her feet — was changing. Colours began to creep in: dark shades of blue and purple at first, so dark that they could barely be discerned against the solid, deep grey. They began to grow brighter and more vivid, and developed veins of something that shone white in the light. By the time they reached the bottom of the stairs, the walls around them were turquoise, violet and gold.

Fabian stopped, so abruptly that Iyamar almost collided with his back. He had not seen the pictures, Serena realised, so the site was a complete surprise to him.

She swiftly discovered that the images she had seen did little justice to the reality. A large cavern opened up ahead, so crowded with incongruous vegetation that Serena could only guess at its true size. The vines and foliage that had appeared so sumptuously tinted in the pictures were infinitely more so now that she stood before them herself. Cerulean and deep purple leaves shone in the radiance of the light-globes; the grass underfoot, in its many luscious green tones, resembled the finest plush velvet; and the river, part of which passed by almost directly ahead, glittered darkly, the deepest black Serena had ever beheld. Everything shimmered and pulsed with a kind of energy that she didn't understand at all; she felt it beating upon her skin. The atmosphere was warm and humid, and the air heady with fragrance.

She could not even begin to imagine how such a place could exist underground. As far as she could tell with a cursory examination, the verdure around her was no sculpture; it lived, and grew.

'Wow,' whispered Iyamar.

'Wow,' agreed Serena.

An air of hushed expectancy hung about the place, so heavy that Serena felt they might even be alone down here. As they advanced into the cavern, however, she soon began to see other people. Scholars from, no doubt, many universities were at work all over the site, examining and discussing everything that they saw, making sketches and taking pictures and samples. For the first time, Serena wondered at its classification as an archaeological site. Nothing that she saw appeared to be ancient, or even aged.

There was still no sign of Teyo and Egg, or anybody who was obviously from the LHB. Serena walked about a little, getting her bearings. Leaning close to Fabian, she murmured, 'We need to split up. If we don't hurry we'll be too late.'

He nodded, and Serena quickly dispatched her brother and Iyamar to different parts of the cavern. The thing she sought had been situated on the banks of the glittering black river, but that proved to be larger than she had expected and apparently ran through the whole of the site. What if they were already too late? The only lead that had emerged in weeks and she'd lost it... she sped up, pushing her way through the thick foliage as she followed the river into the depths of the cavern.

Many strange and unfathomable things met her eye as she anxiously scanned the ground. The riverbank was scattered with rocks and stones in all manner of colours, and an occasional object that looked man-made. Many of them interested her exceedingly, but she did not pause to examine them. She pressed on.

Until she rounded a gentle curve in the river's path and came to a dead stop. Ahead of her, two women stood talking. They both bore the white hair that proclaimed their Lokant heritage, and Serena's eyes narrowed. One of them, she was almost sure, was the same woman who had invaded Baron Anserval's private collection and taken the strange key. The other's face was familiar to her as well, and it took a moment for her to realise why. This woman, dressed in practical shirt and trousers and totally unadorned by any kind of jewellery, was none other than Lady Evastany Glostrum herself: co-founder and chief of the LHB, and a minor celebrity in her own right.

What was she doing talking to the thieving Lokant who'd ruined Serena's mission?

Her gaze travelled down as far as the ground, and she froze. There at the thief's feet was the object Serena was looking for: the tiny, insignificant little thing she had seen on the bulletin board.

It was a round little stone, its shape resembling a seashell. This one was cream in colour and threaded with gold, but Serena was almost sure that she was looking at another "key", if such it was. And the same damned thief had found it first.

She hadn't claimed it yet, though; why not? Perhaps she hadn't seen it, or didn't realise its connection to the first (if there was one). Or perhaps she simply wasn't interested. Serena stayed back, keeping herself out of sight and hoping fervently that both women would turn and walk away, leaving the stone alone. They talked for a few moments longer, their conversation inaudible to Serena, and then Lady Glostrum nodded a gracious farewell and left, rapidly disappearing into the verdure.

As soon as Lady Glostrum was out of sight, the other woman stooped down, grabbed the cream-and-golden stone and slipped it into her pocket.

Serena swore, and pulled out her voice-box.

Teyo and Egg had secured entry to the site easily enough, though the problems had begun soon afterwards. The real LHB was already in residence, and not just guarding the entrance. He'd been prepared to see perhaps one or two stray officials down here, and it wouldn't have been difficult to avoid them. But they were here in force. Even their leaders were here in person. Teyo couldn't guess whether Lady Glostrum and Tren Warvel knew every agent of the LHB on sight, and he didn't want to find out.

Egg's brows rose when she saw the groups of LHB agents, and she swore a bit under her breath. 'That complicates things,' she muttered.

'Yeah,' Teyo agreed. He and Egg shrank back against the cavern wall as a group of three agents went past, faces grim, their eyes scanning the cavern for... what? Did they know something about the Lokant woman who'd taken Baron Anserval's key? Did they know about the second key that might be lying down here? Did they know what the keys were for?

Those were questions for Oliver to answer, he decided, dismissing the problem from his mind. For the present, he and Egg needed to focus on finding the second key before someone else did — either the thieving Lokant woman or the LHB — and without being stopped and questioned by any of the real Bureau agents. Tall order.

But every time he and Egg emerged from their hiding place and attempted to resume the search, barely a minute would pass before another Bureau official (or two, or three) walked past, and they were obliged to duck into hiding again. Once, they turned a corner only to find Lady Glostrum herself just ahead. She was not looking at them, and they were able to dart away without being seen. But it was close.

'Hopeless,' muttered Egg after ten minutes of this. She pulled off the white wig that hid her hair, then stripped off her tunic and turned it inside out. In the low light down here, nobody would notice the exposed seams, and it hid the fake LHB insignia that Serena had painstakingly embroidered into the fabric. Teyo swiftly followed suit, and looked down at himself with a frown. Their attire still resembled the Bureau uniform too closely for his comfort, but perhaps it would pass.

Then the voice-box in his pocket buzzed and crackled, and he hastily took it out. Egg dragged him into the shadow of a cluster of overhanging purple vines and kept watch as he activated the device.

'Teyo?' came Serena's voice.

'Yeah.'

'That woman's here and she's got the key.'

Egg muttered something unfavourable about the woman's parents, but Teyo merely sighed. 'Right. Where is she?'

Serena gave him the best information she could, but it was difficult for any of them to get their bearings down here. Teyo foresaw a frustrating chase around the caverns ahead, and sighed. Serena ended by saying, 'Careful with her, T. Don't take any risks.'

He assented to this, and shut off the box. He stood in thought for a moment or two, a process which Egg knew better than to interrupt.

'She's got the stone in the left pocket of her coat,' he murmured. 'But, I don't think you should try to pickpocket it.'

Egg raised her brows.

'Serena's right. She's too dangerous to get close to.' He dug his hand into his own trouser pocket as he spoke. Curled up in a tiny ball at the bottom was Jisp, who grumbled a protest at being so awoken.

Sorry, he apologised. *We need you, Agent Jisp.*

She loved it when he called her that. Snapping awake, she scurried circles around the palm of his hand, bristling with excitement. *What is my mission?!* she trilled in his mind.

Teyo related to her, mostly by way of pictures, the situation at hand. He suffered some disquiet at using Jisp for such a dangerous task, but his choices were few. Jisp was swift, silent and extremely adept at going unnoticed. She was also remarkably good at causing a ruckus when she needed to.

Egg herself was not entirely enthused about the plan, he thought. In fact, he might have said she was miffed at being passed over in favour of a lizard. He would have to make it up to her later.

He set off in the direction he hoped would lead him to their target. Egg, apparently swallowing her displeasure, followed close behind. She made no verbal protests at all and uttered not even a single acid comment, which puzzled Teyo. How thoroughly unlike her. She was probably speechless with indignation, and planning some truly terrible revenge. He would have to be on his guard for unexpected and undoubtedly fiendish retaliation.

He was glad, now, that he had hitched a ride with Lady Fenella down to the Baron's underground gallery, Serena's displeasure notwithstanding. He might have been in an unusual shape at the time, but at least he had seen the Lokant woman. He scanned the face of every white-haired person they approached until Teyo recognised the features of the woman he sought. He crept up until he was within about ten feet of the woman, and stopped, screened behind a flourish of turquoise-and-jade foliage.

She resembled Lady Glostrum more than a little, he realised with a start. Perhaps it was merely that their ages appeared to be approximately the same, and they had similar posture and bearing, in addition to the characteristic white hair. They were also dressed similarly, in practical trousers and shirts and sturdy boots. His quarry wore a long coat, warm against the autumn chill, and Teyo focused his attention on the pocket Serena had indicated.

Teyo bent slowly down and let Jisp go. She scampered away at once, and he retired to watch. Jisp had to cross the distance to her target, climb up the woman's fine suede coat, slip into her left pocket, retrieve the key, climb back down and return to Teyo, all without being observed. He still thought that she had a better chance of pulling this off than Egg, but he couldn't help feeling a little flicker of concern about the wisdom of the plan.

Jisp quickly disappeared from sight in the midst of the thick velvety grass, and he followed her with his thoughts instead. She took great care in transferring herself from the grass to the hem of the woman's coat, and paused there for several long seconds, waiting to see if she had been observed. The woman made no movement, and Jisp began to climb.

Teyo and Egg stood side-by-side, barely breathing, as they watched Jisp's tiny, bright form inch her way up the coat and into the pocket that held the key. Teyo's heart began to thump a little bit harder somewhere in the middle of this process. What if they key wasn't there? He knew better than to imagine that Serena might have got the pocket wrong, but perhaps the woman had transferred it somewhere else in the meantime.

His mind was soon put at rest on that score, as Jisp gleefully reported the presence of the key. In another second, though, her satisfaction turned to dismay.

It's too big, she told him, and he received a brief vision of her trying unsuccessfully to fit her jaws around the stone.

That brought him up short. Having never had the chance to examine one of these key-things closely, he'd had to guess at its size. When the woman had taken the first one, he'd received the impression that it was tiny indeed, fully small enough for him to carry off himself if need be. But he had sized himself a little bigger than Jisp.

Get out of there, he ordered Jisp, who obediently began the descent — though not without transmitting her abject disappointment to Teyo.

Egg cast him a questioning look.

'She can't carry it,' he told her in the barest whisper. 'I'm going to try.' He began at once the process of shifting himself

76

into his Jispish form, but Egg stopped him with a hand on his arm.

'Wig back on,' she murmured very softly.

He didn't waste time asking questions; he had to trust Egg. Retrieving the wig from the capacious pocket he'd stuffed it into, he restored it to his head. Egg adjusted it for him — hers required no alteration at all, of course — and they effected a hasty inversion of their inside-out shirts. Then Egg nodded significantly at something over his left shoulder.

He looked. A small group of university academics had just turned the corner and were approaching their hiding place. A tall, grey-haired man of fiftyish years shepherded a dumpy woman perhaps ten years younger, while a male student showed them something with the eagerness of the young. So convincing a picture did they make, it took him a moment to remember who they were. He shook his head slightly, marvelling. Fabian and Serena's ability to transform themselves into somebody else entirely never ceased to amaze him; their talents in that direction far outstripped his own, or Egg's, for that matter. And it looked as though Iyamar was a worthy student of theirs.

He exchanged a look with Egg, who nodded. Their target was walking away, but slowly, apparently absorbed in the consideration of something Teyo couldn't see and didn't care about. Serena, Fabian and Iyamar drifted steadily in her direction, talking animatedly amongst themselves.

Teyo moved. Without a word, she left their hiding place and headed straight for their target, her forged LHB badge in her hand. She reached the woman a little before Serena's group, and cleared her throat to catch the woman's attention.

'Excuse me, ma'am,' she said, scrupulously polite, and showed her badge. 'Only full members of the LHB or an accredited university are permitted down here at this time. May I see your identification?'

The woman's brows snapped together with annoyance, a scowl that deepened as Serena, Fabian and Iyamar arrived and she found herself surrounded with chattering academics. 'It has already been checked and approved,' she said stiffly. She spoke Irbellian well, but her accent was peculiar. Teyo couldn't recall ever hearing such an intonation before.

Teyo hastily caught up to them. 'My apologies,' he said with a conciliating smile. 'We've received word that there's been an infiltration and we've got some people down here who shouldn't be. Lady Glostrum sent a bunch of us out to double check.' Jisp began at that very moment to climb up the inside of his trouser leg, and he fought to keep his composure. Her tail tickled.

The woman stiffened visibly. 'I am here at Lady Glostrum's request.'

That gave him pause. Lady Glostrum knew this woman? What was she, some kind of consultant with the LHB? And if so, what was she doing stealing from the aristocracy of Irbel? He didn't like to imagine that the leader of the LHB might have put her up to it.

Between the distractions of his questioning and the chatter of Serena, Fabian and Iyamar as they enthused over every single thing they saw, Egg's job was accomplished without incident. She gave him a barely perceptible nod, and he turned his smile from conciliating to ingratiating and made the woman a servile bow. 'My apologies,' he said. 'We meant no offence.'

The woman gave him only the coldest nod in return, and instantly walked away. Teyo and Egg immediately left in the opposite direction, followed, he trusted, by the rest of their team. Jisp, her climb incomplete, rode his hip with a clinging grip as he quickened his pace. It wouldn't take long for the woman to notice that the stone was gone, and he didn't imagine that it would be difficult for her to guess who might have taken it.

Their progress back through the cavern was slower than he would like. Always there were milling academics in their path, or LHB agents still making their patrols. He dragged off his wig again, hoping not to attract their attention, and all but held his breath until the exit came into sight. He and Egg dashed for it, breaking into a near run as they reached the stairs.

They knew better than to wait for Serena. Egg darted out of the cavern ahead of him and immediately began to shove her way through the bustling throng towards the cart-stop. Only a single cart waited there, which Egg spared no efforts to secure. It was Teyo's task to keep an eye out behind — or, indeed, in front, given the Lokant woman's strange translocation abilities — for any sign of pursuit, of which, fortunately, there was none. A few minutes more and he and Egg were ensconced in the cart and on their way back to Balbater, their wigs and tunics discarded. With their own hair showing and clad only in plain, nondescript white shirts, he hoped they would be unrecognisable as the two LHB officials of a few minutes before.

He also hoped that Serena, Fabian and Iyamar had got out safely, but it would be some time before he would find out. His task now, and Egg's, was to protect the stone and get it safely to Oliver Tullen.

8

'So,' said Serena some hours later, when at last she and the rest of the team had made it back to their apartment. 'What happened back there?'

Teyo eyed her warily from his seat in an overstuffed armchair in their lounge. She was wearing a carefully pleasant expression, but he wasn't fooled. She had a steely look in her eye. All had not gone well, he guessed, after he and Egg had left the site. Was it his doing? She had told him not to get too close to the Lokant woman, and he had.

'I sent Jisp in,' he said in a neutral voice, 'but she wasn't big enough. So we had to do it the other way.'

Serena said nothing, only stared at him with no particular expression that he could discern. He had no idea of what was going on in her head, which made him uncomfortable, and she was unhappy about something, which made him even more uncomfortable. He hated it when she did this. He waited her out, returning stare for stare, until she looked away and sighed, and he realised she was tired. Tired and worried about something.

'Took you a long time to get home,' he observed. 'Was there a problem?'

Serena crooked an ironic, annoyed smile at him and flopped into a chair. She hadn't even taken off her wig and make-up yet, and thus still looked wholly unfamiliar to him. Egg was seated not far away, though she was (for once) keeping her thoughts to herself. Fabe and Iyamar had looked in briefly and gone to change.

'Our thief wasn't happy at being thieved from,' Serena said. Dragging off the fluffy brown wig she wore, she threw it on the floor. Egg scowled and immediately scooted over to pick it up. 'Sorry, Egg,' murmured Serena. 'She pinned us down and caused a ruckus, brought the LHB down on us. We had to submit to a full search before she was satisfied that we didn't have the stone. I'm not sure if our identities held up, entirely.' She reached under her shirt and pulled out some padded stuff that had given her the dumpy appearance of middle age. Teyo watched her with some interest, his knitting abandoned in his lap. She rarely permitted anyone to witness her transformations into the characters she played; the best he could get was to watch it in reverse.

'I could've wished for a more peaceful start for Iya,' Serena continued, dumping the padding heedlessly on the floor, 'but she bore it well, to give her due credit. She's going to be great.'

Teyo nodded. He was struggling with a mild feeling of guilt, remembering the way he and Egg had dashed out of there without a thought for the rest of their team. He knew they'd done the right thing — they had got the stone out, which was more important than anything else — but he didn't like to see Serena looking so strained.

'Oliver's got it,' he said in response to her questioning look. 'We took it straight up to the office.'

Serena nodded. 'I knew you'd get through. Any instructions for us?'

Teyo shook his head. He picked up his needles and began knitting more purple yarn into the half-finished blanket that lay, warm and snug, in his lap. 'He'll be in touch. I get the impression that even Oliver doesn't know a lot about these stones yet.'

Serena nodded and lapsed into silence for a while, apparently deep in thought. 'So, this woman is a friend of Lady Glostrum's,' she said at last, and Teyo realised he was forgiven. 'That could be useful to know. Although, it's also a bit worrying. You don't suppose the LHB is behind the theft of Anserval's stone?'

'Couldn't say,' Teyo replied, frowning at a minor glitch in his pattern. 'But I have to doubt it.'

'You never know with those people,' Egg muttered darkly.

Teyo raised a brow at her. 'It seems unlikely.'

'Oh?' Egg cast him a faintly disdainful expression. 'Are you personally acquainted with her ladyship?'

'No, but I believe the LHB to have a well-deserved reputation for fair dealing. I don't think they'd stoop to theft. Anyway, Oliver's been working with them for the past year. There's a solid alliance there, and I don't think he'd be that far wrong.'

Egg snorted. 'Her LadyGlostrumship is as capable of corruption as the next person, and Oliver's as human as the rest of us. I wouldn't bank on it.'

Teyo regarded her with some curiosity. Egg could be acerbic, but she wasn't usually prejudiced or unfair.

'I think we can leave that to Oliver,' Serena said smoothly, before he could make any reply. 'He's the better person to approach her about that connection, and we have to trust him. He's never gone far wrong before.'

Teyo nodded. Egg subsided, muttering, into the blanket that she had drawn all the way up to her chin.

Serena stood up wearily, tugging at the buttons that fastened her drab, oversized shirt. 'I'm going to bed,' she said with a tired smile. 'I'll see you in the morning.'

Before she had taken two steps there came a knock on the apartment door, and she froze. Exchanging one brief, startled look with Teyo, she murmured, 'Who could that possibly be?'

Teyo shared her confusion, and alarm. The location of their dwelling was supposed to be known only to Oliver, but there wasn't the smallest chance that he was the person at the door.

Serena cast a helpless look down at herself. She was half-in and half-out of costume, and looked a ragged mess. Teyo motioned to her to sit down and went to the door himself, while Egg emerged from her blanket and stood up, wary and alert.

There was a peephole in the door, which Teyo made immediate use of. On the other side stood a tall, regal-looking woman with white hair tied up in braids. She wore sturdy trousers and boots and a plain shirt, along with a mildly troubled expression.

Teyo started back, convinced for a horrified second that the Lokant woman they had crossed earlier in the day had discovered them. Then he thought better of it. This woman was wearing headgear with dark-tinted lenses to block out the light, and she was accompanied by a similarly-equipped man with the characteristic pale skin of a Darklander. The lady was not a full Lokant, then, but a partial, for she was a native of the Darklands to the east of Irbel.

'It's Lady Glostrum,' he said.

'What?' said Serena. 'How can that be?'

'Let's find out,' said Teyo, and opened the door.

Her ladyship was greeted with the total silence of three stunned people. She smiled a trifle uncertainly, and dipped her head in greeting. 'I hope you will forgive the intrusion,' she said in a mellifluous voice. 'It is urgent that we speak with you at once.' When nothing but silence greeted this announcement, she added: 'We saw Mr. Tullen, earlier in the day. He sent us to see you.'

Teyo recovered his scrambled wits. 'Of course,' he murmured, and ushered them inside. Observing the way her ladyship's companion — her husband, Tren Warvel, he thought — glanced guardedly behind himself as he entered the apartment, Teyo took the precaution of triple-locking the door.

Serena and Egg performed a brief dash about the room, preparing chairs for their unexpected visitors and dimming the light-globes as low as they could possibly go. Low enough for the Darklanders to remove their headgear, it seemed, for they both set aside their lenses gratefully.

'I hope we haven't alarmed you,' said Mr. Warvel with an apologetic smile. He offered a note to Teyo, who was nearest to him. The note was clearly in Oliver's handwriting, and arranged with typical terseness. *See these people*, it said, and was followed by nothing save a scrawled signature. Teyo passed it to Serena without comment.

Serena made hurried introductions. Teyo knew her well enough to see the embarrassment she felt at appearing in such attire before such visitors, though he didn't imagine that it was apparent to Lady Glostrum or Mr. Warvel. The two paid close attention to the names of Serena's team, he thought; he wasn't sure why. Reclaiming his former seat, Teyo took up his knitting and prepared to sit in quiet observation. Serena would handle the talking — unaided by Egg, apparently, whose scowl suggested she was keeping a number of unpleasant thoughts unspoken.

Lady Glostrum began without preamble: 'What really happened down at the dig site today?'

Serena considered the question, her eyes slightly narrowed. 'What account did you receive from your friend?'

Neither seemed to require any elucidation of the term "friend". 'Something important was stolen from her today,' Lady Glostrum replied. 'Some Lokant artefact, the identity of which she was not inclined to share.' Her ladyship paused, eyeing Serena's half-costume, and continued, 'The three academics she accused were not academics, I think?'

Serena nodded once.

Lady Glostrum reached into a pocket and withdrew the gold-threaded stone. 'Oliver Tullen called at the LHB headquarters this afternoon, and gave this into my keeping. I believe you know a little more about it?'

Serena's brows rose as she saw the stone, and a look of consternation came into her eyes. 'Ah... does your friend know that you have that?'

'I have not yet told her,' replied her ladyship.

'Shall you?'

'That depends on the outcome of this conversation.'

Serena looked at Teyo. He gazed steadily and confidently back. He and Egg had delivered the stone into Oliver's own hands; if Lady Glostrum possessed both that and a note with Oliver's signature, Teyo felt no reason to doubt her.

Serena nodded once, and related in all due detail the events of Dame Halavere's ball and their subsequent visit to Baron Anserval's house. Teyo noted, with some amusement, the flicker of distaste that crossed both Lady Glostrum's and Mr. Warvel's face when the Baron was mentioned, and wondered how these two knew his lordship.

When Serena came to recount how the Lokant woman had stolen the first stone — or key, if indeed it was — she looked disappointed, which was not what Teyo might have expected. She did not interrupt Serena, however, listening with close attention to the end of her account.

When Serena had finished, Lady Glostrum turned her attention to Teyo. 'That word, "key",' she said. 'It was you who first heard it applied to those stones?'

'Yes. I got it from a contact within the Unspea— within the Yllandu organisation.'

The faint glint of amusement in her ladyship's eyes suggested that she could guess what the rest of the abandoned word would have been, and also that she appreciated the joke. She understood Ullarni, then.

'That's all that you know?' she enquired. 'Do you have any information regarding why they're thought to be keys, and what they might open?'

Teyo shook his head. 'If anybody knows, it will be the higher-ups, and I don't have access to them.'

'Perhaps not even they,' Lady Glostrum mused.

Mr. Warvel cleared his throat apologetically and looked at his wife. 'It does sound as though Ylona's been playing both sides.'

Lady Glostrum sighed and nodded. 'Ylona is the Lokant from whom you took this stone,' she explained to Teyo, Serena and Egg. 'Ylona Duna. She is, indeed, a consultant with the LHB, and one of our liaisons with the Libraries. In fact, the LHB was present at the Balbater site on her advice. She said she expected to find a very important Lokant artefact, though she would not tell me what it was, or why she had reason to believe it would be discovered there.'

She looked a little sad. 'Friend of yours?' Teyo ventured.

Lady Glostrum nodded once. 'But it would not be the first time that a Lokant has turned out to be… not what I thought.' She frowned, and added, 'I wish I could believe that her motives are good, even if her methods are questionable. But I cannot guess at her goals.'

'Halavere?' queried Mr. Warvel.

His wife's face darkened. 'That is another problem, yes. I hadn't suspected her of such dealings. I knew she was close with Ylona, though. I wonder what Ylona promised her?' She gave herself a little shake as if to dismiss her reflections, and sat up a little straighter. 'I will do what I can to wring some more information out of Ylona,' she said decisively. 'Or to trick it out of her, if necessary.' She looked down at the stone in her hand, considering. 'I think for the present this might be safest left with you. It seems certain that Ylona has, as yet, no idea of your identities or involvement. The same cannot be said for mine.'

She made a move to hand it to Serena, but something caught her attention and she raised the stone close to her eyes, frowning slightly. 'There is something written,' she murmured. 'It is a little faded, and in an old Lokant dialect…' she trailed off. 'It says,' she continued at last, 'Seven Realms, Seven Dreams.'

Serena's brows rose. 'Perhaps, then, there are seven stones. Or keys. Or whatever.'

Lady Glostrum smiled with faint irony. 'There are Lokant Librarians involved, so naturally it is destined to become very complicated indeed. Seven stones will be the least of it, I would think.'

'Do you think you can get the first one back from Ylona?' Serena asked.

Lady Glostrum looked doubtful. 'I'd imagine she's taken it back to her Library, which none can access. But I'll try.' She looked at Teyo. 'At the risk of repeating myself: did anything about "Dreams" come up when you talked with your Unspeakable contacts?'

Teyo's lips curved in brief appreciation of her use of the irreverent moniker. 'No,' he said, 'but I can ask around.'

'I wonder if the site is one of these "Dreams",' Lady Glostrum mused. 'It struck me as reminiscent of Ayrien — the Lower Realms. You know that draykoni can manipulate that realm, and the Uppers, into taking whatever appearance they choose? The nature of that site — a jungle underground, the colours, the confused mixture of vegetation and lifeforms, the fact that it appears to be alive but doesn't seem to grow — all of that reminds me strongly of Ayrien. Though I have never seen anything like it within the Seven before.'

'But if this Ylona is so interested in the place, and it contained a Lokant artefact, surely it is a Lokant site?' said Serena.

'Perhaps it has merely been appropriated by them, at some time in the past,' Lady Glostrum mused. 'Or perhaps it is both. Draykoni and Lokants have been known to work together before, you know.'

Serena nodded slowly, thinking. 'Who discovered the site?' she asked abruptly.

Lady Glostrum blinked. 'I don't know,' she said.

'Maybe Ylona had something to do with it,' Serena continued. 'Maybe she knew it was there. If it is one of those "Dreams" and there are six more, maybe she knows where to find those, too.'

Egg finally spoke up. 'If she did, why didn't she just go and take the stone herself? Why report the discovery, wait until it was full of people and *then* go in search of the key?'

'Good point,' Serena conceded. 'But it's not all bad. If her information is limited and there are more of these keys, maybe we've got a chance of finding them first.'

'With zero information,' Egg said dryly. 'The first site was hidden in a hillside near Balbater. What are we going to do, search every inch of every Realm?'

'Anyway, if it's the first site of seven that's been found, how is it that Anserval had one of the stones?' put in Teyo.

Lady Glostrum sighed. 'Too many questions, and I can't answer any of them. Yet. We'll need more information.' She looked at Teyo, and he nodded to her.

'I'll do what I can with the Unspeakables,' he confirmed.

'And I'll do what I can with Ylona.'

'I'll see Oliver,' Serena added. 'He might get the Agency on it, if he thinks it's important.'

Lady Glostrum smiled. 'Ylona is the leader of a Library I've dealt with before, and it wasn't much fun last time. If they are involved, then it is important. And likely to involve a number of things we'd prefer to interfere with.'

'Not only that,' Egg added, 'it seems as though the Unspeakables are heavily involved, too, and they always need a good thwarting.'

Lady Glostrum opened her mouth to say something else, but a sound like a muffled roar crossed with a scream drowned out whatever it might have been. Teyo sat up, dropping his knitting. The scream had been human, but the rest sounded more like draykoni.

Fabian's head appeared around the door. Ignoring the extra company, he barked, 'Teyo, get here,' and vanished again.

Teyo ran to the hallway. There was no further sign of Fabian, but he didn't need to be told that Iyamar was in trouble. He went straight to her room, where he found Fabian blocking the doorway.

'Move,' growled Teyo, and Fabian backed away.

Iya was half-standing, half-crouched in the middle of her room. She was mid-shift, somewhere between human and draykoni; her body had already taken on the polished amber scales and some of the expanded proportions of her draykon form, and her wings were beginning to sprout. What was she *doing*, trying to shift in here? The room wasn't nearly big enough to accommodate her as a draykon. She would break it to pieces.

In another second he realised that she was fighting the change. Her face briefly reappeared, pale and distraught, but the long muzzle, sharp teeth and glittering eyes of the draykon soon reasserted themselves. And she was growing.

With horror, Teyo realised that she had never yet learned to control the shift.

Iya was obviously panicking, and Teyo began to feel panicked himself. Fabian had summoned him because he was the only one who had even the smallest chance of helping her. But what could he do? She had to shift back herself, he couldn't do it for her.

Iya, breathe slowly and focus on your human shape, he told her. *Don't let the draykon distract you. You're a human girl, with pale blonde hair and blue eyes...*

He talked on in similar fashion, but it wasn't working. He couldn't even tell whether she was hearing him. She grew so big that her back brushed the ceiling; her panic grew in proportion, and she began thrashing wildly. Teyo heard the splintering of furniture and the crash of objects striking the ground.

Then he was roughly shoved out of the way, and Lady Glostrum strode into the room. She took a brief, appraising look at the stricken Iya and then shouted: *'Look at me.'* Her voice rang with authority, and Teyo found that he couldn't help obeying her command, even though it had not been directed at him. He stared at her, transfixed.

'You are a human,' said Lady Glostrum firmly. 'You will not shift here.'

Teyo did not seriously imagine that such an approach would work; if it was as simple as speaking to her, he would have done that himself. But... but the draykon was shrinking, disappearing. A minute or two passed agonisingly slowly as Iyamar gradually regained control of herself, her human form appearing more and more solid as the moments passed. She stood, trembling with shock and fear and exhaustion, her thin face stark white. Feeling shaken himself, Teyo went to her at once, gently bade her sit down upon her bed, and wrapped her in a blanket.

'What was that?' whispered Iyamar, staring at Lady Glostrum with a mixture of relief, awe and horror in her young face.

'It is a Lokant ability,' said her ladyship. 'A compulsion. I am sorry. It was brutal, but necessary.'

'That was terrible,' said Iyamar bleakly. 'But... thank you.'

Lady Glostrum nodded, and turned to leave. She was brought up short by the sight of Serena, Fabian, Egg and her husband all gathered just outside the room, staring at her in horror.

'Oh, no,' she said. 'Did you all feel it?'

'I should *say* so,' said Egg acidly. 'Can you all do that?'

'Any full Lokant can, though the degree of talent varies. Very few Partials can.'

Nobody spoke.

'It probably wouldn't have worked if the young lady had been actively trying to shift,' said her ladyship. 'Draykoni aren't so easily persuaded as that, in fact! All I have done is to reinforce her own will.'

This explanation did not do very much to settle the alarms of her ladyship's audience, Teyo's included. The silence continued, and Lady Glostrum began to look a little uncomfortable.

Then Serena came forward, smiling. 'You've saved the roof of our apartment and Iyamar's peace of mind besides. And we are grateful. Just a bit... surprised.'

'Horrified,' corrected Egg. 'Is Ylona the one training you?'

Lady Glostrum nodded.

'So she can do all that?'

'I'm afraid so.'

'Brilliant,' muttered Egg. She spun around, as though literally turning her back on the whole mess, and stalked away.

9

Iyamar, Egg and Teyo were arguing. Loudly.

Serena sat with Fabian in the parlour of their apartment, she sipping from a large mug of steaming cayluch, Fabian half-lying in his armchair with his long legs stretched out before him and his eyes directed ceilingward. His dark hair, unbound, spilled messily over the cushions; Serena guessed that he hadn't brushed it for a day or two. She itched to neaten it for him, but knew better than to interfere.

The raised voices emanating from the next room belonged mostly to Iyamar and, to a lesser extent, Egg. Teyo she barely heard, which surprised her not at all. He rarely spoke above a normal volume, and never shouted.

'But I hate it!' Iyamar yelled. 'I didn't *ask* for it!'

'We didn't ask to have our apartment ripped open by a draykon either,' retorted Egg. 'You put us all at risk by refusing training.'

'Then I'll leave!'

'If you won't let Teyo train you, you'll have to,' said Egg ruthlessly. 'Good luck on the streets. You might want to work on your highwaywoman routine a bit.'

Serena winced. Egg could be vicious when she was angry. Teyo's deep rumble intervened at that point, though she couldn't hear what he said. She took the opportunity to say to Fabian, 'Lady Glostrum said she'd be in touch about the key thing.'

Fabian shrugged, an awkward gesture in his current posture. 'I don't see that it has a lot to do with us from here on.'

Serena smiled coldly. 'But it does, because it has a lot to do with the Unspeakables.'

Fabian raised an eyebrow at her.

'Lady Glostrum thinks that Ylona Duna is using them to find — or steal — the keys. They aren't exactly for hire like that, so if they're consenting to help, they must be interested in these keys, too. And that means it's got to be big.'

'But I'm *not!*' shrieked Iyamar. 'I'm not a draykon! I'm a human, like everyone else! I *refuse* to be anything else!'

There followed a crashing sound, which Serena guessed to indicate Egg kicking something.

Fabian said, 'Anything that's got Lokants *and* Unspeakables involved has got to be big. It's also got to be crazy, dangerous and none of our business.'

'*What* advantages?' shouted Iyamar. 'It's brung nothing but trouble! My own gang kicked me out! They acted like I was a monster, and — and they're right!'

Teyo said something.

'Of course I don't think *you're* a monster!' yelled Iyamar.

Teyo said something else, which apparently silenced her.

'We could make it our business,' said Serena, taking a sip of creamy cayluch.

'Why would we?' said Fabian.

'Because it would be an adventure!' she said grandly, with a dazzling smile. 'Aren't you intrigued?'

'Nope.'

Serena gave a small sigh. 'Well then, because it is our business to oppose the Unspeakables in every possible way, *especially* when they're doing something sneaky, underhanded, mysterious, probably dangerous and potentially disastrous.'

'When aren't they?'

'But I *can't*,' wailed Iyamar in tones of utter despair. Teyo was getting somewhere, Serena thought. She'd gone from furious accusations to dramatic and rage-filled denials and now to despairing under-confidence. Resignation would follow soon enough, and after that — progress. Hopefully.

'You feeling okay, Fabe?' Serena said cautiously.

'Fine,' he said.

She said nothing for a moment, listening to the low drone of

Teyo's voice from the next room. 'Do you want to visit mother today?' she said next.

'Maybe.'

She began to say something else, but Fabian interrupted. 'I found out something.'

'Oh?'

He shifted in his seat. 'About father.'

'Fabe...' Serena said slowly. 'I thought we'd agreed to let it go?'

He directed one swift, angry look at her. 'You agreed. I didn't.'

Serena's heart sank a little. 'All right,' she said in a neutral voice. 'What did you find out?'

'Bironn Astre,' said Fabian. 'We got *him*, but he wasn't the only one involved. There was someone else.'

Serena heard this with mixed feelings. Foreboding and dismay warred with concern for Fabian and... and a rising anger. Much as she tried to put it behind her, she wasn't immune to the feelings that tormented her brother either.

Their father, Thomaso Carterett, had been a small-time landowner in the far south of Irbel, right on the border with Nimdre. He had been able to give his two children a good education, and the family had lived prosperously for some years.

But sometime during those years, he had begun to drink. He drank more, and more, until money was tight and their mother, Theresa, began to wear a perpetually worn, anxious look. One night, Thomaso had got involved with a card game. He'd been very, very drunk, and the game had ended with the total loss of everything he had — their house, land, everything.

Two days later, he'd hanged himself.

Fabian and Serena had never completed their expensive education. Obliged to work as they could to support their increasingly ailing mother, they had learned to rely more and more upon each other, and upon their shared gift for acting. They had worked as players for some years, taking jobs with theatres across Irbel and Nimdre, and all the while they sought to learn the truth about the card game that had ended so disastrously for their father.

At length, they had learned a name: Bironn Astre. He hadn't just been lucky, they found. He had deliberately targeted Thomaso as an easy mark. He was a member of the Yllandu organisation, a fresh recruit, and he'd manipulated the game — cheated, in other words — in order to ensure that Thomaso lost. The Unspeakables required each applicant to complete some kind of con or theft or cheat in order to prove their worthiness, and Astre's had been sufficient to secure his membership. The proceeds of his efforts — Serena and Fabian's family home — had been handed over to the Yllandu by way of an entrance fee, and he'd gone on to perform many more cons as part of the organisation.

Until Serena and Fabian, now members of the Torwyne Agency, had succeeded in catching him. He had been in prison for four years already, and would not be released for many more.

Serena had hoped that was the last of it, though more for Fabian's sake than for her own. While she felt anger, indignation, sadness and a host of other emotions over the fate of her poor father and their family lands, she wanted more than anything to put it behind her and move on. Surely the last thing their father would have wanted was for his family to suffer for his mistakes.

Fabian, though, had been obsessed with it from the day of their father's death, and he possessed a burning need to exact some kind of revenge. It was, she thought, the source of the black moods which sometimes assailed him. Jailing Bironn Astre had been enough, for a little while. Serena was not surprised, though she was dismayed, to learn that he had taken up the matter once more.

She didn't say any of this out loud, of course. Fabian reacted badly to any suggestion that he ought to let it lie. Instead, she merely said: 'Who was this other person?'

'A woman,' he said. 'Her name was Valore Trebel at the time, though I don't think it is any more. I can't find any trace of her.'

A renewed howl of misery from the next room interrupted Serena's train of thought, and she looked to the door, feeling the first twinges of annoyance with the disruption.

'I can't, I can't!' wept Iyamar. 'Stop pushing me!'

Serena tried to school herself to patience. She didn't think that Iyamar was naturally melodramatic or difficult; nothing she had seen until today had suggested it. But the girl was very young, and bitter, and very, very afraid.

'I think it's time to intervene,' Serena muttered, setting aside her cup. She strode to the door and threw it open.

A little parlour lay beyond, much of the cramped room taken up with a table and six chairs. Teyo was sitting at his ease in one of the chairs, his feet set upon the table. Egg stalked about at the back of the room, scowling fiercely. She was probably working herself up to kicking something again.

Iyamar huddled in a corner, clutching herself and sobbing.

'Iyamar,' said Serena. 'You do know that Teyo can shift into other forms besides the draykon?'

Iyamar made no response for a few moments. Then, she lifted her head and stared at Serena. 'You mean like… like Jisp?'

Serena smiled inwardly; she'd hoped that would get Iya's attention. The girl adored Jisp, and frequently abducted the little lizard from Teyo's care. The prospect of being able to join her tiny playmate in a similar shape couldn't fail to appeal to her.

'If you learn to shift between human and draykoni, you'll also be learning to shift into other forms,' Serena continued. 'It's the same thing.'

Iyamar said nothing, but her tears had dried up and she appeared much struck by the idea.

Serena turned her attention to Egg. 'You'd better come in here, Egg,' she said coolly. 'The furniture cannot bear very much more violence today, I think.'

She turned and swept back into the living room, disposing herself comfortably upon the divan once more. A moment later, Egg came trailing in.

'Sorry,' she muttered. 'Only it's just so —so *very*—'

'I know,' said Serena.

Egg nodded and went to the door. 'Got to say, though,' she added, pausing on the threshold. 'Kid doesn't let anybody push her around. I like that.' She left.

Fabian said, 'I'm going to chase it up.'

Serena just looked at him. He stared back, unrepentant and uncowed.

She struggled with herself. It wasn't good for him to wear out his life and his youth in bitterness and schemes of revenge, and she wished so very much that she could do something to change his heart. But she couldn't, and it mattered to him more than anything else in the world.

Fabian added, 'We might… we might get it all back.'

He meant the house and the land. As though returning to the place of their childhood would make everything better; that it would reverse, somehow, the effects of their father's ruin and suicide and their mother's madness. Serena didn't think that it would, but Fabian... Fabian believed it with all his heart.

'I'll help you,' she said.

Fabian smiled.

'But!' she added, her lips curving into a mischievous smile, 'I want your help with the keys, too.'

Fabian grinned. 'It's to be a bargain, is it? That's my sister.' He stood up and stretched, looking suddenly better. She watched him with a mixture of gladness and concern. If only it had been something else — anything else — returning that lively sparkle to his eyes! But he was interested in nothing else. He was as he was, and Serena would have to do what she did best: damage control.

She only hoped she could rein Fabian in enough to avert the total disaster she feared lay ahead. If Fabian felt that something lay between him and his notions of justice — obstacles, people, anything — no power could stop him. He would do whatever it took to remove them, at any risk to himself. And though he never willingly endangered either his sister or his team, his actions couldn't help but affect them, too, sometimes.

Serena finished the last of her cayluch, watching as Fabian left the room with a new bounce in his step. She stood up and wandered to the window, wrapping her shawl tightly around herself. Outside, the sun hung low in the sky, golden and shining with that peculiar autumnal radiance that she loved. The mist of the early morning had gone, the clouds had dissipated, and the day was fine, if chill. The edge of the city was spread before her, and beyond it, fields recently harvested of their bounty. She gazed at all this goodness for some time, reflecting with some little concern on the many complications that were suddenly cropping up in her life. There was Iyamar's training to attend to, if she would permit it; Fabian was on the trail of a second Bironn Astre, and like to grow obsessive over it; full Lokants and partial Lokants and the LHB wandering in and out of her life; mysterious artefacts and strange archaeological discoveries cropping up all over the place; Halavere Morann and Ylona Duna's questionable loyalties; and all of that on top of her regular job. At least Teyo and Egg were stable, steady and reliable, and needed little of her help or guidance.

She hoped, with a long, inward sigh, that the next few weeks would prove to be quiet ones, and that Fabian would soon resolve this new mission and move on.

A glitter of something dark caught her eye, and she raised her gaze to the sky. It was a bird of some kind, or probably a small flock of them. Their behaviour was odd; they were hovering in a tight cluster in the sky, in a fashion wholly incompatible with typical birdly behaviour.

No. It was not a bird, nor anything like. Her unbelieving eyes discerned the shape of a letter forming in the sky, an S, in glittering, inky black. More followed, until a word appeared.

Seven.

She watched, transfixed, her heart pounding. More words appeared, bit by bit, as though someone were writing each letter one at a time upon the sky.

Seven mortal Realms I saw and seven keys had I.

The sentence was written clearly, like dark, silvered ink upon blue parchment. More came.

Seven Dreams I wrought anew and cast them sea to sky.
Find the treasures, win the games and all the world explore,
Live the fables, be the tales, and you will find the door.

There followed a symbol, a round glyph of some kind, which it took Serena a moment to decipher. It was, she realised, a representation of the seashell spiral pattern that characterised the strange stone they had found at the dig site.

'Wha...' she murmured, stunned.

The door opened behind her, and Egg's voice interrupted her stupor. 'Er, Serena? There are words in the air.'

'I know,' she said faintly.

'Any idea what that's all about?'

'No idea.'

'Should be fun,' said Egg, and disappeared again. Serena listened absently to her footsteps fading away, her brain struggling to make sense of what she saw.

One thing only was clear to her: all hope of a quiet few weeks must be abandoned. Things were about to become... complicated.

10

'I want to hire you,' said Lady Glostrum, and smiled.

It was two days later. Serena and her entire team — even Iyamar, who had mostly recovered from her agonies — were assembled in Oliver Tullen's office. They had been peremptorily summoned by note, and urged to make all due haste. That had alarmed Serena, just a little. Oliver was never in a hurry.

On reaching his office, however, she had swiftly discovered that it was not Oliver who wished to see them, but Lady Glostrum. Her ladyship and her husband were comfortably ensconced in Oliver's better chairs, though neither of them looked especially relaxed. They were conferring together in hushed undertones as Serena's team walked in, while Oliver watched the play of images on a portable bulletin board he possessed. Serena felt more than a little covetousness for that device. They were fabulously expensive and had to be given regular maintenance by the sorcerer's guild of Irbel; very few people could contrive to own one.

'Excellent!' her ladyship had said upon seeing them arrive. The smile she had bestowed upon them had been very friendly, but also a little bit calculating. 'That was quick, indeed. Excellent. I do so like promptitude.'

Egg's body had stiffened with displeasure and suspicion upon seeing Oliver's visitors. 'What are you doing here?' she demanded. 'And what are *we* doing here?'

'You are here at my request, Ms. Rutherby,' Oliver had said briefly, without looking up from his board.

Egg had folded her arms and glared. When her ladyship spoke the word "hire", Egg's suspicions hardened into serious displeasure. 'Ohhh,' she said with appalling sarcasm, 'of course you do! It's lucky that we're available to every random person who finds their way in here. Oh, no, wait. We're not.'

Oliver ignored this outburst. Addressing himself to Serena, he looked up briefly from his perusal of the news and said, 'I imagine you will have guessed the nature of the job, Ms. Carterett.'

'Something to do with the riddle?' said Serena. She could not entirely suppress the note of hope that crept into her voice. In spite of Fabian's indifference and Egg's loudly-voiced disapproval, she would like nothing better than to find herself involved with this adventure.

The boards had been full of nothing else since the glittering words had appeared in the sky. The riddle had captured the imagination, and excited the curiosity, of the whole world, or so it seemed. It was talked of everywhere Serena went; everyone had some theory to share; and everyone wanted to know what the keys were, and where the mysterious door might lead.

It hadn't taken the boards' journalists long to make the connection between the Balbater dig site and the riddle that had appeared so soon afterwards, either. Teams of scholars, adventurers and treasure-seekers had quickly assembled and set out to seek more sites like it. Nobody had yet discovered any new site, that she had heard.

Oliver nodded his head at Lady Glostrum, ceding the floor to her. 'It *is* about the riddle!' said her ladyship. 'However did you guess?'

Serena smiled. 'But how can we help? We are not academics or explorers.'

'But I have plenty of those,' she said. 'Team LHB, as some are inclined to call it, already sports a full cast of historians, geographers, anthropologists, archaeologists, cartographers, explorers, linguists and assorted others who all think they can find another site like Balbater dig. I don't need any more of those.'

'What do you need?'

'I need a small group of resourceful people with many

unusual skills, and who are accustomed to working together. And I do not think it will hurt at all if two of them happen to be shapeshifters.'

Serena glanced at her colleagues. Fabian stood to her right with his hands in his pockets, looking as though his mind was only half occupied with the conversation. The other half, she supposed, was mulling over the problem of Valore Trebel. Iyamar hung back near the door, a trace of a frown creasing her young brow — probably prompted by the word "shapeshifter", Serena guessed. Teyo stood with silent attention, showing no sign of either approval or disapproval.

Egg gave a scornful laugh. 'So you just want to pick us up and make use of us at your convenience, is that it? We've got those interesting, *slightly illegal* skills and you never know when you might need them.' She paced in a tiny circle, working herself up into a fine rant. 'You aristocrats! As if owning half the world wasn't enough, you think you can pick up and drop the rest whenever it suits you!'

Lady Glostrum did not appear to be offended by this outburst. On the contrary, she watched Egg with a mild kind of amusement. That, of course, only incensed Egg more.

Serena remembered Egg's words when the riddle had appeared in the sky. *Should be fun.*

'Egg,' she said forcefully, interrupting the next chapter of her enraged musings.

'What?'

'Do you have any objection to the job?'

'Wouldn't miss it for the world,' said Egg promptly.

Serena frowned.

'It's the principal of the thing!' exploded Egg. 'I don't want a snotty aristocrat for a boss!'

'Not to worry. I'll be your boss,' interposed Tren, with a beaming smile. 'That ought to be acceptable, shouldn't it? I am no aristocrat.'

'Married to one,' Egg muttered.

'Still a one hundred per cent, pure-bred commoner,' said Tren cheerfully.

Egg muttered something inaudible and fell silent.

'Excellent,' said Lady Glostrum. 'That's settled.'

Serena felt a flash of excitement. Fabian's lack of interest in the puzzle was mystifying to her, though to be fair, her lack of interest in Valore Trebel was equally mystifying to him.

'Does anybody else have any objections?' she said quickly, and looked around at Teyo and Iya, hoping very hard that they would not. Teyo gave her a gentle smile by way of answer, and Iya said nothing at all. But since she voiced neither objections nor approval, Serena took her silence as assent. 'Great!' she said, beaming. 'What do we know about the riddle?'

Lady Glostrum grinned at her enthusiasm. 'Nothing at all, save that it is most likely of Lokant fabrication. Though of course, we haven't the faintest idea how it might be done.'

The words in the sky were still there, two days later. They had neither faded nor vanished, remaining unchanged no matter the hour of the day. Nor were they confined to Irbel; pictures of the riddle in the skies above the other Realms had flashed up on the boards very quickly. In the Darklands realms — Glour, Orstwych and Ullarn — the words were traced across the night-dark heavens in pale silver moonlight. In Nimdre and Orlind, the riddle's appearance altered with the changing of the light, from sparkling black during the day to ghostly moonlight at night.

'I can't help suspecting some degree of draykon involvement with it, though,' Eva continued. 'Which is why I shan't object to having an extra draykon or two at my disposal.'

Teyo said, 'I don't know of any way to do *that.*'

'No, that's what all the others said, too,' said her ladyship comfortably. 'But we'll figure it out.'

'I don't understand what it's for,' said Teyo. 'The riddle.'

Tren said, 'Yes, good question. A few days ago, we were asking ourselves how to find other sites like the Balbater dig, with no clues whatsoever. They could be anywhere. All we can guess is that there is, or was, one in each of the Realms, although how long ago these sites were created and scattered, we know not. What was the world like in those days? That's why we've got historians and archaeologists involved.

'It did occur to us that the case was virtually hopeless. We'd have to get half the world involved in order to find all the sites, said we. And possibly, someone else had the same thought.'

Lady Glostrum nodded. 'I suspect that whoever's behind this has no more idea how to find them than we do, so they're using us. And what better way to get half the world involved than to set up a giant treasure hunt? It's clever.'

'Fiendishly,' said Serena.

Egg muttered something acerbic and luckily inaudible.

'Where does the door go?' said Iyamar.

Serena looked up in surprise. The girl had been so quiet, she'd almost forgotten her presence. But Iya — interested in spite of herself, it seemed — had drawn closer, and now watched Lady Glostrum and Mr. Warvel with an expression of keen curiosity.

'We've no notion,' said her ladyship with obvious chagrin. 'It's the first mention we've heard of a door. Though I suppose, if we have keys of some kind, there being a door to be opened isn't the greatest surprise.'

'We have people working on that, too,' Tren offered. 'Not that we needed to ask. I think the history faculties at virtually every university in the Seven dropped everything they were doing and started hitting up the books and maps. If they find any mention of mysterious keys or doors or the Seven Dreams, I daresay we'll all hear about it.'

'I don't think they'll find anything,' Lady Glostrum said. 'Remember how nobody knew the draykoni had ever really existed, until suddenly they reappeared? Every mention of them in every book had been excised by Lokants long ago. They're very thorough, when they want to hide something.'

Tren grimaced, and nodded. 'True enough.'

'So,' said Serena, 'what is our task?'

Lady Glostrum just looked at her for a moment. 'I'm not sure you'll like it.'

Serena's brows rose. 'Oh?'

Her ladyship shifted in her chair. 'All right. I have two things in mind.'

Serena waited.

'Firstly, we aren't going to be the first to reach all of these sites. Maybe none of them. Other people are going to find at least some of those keys, and we'll need to get them back.'

'You mean steal them,' said Egg flatly.

Lady Glostrum gave her a cool look. 'If it comes to that. I hope that it won't. But remember, please. We don't know what this is about, but it is certainly a matter of international security. I don't want those keys falling into the hands of whoever's using us to find them; Lokants and power tend to become explosive when mixed together. If I have to use underhand means to prevent that, I will.'

Serena nodded. She didn't like the idea of stealing the "treasure" from people who'd found it fair and square, but she had to admit the justice of Lady Glostrum's reasons. 'Fair enough.'

'The other thing is…' said her ladyship, and hesitated.

'Yes?'

'The first site was underground,' she said. 'That was convenient. But the riddle suggests that not all of them are.'

Seven Dreams I wrought anew and cast them sea to sky. Indeed. 'And?'

'If there are any in the sea or in the sky, we're going to need some way of reaching them.'

'Is that why you want draykoni shapeshifters?' said Teyo. 'To search the skies?'

Lady Glostrum hesitated. 'Not exactly. I understand that the draykoni aren't all that well suited to staying in the air for long periods of time, is that right?'

'True enough,' Teyo admitted. 'Better for short, screamingly powerful, rage-filled and utterly terrifying bursts of speed.'

Lady Glostrum grinned. 'I've travelled by draykon-back before, and I wouldn't like to so burden friends again. I had something else in mind, namely the Irbellian mailships, or something like them.'

That was clever. Irbel possessed an efficient mail delivery system whereby the post was carried by air. The mailships were balloon-based flying machines, slow but stable, and certainly able to remain aloft for long periods. Neither the machines nor the technology were shared with, or sold to, other Realms, nor were they available for purchase or hire, save to the few very wealthy citizens of Irbel who could afford it.

As that reflection crossed her mind, a feeling of foreboding swiftly followed.

'Do you,' she said carefully, 'happen to know anybody with an airship?'

Lady Glostrum coughed. 'I gather from Mr. Tullen that we do indeed know somebody.'

Serena sighed.

'Baron Anserval has a particularly fine specimen,' Lady Glostrum continued.

'I was afraid you were going to say that,' muttered Serena.

'It would give us a huge advantage,' Lady Glostrum said

quickly. 'No one else is going to have an airship to hand! We might find the skyborne ones before anyone else.'

Serena inched a little closer to Fabian and leaned disconsolately against him.

'What?' he said, blinking down at her. 'Oh. He's not all that bad, sis.'

Serena blinked incredulously at her fatuous brother.

'Oh, right,' he amended after a moment. 'No, he really is that bad.'

'It's lucky,' said Serena, turning her attention back to Lady Glostrum, 'that the head of the LHB can just commandeer his airship. No need for me to get involved there.' She smiled brightly, an expression which quickly faded when her ladyship shook her head.

'My authority doesn't extend so far, I'm afraid. Besides, I'd like him to give us his airship voluntarily. Leaving a trail of resentful, powerful people behind me isn't my favourite approach to any job.'

Serena's shoulders slumped, but she made no further objections. Anserval was an idiot and in possession of a particularly repellent personality, but if she had to deal with him in order to pursue this most intriguing of mysteries, she would live with it. At least she only had to put up with him for as long as it took to persuade him to hand over his ship.

'When do you want to leave?'

Lady Glostrum smiled. 'Five minutes ago wouldn't be too soon.'

Her ladyship left Serena with one parting injunction: *Do not, under any circumstances, talk to him about the keys.* He might already be aware of the connection between the riddle and his stolen property, in which case there was little to be done. On the other hand, given the vastness of his collections he may have only a vague recollection of the stone's appearance and may not be aware of its significance at all; and if this was the case, Lady Glostrum wanted to preserve his state of ignorance.

True, if he knew that he might get his stolen artefact back he might be more co-operative. On the other hand, since they had no intention of ever returning it to him, raising such expectations might prove to be horribly awkward later.

In the end, it hardly mattered. The Baron was flatteringly

eager to perform any service for his dear Lady Fenella that he could, and was delighted to minister to her charming fascination with the treasure hunt.

'No doubt it is a product of the liveliness of your mind, my dear!' he declared, kissing her hand. 'Curiosity and an eagerness to learn! How I cherish such qualities.'

Lady Fenella gave a suitable simper. 'Oh, my lord! How kind you are.' She tried her best not to choke on the words as they emerged, and managed the business with only the tiniest catch in her voice. Barely noticeable at all, really.

'I wish,' said he in a low, intimate voice, 'that you would call me Farran.'

Lady Fenella bowed prettily.

'Especially,' he continued, pressing her hand in a most unnecessary manner, 'since we are to be travelling companions! In such circumstances as those, one would wish — would one not? — to be on terms of familiarity.'

Serena blinked. 'We... we are?' she faltered.

The Baron gave a soft, indulgent laugh and squeezed her hand again. Her fingers were growing slightly damp under this persistent attention. 'My dear Fenella! My affection and esteem for you could not be higher, I assure you. You cannot imagine, however, that I could permit my precious ship to be taken out on a lengthy voyage without my attendance and supervision?'

A tiny voice at the back of Serena's mind began to wail something incoherent. 'But, my dear Baron!' said Lady Fenella with a coquettish laugh, 'I must almost begin to imagine that you do not quite trust me.'

The Baron bowed over her hand, kissed it softly, and looked at her with a roguish twinkle in his green eyes. 'My dear Fenella,' he murmured. 'Of course I do not.'

Well, damn.

The Baron proved to be infuriatingly inflexible on this point, and since Lady Glostrum's attempts to find an alternative craft failed, they were obliged to accept the good Baron's irksome company on the voyage.

This pleased her ladyship almost as much as it pleased Serena. The presence of anybody on the ship who was not, and could not be permitted to become, fully conversant with all the facts would certainly create unwelcome complications, even were he likely to prove a congenial colleague. Since there was little chance of the latter, no one was much delighted.

The voyage would go ahead, however. Not all of Serena's team were to go, which disappointed her, but she couldn't fault Lady Glostrum's logic. They would have no use for Egg or Iyamar in the air, and there was little reason to imagine that even Teyo's shapeshifting might prove useful at this stage. The Baron's ship could convey up to ten people in safety, and since three of those must be the pilot and crew, that left space only for her ladyship and her husband, Serena and Fabian (as Lady Fenella and Lord Bastavere), and the Baron, plus two others Lady Glostrum wished to bring. Since these included an expert navigator and one of the best cartographers in the Seven, Serena couldn't fault her choices.

It was not strictly necessary to bring Fabian along, of course, but on this point Serena had been as inflexible as the Baron. Firstly, she refused to be obliged to put up with Anserval's company for days — possibly weeks, who knew? — without the support of her brother; she was not at all convinced that he might not develop some highly unwelcome ideas, otherwise. Also, she hoped that the mission might serve both to interest Fabian in the hunt, and to distract him from his obsessive focus on the matter of Valore Trebel. He was not pleased, but she had insisted. As a result, he was not speaking to her when it came time to board the vessel.

Anserval had his own airfield (of course), situated not far from his stupendous country mansion. The six of them met their host at the entrance, all of them dressed in the thickest, warmest clothing they could find; they had been well warned about the likely temperature far above ground. Escorted to the ship on the Baron's arm, and regaled with many a tiresome detail about the engineering and the cost of the craft, Serena nonetheless felt a degree of excited anticipation she had scarcely experienced before. This only increased when she saw the airship, moored in the centre of the wide airfield and awaiting their embarkation.

Its size alone rendered it an impressive sight. The ship part — or gondola, as the Baron swiftly informed her — was so large, she wondered at Anserval's pronouncement that it would only house ten. This apparent mistake was soon explained when he assured her that she and her brother would have the use of multiple cabins, and that Lady Glostrum and her husband would enjoy the same — because, he told her earnestly, how could he expect gently-bred, aristocratic ladies (and their gentleman escorts) to suffer anything less than the finest accommodation he could offer? Serena, who would have preferred to hand over the extra cabins to Egg, Teyo and Iyamar, was forced to content herself with only a polite demur.

The balloon held her attention for some time (Anserval called it the "envelope", which in Serena's view sounded so absurd, she preferred to think of it as a balloon). It dwarfed even the spacious proportions of the gondola beneath, swollen with (as she was now informed) some kind of gas which would, once the tethers were released, raise it up into the skies. He had a great deal more to tell her about the workings of the airship, but she, being wholly uninterested in such technicalities — especially when related by him — ignored him. Since her brother did likewise, Anserval was left to display his superior knowledge unattended.

Inevitably, the balloon was bright, shimmering gold in hue, but Serena was relieved to see that the gondola had been painted in a much more handsome, dark plum colour. The ship accordingly bore a sumptuous appearance which she found pleasing. It also bore an appearance of such staggering expense that she was a little floored by it. She'd known that Anserval was rich, but this? What else might the infuriating man have at his disposal? And why, when surrounded by so much privilege, could he not manage to be just a little less repulsive?

She and Lady Glostrum were escorted on board ahead of everyone else, even the pilot, and by the Baron himself. He did the honours with so much pomp and ceremony that she was thoroughly exasperated by the time she had been shown to her cabin(s) and left to settle in. She didn't waste long on this task; she wanted to be on deck when the ship took off.

Fabian apparently had the same idea, for she met him on her way back up to the observation deck a few minutes later. He had donned Lord Bastavere's haughty expression, and apparently had no intention of dropping it for her. Serena refused to coax him out of his poor mood. Accordingly, they walked up to the top deck together in silence.

They found Lady Glostrum, the cartographer and the navigator in a cluster on the largest of the viewing platforms. They were discussing something involving papers, which Serena instantly felt that she didn't want to miss. Lady Glostrum greeted her with a smile as she approached, and immediately said,

'My lady Chartre, and Lord Bastavere! How wonderful of you to join us. We were discussing our first destination.'

Lady Fenella responded with a dazzling smile and a curtsey in response to Lady Glostrum's bow. She interpreted these signals to mean that they were to play up the supposed status of her character and Fabian's, and made a note to play along. 'Oh, wonderful!' she said with every scrap of Fenella's limitless enthusiasm. 'And where are we bound?'

The cartographer made her a perfunctory bow, his lack of interest in aristocracy very apparent. His name was Wrob, though she had not been told his family name. He was rapidly approaching fifty, she judged, and he was almost certainly Irbellian in nationality, for he bore the same medium-brown skin as Serena and Fabian. But his hair was much lighter than theirs, almost blond, and greying at the temples. He surveyed Lady Fenella in her expensive silken flight attire with a dispassionate expression in his greyish eyes. 'Here,' he said, and with a little reluctance handed her the maps he had been showing her ladyship. 'I have marked with a cross the three locations we'd want to look at. I suggest that we begin with the Sammerill Peaks.' He smiled thinly at Lady Fenella and added, 'Those are the mountains to the west, bordering Orlind.'

Serena leafed through them, maintaining an expression of vacuous, vague enthusiasm upon her face even as her brain whirred rapidly through the implications of Wrob's choices. The locations he had marked were all in the midst of mountain ranges, and she knew that at least one of them — the mountains that divided the empty realm of Orlind from Irbel — were virtually inaccessible on foot, and known for the constant cloud cover that shrouded the tallest peaks. She nodded her approval, flashing the good cartographer a beaming smile. Anything could be hiding in those clouds!

'Wonderful!' she gushed. 'What a clever, clever man you are.' She handed back the maps, noting in passing the way his lip curled derisively before he recollected himself and smoothed out his expression. She spared an instant to regret that she was forced to play her most vapid character for the entire voyage, and cursed the Baron all over again. She could no longer remember why she had ever found Fenella amusing to play.

Their navigator was a woman of similar age to Wrob, and Serena wondered if they might be colleagues. They certainly seemed familiar with one another. Her skin and hair were much darker than Wrob's, almost black, and she eyed Lady Fenella out of mildly sardonic black eyes. She was introduced as Ayra Delune.

'These places couldn't be a little easier to reach, could they?' she sighed.

Wrob rolled his eyes. 'Complaints, complaints. If they were easy to find, someone would've found them already.'

Ayra rewarded that comment with a withering look. 'Easy for you to say, Mister. You just have to point at the map and say, "Destination confirmed!" The hard stuff is up to the rest of us.'

'Wishing you hadn't agreed?' said Wrob, with a knowing smile.

'Not even for a second.' She grinned, and Wrob grinned back.

The pilot, a middle-aged woman with the friendliest demeanour Serena had ever seen, approached at that moment to receive instruction. Serena stood silent and a little way back, until she realised that the pilot was looking at her.

'Where are we headed, ma'am?' she said.

Ah, yes. As the ostensible leader of this little party, Lady Fenella would have to give instruction.

'I believe our good cartographer has all the answers!' she said airily, earning herself a wry look from Wrob. He went off, however, to give instructions as to their first destination, and Serena could relax. She was happy to do whatever she could on this expedition, but deciding where to go was not something she was qualified for.

The Baron joined them soon afterwards, and Serena was obliged to bear another lengthy lecture on the workings of airships, mixed together with lists of the other rare, wondrous and expensive things the Baron was fortunate enough to own. Serena bore it with as much fortitude as she was able, all the while enviously eyeing Fabian, who had wandered to the rail and leaned upon it with every appearance of ease.

At last, the ship was ready to fly. Serena ran to join Fabian, abandoning the Baron mid-sentence, and proceeded to ignore everything that was going on around her in favour of the view that promised ahead. She watched, breathless with anticipation, as the airship's engines started with a roar and a rattle and the craft began to rise. The ground dropped away much faster than she had expected, and she gasped in delight. She and Fabian gazed in silence as fields, woodlands and streams fell away before them and the world expanded into a vast horizon of green and brown, beneath infinite sky.

Finally, Fabian said: 'I suppose I would have missed this, if you hadn't forced me to come.'

Serena permitted herself a smug smile. 'Still angry with me?'

'Yes,' said Fabian, with a dark, sideways look at her. 'But maybe a bit less.'

11

Teyo folded his arms and stared at Egg and Iya. Iyamar wore a belligerent expression, while Egg looked amused. Annoyingly amused.

'We aren't going anywhere until you two sort this out,' he said firmly.

'We aren't going anywhere anyway,' Egg pointed out, hurling herself into a chair and putting her booted feet up on the table.

Teyo sighed. 'That's not the point.' They were stuck at the apartment with not enough to do. Teyo welcomed the opportunity to continue training Iyamar, but her lessons with Egg had ground to a halt since their altercation of a few days ago.

'I don't see what Fabe and Serena have to do on this voyage that we couldn't,' Egg added.

Teyo said nothing. Privately, he agreed with Egg; he'd been disappointed not to be taken along on the airship when some of his team were going. Serena had left him in charge, though, and he had to be professional.

Besides, the job they'd been given was important too, whenever it finally got started. Lady Glostrum had said, *About half the world's out looking for these Dreams, and it won't take long before somebody finds one, and a key along with it. When that happens, I need you to go get it back.*

Teyo made a few trips out to the city boards every day to

keep an eye on the news. That way, when the next site was discovered, he'd know about it within a few hours.

Egg had declined the honour of participating in this duty, deeming it a boring run-around, and had instead devoted herself to the completion of a couple of new wigs for their collection. Not a wholly unproductive activity, as it went, but not quite what he'd had in mind either.

Under normal circumstances, Iyamar could be even more taciturn than he. She was voluble when she grew excited about something, but otherwise her young mind appeared to be too busy with her own thoughts to bother much with talking. The recent drama had been an exception, to say the least. She had nothing to say now, apparently. She merely stood, watching Egg with a wary expression and a posture that said she had no intention of apologising. She had apologised to Serena and Teyo days since, but she would not forgive Egg's behaviour.

Teyo decided to appeal to their better sides, supposing either of them had one. 'Please,' he said, lowering his arms. 'We've got a job to do, and it's important, and we'll mess it up if we can't work together properly.' That elicited zero response, so he continued, 'Anyway, do you have any idea what Serena will do to me if we don't get those keys when they turn up? She left me in charge, so it's going to be my guts on the line.'

Egg smirked.

Iya glowered.

Teyo sighed and threw up his hands. 'I have no idea how Serena puts up with any of us,' he muttered, and walked out.

He also had no idea how Serena ever got anybody to mind her. Somehow, she did. She had talked Iyamar into accepting shapeshifter training with a mere few, clever, well-timed words — drawn, he thought, from a clearer understanding of her character than any of the rest of them had yet achieved. She was perceptive.

Egg she managed through a mixture of bribery, cajoling, crisp commands and wry jokes. Somehow she always knew which ones to apply and when. Apparently she understood Egg pretty well, but he couldn't say the same for himself.

He just didn't have the knack of it. He wasn't given to fretting, but he was beginning to worry just a little bit today. What could he do if his team wouldn't obey him and wouldn't listen to each other? How could they expect to accomplish anything useful if two-thirds of their vestigial team weren't even speaking to one another?

It would take a while yet before anybody found another Dream, he consoled himself. They were incredibly well-hidden. They had to be, or they would've been found long ago. And nobody had any clues, save for the riddle that still hung eerily in the skies. Nothing much would happen for a few days, at least. Time enough for him to figure out what to do with his frustrating colleagues.

Even as he formed this thought, the voice box he carried in his pocket buzzed violently, and he jumped. He always had the thing on him at the moment, but this was the first time it had done anything.

He scrambled to retrieve it and switched it to transmit, then announced his name.

'You're up,' said Oliver's voice, and the box went dark.

Teyo stuffed it back in his pocket, grabbing for his coat with his other hand. He charged down to the bulletin boards at a run, and ruthlessly shoved his way through the crowds of people already gathered around them.

He swore a little under his breath when he saw the headlines. SECOND DREAM FOUND, proclaimed the board. Teyo watched in silence as pictures of the site scrolled past. This one was under water, apparently, and constructed entirely from eerily pale crystal. It looked cold and ethereal and strange, and he shivered involuntarily.

After the images of the site came a short article describing the circumstances of the discovery. It was situated at the bottom of an isolated, very deep river which wound through the highlands of Orstwych. The article noted that eight people had drowned while exploring the river and a ninth had died trying to access the site, which made him blink. No one had any idea what the keys were for or where the supposed door might lead, yet they were taking life-threatening risks over it? He felt simultaneously saddened and befuddled, and slowly shook his head.

And then, froze. The LHB were on site, he read, and had already secured what they considered might be the *key* the riddle spoke of. The next image confirmed that: a woman held a black stone streaked with violet. It bore the same shape as the others, and the same inscription, though it had not yet been translated.

He did not have time to feel relieved that it had fallen to the LHB, however, because the woman depicted was Halavere Morann. An LHB official she surely was, but what else was she? Teyo had no doubt at all that the key was destined to end up, one way or another, in the hands of the Yllandu — and Ylona Duna.

He returned to the apartment at a run.

Egg still sat with her enormous boots propped up on the table. She was nonchalantly eating some kind of nuts out of a tiny paper bag. There was no sign of Iyamar.

'Everything all right?' she said, eyeing his hastily-donned coat and his air of urgency with interest.

'Maybe,' he returned. 'We've got about six hours to get the next key off Halavere Morann before it's absorbed by the Unspeakables.'

Egg stared at him. 'Right,' she said at last, and took her feet off the table. 'Okay then.' She swallowed the contents of her snack bag in one mouthful and chucked the paper aside. 'Where'd Iyamar go?'

Teyo blinked. 'I don't know. Isn't she here?'

'She left, right after you.'

'As in, left the building?'

'Yeah.'

Teyo felt a headache coming on.

But the door slammed an instant later, and Iyamar came whirling in. She held in her hand a paper bag like Egg's. Actually, she held three. She tossed one to Egg, who caught it with an air of surprise, and offered the second to Teyo. Peace offerings?

'Where have you—' began Teyo, but then shook his head. 'Never mind. Thank you. Are you ready to head out? Job's starting.'

Iyamar flashed him a smile of such dazzling brilliance she could only have learned it from Serena — or, perhaps, Lady Fenella. 'Yes, please. Can we go right away?'

Egg was already on her feet and heading for the door. 'I'll pack,' she called back over her shoulder. The animosity that had choked the room half an hour before had dissipated completely, and Teyo heaved an inward sigh of relief. Perhaps all any of them really needed was something difficult and potentially life-threatening to do.

'Leaving in thirty minutes,' he told Iyamar, and she saluted.

113

'Right you are, boss!'

The downside to the job, Teyo reflected en route, was that they would be obliged to access the LHB office in Iving. That the key was there, he did not much doubt. Halavere Morann had been pictured standing outside the building with the key in her hand, and it was an obvious repository for it for the time being. He suspected that a break-in was likely to be staged by the Unspeakables that night, after which Halavere — unaware that her connections with the underworld were known to her superiors — would deny all knowledge, and declare the key sadly lost. They'd have to get their hands on the key before then.

Fortunately, Lady Glostrum had anticipated problems of this nature. She herself expected to be out of reach for the next while, but she had given him the name and contact details for a trusted subordinate in the Bureau. Teyo took out his voice-box. It was the work of a few moments to adjust its designated contact, and then he depressed the authorisation tab. The box buzzed promisingly.

The response came quickly. 'Devary Kant,' announced a male voice.

'Teyo Bambre,' Teyo replied. 'I'm—'

'I know,' Devary cut in. 'What can I do for you?'

'I need access to the Iving HQ.' Teyo rapidly explained. He was prepared for opposition, but Kant merely said, 'Right,' in a reassuringly crisp tone. 'I'll set you up with access to the necessary stuff,' continued Devary, 'but I can't make it easy for you. Halavere's got allies at the HQ but we aren't sure who they are yet, and she knows we haven't taken on any new recruits lately. It would be better if you weren't seen.'

Teyo understood the unspoken subtext well enough. Kant could get him through the weird Lokant security, but they'd have to sneak in and out. Ah well. They were well practiced at that.

The building wasn't especially large nor, he estimated, all that difficult to get into. He'd been there once before, and remembered it as an unprepossessing stone construction, a former townhouse pressed into duty as an office. Its doors and windows were standard, and external security wasn't all that high; it wasn't a safehouse or (usually) a repository for anything valuable.

He, Egg and Iya would have to get the job done quickly. The

hour was already advanced. He estimated they had about two hours of natural daylight left before the Day Cloak came in, and it wouldn't be long after that before they could expect a visit from the Unspeakables.

In spite of Devary's words, they dressed and wigged as LHB agents. If anyone *did* see them, he hoped their costumes would prove passable enough to fool anyone who wasn't looking too closely. Their attire lacked Serena's or Fabian's special skills and eye for detail, and they had no badge for Iyamar, who looked awfully young to be an officer of the LHB, besides. Perhaps she might pass for a trainee? The lack of finesse was regrettable, but they hadn't the time for an elaborate masquerade.

The nearest railcar station was a few minutes' walk from the LHB HQ. Unable to shake his feeling of urgency, Teyo pushed the pace, leading Egg and Iya at a half-trot. They slowed to a more relaxed walk once the building came within sight, and Teyo took a few moments to examine it closely.

It was a plain, unprepossessing structure of drab grey brick. It had originally contained two semi-detached houses, he guessed, though it had probably been combined into one when the LHB took it over. A quick survey revealed at least five possible ways of getting in; that wouldn't be the problem.

No problem at all, in fact. Office hours were just about over. As Teyo watched, an LHB officer in a long coat came out of the front door and stepped briskly down the short path to the street, setting a neat black hat upon his head as he went. He didn't lock the door.

Promising, but Teyo didn't dare dash heedlessly across the road and shove his way inside. What if there were other agents on their way home for the day? But if there was a front door left unsecured, Teyo reflected, there was probably a back door as well. Or a side door. Something.

They circled around again and came at the building from the rear. The back door was swiftly eliminated, as a kitchen lay directly beyond, within which a pair of agents stood lingering over some kind of beverage. It came down at last to a tiny side-door which was, typically, locked fast.

'Allow me,' said Egg with a smug little smile, and bent to the job, picks in hand. Teyo looked at his watch.

'Twenty-two seconds,' he reported when the lock gave that promising *click*. 'Not your best.'

Egg merely grinned at him. She opened the door barely an inch and peeked into the gap. 'All clear,' she whispered, and they slipped inside.

They room beyond appeared to be a storage room, as it was piled high with crates and boxes. They were lucky there was a route to the side door at all, Teyo thought, until he saw a large sign proclaiming the presence of a fire exit. Ah, safety considerations could be so convenient sometimes.

It was perfect for the next part of his plan, Teyo reflected with satisfaction. Egg sat cross-legged atop a stack of crates out of sight of the doors, while Teyo drew Iya aside.

'Are you sure you're all right with this?' he whispered.

Iyamar's eyes held a scared child look that gave him grave doubts, but she lifted her chin and nodded. 'I can do it.'

'Sure, now? No shame in letting it go. Better not to risk it, if you aren't certain.'

Iyamar developed a grim look which told him she would do it or die, and she nodded. 'I can do it. It's been better since Lady Glostrum.'

He nodded. 'Right. You first, then.'

Iya took a deep breath and closed her eyes. For a while nothing happened, though Teyo could see her hands beginning to shake with effort. Then her human form vanished all in a rush, and seconds later a tiny Jisp-like creature sat on the ground. She'd matched her colouring to the floor, he noticed with approval, and she'd done an excellent job of it too. He felt a brief flash of pride; she was a fast learner, and for someone who'd howled with agony at the prospect of shapeshifting only a week or so ago, she was doing well.

Good, he told her the silent way, and felt a glow of satisfaction from her in reply. He took Jisp out of his pocket and set her down next to Iyamar, then shifted his own form. Iya's and Jisp's miniscule bodies swelled in his vision as his own stature shrank, and then three little Jisps crouched together upon the floor.

They didn't pause to confer, but ran immediately for the door. They were small enough to slip easily underneath, and within moments they were scurrying furiously away, spreading out over the three floors of the LHB building. Teyo had arranged that Iya would cover the ground floor, because he felt it would contain the fewest threats. It was dedicated mostly to kitchens, dining areas and storage; few agents would be in evidence, and he doubted the key was down here.

He and Jisp ran for the stairs and dashed up them. It was always disconcerting to find his legs suddenly so short, Teyo mused as he laboured to reach each step. It was fortunate that his tiny body was nimble enough to make up for it — most of the time.

Jisp darted away at the top of the first flight, and Teyo continued up to the top floor. He slowed to a more cautious pace, alert for any signs of activity. His sensitive nose caught a whiff of something human behind the second door he passed, and he gave it a wide berth. Most of the rooms were empty, fortunately, and he scrambled beneath each door to check the contents inside. Office, office, a filing room, another office, a water closet... nothing interesting on this side. Turning about, he dashed furiously back to the staircase and away to the other side, keeping his senses alert for any communications from Jisp or Iya as he ran.

He found the treasure room, as he liked to think of it, a few moments later. He knew it by the box of strangeness that was attached to the door, a white light blinking upon its surface. It was a stupid security system to employ, when every other door around here used a normal lock and key. One might as well hang a sign on the door saying, *Here is all the good stuff!*

On the other hand, he was pretty sure that was top-level Lokant technology guarding the portal to the goodies, so perhaps it wasn't so stupid.

He dismissed Jisp and Iya back to Egg, and — steeling himself in case something weird and painful should occur — made a mad dash under the door.

The room was empty, as his nose had already informed him. Tall cabinets soared away to impossible heights on either side of him, lining the walls like rows of stern sentries. Each one of those bore a similar lock on each and every drawer, which was both promising and devastating at the same time. He hoped Kant had got him access to these, or he was going to have a problem.

He shifted back to his human form, praying that he wouldn't set some screaming alarm off in the process. Nothing happened to break the silence, and he breathed a little easier.

Okay, drawers. He looked closely at the nearest ones, hoping for some guidance as to its contents or how to open it. Nothing. The drawers were all unmarked and identical. They didn't even have handles. Gingerly, he set his fingers to one of them, probing for something — a handle, a catch, anything.

An alarming red light began to glow before his eyes, and a voice from nowhere said, 'Access attempted.'

Teyo jumped back.

'Teyodin Bambre,' continued the voice. 'Welcome.' The drawer he'd touched slid open.

Teyo sagged a little in relief, and blessed Devary Kant. The man was certainly efficient. Cautiously, he approached the cabinet again and peered inside the drawer.

He saw a great many gadgets nestled inside, none of which he recognised. They were so far beyond his comprehension, in fact, that he felt an obscure shudder at the mere sight of them, and quickly moved on. The stone wasn't there, anyway. He touched the next drawer down, which slid open exactly like the first, and perused its contents.

Ten minutes and half a room later, Teyo found the key. It lay snugly inside a little velvet tray, thoughtfully cushioned upon silk, its black stone veined with silver and white. Teyo could picture Halavere Morann, the dedicated and triumphant agent, coming in here with a colleague or two and showily placing it inside a secure drawer within the most secure room in the building. When it was stolen later on, nobody would be blaming *her*. He grabbed it, stuffed it into his pocket, and shut the drawer.

Next problem: exit. The door looked thoroughly impregnable, but if he had access to the drawers, he probably had access to the door as well, right?

Right. He touched it and the same disembodied voice announced his name. 'Have a pleasant day,' it added, which Teyo thought was a nice touch.

Still human, he made his careful way back to the stairs, keeping eyes and ears open for wandering agents. He didn't dare shift at this point. If he took a tiny shape like Jisp's, the chances of being seen were minimal, but how could he convey the key? Anything larger would attract a lot more attention than a middle-aged man in LHB uniform was likely to excite. So he risked it.

He saw no one, and made it all the way back down to the ground floor without being stopped. He was just beginning to feel that everything might be all right when a door suddenly opened and a woman stepped out. She was tall and white-haired and just a little bit haughty. For a heart-stopping second Teyo thought it was Halavere Morann, but a moment's scrutiny revealed that she was not. His feelings of relief were short-lived, as he realised that he recognised her. This was the same woman that had taken the key from Baron Anserval's treasure store.

Teyo instantly averted his face and walked on, hoping hard that she would ignore him. But she didn't.

'Excuse me?' she called after him.

Reluctantly, he turned.

'It's late,' said the woman sternly. 'What are you still doing here?'

'Working late,' he said gruffly.

'Whatever it is you're doing can wait,' she decreed with decided hauteur. 'Off you go.'

Teyo needed no further invitation, and took himself off at once. She had been almost as displeased to see him as he was to see her, he judged; she must be here for the key, and had expected the building to be empty by now. Well, he was happy to oblige.

To his relief, he found Iyamar human again and sitting companionably with Egg, Jisp perched atop her left knee. He'd been half afraid that they might get into another altercation if they were left alone together for long — or worse, that Iya would get some crazy idea into her head of following him up to the top floor and "helping" him out. Youngsters got those kinds of notions sometimes.

'Time to go,' he said tersely. 'Now.' He all but threw the exterior door open and charged out into the soft light of the Evenglow. There had been a tinge of suspicion in the woman's gaze that he didn't like.

The three of them left the vicinity of LHB HQ at a run. Teyo didn't permit them to slow down until they'd reached the station and boarded the nearest railcar. He slumped down into his seat and let out a long sigh.

'Did you get it?' Egg whispered urgently.

'Teyo nodded once, earning himself a broad smile.

'You were both great,' he said, smiling back. 'Thanks.'

'Oh, yeah,' Egg said, grinning. 'I can sit on boxes with the best of them.'

His lips curved in a lopsided smile. 'You got us into the

building, Egg.'

'Yep, that's my contribution. Twenty-one seconds of work.'

'Twenty-two,' said Iyamar.

'That extra second makes all the difference,' Teyo agreed.

Egg made a rude gesture at them both, and turned her head to look out of the window as the railcar began to move.

'How was the shifting?' Teyo asked Iya.

'It was great!' she said, sitting up straighter. 'Much easier this time. And it was fun.'

'Being a Jisp-a-like, or conducting reconnaissance?'

'Both!' she enthused. 'It was fun and exciting.'

So she liked the danger, did she? Teyo made a mental note of that. For himself, he more tolerated than enjoyed those aspects of the job. If he felt entitled to free choice, he would be running a small fruit farm near the south-eastern coast of Nimdre and spending his days in peace. But that was his own fault. He'd messed up as a youth, and done a lot of things he shouldn't. Until he was finished paying his self-imposed debt to society, he would have to stick to only dreaming about orchards and fresh milk in the mornings.

'So,' said Egg slowly, without turning her gaze away from the window. 'It's back to waiting?'

'Reckon so,' said Teyo. Egg's posture betrayed her displeasure at this idea, and Iyamar's excited expression faded into chafed disappointment.

Teyo, in contrast, felt a flicker of satisfaction, or possibly relief. He could put up with the "excitement", as Iya called it, of breaking and entering and thieving and running, but he liked to have a nice, calm interval in between episodes. It usually took a day or two for his heart rate to slow down.

12

Ayra Delune's navigational plan worked perfectly, right up until the wind got involved.

'I don't see that anybody invited it,' said Lady Fenella petulantly, after a few frigid, windy, miserable hours of trying futilely to penetrate the fog bank that hovered above the highest peaks of the Sammerill Mountains. The area it covered was not vast, but it was surrounded by some kind of endless cyclone which repelled every attempt the pilot made to steer the airship into it. Some damage had been suffered in the process, and the Baron had at last declared a halt to the endeavour.

'Quite right,' said Lord Bastavere, his hands shoved deep into his coat pockets against the biting cold. 'Stand aside! I shall simply *order* it to take itself off. It cannot possibly refuse me.'

'A job for darling Eva, perhaps?' responded Lady Fenella, not quite in jest. If Eva (for as bosom friends they had of course progressed to first names by now) could order Iyamar back into her human form, who was to say she couldn't order a cyclone around as well?

Her new best friend shook her head, amusement glinting in her eyes. 'How lovely that would be! But no. The weather has no will, you see, and therefore I can have no effect upon it whatsoever.'

'If you could,' put in Tren, 'no cloud would ever dare rain upon you again.'

Eva's face lit up.

'And!' her husband added, 'you wouldn't be cold anymore, either.'

Eva did indeed look just a shade or two more miserably frozen than the rest of them. She was swaddled in so many layers her own shape was completely indiscernible beneath them, and she wore at least two scarves that Serena could see. Despite this, she was shivering violently and her face was stark white.

Eva sighed. 'Stop tormenting me.'

At the Baron's instruction, the pilot had directed the airship away from the circling winds that guarded the skies over the peak. They did not appear to be regaining any particular course, Serena noticed; the force of those winds emanated a long way out from the peak, and the ship flailed helplessly under it, drifting and turning apparently at random. The shuddering, jerky motion had become familiar over the last couple of hours, and everybody was stationed near to something solid they could hold onto — and as far from the ship's rails as possible. Serena had considered going below, thus avoiding the dangers of the deck and some of the cold. But to be shut into a small cabin and thus miss all of the developments above was an intolerable prospect, and besides, she was afraid that the motion of the ship would soon make her ill.

She was nonetheless engaged in eyeing the distant railing with distinct misgivings when the Baron strode up to the little shivering knot of people. The man was insane as well as infuriating, Serena had long since concluded; he made no effort whatsoever to protect his own safety, instead striding about the deck as though he were invulnerable to incidental forces of nature like screaming winds.

'I've spoken to my pilot,' he announced, his voice raised to shout. 'She's trying to get us out, but it will take some time.' He looked uneasy, Serena thought. It could not be the prospect of personal injury or death that troubled him; perhaps it was the prospect of costly damage to his precious ship.

Or something else?

Eva said: 'Do we know where we are?'

The Baron's unease grew more visible, and he shook his head, his lips tightly pressed together. 'We have gone about too many times for Ayra to keep track.'

Eva glanced around, the Baron's discomfort echoed in her

face.

'What is it?' said Serena.

Eva sighed. 'We've been blown well over the mountains, I suspect. I fear we will end up in Orlind, if we haven't already.'

The word "Orlind" operated powerfully upon Serena. The mythical Seventh Realm had been abandoned and desolate until a couple of years ago, when an expedition led by Eva herself and the first draykoni, Llandry Sanfaer, had made some startling discoveries there. There had been talk of late of its being resettled by one of the new draykoni clans, though she was not sure whether anything had come of it.

Why any of this, or their proximity to it, should trouble Eva, was unknown to her. A question sprang to her lips; at the last instant she remembered the Baron's presence and her own role, and changed it to a rapturous expression and a tiny bounce upon her toes.

'Oh, but would that not be marvellous!' she uttered, every word dripping with joy. 'Only think! Orlind itself! How much I shall have to tell my friends on our return.'

Something flickered across Eva's eyes, possibly annoyance, and she shook her head. 'I haven't been back since... well, since two years ago. And at *that* time, it was — not habitable. Not logical, or stable, or ... it was very dangerous. Especially to anyone airborne.'

It was unlike her ladyship to be so inarticulate, Serena thought with a flicker of alarm.

'Airborne?' echoed the Baron sharply. 'Why?'

Eva merely shook her head, her vocabulary apparently exhausted. 'I can't explain.'

'We went draykon-back,' offered Tren. 'Flew in over these mountains, though we never came up this far. Once we entered Orlind, it was as though... as though up and down had turned themselves around, or ceased to exist altogether. We didn't know which way up we were, let alone which direction to go in. We were very lucky not to be injured.'

'Or killed,' added Eva bleakly. 'We owe that to our draykoni friends, I think. They kept their wits about them, and landed us safely. I'm not eager to repeat the experience in an airship.'

Nobody said anything for a while. The prospect of sailing helplessly into Orlind only to be upturned, spun about and ultimately dashed to pieces thrilled no one. Even the impervious

Baron was visibly disturbed.

'How experienced is your pilot?' said Tren at last.

The Baron's lips tightened further. 'Enough. I hope.'

An hour passed, or so Serena's watch believed. To her, it felt more like two or three days. The wind's unsettling influence upon their ship gradually lessened as time passed, and the beleaguered craft ceased to shudder and rattle so badly. However, this could only be because they had been pushed farther and farther away from the fog over the peak, and closer and closer to Orlind. Without Eva's and Tren's stories, Serena would have welcomed this as a good thing. Now she wasn't so sure.

At least she felt less like she might topple over the side at any moment, or throw up over it, whichever happened first. She and her brother stuck closely together, a little apart from the rest of their group. She thought that Fabian was doing some protective hovering, which was touching, since it wasn't especially like him. If the worst happened, hopefully he would catch her, thus preventing her untimely death — always supposing they didn't hurtle over the side together.

Eyeing his taller, bulkier frame, she wasn't at all sure she would be able to return the favour.

The Baron had gone back to harass the poor pilot. Whether his assistance would improve or hinder their prospects, Serena wasn't sure. She could only sympathise with both the pilot and Navigator Ayra, who hadn't moved from her position by the helm in the last few hours.

Serena was just beginning to relax a little when the airship lurched horribly to one side, dashing her to the floor. Fabian narrowly missed crashing down on top of her, for which she was extremely thankful. She lay still, waiting for the craft to right itself, but it did not. It leaned further, shuddering, until Serena was heart-poundingly certain that it would overturn altogether. She stared anxiously above, searching for any sign of damage to the balloon. They were falling! Were they falling? She couldn't be sure; perhaps it was only her fears talking. Or perhaps they had finally crossed into Orlind, and they were actually sailing higher? Unhelpful thought. She clung to Fabian and, hopelessly confused, closed her eyes...

...and the ship settled back with a snap and a creak. The

deck felt level again, and after a moment Serena pushed herself up onto her elbows.

The pilot was yelling something. Had someone gone overboard? She could see Eva and Tren, and Fabian still lay nearby, but what about Ayra and the Baron? Steeling herself, Serena dragged her aching, frozen body to her feet and dashed forward.

She saw three figures assembled at the helm, as expected, and relaxed for a moment. All accounted for; no one overboard. Then her gaze travelled upward.

'Draykoni sighted, southwest!' hollered the pilot, still struggling with the helm. 'Somebody get that Lokant woman!'

Draykoni, up here? That seemed unlikely. But the oncoming creatures were indeed draykoni, Serena realised, staring in wonder at their approach. There were two of them, their scales shining deep purple and white in the muted sunlight. She had seen draykoni before, of course, for Teyo had shifted a few times in her presence, and she'd seen Iyamar in that state. But she had never beheld them in flight, and from this altitude. They were impossibly graceful for such enormous creatures, and sailed gloriously through the skies as though they owned the air itself. She felt a swift, surprising stab of envy for a brief moment; not even Teyo's magnificence up close had ever yet made her feel that she would like to try it herself.

The draykoni caught up to their ship very quickly and began to circle. Whether their intentions were peaceful or otherwise was not immediately clear. The humans on the deck gathered nervously into a knot, Serena with them, as though proximity to each other might protect them if the draykoni attacked. Was it her imagination, or was one of the draykoni eyeing the balloon that held them aloft? If it chose to use its fearsome claws and teeth upon it, their ship would be on its way swiftly downwards in seconds.

Eva came running up, yelling something. Serena was by no means ignorant in the matter of languages; she spoke Nimdren fluently in addition to her native language, and she was proficient in Glinnish and two of the Darklander tongues as well. But whatever Eva was saying was like nothing she'd ever heard before, and the sounds were completely alien to Serena's ears.

They appeared to have some kind of an effect upon the draykoni, for the subtle menace to their movements faded. They continued to circle, but with a fluid grace which spoke of a relaxed state of mind to Serena's eyes, and she relaxed herself a little bit.

But only for an instant, for one of them suddenly flew directly at the ship at some speed. Serena jumped, heart pounding, and tried to scramble backwards; a futile instinct, for where was she going to go? But there was no juddering impact, no attack whatsoever. In the blink of an eye, the vast draykon with the glittering, deep purple scales vanished and a human woman fell, rolling expertly, onto the deck. She wore a set of slim eyeglasses like Eva's, proclaiming her Darklander heritage. Her dark curls were bound back into a neat ponytail, and her clothing was as purple as the scales of her draykoni form.

And she was known to Eva, apparently, for her ladyship went flying forward and wrapped the woman in a huge embrace. 'Avane!'

The woman, Avane, returned the salutation with every bit as much enthusiasm, and repeated this ritual with Tren, who had by this time joined the party. The three fell instantly into animated conversation. They were speaking some bizarre mixture of Darklander tongues with some of those strange words Eva had used mixed in — were they a draykoni language? They were also speaking at such speed that Serena couldn't follow most of it, but she picked up a few words. Avane and her friend were on patrol duty today, she guessed, and they'd come to investigate the airship that had wandered so close to the Orlindian border. There followed a lot of irrelevant conversation, principally relating to people called Lyerd and Ori. After a while, Serena tuned this out.

Eventually the conversation was over. Avane ended with, 'And you know they would *love* to see you,' or something like that. Eva turned back to her airship companions — forgotten for the past several minutes — and made an "everything is fine" gesture.

'It's safe,' she announced unnecessarily. 'These are friends, and we can safely go into Orlind.'

Serena, Fabian, the Baron, the pilot, Wrob and Ayra remained in their nice, secure knot of human flesh, and nobody moved.

'We aren't going to die!' insisted Eva. 'Honestly! I don't yet understand what they've done or how, but Orlind's different. We

126

can fly there.'

'What about the peak, and the Dream?' demanded Anserval, drawing himself up. 'After all,' he added pompously, 'that is why we are here, and it is just a little bit pressing, don't you think?'

Eva, Tren and Avane all turned identical contemptuous stares upon Anserval, who seemed oblivious to this derision. 'We may be able to help you with that,' said Avane coolly. Her tone implied an addendum: '*If* you aren't too obnoxious.'

Anserval looked as though he wanted to object further, but he was caught and he knew it. Their attempts to reach the peak unaided had utterly failed, and had, moreover, brought both ship and passengers into danger. He disliked the feeling that the direction and control of the airship had been wrested from him, though everyone else had known from the beginning that Eva was in charge. Serena watched with mildly vindictive amusement as he struggled, and finally capitulated.

'Very well,' he said grandly. 'Perhaps we may visit Orlind for a little while. Not too long, mind! We have an important task here!'

Avane turned her back on him without comment. She seemed to have got his measure very quickly; either she was very observant indeed, or Eva and Tren had forewarned her about the Baron somewhere during that hasty conversation. These reflections left Serena's mind in an instant as Avane ran towards the rail, vaulted over it and disappeared into thin air.

'Wha — what did she—?' Serena spluttered, and ran to look. Could she shapeshift in mid-air like that? She could, apparently, for there was the dark purple draykon some way below, turning a playful somersault in the air.

Serena turned to find Eva and Tren behind her, a strange smile curving Eva's lips. 'She's gained confidence, wouldn't you say?' she murmured to her husband.

'Marvellously,' he agreed.

Serena looked for Fabian, and found him still standing with Wrob, Ayra and the pilot whose name Serena still hadn't caught. They were discussing something earnestly, or three of them were; Fabian stood ostensibly listening, but Serena recognised the look on his face. He wasn't paying all that much attention. Even the prospect of seeing the mythical Orlind — a prospect which thrilled *her* to no end — couldn't interest him much compared with the prospect of revenge.

She sighed, and turned away.

13

Jisp was in love.

Iyamar's Jisp-a-like form had been attractive, undoubtedly, but Jisp's response to it seemed far out of all proportion to Teyo. The little orange creature had taken to following Iya around, mewling plaintively, until Iya gave up and shapeshifted. Jisp's extreme joy on beholding the object of her affection fell somewhere between heart-warming and befuddling, Teyo felt, with some annoyance. After all, he and Jisp had been friends for a long time and she'd never felt that way about him. (Not that he wanted her to; that would be awkward. But still).

Iyamar didn't seem to mind, and since they were both ladies, there was no chance of a litter of tiny Jisps arriving anytime soon. Teyo hoped that it would help Iya grow more comfortable with her shapeshifter abilities, and so he let it be, content to watch Jisp's lovesick antics with tolerant amusement.

Until Jisp began with the poetry.

To the Glory of Thy Tail was the title of the first one. Jisp shyly approached Iyamar when she was looking particularly lizardly and gorgeous, her scales pearly white and shining gloriously. Jisp dropped a mouthful of bright red berries before her, and announced the title of her composition. Then she lifted her tiny head and began:

Your tail is so long,
So very long,

129

And so scaly.

She paused for a response, radiating hope.

There was a long silence. Teyo sensed confusion, embarrassment and amusement from Iyamar, all of which he hoped she was managing to hide from Jisp. She made an encouraging noise and Jisp, blazing happiness, continued.

There is nothing so pearly
as your scales
which are...

Jisp paused grandly.

Pearlier than pearls.

That appeared to be the end, for Jisp sat back on her haunches, beaming a lizard-grin, and gazed adoringly at Iyamar.

Iyamar flailed. *That was...* she began.

Jisp beamed yet more widely.

Amazing, finished Iya weakly. This feeble praise appeared to satisfy Jisp, for she hurled herself at her friend and rubbed her tiny body all down the length of Iyamar's, quivering with pleasure.

Teyo felt an almost insurmountable desire to laugh. He was obliged to cough hard to dispel the feeling, which sent a gust over his worktable and propelled bits of drying clay all over the polished wooden floor. Oops. He'd made an appalling mess of the parlour with his new project, which he'd better clean up before Egg saw it. Considering her foul mouth, raging temper and total indifference to attire or trinkets it seemed out of place, but she was a stickler for cleanliness, and insisted on perfect neatness in their abode at all times.

He surveyed the object he'd made with a critical eye. It wasn't a bad piece of work, actually, which relieved him somewhat, as he hadn't worked with stone or clay in some years. He picked up a tiny brush and carefully applied a little more paint. There, finished. Hastily — noting in passing that Iya and Jisp were now curled up together in the crook of an armchair, whispering about something — he began to sweep up the clay.

Not fast enough. The front door slammed and three seconds later Egg came stamping in like a little whirlwind, shivering theatrically and rubbing her arms.

'It's damned cold out there!' she announced, then stopped dead. 'What's all this crap?'

'Soon to be taking up its new residence in the bin,' Teyo said in a soothing voice. 'Pretend it never happened.'

Egg aimed a kick at his side, which thankfully she did not quite land. She tended to wear enormous boots with steel in the toes, which his ribs fervently objected to.

She might have said something else — something rude, most likely, and loudly voiced — but her eye fell on the Jisp-and-Iyamar snuggle that was still ongoing in the armchair and she stopped, mouth open.

'You know,' she said after a moment, her eyes narrowing, 'for a girl who screamed blue bloody murder at the prospect of having to shapeshift, she's sure doing a lot of it lately.'

Regretting his undignified posture upon the floor more with every moment, Teyo tried to catch her eye to deliver a warning look, but she wouldn't look at him. 'Yes, Egg,' he said, busily sweeping, 'isn't it great?'

Egg smirked. 'Very touching.' Teyo stood up just in time to witness her rolling her eyes expressively and turning her back on the cute couple.

Iyamar chose that moment to disentangle herself and run down the arm of the chair, gaining the floor just as Egg reached the doorway. In a flash she was human again. 'Hey!' she yelled after Egg. 'Jisp's *much* nicer than you!'

Egg cast her a withering look over her shoulder. '*Everyone's* nicer than me, darling,' she retorted, and wandered off.

Iyamar turned to Teyo and shrugged. The gesture was nonchalant, but Teyo thought she looked a little injured. He paused to think for a moment, stretching his back (ever since he'd turned forty, aches and pains had seemed to develop much faster than he could like or approve of).

'The shifting's coming along nicely,' he offered with a smile.

Iyamar's face instantly transformed into enthusiasm, followed by trepidation. She could be deadpan when she needed to be, but when she wasn't trying, her every thought was lamentably obvious, prominently displayed upon her pale face. That was youthful enthusiasm for you, Teyo thought with a pang of regret. He couldn't ever remember being that excitable.

'Only the smaller things, though,' Iyamar cautioned. 'I mean, nothing that would — nothing that's likely to — just the little ones.'

Teyo unravelled this incoherent speech without much difficulty. 'Still not ready to try your drayk again, then?' he enquired.

Iyamar shook her head vehemently. 'No!'

'But,' Teyo said carefully, doing his best not to look confrontational, 'you used it when we first met you. On the road? When you held up the carriage?'

Iyamar flushed miserably. 'Not deliberately.'

'Ohh.' Teyo took a step back.

'It happens when I panic, sometimes,' she continued in a tiny voice.

'Shapeshift?'

'Yeah.' She shuffled her feet, staring at the floor. 'It all went wrong, and I was hungry and I had nowhere to sleep and the carriage was about to leave and… I panicked.'

Teyo felt a stab of sympathy at this speech. He hadn't been certain what to make of Iyamar's ill-fated hold-up, though as he had got to know her better, he'd felt reasonably sure that she had been driven to it out of desperation rather than thrill-seeking or anything else so daft. He'd been right. He didn't like to think of such a young person homeless and hungry like that, especially if it had come about because other people hadn't liked her draykon heritage.

'That's why you didn't attack the carriage,' Teyo said in sudden realisation. 'I wondered about that.'

'Right.' Iyamar sighed. 'I was busy trying to turn back into… me.' She fell silent, frowning, and Teyo waited for more. Nothing else followed.

'We can talk about it later,' he offered, when her discomfort didn't abate.

'Sorry,' Iya muttered, and slunk away.

Watching her go, Teyo found himself thinking of the fit of panic she'd had when he had first tried to encourage her to shapeshift. She was prone to panic, it seemed, which was a shame; once she calmed down and thought things through, she had considerable strength and talent. Had he ever got so worked up about things in his own youth? It seemed a very long time ago — it *was* a pretty long time ago — but he had. Oh, certainly. He had far, far outdone Iyamar in overreacting, although a small part of his mind still insisted that he hadn't been overreacting at all. Not one bit.

At her age, he'd been a moderately prosperous stonemason's apprentice. His father had been the mason, and Teyo had begun learning the trade at the age of ten. By the time his seventeenth year rolled around, he was fairly skilled and beginning to take on jobs for his father's business. Then everything had changed, and Teyo had... lost it, for a while. For a long while.

He still didn't like to think about it. Stooping carefully, he picked up a final, stray piece of clay that he'd missed and added it to the dustpan he held in his hand. He went to the bin, emptied the pan into it and mentally threw all thoughts of his past transgressions away along with the clay dust. Then he retrieved his coat, stepped out of the door and wandered back to the city square to check the boards again.

It was two days later when the knock finally came at the door to their quiet apartment.

'Finally,' muttered Teyo, which earned him matching enquiring looks from Egg and Iyamar. He ignored these. The two of them had commandeered the parlour table and Egg was showing Iya how to make a simple wig. He wasn't sure why. Iya had taken to the project with surprising enthusiasm, showing an equally surprising creative flair — if slightly questionable taste along with it. The wig she was making was rainbow coloured and covered in glass jewels. It was a little garish to his eye, but Iya clearly loved it. So, more curiously, did Egg. They were getting along comfortably enough, with only a little sniping and grouching from time to time, so Teyo didn't interfere.

He gestured to them to remain seated and went to the door alone, dusting off the front of his jacket as he went. He'd managed to pick up some clay dust and hadn't even noticed until now. Pausing before the door, he took a moment to cross his fingers, both literally and mentally.

He opened the door.

Ylona Duna really was an extremely handsome woman, he thought upon beholding her again. So was Lady Glostrum. Was it the Lokant heritage? They had such regal bearing, such lustrous, snowy hair, and such stupendous figures. Teyo gazed at her in silence for a moment, frowning slightly, but abandoned the train of thought. With a sample size of two, it was impossible to draw any useful conclusions. No, three! He mentally factored Halavere Morann into his thinking, which did no harm to his theory whatsoever.

Ylona returned his stare with one every bit as measuring, and smiled. 'Hello,' she said in a pleasingly low, smooth voice. 'I believe you have my stones.'

Teyo smiled back. 'I own a stone or two, I think.'

Ylona leaned against the door frame, hands in her pockets, and surveyed him a little more. Well, Teyo could match her for nonchalance. He stuck his hands into his own pockets, fixed a pleasantly vague smile upon his face and waited.

'This big, dumb routine,' said Ylona after a moment. 'It's well-practiced, I'll give you that, but I don't believe it.' Her accent was enthralling, Teyo decided, and instantly resolved on prolonging their conversation for as long as possible.

He widened his smile and his eyes, and said nothing.

Ylona's smile twisted. 'Good, yes, but it *is* a waste of my time. Where are my stones? Hand them over and we can all go back to our lives.'

Teyo shrugged. 'I don't have them.'

Her eyes narrowed. 'Is that a lie?'

Teyo felt a whisper of compulsion begin to bear down upon him. It began as an echo of that he had felt when Lady Glostrum had rescued Iyamar from her involuntary shapeshift, though it swiftly grew much, much stronger. 'No,' he managed to say, thankful that it happened to be the truth.

'Hand them over,' she said again, and this time it bore the full force of a Lokant's will behind it. She was as powerful as Lady Glostrum, easily. Perhaps more so.

Teyo's right hand emerged, involuntarily, from the pocket of his trousers and plunged instead into the pocket of his jacket. His fingers closed around the little round stone that lay there and he brought it out to show her. It was black, veined with silver and white, and it felt warm in his hand.

Ylona took it immediately. 'And the other one,' she ordered.

Teyo's left hand repeated the same process and, shaking with the effort to resist, it obligingly handed over a cream stone threaded with gold. Ylona rewarded him with a cool smile and a murmur of thanks, which intrigued him. Why bother to be polite when she had forced his compliance in the first place?

'Your team is very good,' she said as she turned away. 'My compliments.'

Well, that was nice. Teyo tried not to stare at her backside as she walked away, and mostly failed. He would get used to women wearing trousers someday, he supposed, but it might take a little time.

He went back inside and shut the door.

'What the hell was that?' Egg demanded as he joined his companions.

'Ylona came for the stones.'

'I gathered.' She was on her feet, arms folded, staring at him in undisguised disgust. 'And you just let her have them?'

'I was compelled!'

'Uh huh.' Egg looked him up and down, frowning. 'Why aren't you more upset? Serena's going to kill you. Actually, she'll kill all of us.'

Iyamar was laughing. 'Egg, if you hadn't been so annoyed about all that clay everywhere you'd know why he's not upset.'

Egg lifted a single eyebrow at her, with speaking contempt. 'When you've finished laughing at me, Iya dear, do please explain.'

'She's taken duplicates,' Teyo said hastily, before the situation could deteriorate any further. 'I made them yesterday.'

Egg blinked at him. 'Duplicates?'

'They look just the same.' Teyo smiled.

Egg looked both suspicious and thunderstruck. 'You made them? How?'

'Well, I used stone, and a bit of clay moulding, and some paint —'

Egg held up a hand. 'Never mind. I don't want the details.' She gave a grudging nod. 'Good. How did you know she was coming?'

'She saw me, on the way out. She didn't suspect anything at the time, but I thought she might work it out once she realised the stone was gone.' He paused, and added apologetically, 'I didn't really steal it. The security box-thing knew me and let me in the drawer. I imagine she got my name out of it later.'

'Eh? How did it know you?'

He shrugged. 'Lady Glostrum arranged a contact for me at the LHB. He set it up.'

Egg sighed. 'Okay well, nice job on the duplicates. Won't fool her for long, though.'

'I shouldn't think so,' Teyo agreed. 'We'd better decamp. We're in Tarvale for the next few days. Oliver's set it up.'

Egg was already striding to the door. 'Where?' she threw back over her shoulder.

'Tiny village-type place. Twelve miles southeast. Oh, Egg! Hang on a second.'

Egg stopped and waited while Teyo fetched the purple blanket he'd finished knitting. 'Here,' he said, holding it out to her.

Egg stared at it and didn't take it. 'What's that?'

'It's a blanket.'

'I can see that.'

Teyo began to feel awkward. 'It's for you.'

She blinked at him. 'You… made that for me?'

Teyo nodded.

Egg hesitated, then took it and stuffed it under her arm. Muttering a gruff thanks, she left the room without meeting Teyo's gaze.

'She likes it,' Iya decided. 'Otherwise she'd have thrown it at you.'

Teyo smiled. 'Yeah. I know.'

14

Based on Eva's descriptions, Serena had expected to arrive in Orlind to find a small, barren island of bare rock, separated from the mainland by a long stretch of water.

That was not exactly what happened.

They travelled to Orlind under escort, following Avane and with her companion flying behind. When the airship finally crested the last peak that divided them from the Seventh Realm, the vista that lay before them revealed no miserable lump of rock at all, but a flourishing island of considerable size.

Serena, Anserval, Eva and (to Serena's delight) Fabian stood at the viewing deck together. When Orlind at last came into view, they were all taken by surprise. Even Anserval stopped mid-sentence in the middle of one of his monologues.

The glittering expanse of water that lay between the mountains and the island was barely a few miles across, Serena judged, and it was surprisingly serene. Where it met the foot of the Sammerills the water was of a typical greyish hue tossed with green; as it approached the island, however, the grey gave way to blue and the green to purple, turning it a mesmerising twilight-violet colour where it met the shore of Orlind.

The island itself was no less startling. A short beach of silvery sand gave way to a forest of tall trees with thin, curving trunks and silvery bark, their leaves in all shades of blue, green and purple. The tiny shapes of coloured birds were just visible wheeling and diving above the treetops, and fishing out of the strange sea that surrounded their home.

As the airship grew closer, Serena discerned more details: the trunks were striped in colours, weirdly contorted seashells in strange hues lay littered across the beach, and flickers of movement revealed the presence of darting animals among the trees.

'What's all this?' Serena breathed.

Eva shook her head. 'I don't know. Last time I was here… it's been almost two years. I realised — I *hoped* — it might have changed, but this is… this is beyond anything.' She sounded awed and a little breathless. Tren merely stared and said nothing at all. She wondered what he, with his draykoni heritage, made of this sight. He was no shapeshifter, but as a powerful sorcerer he must possess strong draykon blood. Did he see or sense anything that Serena did not? Did Eva? She wished, suddenly and fiercely, that she hadn't left Teyo behind. She wanted his thoughts and his unique perspective on this dazzling place. More than that, she wanted him to see it.

There was nowhere in all of this for their ship to land, but Avane made no move to stop or slow down. They sailed serenely over the tops of the trees and found, on the other side of the forest, an open area of lush bronze grass. Arrayed around the edges of this peculiar meadow was a variety of structures. Some were built from branches and grass and leaves and resembled enormous nests, although they appeared to possess several levels like some human dwellings. They were decked in jewels and flowers which appeared to be growing out of the sides. Others were clearly houses in a more traditional style, though they were built into the sides of jutting outcroppings of bronze-coloured rock. Serena couldn't tell what they were made of, except that it vaguely resembled the goldish wood of the silner trees of Irbel, albeit with an eerie glitter she didn't recognise at all.

And there were draykoni everywhere, wildly varied in shape and hue and even size. Serena was surprised to see some very small draykoni flitting amongst their larger brethren. Having only ever seen Iyamar's very large drayk-shape and Teyo's still vaster one, it hadn't occurred to her that some of them might be very diminutive as well.

She was also surprised and delighted to observe a fair

number of humans working and living in apparent comfort alongside the draykoni. Some of them were probably shifters themselves, but perhaps not all?

Anserval's airship came down slowly in the centre of the meadow and their party was free to disembark. Eva and Tren reached the gangway at the same time as the Baron, and the three of them paused to eye each other.

'Watch Anserval try to steal it,' Fabian muttered in Serena's ear.

'He'll try,' she murmured back. 'I doubt Eva will have it, though. This is her territory.'

Baron Anserval drew himself up with an oily smile, and actually smoothed his luxuriant moustache. His expectation that he would, of course, be the first to set foot in the unexpectedly glorious Seventh Realm was evident in his posture, his smug expression and the air of entitlement he never lost no matter where he went.

Eva lifted her chin very slightly and stared at him, her face devoid of expression save for a faint question in her eyes.

The Baron coughed, and bowed smoothly. 'After you, your ladyship.'

Eva nodded once, the barest gesture of courtesy. 'Thank you.' She swept past him and down towards the ground. Tren followed, utterly failing to hide his smile, and the Baron consented to a poor third place.

Serena glanced at Fabian. His blond Bastavere hair was wildly disordered; the high winds had made a mockery of his attempts at neatness. Tutting, Serena stood on tiptoe and neatened it with her fingers. Perhaps it was silly, but she didn't know who they might meet down there in Orlind, and she wanted them both to make an acceptable impression. Only belatedly did she remember that neither her character nor his would ever consent to appear in public in a disordered state.

'Fix my hair,' she ordered. Fabian raised his brows at her, but he complied competently, if slightly clumsily.

'You'll do,' he pronounced. Ayra and Wrob had already preceded them down the gangway. Serena linked her arm with Fabian's and they made the descent together. Her eyes darting everywhere to take in the sights and her mind and spirits almost overwhelmed with awe and excitement, Serena had never found it harder to play a role. What she really wanted was to bounce down the gangway and hurl herself into the beauties and intrigues of this marvellous place. Instead she forced herself to keep her enthusiasm within the bounds that suited Lady Fenella, and to keep her chin as high as her character's obvious superiority demanded.

The Baron was awaiting her at the bottom, his back pointedly turned to Eva and Tren, who stood not far away. Serena had enjoyed some hopes that his admiration might be turning in the direction of Lady Glostrum's compelling beauty, but her ladyship had fallen well out of favour today. Thus, Lady Fenella was restored to all the dubious honour of the Baron's charming attentions. With an inward sigh, she accepted the proffered arm and forced herself to stand still and calm, and follow Eva's lead.

Which was to wait, apparently, though she was not sure what they were waiting for. Eva and Tren stood closely together, an air of delighted expectancy about the pair of them and their faces turned away from the airship. There was no sign of Avane or her erstwhile companion. Ayra, Wrob, the pilot and the airship crew were all wandering about exploring the meadow, and Serena would have liked to join them, but something told her to stick with Eva for the present.

The air was surprisingly warm, and within a few minutes Serena was glad to strip off the heavy coat, scarf and gloves she had been wearing up in the air. It was as she was engaged in unwinding her scarf that she realised there were two suns in the sky: one large, golden, normal one, and a second, much smaller one which shone faintly pink. The Seven Dreams riddle was visible here, as well, and from her current vantage it floated neatly between the two.

'How is that possible?' Serena said to Fabian, pointing out the second sun.

Fabian stared at it for a long moment, and then turned a few circles, searching the sky for... something? She couldn't read his expression. 'Odd,' he finally pronounced. 'I didn't realise we were going off-world.'

'We have? How?' It was not possible to travel to one of the adjoining worlds — the Uppers or Lowers, for example — without passing through a gate, and that was noticeable because it was painful. Nothing like that had happened; they had sailed gently and serenely into Orlind's airspace and landed and that had been that.

Fabian shrugged. 'I don't know, but how else can you get one sun back in Irbel and two just over the Sammerills?'

Serena cast a look of enquiry at Eva and Tren, who shook their heads and shrugged in similar *I don't know* gestures. Lady Glostrum and Tren might have been some of the first people to set foot in Orlind in modern times, but they were out of touch, and obviously as out of their depth here as she.

A diminutive figure appeared out of nowhere and hurled itself at Eva, who staggered. Serena, startled, wondered briefly whether this sudden assault was friendly or not, but was soon reassured, for a delighted, three-way embrace was going on between Eva, Tren and the newcomer. It was much like their reunion with Avane, only this time there was a great deal of excited chattering and squealing attached to it. Serena wondered idly who this might be, and inspected her nails while she waited to find out.

'Rena,' said Fabian, watching this display impassively. 'What are we doing here?'

Surprised, Serena said, 'In Orlind?'

'Yes. Well, yes, but I meant, on this journey. Why were we on that ship?'

'Eva invited us.'

The look he gave her was both amused and knowing. 'She invited *you*, you mean, and you dragged me along in hopes of distracting me.'

'That's not true,' Serena said reflexively, even though it was.

'Yes it is, but let's not get side-tracked. What have we contributed so far? Nothing. We are spectators. I don't see why she wanted either of us, if Teyo and Egg weren't needed.'

Serena frowned. 'It's on account of the Baron,' she replied hopefully. 'We needed his ship, and he's fond of Fenella.'

Fabian scoffed at that. 'Come on. Lady Glostrum could've charmed it out of him, if she'd wanted to.'

Serena couldn't deny that. It hadn't occurred to her before, but she had been little acquainted with her ladyship before the voyage began. Witnessing the way Anserval's eyes had repeatedly strayed towards Lady Glostrum, though, she couldn't deny that Fabe had a point.

Which made her, what? A bystander? It was lowering to think of herself as so wholly unnecessary on so exciting a voyage, and it made no sense either. Why would Lady Glostrum make a point of including her, if there was nothing for her to do?

'There'll be something,' she said, trying to sound confident. 'She just hasn't said what it is, yet.'

'Hmm.' Fabian said nothing further. His eye had travelled to the Baron Anserval, who had wandered off somewhere — unaccompanied by Serena, who had refused his offer of escort — and had now come back again. He wore a wide, satisfied smile, and glanced towards her ladyship and her chattering colleagues with an indulgent air of geniality. Perhaps he thought Lady Glostrum had somewhat sacrificed her dignity with the squealing, and was back in charity with her.

'Touching display, is it not?' he observed. 'Do we know who these people are?'

People? Belatedly, Serena observed a second figure standing a tiny bit apart from Eva, Tren and the first of their visitors. He was now visible, having separated at last from the crushing embrace. They made a strange-looking pair, Serena immediately thought. The diminutive one was female, with the darkish brown skin and vast wings of the people of Glinnery. Her black hair was neatly braided, and she was dressed in trousers, boots and a shirt like Eva. Almost exactly like Eva, in fact; Serena might have guessed that they were outfitted by the same tailor.

The other, who had not participated in the physical display of affection, was male, and rather taller. His skin was also a few shades lighter than his friend's, though his hair was as dark. His eyes were startlingly blue, no shade that Serena had ever seen before in a human. His clothes were a little unorthodox, too; he wore essentially the same shirt and trousers combination as his companion, but his clothing was cut a little oddly, as though he might have designed them himself without much idea of how a shirt was put together. They were also oddly coloured, and decked in strange accessories.

The Baron's shamefully rude question was overheard, and all four looked up. 'Allow me to introduce my friends,' Eva said after a moment, and without an apology. 'Lady Draykon Llandry Sanfaer, and her mate, Pensould.'

'LadyEva,' said Pensould, in the midst of a sinuous and slightly alien-looking bow in the Baron's general direction. 'I do not know why you insist on using these silly human words when

142

we have much better ones.' He pronounced the name as though "Eva" and her title were all the same thing.

Silly human words? This, then, was no human who could shapeshift into a draykon, but rather a draykon who could shapeshift into a human. He was undoubtedly extremely old, and... alien. Serena's curiosity and interest were caught at once, and she hoped she would have chance to get to know this Pensould better.

Eva's lips twitched. 'You're quite right, and I apologise. When will I learn? This is the Baron Anserval, dears; Lady Fenella Chartre; and her brother, Lord Bastavere.'

Serena performed the expected curtsey, coaxing Lady Fenella's dimple into her beamingly smiling cheek and a bright sparkle into her eye. 'Lady Draykon!' she gushed. 'My word, that is a fine title. I had not thought to meet with such eminence in mythical Orlind!' Her mind was busy as she spoke, reflecting on the significance of that title. It was rare indeed. It had been bestowed upon only a handful of people, all of them shapeshifters who had performed significant services to their various realms and homes. They tended to serve as ambassadors between the draykoni courts and their home realms.

Such importance did not appear to suit Llandry, however, who blushed and said with surprising awkwardness: 'Eva, you did promise not to use that silly title.'

'Gracious me, I am in everybody's bad books! It is your own title, Llan, and you earned it fair and square.' Receiving only a reproachful look in response, she relented. 'All right, I will not use it if you prefer.'

Anserval was oddly silent, nor had he moved. She expected that from Fabian, but why would the good Baron pass up his chance to charm these fine people? Serena glanced sideways at him. He was smoothing his moustache, his face thoughtful and devoid of the fatuous pomposity she had come to expect from him.

'Shall we dispense with this absurd charade?' he said abruptly. 'I am not the Baron Anserval, in point of fact, and there can be no sense in continuing the pretence out here. My name is Farran Bron—' here he paused to bow once more to Llandry and Pensould, though without the oily grace that had characterised his courtesies before '—and I am in the employ of G.A.9.'

Serena stared.

GA stood for Government Agency, which was terrifically unimaginative but nobody cared; they were about efficiency, not creativity. Irbel's ninth agency was devoted to… well, nobody knew quite what, save for those on the inside. That they dealt in espionage, there could be no doubt, but what else they might do? Perhaps it was best not to know. They had a reputation for a cool kind of ruthlessness which made them somewhat unpopular.

'It's their airship,' Anserval — or rather, Bron — continued. 'And this is their mission, I'm afraid. The LHB will have to stand aside.'

Serena found her voice. 'Why couldn't you have said that to begin with? Why were you pretending to be Anserval?'

He just looked at her. 'You really didn't know?'

Serena lifted her chin and made no reply.

Bron began, with impatient movements, to strip off the facial hair he wore. 'Same reason you were pretending to be Lady Fenella,' he returned. 'Not a bad act, by the way, although I could've wished her a little less gushing.'

'I could've wished Anserval a little less obnoxious!' Serena replied, stung.

He ignored this. 'Bastavere, on the other hand, is pitch-perfect.' He awarded Fabian a grand nod, a professional according a high compliment to another.

Fabian said nothing. He was thinking deeply; Serena recognised that posture and the intense silence that went along with it. He was doing the same thing she was doing: thinking back over all the dealings they'd had with "Baron Anserval" and trying to work out what it all meant.

Serena failed there. 'Anserval is a major masquerade,' she said, frowning at the erstwhile Baron. 'Lady Fenella's just a persona, with a carriage. But the Baron? The house, the servants, the collections?'

Bron shrugged. 'The aristocracy's frequently up to no good, both in Irbel and abroad. G.A.9 likes to keep an eye on them, and for that, you need someone on the inside. Someone fully accepted, not just an occasional character. They chose me.' He evidently considered this an achievement, but Serena wasn't so sure. His acting talents were undeniably superior, but in his place, she wasn't sure she would have been pleased to be assigned such a long-term role.

'I don't buy that,' Serena replied. 'All that, just for basic surveillance? Come on, really. What was the game?'

'Nothing to do with you,' he said briefly. 'You were a useful cover once or twice, I admit. And then you provided an easy entrance into all this riddle stuff.' He cast a scornful glance at the Seven Dreams rhyme still glimmering in the sky, making his feelings about the whole assignment painfully clear.

'So you knew about the key all along?' Serena said. 'The one that was in "Baron Anserval's" collection?'

Bron hesitated. 'Yes,' he said.

He was lying, and making a remarkably inept job of it considering his apparent aptitude for deceit. Serena hid a smile, and did a horribly inept job of that, too.

'All right, no,' said Bron irritably. 'We don't know where it came from or how it got there. Probably we got it as part of a job lot of old rubble. Stuff to line the shelves, you know.' He eyed Serena, and his irritable manner vanished behind a smooth smile. 'Did you think we were infallible?' he said, eyes sparkling with amusement. 'That's cute. We do our best, of course.'

Serena opened her mouth to offer some deservedly harsh retort to this nonsense, but she was distracted before she could speak. Fabian moved. In one gesture, he ripped off the blond, perfectly styled Bastavere wig he'd been wearing so much lately, and threw it. It sailed a long distance, and landed in the waters of a tiny, swift-flowing beck that passed nearby.

'You just pissed Egg right off with that, there,' Serena commented.

'Um,' said Fabian. 'Yeah. Oops.' He shook out his much longer dark hair and tied it back into a tail, already looking more comfortable. So much more so, in fact, that Serena felt a moment's gratitude to Anserval or Bron or whoever he was. Maybe Fabian just needed to stop pretending for a while, and he'd be okay.

By the time Anserval-Bron had finished removing the immediately disposable articles of his disguise, he looked very different. He was younger than Serena had supposed, and he'd lost the Baron's smug manner and air of self-satisfaction — though he had gained more than a hint of cockiness and self-importance to balance it out. Serena still felt little liking for him, although perhaps that was merely discomfort; all her fine efforts as Fenella, wasted! She was downright embarrassed to think that he had known all along that she was acting, but she hadn't guessed that about him.

'Don't feel bad,' he said kindly. 'We've worked with Torwyne before. You do all right, with what you've got.'

He probably meant it well, Serena was charitable enough to concede, but his comments still rankled. He was magnanimous, as though her precious Agency was a minnow compared to the shark of G.A.9, and she and Fabian were children flailing about with a few cheap toys. 'Thank you,' she said stiffly, earning herself a knowing grin in response.

Damn him.

It occurred to her that Eva and Tren were silent in the face of these revelations. Llandry and Pensould merely looked confused, but Eva looked nicely composed. She caught Serena's eye, and Serena detected a faint twinkle before her ladyship looked away.

Oh, dear. Eva had known. She had known! How mortifying. But then... Serena's quick brain flashed through the connotations of that, and came up with an answer to Fabian's questions of only a little while earlier. What was she doing on this flight? She was here to counter Bron, that's what. Eva had needed an airship to go after the keys, but the LHB couldn't muster the funds for that; only G.A.9 had that kind of money. So she'd used Serena's — or rather, Lady Fenella's — connections with a man she knew to be a G.A.9 agent to gain access to his ship, knowing that, sooner or later, he'd break cover and take over the expedition.

He'd try to commandeer any keys they found, too, and that was where Serena and Fabian came in. Eva was relying upon them to prevent Bron from walking off with the keys, by any means necessary.

She smiled inwardly, feeling at once much better about everything. Bron thought that she and Fabian were just little amateurs, did he? He would regret that. She'd make sure of it.

Catching Fabian's eye, she gathered at once that he'd grasped everything she had and felt much the same way about it. They exchanged a tiny nod, and an even tinier smile. In that moment he looked more like the Fabian she remembered, and she could've blessed the idiot Baron Bron for his subterfuge and manipulation. For the first time, Fabian was interested in the job at hand; his pride was injured, and he'd do anything he could to outdo the other agent.

The next few days would be very interesting indeed.

'So,' said Llandry with a frown, 'You are not Lady Fenella Chartre after all?'

Serena cleared her throat. 'Uhm. No, in fact. I apologise for the deceit, only it was… well, it was…' she searched for the right word. Necessary? More or less, but that wouldn't make sense without a lengthy explanation. Fun? No, how inappropriate. Also untrue, on this occasion; her joy in Lady Fenella's character had gone, and she wouldn't regret leaving the role behind.

Fabian saved her with a little of the charm he rarely showed, but which tended to conquer when he did. He made Llandry a graceful bow, smiled winningly at her and said, 'It's complicated. While my sister searches through her vocabulary, allow me to introduce myself? I am Fabian Carterett, of the Torwyne Agency of Irbel. The lady is Serena, the younger and much finer Carterett.'

'And why were you all pretending to be other people?' interrupted Pensould, with a sweep of his arm which took in the former Baron Anserval as well as Serena and Fabian.

'It's our job.'

Pensould stared at him. 'You mean that somebody pays you to pretend to be fake people?'

'Exactly.' Fabian smiled. 'Pays rather well, actually.'

Pensould threw up his hands in disgust and turned away. 'Never will I understand you humans.'

15

'I have a plan,' announced Teyo.

After two days of waiting around in a tiny, run-down farmer's cottage in Tarvale, which was damp and cold and not at all the kind of hideout that any of the team would have preferred, Teyo was growing bored and Egg and Iyamar were bickering back and forth all day long.

Simply waiting for somebody else to do something remarkable had never been high on Teyo's list of priorities, and if he didn't find something for his esteemed colleagues to do, he might end up killing them both. Or himself.

At this promising pronouncement Egg and Iyamar instantly stopped sniping at each other and sat looking expectantly at him. They were huddled in the cottage's tiny and ill-equipped kitchen, gathered around the small fire in a largely futile attempt to stay warm. The three of them were certainly well-hidden and out of the way, but Teyo couldn't help wondering what they had ever done to Oliver to deserve these privations.

'Two keys have been found, not including the one from the Baron's collection,' Teyo began. 'The two we know about were discovered in Irbel and Orstwych. Meanwhile, according to the rhyme we can expect to see one coming out of each realm. With me so far?'

'Six of them, anyway,' Egg pointed out, 'since the Baron already had one from who-knows-where. So, one of the

"Dreams" must already be missing its key.'

'Right. No way of knowing which one that is, at the moment. For now, we can assume that any of the following realms may produce a key, and four of them certainly will: Glinnery, Glour, Nimdre, Ullarn and Orlind.'

Egg and Iyamar nodded.

'We can't reach Orlind, nor Ullarn either, as the Tillikor Mountains are virtually impassable this time of year. So that leaves us with Glinnery, Glour and Nimdre.'

'Okay,' said Egg. 'Where are we going with this?'

'We're going to Glinnery, Glour or Nimdre,' Teyo said. 'That's what we have to decide.'

'What?'

'There's no point sitting here waiting for someone to find a key. It could be days, weeks or months, and besides, by the time we reach the site the key's long gone and it gets harder to track it down. What if we're already there when it's discovered?'

'But how do we know which one will be discovered next?' said Iyamar reasonably.

'We don't. It's a bit of a gamble.'

Egg raised her brows. 'How much of this has to do with being bored out of your head, Tey?'

'Um. Some of it might be because of that, yes.'

Her response to that was to climb to her feet with a slightly disturbing cackle. 'I'm bored with Nimdre and I don't like the Darklands,' she informed him.

'Glinnery it is, then,' Teyo said, beaming. 'Is that okay with you, Iyamar?'

'I… um, yes, but isn't Glinnery north?'

'More or less.'

'And Nimdre is south?'

'Right!'

'What if we go north to Glinnery and the next key is discovered in the south, in Nimdre? We'll be way out of position to get it.'

'Not much more than we are already,' Teyo argued. 'Anyway, it's a free-for-all out there. Tracking down and retrieving the keys is going to be really hard whatever we do. Might as well do something proactive, and have a bit of fun while we're at it, right?'

Iyamar looked dubious. 'It's a rubbish plan, Captain.'

Teyo sighed. 'I know, but it's the best one I've got. Unless you'd rather sit here and argue with Egg for the next three weeks?'

Iyamar blanched. 'When you put it like that…'

Egg grinned. 'Good choice. I can make your life *really* miserable, girlie.'

'Like you aren't already,' Iyamar muttered.

'I heard that.'

This plan was reinforced the next morning. They left early, provisioned for a considerable stay, and stopped at the bulletin boards on their way to the railcar station in central Irbel.

DREAM FOUND, BUT WHERE IS THE KEY? shouted the central board.

'So much for Nimdre,' Egg said cheerfully, hefting her pack.

Teyo read quickly. A group from the University of Draetre, and other organisations, had found a skyborne Dream in eastern Nimdre, near the border with Ullarn. No key had been found within. The Dream itself had been floating in an enormous bubble, the boards proclaimed, though Teyo had trouble visualising that. It had been secreted behind a ring of peaks so high that no one had ever explored them before. Curiously, the bubble had been filled with water, or something very like it, rendering it both airborne and underwater at the same time. Teyo saw pictures flash past bright with colour: the water was more lavender than blue, and filled with watery fauna the likes of which he had never seen or heard of before. Everything shone with a pearly radiance that was mesmerising to the eye. He wanted to stay and read everything about it, and look at every single picture, but his interest was not shared by his colleagues. Egg was already striding away, and Iya seemed more inclined to follow than to try out her fledgling reading skills on the text. Disappointed, Teyo turned away. He could catch up with the report later, maybe.

The important thing was that their three choices had now been reduced to two: Glour or Glinnery. That gave them good odds of finding themselves in the right(ish) place at the proper time. It also explained which realm the Baron's key had come from, which gave them an advantage; as far as he knew, few of the searchers were aware that three keys had been found, not two. A lot of people would waste a lot of time searching

Nimdre, while his team would be well away.

Shouldering his pack, Teyo trudged after Egg in the direction of the station, his pace much slower than her brisk step. They were disguised again, judging it best given Ylona's discovery of their last hideout. Teyo regretted this, since he secretly hated the wigs. They made his head itch, and he had to resist the temptation to scratch. But it was necessary. They were attired as farmers, which seemed apt given the rural location they had been hiding in, and Teyo did his best to stare around himself in awe, just like a real farmhand might do on his first visit to the big city. He made a hash of it, of course. Serena and Fabian would do it perfectly; he'd hardly know them himself. Teyo wished they were here, not rambling around all over somewhere without him.

Never mind. He was doing the best he could, and nothing catastrophic (or unsalvageably so) had happened so far. He tried to enjoy Iyamar's obvious enthusiasm for the venture and set aside his gloomy reflections. If he was leading his reduced team wrongly, well… they would deal with it later.

He was somewhat heartened to notice a stray corner of Egg's new blanket sticking out of the top of her backpack.

Teyo had been to Glinnery only once before, in his youth. He had gone with his father to the market of Waeverleyne, Glinnery's capital city, to buy new and rare materials for their business. Glinnery was a remarkable place, and the market was justifiably legendary; he had held fond memories of that trip, until the death of his parents had tainted all such recollections forever.

This being the case, he had privately hoped that his team might pick any realm to go to except Glinnery, though he would rather have died than admit it. Especially to Egg. And now, here he was; not only in Glinnery, but back in Waeverleyne as well.

Admittedly, it had changed a great deal in the quarter of a century that had passed since his last visit. Or, some of it had. The route from Iving through southern Glinnery to Waeverleyne remained as remarkable and glorious as Teyo remembered: all rolling hills and valleys spread with bright grasses and vibrant flowers, and dotted everywhere with clusters of the strange Glinnish glissenwol trees that were seen nowhere else. They were not like the trees of Irbel, which were clad in coloured bark and decked in wide, frondy leaves. Glinnery's trees were vast —

much, much taller than those of Irbel or Nimdre — and they bore neither bark nor leaves. Their trunks were toweringly tall, wide and gracefully curved, and topped with enormous, spreading caps, plumply rounded and shining blue and purple and silver in the eternal Daylander sun.

The same trees populated Waeverleyne. In fact, most of the city's buildings were constructed up and around those graceful trunks, easily accessible to the winged folk of the realm. But here, things had changed. The city had been the site of a brief but brutal war between some of the returning draykoni and the human inhabitants of Waeverleyne. The attackers claimed that the realm had been theirs, many centuries before, and they sought to reclaim it from the human settlers. They had been defeated, but Waeverleyne had borne heavy losses. Teyo saw painful gaps where once majestic trees had grown, still unfilled two years later. Worse, there was the appalling sight of half-burned glissenwol trees, one or two buildings still clinging bravely to their trunks but the upper storeys lost forever.

'Why are the trees burned?' demanded Iyamar as they neared the centre of Waeverleyne. 'Come to think of it, why are the trees so *weird*?'

'They're "weird" because they're glissenwol, and they're burned because there was a war,' Egg said. 'Surely you can't have missed that?'

'I dunno. When was it?'

'About two years ago?'

Iya shrugged. 'I would've been busy trying to eat, around then.'

'That's no excuse for ignorance,' Egg snapped.

Teyo quickly intervened. 'I asked around, and there's a decent inn a couple of streets from here. Shall we get settled in? We'd be close to the boards for the news.'

Egg grumbled something, but thankfully it was inaudible. Iyamar said nothing at all.

'Excellent,' Teyo said with a bright smile. 'Let's go, then.'

Their stay was destined to be short, in spite of the inn's many comforts. Teyo was woken in the middle of the next night (such as it was in daylit Glinnery) by the ferocious buzzing of his voice-box. He leapt to answer it, kicking his blankets out of the way and slamming his hand into the activation button.

'Teyodin Bambre, division three.'

'Teyo, this is Rulan Trame, division five,' said the box. 'Got a tip-off for you. I'm stationed at Aravin. They've found something up here, and I think it's going to be the one you're looking for.'

Teyo felt a flash of excitement, and relief. 'Aravin's north of Waev?'

'Due north. The site's near the coast, about six miles west of the border with Glour.'

'Gotcha,' said Teyo. 'Thanks.' He switched off the box and ran to wake his team.

'Got a proposition for you both,' Teyo said a little while later, as they collectively shoved food down their throats prior to departure. 'We need to get up to Aravin *fast*. We don't have time for carriages. I'm going to shift, and I've got two options for you.'

Iyamar stopped eating and stared at Teyo, horror-struck.

'I can either carry both of you, or Iya can shift and one of us can take Egg,' he said. He gazed back at Iyamar, trying to convey by his expression an air of confidence and calm. He knew Iya could do it, even if she didn't.

Egg glanced sideways at Iyamar with more than a hint of derision, but to Teyo's relief she didn't complicate matters by offering any comments. The silence stretched as Iyamar struggled with herself.

'I can't,' she said finally. The statement bore none of the panic or fury of their legendary debate a couple of weeks ago, but it was nonetheless inflexible. Resigned, defeated, and depressed as well.

'Why not?' said Teyo gently. 'Here, try something right now. Shift draykon, but do a tiny one. This big.' He held his hands a few inches apart to demonstrate the size. 'You won't be a danger to anybody. It'll be almost the same as turning Jispish.'

The subject of this latter addition twitched at the mention of her name, and looked up. She was ensconced atop the table with a dish of cream, which she had been greedily slurping without pause since Teyo had put it down for her.

Iyamar glanced uncertainly at Jisp, and then back at Teyo. 'Do you think it will be all right?' she said uncertainly. 'What if I lose control of it again?'

'You won't.'

'But what if I do?'

'You won't. It'll be fine.' When Iya glanced uncertainly towards the door, he added, 'no one will come in.'

You can do it, declared Jisp adoringly, and proceeded to radiate the kind of serene, worshipful confidence nobody had ever felt for Teyo.

Iyamar bit her lip, and then — before Teyo had even realised she planned to try — she was gone, and in her place hovered a tiny draykon. She'd panicked a bit, though. The proof was clearly evident.

'You've got the head on backwards,' Teyo said calmly. 'Give it another try.'

Iyamar had realised this and was flapping madly in circles, shrieking. The girl had a point, Teyo was forced to admit; had she done this full-size, the damage could have been considerable.

It took her a minute or two to pull herself together, and then she shifted again, correctly this time. Her miniature draykon was perfect in every detail. Her joy at getting it right was palpable, and Teyo grinned. 'Good! See, I knew you could do it.'

Iyamar whuffed through her nostrils and nuzzled at Jisp, who had thrown herself at the little draykon with a piercing howl of admiration. Egg rolled her eyes and turned her back, munching her sausages and bread with cheerful obliviousness to the screaming congratulatory victory lap going on behind her.

'So, if we get you somewhere out in the open, I reckon you could do a full-size one,' Teyo urged. 'You've got it down!'

The joy-party stopped abruptly and Iyamar-as-draykon keeled over in a dramatic faint.

'It's not that bad,' Teyo said, laughing. 'If you end up with your tail growing out of your nose, we'll just fix it.'

Iyamar, apparently dead, made no response.

Teyo solved that problem by simply picking her up and stuffing her into his pocket. He added Jisp, too, to keep them both quiet, then hauled Egg away from the remains of her very generous breakfast and packed them all off northwards.

They soon found a reasonably unoccupied meadow to use as a testing ground. Teyo decided it was time to apply just a little bit of pressure, and made a show of checking his timepiece. 'If we don't get going soon, we'll be too late,' he observed. 'Rulan won't be able to hold off the hordes forever.' He held Jisp in one hand and Iyamar, still in her tiny draykon form, in the other.

'Ready?' he asked. 'Good!' And he chucked her up into the air.

Her wings stretched out instinctively, and caught her before she fell. She soared some distance away, turned a few loops in the air (showing off for Jisp's benefit, Teyo thought, feeling the tiny lizard vibrating with awe in his curled left hand), and then began to grow. It happened fast. Teyo had noticed that about Iya before; she procrastinated, shied away and generally gave in to all manner of specious fears, but once she gathered the resolve to do something, she did it, instantly and without delay. Within seconds, a fully-sized draykon was soaring majestically over their heads, her amber scales flashing gorgeously in the sunlight.

Teyo forgot himself so far as to jump into the air and let out a wild cheer. Egg greeted this with a sardonic look and a roll of her eyes. Chastened, he stopped, coughed, and confined his raptures to mindspeak.

Amazing! he called. *Fabulous! Fantastic! You're the best!*

I hate you, Iyamar replied.

I suppose that's fair. Teyo handed Jisp off to Egg, who tucked the tiny creature into her pocket with surprising tenderness, and then he shifted into his own draykon shape. He *loved* it so much, which was a thing he would never admit. The sheer size and power of it! In this shape, he didn't feel guilty about the past, or troubled about the future, or worried about anything at all. He was content to simply be, and enjoy the miraculous joy of flight. He waited with forced patience as Egg clambered onto his back and settled herself and their belongings, tying the latter down with rope. Once all was ready, she tapped him between the shoulder blades in their agreed signal, and he spread his wings.

His favourite way to take off was simply to jump into the air and burst into flight; it felt exciting and fabulous and powerful. He was careful today, though, mindful of Egg and the baggage, and rose slowly and steadily into the air. Iyamar was still turning loops ahead of him.

Time to go, he called.

Iya span in a few frenzied circles and then stopped, with a visible effort at controlling herself.

Lead on, Captain, she said crisply, and Teyo did.

16

As if being an unwelcome, unwanted and uncongenial companion were not enough, Farran Bron had the bad taste to be extremely good-looking underneath all the false hair and ageing make-up he had been wearing as Baron Anserval. He was no more than thirty in truth, Serena judged, and he was blessed with all the regularity of feature, blueness of eye and glowing good health that tended to bestow considerable beauty.

Which wouldn't matter at all, except that he appeared to expect Serena to be impressed by it. As though good looks had ever made up for an obnoxious personality, she thought grumpily. His manner towards her was only slightly less condescending than it had been as the Baron, and he regarded her with a knowing twinkle in his eye that said, *I know I am gorgeous, and you know it too? Don't you?*

Serena took great pleasure in ignoring him.

The inhabitants of Orlind were aware of the circling winds over the tallest peaks that neighboured their domain, as it turned out, though they had not yet launched an investigative expedition. The rejuvenation of the realm was difficult and sometimes dangerous work, and their numbers were, as yet, relatively few. They were willing enough to explore to the peak, in preparation for which Serena and her friends were honoured with a tour of the land on draykon-back, which thrilled Serena enormously. Serena and Fabian were assigned to be carried by a pair of draykoni who, in their human forms, were slight and diminutive and looked to be of Ullarni heritage, if anything. As draykoni, they were shimmering green and pale yellow respectively, and as fearsome and impressive as any of their brethren.

'We have been reclaiming the land,' Llandry explained. 'It wasn't as far sunk as we initially thought. It's hard work, but it's worth it.'

It was indeed, Serena thought, as she flew over grassland and valleys and woods surrounded on all sides by that strange, blue-purple sea. Compared to the other realms, it was still tiny, a mere insignificant island. What it lacked in size it made up for in lushness, rarity and beauty, however, and their work was but barely begun. Reclaiming sunken land was one thing; how they had contrived to populate it with so much vibrant life in such a short space of time confounded her completely. Draykoni sorcery of some kind, no doubt. Perhaps Teyo would understand it.

'Come back in about five years,' Llandry said to Eva with a smile. 'Then it will be truly remarkable.'

The same company assembled the next morning to explore the winds at the peak. Bron was mounted draykon-back as well, much to his disgust. He had been forced to admit that his precious airship was not best suited to the requirements of the day, and fear of damaging it had obliged him to consent to leave it behind. It did not suit his consequence, Serena supposed, to travel as merely one of a group, rather than in splendour as the captain of a grand airship which nobody else could contrive to boast.

Eva and Serena had asked a great many questions of Llandry, Pensould, Avane and their companions, but no one had any more notion what the keys were for, or what the rhyme in the sky meant, than they did. They were able to establish that the words had appeared over Orlind at the same time as they had materialised for the other six realms, but the draykoni of Orlind had no further information to offer.

They were as intrigued as anybody else by the mystery, and several volunteers were speedily found to carry the human members of the exploratory party through the winds. Remembering the severity of the currents, Serena had her doubts about the success of the mission. Llandry and Pensould seemed unfazed by it, however. Draykoni must be stronger than Serena had ever realised. Once again she missed Teyo, and wished she had brought him along.

Given the risks involved in penetrating the cyclone, the draykoni passengers had been securely strapped to the backs of those carrying them. This held its own dangers, and Serena had endured a lengthy lecture first thing in the morning regarding What Not To Do If Your Draykon Gets Into Difficulties. The lecture had mostly served to put horrific ideas into her mind, which she tried and failed not to dwell upon.

But once the expedition launched and they were underway, she began to forget her fears in enjoyment of the journey. The sensation of flying was always delightful to her, and she could gaze at the flourishing, if peculiar, vegetation and dazzling colours of Orlind all day. It did not take long for their party to reach the high peaks separating Orlind from the realm of Irbel, and the glittering scenery fell away behind them.

These peaks had been considered part of Irbel for longer than anybody could remember. But it was Eva's theory that, long ago before the destruction of Orlind, they had been part of the Seventh Realm instead, and hence, it was Orlind's key they were now seeking. The notion piqued Serena's curiosity, and she pondered the arbitrary nature of geographical boundaries and their inevitable fluidity all the way to the tops of the peaks.

The winds could be felt some distance away, initially as a moderate breeze but rapidly swelling to grander proportions. As the winds grew to a gale and began to snatch violently at her clothing, Serena's fears returned a little more than she would like. When the enormous, powerful draykoni beneath her began to be buffeted about by the winds and had frequently to adjust his course, those fears grew a little more. She set her jaw, clung tighter to the makeshift harness she'd been strapped into, and thought grimly determined thoughts as their party's leader gathered himself and plunged headlong into the cyclone ahead of her.

Two draykoni had volunteered as the advance party, neither of whom bore passengers. Their task was to ascertain whether the circling gale could be successfully penetrated at all; whether it could be safely done with passengers in tow; and whether there was, in fact, anything on the other side. The prospect that the winds might have nothing to do with a Dream or a key or anything of interest at all had certainly occurred to them, and it was a most unwelcome reflection.

Serena, Fabian, Eva, Tren, Bron and their mounts waited outside the pull of the winds for their comrades to reappear. It took much longer than Serena might have expected, and her nervousness grew. What if they had got into trouble down there? Serena could see nothing at all, for a thick, white mist obscured her vision in every direction. She could not even see the tops of the mountains that surrounded them; she could barely discern the tips of the wings of Fabian's mount, which hovered perhaps twenty feet away.

Draykoni had mind-speak, though, she reminded herself. If anything appalling had happened, their friends would be aware of it by now. Her draykon mount shifted beneath her, and Serena wondered helplessly what it meant. If only she could speak mind-to-mind with draykon-kind as well!

Abruptly, her mount gathered himself and charged forward, and Fabian's moved as well. She guessed that the all-clear had been sounded, and spared a brief wish for more advance warning. She had no time at all to prepare as her draykon dived into the mists and winds that surrounded the icy peak, and her vision dissolved into nothing but fog.

The next minute or two were some of the most horrific of Serena's life. If she had thought that the circling gales of a moment before had been alarming, plunging into the heart of the cyclone was… indescribable. Her world descended into pure chaos; a confusing, terrifying mess of mist and clouds and winds pulled violently at her clothes, her hair — her mount was circling and descending and then rising and circling and spinning about and — and then it stopped. All of it, all at once. Even the mist vanished. Serena's draykon mount landed on something blessedly solid and stopped moving.

Serena took a moment to breathe, hoping that her wildly pounding heart would slow to a more reasonable pace. She was trembling and sweating with fear and shock, though the sight of her brother calmly dismounting not far away soothed her a little. If Fabe was unfazed by it, she could pretend to be as well.

After a few minutes she untangled her freezing hands from the leather straps of her harness and began to think about getting down. Her legs still felt weak, but they would probably hold her. She gazed down doubtfully at the ground they had landed on. 'Is this… a cloud?'

It looked like a cloud. It was whiteish, and fluffy-looking, and plumply billowing, and pouring billows of eerie mist, and damp-looking; all the things one would expect of a cloud. But her draykon not only did not plummet straight through, his feet were not even sinking. He stood perfectly solidly, making slight bouncing movements which she interpreted as invitation to dismount.

Nobody heard her question. All the draykoni had landed around her, and their passengers were swinging themselves down from their mounts with every appearance of insouciance, enthusiasm and eagerness. Abashed, Serena hastily unstrapped herself from the harness and slithered down the draykon's back to the ground. Despite the evidence of her eyes, she half expected to sail straight through and fall about eighty thousand feet to the ground. But she didn't. The ground felt soft and spongey beneath her feet, like very wet mud. But it held her.

She drifted towards Fabian, who stood not far away, and then stood staring in awe. The cloud, if it was that, was vast, stretching away apparently for miles in every direction. Its surface, shrouded as it was in translucent mist, still revealed splashes of colour dotted everywhere — flowers growing cheerfully in this environment that wholly lacked soil, their delicate petals unfurled in the eternal light. Serena saw rose and peach and lemon and cerulean, jade and violet and lavender and all manner of hues. It was like a rainbow shattered into splinters and then shaken all over the surface of this peculiar place.

There were trees, too, of sorts. Some were mere bushes, while others rose some way over Serena's head. These were eerily insubstantial: their trunks and branches appeared to be wrought from nothing but silver and golden light, and in place of leaves they bore tufts of pearly, cloudy… something, which pulsed slightly as Serena watched.

She saw no animals at all save for one species: a flying creature resembling the irilapters that were familiar to her. Their tiny, sinuous bodies were covered in soft, downy fur of all manner of colours, and their prismatic wings fluttered busily as they darted from flower to flower, sticking their long, curling snouts into the heart of each bloom.

It was no more fanciful and bizarre than a lush forest and attendant wildlife growing merrily underground, but it felt much

160

more remarkable to Serena. Perhaps because she had seen forests before, albeit never one quite like the specimen at the Balbater dig site. But the experience of standing with blithe unconcern atop a cloud surrounded by trees made of light was wholly new.

A clear sheen and a sparkle caught her eye and she followed, frowning. An expanse of something like glass rose up before her, some forty or fifty feet away from where she had been standing. Following its curving arc upwards with her eyes, she guessed that it formed a dome enclosing some part, or perhaps all, of the cloudy Dream she stood in. But while it looked like glass, when she reached out to touch it she found it to be insubstantial; her hand went straight through. There was a point in there somewhere, though, where the temperature changed from acceptably chilly to painfully frigid, and she hastily withdrew her hand back into the relative warmth of the Dream.

'Very well, let's not get carried away,' Bron called grandly, even though nobody was doing anything more questionable than wandering about looking at everything. 'All of this will need to be properly studied and catalogued.'

He was right about that, more or less. The other sites had been swarmed under the moment they had been discovered, which was terrible for the archaeological finds contained therein. At Balbater, Serena had seen several teams of archaeologists desperately trying to salvage and record as much as possible before it was trampled over or stolen by heedless enthusiasts. This site had the advantage of being inaccessible to the majority, so it offered the first real opportunity for serious study.

That much acknowledged, Bron's attempt to assume control of the proceedings irritated her. He had no authority, for they had not even used G.A.9's airship for this part of their journey. But he liked to be in charge.

Nobody paid him any attention, which gave Serena a moment's reprehensible satisfaction. Admittedly, it was partly because at that moment a wave of purple colours washed over the cloud they were standing upon, emanating from Avane. She looked up at Eva and Tren, and grinned. 'Looks better that way, doesn't it?'

'Hmm.' Tren poked at the purple cloudy stuff with his toe. 'Draykon magic, then?'

'Most certainly.'

Serena joined them. 'I thought this was Lokant business? The keys, and the rhyme, and everything?'

'Oh, it is,' Eva said, 'undoubtedly. But draykoni and Lokants have sometimes worked together, in the past.'

Interesting. Serena wondered anew what might lie behind the door spoken of in the rhyme. Something that Lokants and draykoni felt an equal interest in hiding? That raised more questions and answered none at all.

'Let's spread out and see if we can find that key,' Tren said.

Serena picked a direction nobody else seemed to be heading in and set off. She soon left the rest of her party behind, and a sensation of peaceful isolation came over her. Little sound reached her ears save for the muted, soft crunching noises her feet made as she trod through the cloud. She couldn't see her own feet through the layers of swirling mists that obscured the surface.

Where might they have put a key, in this wide space? Could its creators have simply thrown it anywhere, trusting to the randomness of the act to keep it hidden? If so, how would they ever find it? If it lay somewhere on the floor, it might be hidden forever by the white mists that seemed to cover every inch of it.

They wanted it to be found, though, whoever had made this place. If the intention was to keep the keys hidden forever, they would have been buried in a deep, dark hole somewhere and left, or even destroyed. All of this elaborate game — the Dreams, the rhyme — suggested that the intention was to hide them *well*, so that no casual wanderer would stumble across them, but to render them accessible to the very determined. And if somebody had made it all the way up into the tallest peaks between Irbel and Orlind, an area impossible to reach on foot, and had survived the howling cyclone that guarded the Dream, such a person must qualify as very determined.

She did not think, then, that the guardians of these keys would have tossed it into the cloud and walked away. They would have put it somewhere more or less visible, surely? Perhaps the trees. Serena lifted her gaze from the impenetrable mist and began to scan the nebulous flourishes of light that passed for trees around here. On a hunch, she stretched out her hand to touch one. It was surprisingly solid, just like the cloud. Were they simply illusions, these visions of clouds and light? Perhaps that was the nature of the "Dream": they were standing on bare rock, but their eyes saw all manner of wonders.

These thoughts had barely passed through her mind when she tripped, fell onto her hands and knees, and received a small, painfully solid object in the eye. *Ow.* How had that happened? Something lay hidden under the mist, which was certainly its prerogative, but whatever it was didn't *have* to throw things at her.

Her groping hand swiftly found the offending object, and lifted it above the fog. It was a little round stone, its colour pale like marble and striated with dark crimson. It bore the spiral pattern of some kind of seashell.

Serena gripped the key in frozen wonder for a long moment, her mind whirling. How had she found it? She hadn't found it. If anything, she might have said that it had found *her.*

A flare of light caught her attention and she turned, staggering to her feet as she did so. Some kind of image was flickering to life a few feet above the clouds, emanating, she supposed, from something lying hidden beneath. This was not like the boards, though. The picture hovered above the ground, cast upon the air itself; no gadgetry of any kind supported it. Engineering, or draykon magic, or Lokant trickery?

A face appeared. He was old, Serena immediately thought, as his hair was pure white and fine. His face, though, was largely unlined, and showed no signs of the advanced age that would match his hair. A Lokant, then, and probably no partial-blood at that. His eyes were green and calm, his expression intent. She thought he possessed a slight air of sadness.

He appeared to be staring straight at her, but that was impossible. Serena waited under this apparent scrutiny, wondering what the image would do next. Then it began to speak, and belatedly she realised she ought not to witness this alone. She lifted her voice and hollered for her companions.

I don't know who are, said the vision slowly, *but you have The Key of Orlind, and I hope you are a worthy bearer of it.*

The vision paused. Tren and Fabian came running up together, Eva not far behind. *I have no doubt you will find the rest,* continued the face. *Perhaps you already have. I cannot guess at why you seek the repository, but please: use it wisely.*

The repository? Serena had never heard any mention of such a thing before.

In the meantime, added the man, with a faint smile, *I hope you are enjoying the work of my children. Is it not fine?*

Nothing more was said, and the vision gradually faded away.

'I'd better take that,' said Bron, and held out his hand to Serena.

Team Carterett had prepared for this possibility. The crimson-streaked stone was safely hidden in a pocket; the one she now held in her hand was similar in appearance but paler, with some artful-looking orange swirls decorating its surface. Bron had never seen the real one, so he couldn't know that the colours were wrong.

But it was necessary to keep up the pretence. 'If anybody is to keep it, it should be Lady Glostrum,' Serena said. 'This is clearly Lokant business, and as such must be the province of the LHB.'

Bron shook his head. 'In borrowing G.A.9's equipment, the LHB tacitly ceded control of the exploration to my employers. As their representative, I must insist upon retaining any important finds.' He held out his hand. 'If you're concerned about its safety, I need hardly tell you that G.A.9 is by far the best equipped to keep it out of unfriendly hands.'

Why did G.A.9 have to be so pushy, just because they were bigger, stronger, richer and altogether more impressive than everyone else? Serena handed over the stone with a perfectly real display of ungraciousness, and managed, with a heroic effort of will, to ignore the satisfied smirk with which Bron received the treasure. He awarded her a comradely nod and said, 'Right decision.' With a sideways glance at Fabian he added, 'And don't even think about trying to steal it back. I'll be on guard for any shenanigans.'

Serena adopted an innocent smile, hoping all the while that he would indeed be on his guard. She and Fabian would give him a fine show between them. Hopefully he would be so busy trying to fend off their attempts at stealing back the key, it would never occur to him that he hadn't been given the real one to begin with.

Thanks, Teyo, she thought silently, with a mental hug for her friend and colleague. It had occurred to him before they had separated that a few fakes might not go amiss, and he had found time to prepare two for Serena. He'd also taught Fabian how to make more, in case of need (Serena had passed on this tutorial, owing to a lamentable lack of skill in the area of arts and handicrafts. She was liable to get as much paint on herself as on the object at hand, and equally liable to saw off something vital of her own if given a sharp implement to use).

Later, she would hand over the new key to Eva, who would spirit it away somewhere together with the Balbater key.

17

It was market day in Aravin. This complicated matters a little, since the town was much more populous than Teyo had been expecting. On the other hand, it provided useful camouflage. They'd had the presence of mind to stop on the outskirts of the town and walk in, in human shape and on foot; a pair of draykoni flying in with a passenger would attract far too much attention. They needed to hear the news, while keeping as low a profile as possible.

It didn't take long to find the information they needed. The three of them wandered through the market separately, purchasing a few provisions here and there and keeping their ears open. Conversation buzzed regarding the large team of explorers who had passed through Aravin a few days ago, boasting that they were about to find the next key. They had gone up to the coast, as Teyo's contact had said. Teyo got the directions easily enough, then took out his voice-box to call Egg and Iya to join him.

But when he retrieved it, it was already lit up and rattling. He hadn't noticed in the tumult of the market. He switched it on and held it near his mouth.

'Teyo,' he said, trying to keep his voice low.

'Tey!' came Serena's voice. 'Great news. Mission successful.'

'Congratulations,' he replied, smiling. 'Did you use the toys I gave you?'

'Yeah. Thanks for those.'

'All going according to plan, then?'

'So far, so good. Can't wait to tell you all about it. Where are you right now?'

'Aravin.'

'Which is where?'

'Northern Glinnery. Can't stay, we're pressed for time.'

'Good luck.' The box went dark. Teyo reactivated it and called Egg and Iya. Fifteen minutes later, he stood at the north gate of Aravin watching as the two of them approached together. Judging from the matching scowls, they were arguing about something.

'We're going that way,' said Egg, pointing.

'Yep,' agreed Teyo.

'See?' Egg said to Iyamar. 'I told you he'd already know.'

Iya shrugged. 'Whatever.'

'Let's walk a half-mile or so and shift, all right? We're in a hurry.' The people of the market didn't yet seem to know that someone had (or might have) found something significant up there, but it wouldn't be long before that news spread. Teyo didn't want to have to fight his way through hordes of excited villagers.

Airborne, they had no difficulty finding the site. It wasn't swarmed under, but it was busy enough. As soon as Teyo spotted a knot of people on the horizon, he led Iyamar back to the ground and they shifted human again. The coast was rocky, and ended abruptly in tall cliffs which plummeted a long way down to the sea. The site, if it was a true Dream site, must be situated underneath them. Thank goodness it wasn't underwater.

'Who are we going to be?' he said as they halted just within sight of the crowd. 'LHB again?'

Egg shook her head. 'It's a bit early for them to show up, don't you think?'

'Right. Um, what then?' He scanned the gathered people, trying to work out what they were doing and who they were.

'Does it have to be human?' Iyamar asked.

Teyo blinked. 'Well, no. Not all of us have to be.'

Iyamar promptly shifted into the shape of a swift, sharp-clawed, bushy-tailed rodent that he'd seen darting about among the glissenwol trees on the way here. Her fur was powder-blue, which was very pretty, but wouldn't work very well underground. He didn't have to tell her. In an instant, her fur changed from blue to a sleek grey which wouldn't stand out at all among rock.

'Go on,' Egg said, waving him in Iya's direction. 'I'll probably have an easier time getting in alone than with two companions.'

Teyo knew better than to argue with her. He swiftly copied Iyamar's shape, and the two of them raced away towards the site. He let her take the lead. Judging from the way she was swishing her tail around, she was enjoying herself.

Clustered near the cliff face was a group of eight people wearing uniforms. They had spread themselves out and stood in uncompromising poses; clearly they considered themselves to be on guard. Their uniforms were crisp and identical, all coloured in blue and white. The group comprised an even mixture of men and women, all of whom were both young and white-haired.

They didn't waste any time, Teyo said to Iyamar. He felt more than a little dismay upon seeing them; here he thought they had been among the very first to reach this site. How had a Lokant group learned about it so quickly? Perhaps they were the ones who had discovered it. Were they Ylona's people? Had they already secured the key?

The entrance to the site was behind them, of course. Teyo saw a jagged splinter in the rocky face of the cliff, surrounded by rubble. Had somebody blown it open? How had they known to try that just here?

Let's split up, he told Iya. *See if you can sidle past on that side.*

He hung back and watched as the small, furry form of Iyamar inched her way past a pair of uniformed Lokant guards. She was clever enough to dawdle, foraging with her nose in the ground as though looking for food. These creatures ate worms and beetles which they dug out of the soft earth; there was no chance of finding food in this rocky terrain. But he didn't expect these Lokants to realise that, and indeed, nobody took any notice of the little creature. Once she had disappeared into the crack in the cliff, Teyo followed.

Nobody had yet had chance to set up any lights here, Teyo supposed, as the passage that lay beyond the entrance was pitch dark. Fortunately, Teyo had excellent night vision in his current shape. He wondered whether Iyamar had foreseen that, or whether it had been a lucky choice. Neatly-cut stairs spiralled down into the darkness. The topmost two or three had been damaged in the explosion (or something) that had broken open the passage, but the rest appeared unharmed. Iyamar was already scrambling down them.

Teyo started after her. He was too tiny to navigate them easily, and his long claws skittered on the smooth stone surfaces of the steps; he had to go carefully. Or rather, he *chose* to go carefully. Iyamar, heedless with youth, all but fell down the stairs. Actually, she *did* fall down a couple of them, tumbling end-over-end and giggling as she went. Teyo sighed inwardly. Teaching that one caution might be an interesting task.

The bottom of the staircase had just come into view when the stairs abruptly disappeared. Teyo barely had time to register that something like a tree had taken their place as he utterly failed to catch hold of it, and plummeted a long way down. It wouldn't have seemed like much in his human shape, but as small as he was, it felt like a very long way indeed. He landed painfully, bounced and landed again, even more painfully than before. Dazed, he lay for a few moments, panting, before his confused brain remembered Iyamar.

Iya? He scrambled up and dashed about in circles for a minute, trying to see her.

A stray giggle reached his thoughts. *Interesting,* she said.

Teyo discovered that he couldn't roll his eyes while he wore the shape of a small, furry thing. He tried hard, though.

He stood up and shook himself, enjoying the way his thick fur felt as it flew out and then settled smoothly back down again. The way his bruised muscles felt was less pleasurable. He made a few absurd gestures with his paws before realising that he couldn't brush himself down. His cheeks made a fair effort at blushing, and he hoped Iyamar hadn't seen.

Are you coming or not? she demanded, and he heard her paws pattering away. He hurried after her, taking note of his surroundings as best he could. The stairs had indeed become a tree, a very tall one which stretched away without apparent end. He hadn't fallen *that* far, he was sure, or he could not have survived. What was going on with this place? He left the tree behind as he ran after Iyamar. There was grass of some kind under his paws, and his twitching nose detected the presence of some delicious worms underneath. This was no illusion, he realised with wonder. The earth was real, and populated with all the wildlife he would expect to find. The grass growing atop it was real, too. He thought back to the underground Balbater site and its gorgeously coloured, vibrant trees and vines. How was any of it possible?

The sensation of the springy grass and moist earth beneath his paws was delicious, and no dangers threatened. He threw caution to the winds and raced after Iyamar, his tail streaming out behind him. He felt free and wild and overcome with joy, almost demented with happiness. He didn't remember ever feeling like that before.

The sensations lasted until an enormous pair of human legs appeared suddenly before him, as vast and immoveable as tree trunks in his perception. He came to an abrupt halt an instant before he ran into them face-first, and sat down on his haunches, panting for breath. Iyamar sat not far away.

So much for teaching *Iyamar* caution. What had got into him? There was something in the air down here, he decided; something strange about the place.

He looked up. The human was by no means as oblivious to their presence as he'd hoped. It was a woman, he judged from the skirtish thing she was wearing; he couldn't see her face clearly. He could tell, however, that the face in question was turned in his direction.

The human said something in a booming voice, hands planted upon her hips. It wasn't in any language Teyo understood. She bent down to examine them, and before Teyo could move an inch he was grabbed by a pair of ungentle hands and hauled skywards. He wriggled and struggled, claws flailing, but she was firm. She said something else, in Glinnish this time, but Teyo's grasp of the language wasn't up to deciphering it. She cycled through a couple more languages, and finally spoke in Nimdren.

'How about this one?' she said. Teyo responded with another wild attempt at escape, which failed.

'Ah! I see we're getting somewhere,' said the woman in Nimdren. 'It's a lovely job, but I *do* think you ought to take your proper shape, don't you? Skulking about like this! It is very rude indeed.'

She put him down, and grabbed the end of his tail before he could run away. Having snared Iyamar likewise, she crouched there implacably, waiting.

What do we do? squealed Iyamar silently.

No help for it, Teyo replied, and shifted human. He turned to face their persecutor, dusting off his garments with what he hoped was a casual air. 'Good morning,' he said gravely.

Iyamar flashed into human shape beside him, though she adopted none of his calm. She stood with her arms folded, glaring accusingly at the woman. 'You hurt Teyo!'

The woman — who was, not unexpectedly, white-haired — stared critically at Teyo, and looked him over. 'Not very much, I think. What are you both doing in my dig site?'

She may be white-haired, but she was elderly enough that Teyo wasn't positive she was a Lokant. Probably she was. Her face was traced with fine wrinkles, and deeper ones marked her eyes and mouth; laugh lines, he thought, though she was not smiling now. Her hair was long, but very fine, and swept up into a messy bun at the back of her head. She looked to be of considerable age, but she possessed an air of vigour that belied her years, and her eyes were peculiar indeed: pale purple, and very intent upon Teyo. No mere human, this.

'We're looking for keys,' Teyo said bluntly, 'like everyone else.'

'Yes? And which one are you working for?'

Teyo blinked in confusion. 'Which one? What?'

'Which Library. You're probably Ylona's people, aren't you? She said, years ago: humans would get it done. I imagine she's got a lot of you running about by now. We evicted a few when we arrived.'

A flash of red curls caught Teyo's eye: Egg was sneaking up behind their interrogator. He managed not to look at her, but something alerted the fierce Lokant woman, for she whirled and caught Egg before she could take so much as another step. 'More! Are there many more? Did you bring a whole army?'

Egg rolled her eyes and sagged in the woman's grip. 'Honestly, Teyo. I get past eight guards in my *human* shape and you two get yourselves caught, *and* me, within five minutes? So much for your amazing draykon powers.'

'That's the last of us,' Teyo volunteered, and wondered at himself. 'And we aren't working for Ylona. We're working for the LHB.'

He shut his mouth abruptly, and frowned. Egg stared at him with a *what are you doing?!* expression, but he couldn't help it. It was that damned compulsion again, although this was much more subtle than anything he'd experienced before. He hadn't even noticed her doing it until his mouth had opened and all manner of things had fallen out.

'What is this "LHB"? enquired the woman.

'The Lokant Heritage Bureau. Actually, it's called the Lokant Heritage Information and Training Bureau, or something, but that's a whole mouthful of words, isn't it? So everyone just calls it the LHB.'

The woman nodded repeatedly with an impatient expression. 'Yes, yes, fine, I don't care about that. Who is your employer? Why do these "LHB" people want the keys?'

'We're working for Lady Glostrum,' said Teyo despairingly, his mouth running on and on without his consent. 'She wants the keys because she doesn't want any of you to have them. Says you can't be trusted.'

The woman stared hard at him, her expression indecipherable. Then, shockingly, she broke into laughter, and the compulsion upon Teyo relaxed. 'Hah! Is that what she thinks? She's entirely correct, of course. Shouldn't trust any of us as far as you can throw us. I believe that's the expression?' She surveyed all of them, smiling, as congenial as she had previously been fierce. 'So you're working with Eva? Hmm. Do you know her well?'

Teyo exchanged a look with Egg. Her face said the same as his, he imagined: *what in the world is this now?*

'Not well,' Teyo said carefully, pleased to discover that he could speak as he chose once more. 'We only met recently, and briefly at that.'

'Pity,' said the woman. 'Still, it's a link. Better than I expected. Oh, but let us introduce ourselves! You may call me Mae. I won't trouble you with my full name. It is far too long and complicated to bother with. And you are?'

She was polite enough not to compel any of them to answer. A moment's silence passed as all three hesitated, uncertain.

'Oh, come on! I'm sorry I pulled you about earlier,' she said to Teyo. 'I thought you were Ylona's, you see. It's different, now.' She smiled at Teyo. 'I already know your name, thanks to your friend here. You're Teyo, correct?'

Teyo sighed. 'Correct. You can call the others Iya, and Egg.'

An eyebrow went up. 'Egg? Very well. I daresay there is a

story behind it. You'll tell me, perhaps, when we are better acquainted.'

Egg's face took on a worried look. 'Better acquainted? Are we planning to be?'

'Oh, bound to be!' said Mae cheerfully. 'You're working with Eva. Can't be helped.'

'So you know her?' said Teyo.

'Not yet, not yet. All just a matter of time.' Mae beamed upon them all.

Teyo squinted at her. 'Just who exactly are you?'

'Mae.' She smiled.

'Mae who? You're a Lokant of which Library?'

Her eyes opened wider. 'What do you know of the Libraries, dear?'

'Nothing at all,' Teyo admitted.

Mae grinned. 'I'm not of any Library.'

'Oh? I thought all Lokants were part of some Library or other.'

'You really don't know anything about Lokants, do you?'

Teyo smiled a little sheepishly. 'I guess not.'

Mae turned away and began to walk. 'Most Lokants are,' she said over her shoulder, apparently trusting to the three of them to follow. 'Not all. I find it's much more comfortable not to be. Can't think why everyone gathers together like that. Are they afraid to be alone? Leads to all manner of unpleasant politics. I prefer to keep to myself.'

'And yet,' Teyo said, hastening to keep up with her surprisingly brisk pace, 'here you are, involving yourself in some grand Lokant venture.'

Mae rolled her eyes. 'Yes, well. Sometimes people are idiots, darling, and somebody has to sort them out.'

'So this is about some Lokants being idiots?'

Mae glanced at him sidelong. 'Don't think I don't see you fishing, Mr. Teyo.'

'Damned secrets,' Egg muttered. 'We're up to our collective necks in this mess, and no one will tell us what it's about.'

'Perhaps you'd rather not know?'

'How can I tell that without knowing?' Egg retorted.

'An intriguing point,' Mae said. 'We'll discuss it sometime.'

The environment around them abruptly shifted. The grassy meadow disappeared, along with the insects and birds and flowers and everything else. The landscape transformed into cool greyish-silver rock littered with chunks of what appeared to be crystallised sugar, though surely it could not be. The cavern roof overhead disappeared behind a cape of swirling white mist, almost cloud-like in its density. The air smelled, oddly, of hot, spiced cayluch.

Mae's stride didn't falter for a second, and she took no note whatsoever of the alteration.

'What *is* that?' Iyamar said, staring around herself in unabashed amazement.

'Draykon trickery,' said Mae indifferently. 'Though it's a bit more impressive to manage it here, I admit. They had some powerful help.'

There were few people around; Mae's guards were doing (on the whole) a good job of keeping the crowds away. Teyo saw no one at all, until another uniformed Lokant came running up and said something, breathlessly and incomprehensibly, to Mae. She replied in the same language, an expression of relief crossing her face, and received into her hands a key. This one was pale blue with cloudy swirls of purple covering its surface. Teyo barely had time for a glimpse before it disappeared into Mae's pockets and she turned crisply about.

'That's that. What do we have left?'

Since she was speaking Nimdren again, Teyo assumed the question was directed at him. 'Ullarn and Glour still unaccounted for,' he said.

'Two left. Right.' She narrowed her eyes at him. 'I don't suppose you'll tell me where the rest are?'

Teyo considered this. She hadn't compelled him, which she could have. He took that as a gesture of good faith. On the other hand, he didn't want to give up all their secrets.

'I know that Ylona has one,' he said. 'The rest are… safe.'

'The rest being three,' she said.

'Right.'

'Four for our side, one for Ylona's. Not bad.'

Our side? Teyo raised his brows at that, but he didn't question her about it — not least because she gave him no opportunity. She was off and striding away once more, heading for the exit this time. Teyo felt some mild regret that he couldn't stay just a little longer. He was fascinated by this site's changefulness and curious to discover what other forms it might take. But Mae was right: business wouldn't wait. Perhaps he could return some other time.

'Come along,' Mae called over her shoulder. 'We have a lot to do, and never enough time.'

That called for a question or two. 'We?' he echoed.

'I'll be joining up with your employer soon enough,' Mae said. 'And since you three and I clearly have the same goals in the meantime, we'll be working together.'

'I don't think so,' said Egg. She stopped walking. 'I answer to Teyo, and until he decides what we're doing, I'm going nowhere.'

Mae stopped, turned, and surveyed Egg with an air of exasperation. 'Very well. Mr. Teyo?'

Teyo sighed inwardly, wondering anew how Serena put up with it. 'She's got the key,' he reminded Egg. 'Serena would probably want us to stay close to it anyway.'

In order to steal it back, he thought but didn't add.

'Not with any view to purloining the key for yourselves, I hope?' said Mae, with a piercing look at Teyo.

He suffered the uncomfortable feeling that she was reading his mind. Surely that wasn't possible. He swallowed. 'Um, no,' he lied. 'Certainly not.'

Egg shot an accusing look at Teyo. 'You've got an answer for everything,' she grumbled.

'Um,' said Teyo. 'Aren't I supposed to?'

'Are you?'

'I mean… that's my job, isn't it? Until Serena gets back.'

'Right,' said Egg. 'Keep on keeping on, Tey.'

He frowned, confused. Was Egg annoyed with him or not?

She's just grumpy because she didn't get to steal anything today, Iya told him silently. *And we weren't impressed enough about her sneaking past those guards.*

She might be right, certainly about the latter part. Egg would never show it, but she suffered from some feelings of inadequacy on occasion. Here she was in a team of five. Two of them were draykoni shapeshifters, and the other two were accomplished actors and masqueraders and were unquestionably the leaders of the group — at least when they were here. Egg sometimes felt that she had too little to offer. Nobody else felt that way, but it was never entirely possible to convince Egg. He was impressed that Iya had figured that out; Egg wasn't easy to

175

read. The girl had discernment.

Teyo made a mental note to be suitably admiring later, towards both of them. It was one of the things Serena did well: complimenting and praising her team's efforts without being patronising or condescending. She was great at encouraging everyone.

Mae stopped near the entrance to the site and stared upwards. Neither the stairs nor the tree were presently occupying the space; nothing at all was.

'That being the case,' Mae said, as though they had been discussing the problem, 'let's do something else. Hang on to each other.'

'What?' said Teyo.

'Quickly, quickly. We're pressed for time.' When they still didn't move, she grabbed Teyo's hand and mashed it together with Egg's, then repeated the process with Iyamar. 'Hold on tight!' she said merrily, then took hold of Iya's free hand in one of her own.

The next few seconds were vile. Teyo felt a sucking, rushing, squeezing sensation which brought with it violent feelings of nausea and dizziness. The world around them went dark — darker — and then brightened suddenly into glaring sunlight. It also became a great deal busier in an instant. People surrounded them on all sides, and the noises of talking people, rumbling wheels and assorted other human sounds rose abruptly to tumultuous levels and sadly assailed his ears.

Looking around numbly, he saw tall buildings of wood and silvery metals winding around the trunks of vast trees. Colour was everywhere, rich shades of indigo and teal and jade and many more. The people around him were a glorious mixture: pale skins and dark, winged and wingless, all ages and shapes and sizes. And in the near distance, he saw the glittering sea.

They were, in short, in the middle of Tinudren, the largest coastal city in Nimdre and its main trading port. It was a city Teyo had known well at one time, though he preferred not to remember those days.

'How did we get here?' he said faintly.

'Don't think about it too much,' said Mae. She was already off, aiming for the bank of bulletin boards that occupied the centre of the city square. He saw dazzling images flashing past of site after site, some he recognised and others he did not. The headlines accompanying them were not familiar.

Wirllen: Fourth Site Discovered!

Wirllen was in Ullarn, Teyo remembered vaguely. This wasn't a site he had heard about yet. Reading on, he learned that the discovery had been made in the last few hours by the Torenn Institute, and they had secured the key. The media didn't appear to have learned about the Orlind or Glinnery sites yet, so this was actually the sixth site. One to go.

'Torenn,' said Mae disgustedly. 'That's Ylona.' She chewed absently on a fingernail, a habit which surprised Teyo to see in so powerful and imposing a woman, and finally sighed. 'So it's a race to the last key. I hate that.' She turned abruptly to one of her ever-present aides and said, 'Glour?'

The man nodded.

Mae turned back to Teyo. 'Where was Eva going to?'

Teyo hesitated. He didn't precisely know where Eva was, so he couldn't give away her location. But did he trust this woman enough to tell her what he did know?

No. Eva was right: Lokants were tricky. How did he know she wasn't working with Ylona, and all her apparent distaste for the woman was merely an act?

Mae sighed again, more deeply this time. 'I am sorry to do this. I prefer not to, you understand. But this is important.' The feather-light compulsion settled upon Teyo again, and when Mae asked, 'Tell me what you know of Eva's location,' he replied instantly, 'She went up by airship.'

'Airship.' Mae nodded crisply, and turned back to her aide, who had retrieved a map from somewhere. He pointed to three locations.

'No,' said Mae to the first. 'Ullarn site is found. And no, not likely.' She inspected the third point closely, then nodded. 'Orlind it is.' Before Teyo had time to process her intention, let alone object to it, she had grabbed the three of them once more and away they went, hurtling through space — or were they simply stepping through some kind of doorway, albeit one that was far too squeezingly small? Moments later, Tinudren had vanished and instead they were standing in a lush, richly-coloured forest. The air was warm and damp and full of fragrance. Was this Orlind?

Teyo stared, briefly, and then he closed his eyes. The way it *looked* was remarkable, but the way it *felt* was... he struggled to

177

find the words. This was unlike any place he had ever been before. He felt in tune with it in an unfamiliar way. Energy thrummed gently through his bones, imparting a sense of well-being, of harmony, of happiness... of *belonging*. He felt soothed and calmed and energised, all at the same time. He also felt empowered, as though everything he could do — everything *draykon* he could do — was amplified.

Iyamar wore a similarly poleaxed look on her face, he noticed when he finally opened his eyes. Egg merely looked annoyed.

'Special, isn't it?' said Mae, nodding. 'No wonder it spawned a civil war.'

Teyo groped for some words to offer, and found none.

'All right, you pull yourselves together and I'll come back for you later,' said Mae, more or less kindly. 'I want to find out if Eva is here somewhere.' She strode away, two of her aides trailing loyally in her wake.

'So,' said Teyo weakly. 'This is unexpected.'

'Right,' said Egg, but then she seemed to realise that their sudden transportation to Orlind wasn't quite what Teyo had meant. She looked from him to Iyamar and back again, her air of disgust growing. 'Oh, crap. This is another one of those things you two get but that I'll never understand, isn't it?'

Teyo and Iya exchanged an uncomfortable look. 'Um, sorry,' Teyo mumbled.

Egg made a revolted noise and turned her back. 'I'm going somewhere else,' she announced as she walked away.

Teyo felt a headache gathering between his brows. 'I really, really hope we get Serena back soon,' he said to Iyamar, and instantly regretted it. It wasn't professional. He was supposed to be exuding an air of unflappable composure.

But Iya nodded. 'Me too,' she said fervently.

Teyo tried not to feel offended.

18

'Nice try,' said Bron in a smirkful voice. 'Really, you've got to try harder to get around me. Oh, not that I mean to disparage your skills. You're amazing! Really! But G.A.9 is different. You don't get training like that anywhere else.'

Serena had been caught attempting to sneak into Bron's quarters on the airship. She had waited until he was busily occupied with a group of draykoni, all of them deep in conversation. Bron had been doing most of the talking, she'd noted with disgust. The primary topic of conversation was probably himself.

But here he was, catching her red-handed only a few minutes after she'd entered the ship. How he had managed to extract himself without her noticing, follow her here and creep up upon her unheard, she didn't know; he really did have impressive skills. But it didn't matter. Eva still had the real stone, and Bron was still protecting an appealing fake.

Serena bit her lip with a show of disappointment and embarrassment, and hung her head. She had begun to develop a whole new Serena over the past couple of days, without precisely planning to. The new Serena was a little in awe of Bron, much more impressed by his superior abilities than her pride wished to admit, and prone to bouts of self-doubt each time she failed to steal back the key. This persona flattered Bron's ego and kept him happy, and as long as he was occupied with his boasting, his swaggering, and his kindly attempts to teach her some of his magnificent abilities, he wasn't thinking too closely about his shiny stone, or what might have happened to it before he received it into his own hands.

'Actually, I'll be honest,' Bron continued. 'Part of it's about superior equipment. Look, see this thing?' He reached up over the top of the doorframe and detached something. It was tiny, dwarfed in the palm of his large hand, and composed primarily of metals. 'It's hooked up to something I wear on my belt. Warns me when someone comes in here.' He put the gadget back where it had come from, and smiled at Serena. 'Expensive stuff, I'm afraid. I know Oliver would love to have some of those little trickies.'

Serena forced an expression of grudging admiration into her eyes, and nodded. 'Um, how do they recruit at G.A.9?' she asked.

Bron laughed. 'Wanting to switch teams? Can't say I blame you, but I don't think it will happen. They take people young, and there's years of intensive training to go through before you get to go into the field.'

Serena encouraged him to chatter on in this vein for a few minutes, until she was sure his thoughts were suitably diverted from the key. Keeping her indignation hidden was the most difficult part of the task, but she was growing used to Bron. His absurdities were as likely to incite laughter as aggravation. Fortunately, she was a champion at maintaining her composure.

But then there came an abrupt change of conversational direction. Bron leaned closer, twinkled down at her out of his undeniably gorgeous eyes and said, 'Ah, so. One of the guys told me about a special glade on the north shore of the island. It's got a pool that's suitable for swimming. Do you fancy taking a look, later?'

All Serena's composure deserted her for a single, agonising instant. *What?* Was Bron actually, truly, seriously thinking of courting her? Not as Baron Anserval, in a pursuit as insincere as his persona, but for *real?*

What in the world could she *say?* She had caught herself in a neat trap, here. The new Serena she'd so cleverly cultivated would probably accept, and as far as her goals went it would be the sensible thing to do, for she could keep him nicely distracted. But the prospect of having to spend a lot more time with him was intolerable, especially since she would have to pretend to *like* it as well.

The possibility that this new pursuit was no more sincere than the last floated through Serena's mind, but it was of no comfort to her. Pretence or not, it required the same response. She opened her mouth, summoning her resolution to say something, *anything*, to deflect the attack. Nothing came out.

Nothing! Serena had not been left speechless and resourceless in a very long time.

Just before her silence became awkward, she was saved by the approach of Fabian. His footsteps were recognisable long before he came into view; he dragged one leg ever so slightly, and his footsteps were fractionally uneven.

'Hi, Fabe,' she said brightly just before he came into the room.

'Thought I might find you two here,' he said, lifting his brows.

Serena's heart sank. Were people noticing when she and Bron were both absent, and drawing conclusions? Ugh. Intolerable. Worse when it was *Fabian* doing it. He ought to know her better than that! She couldn't even glare at him. She could only hope, for his sake, that he was shamming.

'Something weird's happened,' Fabian continued, oblivious to her indignation.

'Something else weird, I think you mean?' said Bron with a tentative smile. To Serena's irritation, his manner towards *her* was patronising but he treated Fabian more or less like an equal. He even appeared a tiny bit hesitant around Fabian sometimes, as though he were searching for the best way to impress him and coming up short. It made no sense to Serena, but it galled.

Fabian smiled briefly at this mild wit, and nodded. 'Yeah, so. Tey's here, and Egg and Iya.'

Serena stared. 'Here?' she managed at last. 'How?'

'Some Lokant woman brought them.' Fabian shrugged, as though this occurrence, and the identity of the Lokant woman in question, were of zero importance and even less interest to him. 'I think she knows Eva.'

Serena relaxed a little at this news. Anyone Eva knew was probably okay, and *probably* not here to pinch all the keys. 'Where are Tey and the others?' she enquired. The presence of her team was a relief; it always felt strange to be out and doing without them.

'Azure Glade,' Fabian replied. In an attempt to find their way around without getting hopelessly lost, they'd taken to naming various parts of the island after their predominant colours. The Azure Glade was characterised by glorious leaves in shimmering shades of blue, primarily azure, and its flowers bloomed a blazing white. It was one of Serena's favourite places in Orlind; she spared a brief hope that Teyo would like it.

'Onward!' she ordered, pointing imperiously towards the door. Fabian grinned at her and ducked back out into the hallway. Serena followed, without waiting for Bron.

'So, you are my great-great-great-great — how many greats? — grandmother, is that it?'

Eva stood with arms folded, glaring at a tallish, elderly Lokant woman Serena had never seen before. Tren hovered just behind, looking uncertain, while Wrob and Ayla were vigorously interesting themselves in something on the other side of the glade, their backs discreetly turned. There was no sign of Teyo, Egg or Iyamar, to Serena's disappointment.

'Let's not dwell on the timeframes,' said the newcomer with a theatrical shudder. 'But I most certainly am your direct ancestor. Isn't it marvellous? I have been wanting to meet you for the last *age*. Don't call me grandmother, though! Gracious, how lowering. Mae will do.' She smiled.

'Then why are you only just making your appearance?' Eva's voice was thick with suspicion, and her body language spoke of a total rejection of the connection. Why might that be?

Mae made a careless, dismissive gesture and gave a short laugh. 'Business, business. There was an anomaly in the Enarior Cluster. They let the anteropticon drives overrun *again,* would you believe it? It took me a few oras to sort that one out, and when I next looked in on you, there you were all grown and married and quite, *quite* busy, I think.' She smiled.

'What is an ora?' said Tren. 'Same question about the — the drives, too.'

'Yes, sorry. An ora is a unit of time, like a year, you understand? Only it's not fixed, the way yours are; it's more relative. You see, worlds like yours are awfully small, all things considered, and your perception of time is very narrow. No offence intended, dear, we all do the best we can with what we've got.' She began to speak more rapidly, gesturing occasionally in her enthusiasm for the topic. 'But the worlds all have different ways of measuring time, and often different timestreams altogether, and they are so *vastly* different sometimes that we couldn't settle on anything so simple as a week, or a year. So an ora —' She broke off as Eva cleared her throat, and smiled a little sheepishly. 'Ah… a discussion for another time, perhaps.'

'First we need to clear up the question of who you are, and what you're doing here,' Eva said coldly. Mae began to speak, but Eva held up a hand. 'I don't want to hear any more about my ancestry. Even if you are my infinitely-great grandmother, I don't choose to acknowledge any Lokant as family.'

Mae considered Eva carefully and seriously, her congenial smile gone. 'I ought to have stepped in sooner,' she decided at length. 'Perhaps the Enariors could have waited. Only, you can't always trust someone else to do the job right, can you?'

Serena had heard Eva utter a similar statement once or twice, but her cold demeanour remained inflexible.

Mae rolled her eyes and sighed. 'I have a *lot* to say to Limbane when I see him,' she muttered.

That got Eva's attention. 'You know Limbane?'

Mae wrinkled her nose slightly. 'You shouldn't judge all of us by Limbane's standards, dear, and certainly not by Krays's. Although, it doesn't hurt to be wary. Some of us *will* stab you in the back at a moment's notice. But we're like humans in that respect, aren't we?'

'Yes, and my human family weren't up to much either,' said Eva shortly.

Mae nodded slowly, a hint of sympathy creeping into her eyes. 'I see.'

Eva's scowl deepened. 'As I was saying. What are you doing here? Since you brought the rest of Serena's team with you, I don't think it is merely a social visit.'

'Ah! No! Yes, exactly,' said Mae incomprehensibly. Serena received the impression that Mae, for all her apparent breezy confidence, was a little unnerved by the demands of this meeting. Having tried a bit too hard to impress her descendant, she was now becoming flustered.

'This is weird,' said Fabian in a low voice, right in Serena's ear. She nodded her agreement.

'I don't think we should be watching, anyway,' she whispered back, with a swift feeling of guilt. So absorbing had this strange meeting been, she had been entirely too slow in remembering her manners.

Serena stepped forward. 'Where *are* the rest of my team, incidentally?' she enquired.

'They went looking for you,' Tren replied. 'They went in the direction of the — oh, no, hang on. Here they are.' He pointed.

Teyo appeared from between the trees edging the glade. He was clad in his favourite dark green trousers, enormous boots and loose shirt, though the pleasant heat of Orlind had encouraged him to leave off his fur-lined coat. His mid-brown hair was more tousled than usual, as though he had been fidgeting with it, and Serena detected the unmistakeable signs of strain around his eyes and mouth. But he smiled when he saw her, and some of his apparent tension dissipated.

Egg and Iyamar were dressed so much alike, only the flame-bright flag of Egg's hair and Iya's icy blonde locks differentiated one from the other. This was odd. Last time she'd seen the two of them, hostilities had been high; but wasn't that Egg's second-favourite black coat Iya was wearing? She made a mental note to ask Teyo about it.

Leaving Eva, Tren and Mae to their discussions (or squabbles), Serena went straight up to Teyo and collared him in a bear hug. 'How's it going, deputy?' she said when she released him. His smile was infectious, and she found herself beaming in response.

'We're all very glad to see you,' he laughed. 'Poor Egg and Iya have had ample opportunity to see how awful I am at doing your job.'

Iya winced in sympathy and shook her head at Serena, but Egg instantly said, 'Too right, Tey, not that you didn't try hard. Was a good effort.'

Serena laughed. 'We missed you as well. Let's hear the news.'

The team went into a tight huddle as they rapidly brought each other up to date with their various ventures. Serena was pleased to observe that Iyamar, while quiet, was by no means silent, and she took her place in the group with no sign of discomfort. Her quarrel with Egg certainly seemed to have eased.

They had mostly completed this process when they were interrupted by a strident voice from somewhere behind. 'Well,

Team Carterett!' hollered Mae. 'What a charming picture you make! Such congeniality among a team of colleagues is just what I like to see. Especially in one I'm planning to hire.' She strode up to the group and stopped, smiling, right in their midst.

'Oh?' said Serena carefully. 'What's the job?' She glanced around for Eva, and spotted her with Tren a few feet behind. They were rapidly on the approach.

'I need those keys from Ylona,' said Mae without preamble. 'Imagine my delight to find that my clever grand-daughter has exactly the right sort of people in her employ! I want you to get them back for me.'

Serena glanced uncertainly from Mae to Eva, who had drawn level with the group by this time. Eva merely gazed back at her, her expression revealing nothing at all.

Tricky. Was Eva in support of this plan? In accepting Mae's assignment, would they be working with Eva or against her? Since Lady Glostrum held two of the keys, it was an important question.

'What, exactly, is all this about?' said Serena.

Mae blinked. 'What?'

'The keys, and the floating riddles, and the bubbles. What's it all for? Where does the door lead?'

Mae frowned. 'We've already discussed this.'

'Not that I recall. I can't and won't commit my team to any more assignments relating to these mysterious keys until I get some answers.'

Mae cast Eva a brief, annoyed glance. 'A joint attack, darling? Beautifully conducted, I admit.'

Serena raised an eyebrow.

'I said the same thing,' said Eva, her lips quirking.

Serena grinned. 'Well, how about it?' she said to Mae. 'I think we're all getting tired of being used as Lokant puppets.'

Mae chewed upon her lower lip, her eyes narrowing. 'Couldn't you just trust me?' she said, rather plaintively.

Eva laughed. 'Trust *you?* No one in their right mind would trust a Lokant.'

'Well!' said Mae with a touch of asperity, 'I don't find it at all difficult to trust you lot.'

'You're in the stronger position,' Serena pointed out. 'It's not so hard to trust people from that vantage point. But I don't think there's much trust involved when you won't confide in your colleagues.'

Mae sighed. 'I'm fighting to keep some important secrets hidden, precisely *because* they're too dangerous to be spread around.'

'Then you'll have to trust us not to spread them around,' said Serena with a sweet smile.

Mae pointed a finger at Serena. 'You, young person, are far too glib for your own good.'

'Thank you,' said Serena modestly.

Fabian turned around and walked away. 'I've had enough fun in the wilds of Orlind,' he called back over his shoulder. 'Let me know when something worthwhile comes up.'

Egg rolled her eyes in disgust and followed Fabian. 'Yeah, I think we're done here,' she said, pulling Iyamar after her.

Teyo merely stuck his hands into his pockets and stood, stoic but deeply unimpressed, his brows slightly raised and his expression somewhere between incredulous and exasperated.

'Last chance, Mae,' Serena said softly. 'At this point, I don't see why I shouldn't give all the keys to Ylona and let her do what she wants with them.'

That got Mae's attention. She turned pale and shook her head vehemently. 'No! No, you mustn't do that.' She sighed deeply, swaying a little, and gave a single nod. 'Very well, but it won't be easy to explain. It's no simple matter.'

Serena waited.

Mae chewed a bit more on her lip. 'I think it's better if I show you,' she said at last.

'Oh? How is that possible?'

'It's a secret.' Mae grinned. 'This isn't a good place. Find me somewhere private, and I'll show you everything you need to know.'

'The airship?' Tren volunteered.

'But do you mind if Bron…?' Serena said vaguely.

'If Bron what?' Bron himself stepped forward from somewhere and flashed Serena a dazzling grin. 'Didn't see me there, did you? I'll teach you that trick sometime.'

Serena sighed. 'I suppose it's too late to keep you out of our hair.'

Bron nodded gravely. 'Much too late. Shouldn't have borrowed my ship.'

'It's not your ship, though, is it?'

Bron acknowledged this perspicacious sally with an ironic bow.

Mae adopted a steely expression. 'Mr. Bron understands, I'm sure, that if any sensitive details should escape through his agency, I will be obliged to hold G.A.9 responsible.' Her tone left no doubt as to how unpleasant *that* would prove to be.

Bron gave her his most charming smile, and another bow. 'Yes, ma'am.'

Mae's curious, bouncing congeniality abruptly returned, and she smiled radiantly upon them all. 'Then that's settled! Shall we go?'

Later, Serena's team assembled with Eva, Tren, Ayra, Wrob, Bron and Mae in the airship's largest cabin. Mae had brought some kind of construct, the likes of which Serena had never seen before. It was boxy and sharp-edged, and blinked with strange lights. It looked nothing like the Irbellian engineering she was used to, not even the most sophisticated examples.

'Are we all ready?' said Mae. 'If you need to use the facilities, now would be a good time. There will not be an opportunity until much later.'

Nobody moved.

'Very good!' said Mae brightly. She took a spherical, shining thing from a pocket and inserted it into the boxy thing. Some more lights flashed, and a whirring sound began to emanate from the top of the device.

Mae did some other things which Serena didn't understand, pressing various buttons and running her fingers over the device in a manner which looked utterly futile to Serena. But finally she nodded, and said, 'Good. We're ready. Take a seat, everyone.'

Serena looked around, but there were no seats left. Teyo caught her eye and instantly began to rise, but she gestured for him to stop. It was typically considerate of him to offer her his seat, but she had a better solution. She perched on his knee instead, patting his head gently in appreciation.

'Thanks,' she murmured.

'You're quite heavy,' Teyo whispered back, surprising a laugh from her.

'I'm sure it won't be all that long,' she replied in a soothing tone.

Teyo merely grunted.

Something was happening with the boxy device. Colours whirled through the air directly above it, gradually forming into an image: a man's face. He bore the pure white hair of a Lokant, but he was reasonably young; if he was human he would've been somewhere in his forties, Serena guessed. With a start, she realised she had seen this face before. His had been the visage that had appeared in the Dream of Orlind, when she had found the key. The image expanded until his entire body could be seen, and continued to grow, spreading to comprise several other Lokant figures. The vision expanded until it filled the room, and then something peculiar happened. Abruptly, Serena was no longer viewing the images as external visions; they were inside her mind, and as vivid and absorbing as though she stood in the same room with these people.

The chamber was as strange to her eyes as the device: the walls curved oddly and glittered with faint colours, constructed from some strange, pale, crystalline material she'd never seen before. The peculiarly-shaped furniture was wrought from the same pale, glittering stuff and seemed to grow out of the walls. The Lokant man whose face had first appeared stood in the centre of the room, surrounded by six other Lokants who looked younger than he. He was casually dressed in loose trousers and a shirt, and his feet were bare. No formal audience this, then.

'They're all ready, father,' said one of the younger Lokants, a young man with a shock of wild white hair and a penchant for dark clothing.

His father smiled. 'I knew you'd do well at this task,' he said. 'I'll see them, of course, but we must conceal the keys first. Matters are growing urgent.' He unhooked a bag from his belt and opened it. The first item he drew from within made Serena catch her breath, for she recognised the seashell shape and the cream and golden colours. He handed the little stone to his son, and then proceeded to give another stone to each of the other five assembled Lokants. The last one went into his own pocket.

'Quickly, quickly,' he said.

'Yes, father,' chorused the six young Lokants. Then, one by one, they began to vanish, blinking out of existence until only their father remained in the room. He removed the final stone from his pocket and smoothed his thumb over the sky-blue surface, his expression a little sad. Then he, too, disappeared.

'That is Rhoun Torinth and his six children,' came Mae's voice, cutting through the vision. 'With draykon help, they created the Dreams as hiding places for the seven keys. It was overly elaborate, perhaps, but they were all highly creative. I believe they gloried in the project, as necessary as it was. Anyway, let's move on.'

The glittering chamber vanished and an inky, consuming darkness filled Serena's mind for several discomfiting moments. Then her mind's eye flared with colour and light once more. She was looking at... a library? The word was far too pale and feeble to describe the sheer, mind-bending glory and complexity of what she was seeing. She seemed to be standing in the centre of a chamber so vast, her mind couldn't take in the enormity of it. Shelves lined every inch of the curving walls, even spanning the ceiling; how the books contained therein didn't fall down onto her head, Serena couldn't begin to imagine. Round doors appeared everywhere, each one made from the same pale, glittering substance that Serena had seen in Rhoun Torinth's room. These, too, were scattered all over the ceiling as well as the walls, cheerfully ignoring the usual rules of the physical world.

Not every shelf contained books in the way that Serena understood the term. There were plenty of those, certainly, but many shelves bore row upon row of spherical, shining objects similar to the one Mae had inserted into the device. Did they, too, contain visions of past events?

This was merely one room in this vast and complex Library. Serena had no doubt that every single one of the many doors led into similar chambers. The probable extent of this labyrinthine place almost overwhelmed her mind. How much knowledge, how many ideas, must be stored here?

'The repository,' she said aloud, as her mind made the connection.

'Yes,' responded Mae. 'It is often called that, though its true name is *Teoricq*.'

'It's a Library?' asked someone else — Tren, probably.

'Something like that,' Mae said.

This was what the keys were for, Serena realised in an instant. This repository, containing unfathomable knowledge, was locked away somehow and the seven keys would open it. 'Who made this?' she asked.

'It used to be the focus of all of our efforts,' Mae replied. 'Every Library would contribute copies of every discovery they made, on any topic, in any world. But it grew too large, and too powerful, and many of the secrets it contains are dangerous. There was talk of disbanding the repository, and redistributing its contents. Some were in favour of destroying it altogether.

'It was Rhoun Torinth, in the end, who sealed it off. He was gifted with remarkable foresight; some said he could see the future, or at least glimpses of it. He foresaw the conflicts over Orlind, the site of the greatest and most powerful of our Libraries. There was nothing we could not do with such a tool! He saw that there would be war over it, and that the Library would be destroyed. And he knew that the disagreements regarding Teoricq could easily reach those levels — would inevitably do so, if we weren't stopped. So he sealed it, and he wouldn't tell any of us how to undo it. It made him somewhat unpopular, as you may imagine.'

'But he made the keys,' murmured Serena.

'Yes. Not that any of us knew it, at the time, save for his children. He also foresaw that a day might come when we would need some of the contents of Teoricq urgently. The keys were meant to allow for a way back, but only in the case of dire need.'

'Why hide them on this world?' asked Eva. 'There are more. Many more. And Lokants go everywhere.'

'Because of Orlind,' said Mae simply. 'This world was special to us at that time. Many of our greatest works were completed here, using the peculiar and as yet unequalled energies and facilities that Orlind provided. And when I say "Orlind", I mean both the realm and the Library. The latter... well, it was our best. I doubt we'll ever see another like it.' She paused. 'Personally though, I think that Rhoun also knew that we'd drift away from this world, after Orlind's destruction. All the better for a hiding place.'

'So, what's the dire need?' Teyo asked. 'Why is Ylona trying to dig all of this up? And how did she find out about the keys?'

'Ylona Duna is her wedded name,' Mae replied. 'Her true name is Ylona Torinth.'

Serena thought that over. 'She's Rhoun Torinth's daughter? But then she helped him make all this.'

'Yes, she did, in some part. But Rhoun didn't even trust his children with the entirety of the secret. They helped him to create the Dreams, but I don't think they knew where all seven of them were placed, or where the keys were hidden.'

'So Ylona knew roughly how to open Teoricq, but she lacked the details,' said Egg. 'Fine. But why is she trying to get at it now? What does she want from the repository?'

'Something came to light recently, among Lokant society,' said Mae. 'Some of Rhoun's notes surfaced. He was a far more remarkable man than anybody realised. Quite brilliant. We still don't know how he could see, or sense, events that were yet to come, and we never before knew that he'd developed a way to travel back to events long past.'

Serena blinked. 'Time travel? That's what Ylona is after?'

Egg snorted. 'Oh, come on. That's not possible.'

The vision of the repository finally faded, and Serena stood blinking, confused, in the sudden absence of it. Her gaze focused on Egg who stood, arms folded, an expression of irritated incredulity on her face. 'Lots of pretty weird things have happened lately, I grant you. But time travel?'

Mae raised an eyebrow. 'You can be spirited across the realms in the blink of an eye; talk to someone far away with the aid of a box of metal pieces; use the most powerful sorcery to create the Daylands and the Darklands; communicate with animals as though they were human; shapeshift into myriad alternate forms and sail the skies as draykoni, but time travel is too much for you to swallow?'

Egg looked briefly disconcerted. 'Well — but —'

'But what?' Mae interrupted. 'Rhoun Torinth was always a bit of a mystery to us. The discoveries he made, the things he knew, were unthinkable to most of us. In your parlance, he was a genius. Lokants bend time habitually; our Libraries hold it more or less in stasis, in fact. These things are common to us. But to wander backwards through time as easily as we wander forwards? Or to jump ahead to a future era, as easily as hopping over a puddle? That's different. That's awe-inspiring. And if Rhoun could do such things, that explains a great deal.'

Serena began to feel a sense of mild foreboding. 'You talk about him in the past tense,' she observed.

Mae nodded at her. 'Rhoun Torinth was killed in the Orlind conflict. He almost certainly saw it coming, but he chose to seal off Teoricq anyway, and by doing so he closed the door on the one thing that could have reversed his death.'

'Why?' Serena asked. 'Couldn't he have used it to reverse the Orlind conflict? To change something so it never happened? Maybe it would have been a good thing, to share the time travel secret with the rest of you.'

'That conflict isn't the kind of thing that could be stopped. Rhoun was a genius, but he was still just one man. What could he have done? Even if he killed the people who principally drove the war, there would be others. That was the future he saw: endless conflict, endless war. Lost the battle? Never mind. Hop back in time and try again. It could have gone on forever.'

Serena sighed. The story of Rhoun Torinth was tragic, and it touched her heart; not least because her thoughts jumped inevitably back to her own father. If she had the power to go back to the events that led up to his death and change them somehow, would she take it? Her heart wanted to say yes, but her head knew that the question was infinitely more complicated than it seemed.

She sneaked a glance at Fabian, who sat on the other side of the room. He had been wholly silent throughout this exchange, but she could easily guess his thoughts. If he could bring back their father somehow, he would do it without hesitating and hang the consequences.

Which troubled her a little. The keys were almost all found, and the way to the gate was open. She gathered from Mae's comments that their self-appointed Lokant leader was in favour of keeping Teoricq sealed. Would Fabian agree?

Did she?

To Serena's surprise, Iyamar spoke up. Her young voice was tentative but clear as she said: 'If all Ylona wants is her father back, why can't you all just let her do it? It's not much.'

Mae surveyed the youngest member of Serena's group, her expression grave. 'It doesn't seem like much, does it? But Rhoun Torinth was no ordinary person, as we've seen. If his death were averted, who knows what would happen? We can't even begin to guess. And it's not just the special people. If I died tomorrow, I wouldn't live to have an impact on the world around me in the future, and as a result, something else would have to happen instead. Those things could be very important. How am I to know?

'And then, what if my death is reversed, I live another ten years, and at the end of that time I am responsible for someone else's death? Whether I intended it or not, I have killed someone. If I had not been brought back, the person I might later have killed would not have died. You would, in effect, be trading someone else's life for mine. The consequences to actions that seem very small can be significant, and it is all entirely beyond anyone's comprehension. Do you understand?'

Iya thought about that, and finally nodded.

'Good,' said Mae with a smile. 'Anyway, I am by no means sure that Ylona merely wants her father back. She may want a great many more things besides, including the resurrection of the Library of Orlind; or if she doesn't, someone else will. And these "Yllandu", as they call themselves, what of them? What has she promised them, in return for their aid? The whole thing is unthinkable. It's far, far too dangerous to allow anybody to enter Teoricq.'

A long silence followed Mae's words. Serena thought it felt like a doubtful silence. Her own thoughts were disquiet. She could see the sense of Mae's words clearly enough, but she could guess at Ylona's feelings, too. Couldn't there be some kind of compromise?

'I'm glad we all agree,' said Mae at last, in a dry tone. 'If we are fortunate, the whole business will be cleared up in a few more days, and then you may all go about your lives and forget such matters as Lokant Libraries, secret repositories and time travel altogether.' She smiled beatifically.

To Serena's mind, this vision of uncomplicated peace sounded rather dull.

19

Some time later, Teyo sat comfortably tucked up in a storage cupboard near the heart of Bron's airship. It was primarily used for storing cleaning equipment, judging from the plethora of scrubbing, mopping and polishing accoutrements between which Teyo was now nestled. In his lap lay half of a blanket; his hands were busy knitting the rest. He was using a particularly soft yarn dyed rose, peach and pale gold: sunset colours. Just looking at it was restful.

No one had assigned him a cabin. Bron had said, very coldly, that the rest of Serena's team had not been invited aboard precisely because there was no space. Looking at the size of the ship, Teyo doubted it. Bron apparently harboured some kind of ill-will towards the three subordinate members of Serena's team, and perhaps especially towards Teyo himself. The reason why was unclear.

The cupboard was comfortable enough, however, and most importantly, it was private, at least until somebody decided it was cleaning time above decks. He had made a tolerable seat out of a few buckets and layers of cloths, and Jisp sat snoozing on his knee, her head resting against the soft ball of yarn. He had peace and leisure, at last, for the contemplation of Mae's various revelations.

Lady Glostrum had lost no time in warning them that Lokants withheld information. Mae probably hadn't lied, she said, but she probably hadn't told them the whole truth either. The message was clear enough: Mae could only be trusted so far, and Ylona probably much less. Her ladyship appeared to feel some resentment on this score, which Teyo could understand well enough. The keys, the riddle in the sky, the endless mysteries: these Lokants were using the people of the Seven as puppets to get the tiresome work done, without any intention of sharing the rewards. The riddle may speak of "finding the door" and winning prizes, but he agreed with her ladyship: the chances that Mae, or the rest of her kind, would permit any denizen of the Seven Realms to step through this door into the Teoricq Repository were non-existent. The whole thing was a false promise, and that was poor show indeed.

But Teyo felt no especial concern about this. What bothered him more was the unanswered questions. Who had put the riddle in the sky, thus sending all seven realms on what was, for them, a wild goose chase? Mae had strongly implied that it was Ylona, but she hadn't said so outright. What if it had been Mae? Was she blaming Ylona for her own actions? Were Ylona's motivations really as Mae had said?

And what of Teoricq? It wasn't just about Rhoun Torinth, and his story, as told by Mae, couldn't be relied upon as the absolute truth either. What else was hidden away in the repository? Had it really been sealed off and inaccessible for so many years? Or was Mae protecting something she saw as her own? She wasn't a member of any Library, she had said. Perhaps that was true, and perhaps not. Either way, she was remarkably high-handed in deciding, for everyone, what should or shouldn't be done with Teoricq.

He was growing increasingly troubled about their involvement in the whole peculiar business. In theory, they were available for hire for any job that didn't involve violence, as long as it had Oliver's support and approval. This one did; their boss was fully in favour of their helping Lady Glostrum with anything she required. But why did Oliver feel that way? Did he know something they didn't? Asking him was useless, for he was unrivalled at impenetrability.

Lady Glostrum's motives were clear enough: she distrusted the Lokants (apparently with good reason), and wanted to intercept whatever it was they were doing before they could do any harm to the Seven. That he could support, whole heartedly.

But Mae had gradually, but inevitably, taken over the mission, and she was much more inscrutable. What did she expect to do with the keys, if they managed to acquire all seven? It was his job, his and his team's, to get those keys back from Ylona and deliver them to Lady Glostrum. Or to Mae, if she succeeded in swaying Eva to her cause. Did Teyo really want to be involved with this?

If they could talk to Ylona, perhaps they could get a more balanced perspective. On the other hand, she would probably lie to them as well. The problem was insoluble, and Teyo frowned severely at his knitting as he struggled with it.

His reflections were interrupted by the sound of the door opening. He jumped, startled by the interruption, and dropped one of his needles. Was this the crew, come to start the cleaning? The cupboard was dark, and he couldn't see the face of whoever was peering around the door.

'Tey?' hissed a young, female voice.

'Iya?' he replied. 'How did you find me in here?'

'Scent,' she replied laconically. Squeezing herself into the crowded cupboard, she shut the door behind her, leaving them both in near darkness. Teyo's tiny light-globe only illuminated his knitting; he couldn't see more than a few inches beyond it.

'Good use of shapeshifting,' Teyo said, remembering his duties as mentor. 'You're really coming along with that.'

He felt, rather than saw, Iyamar smile, and she puffed up a bit with pride. 'I don't know what I was so worried about,' she said. 'It's really fun!'

Teyo smiled, a little wistfully. He couldn't remember the last time he'd felt the kind of burning enthusiasm that seemed to afflict Iyamar daily. 'And drayk-shape?' he enquired.

Iya hesitated slightly. 'Okay, that one still troubles me a little. But it's going better.' She paused. 'I just feel so… huge and deadly like that. You know? As if I've been given the biggest, deadliest weapon in the realms and told to go have fun.'

Teyo laughed. 'I know what you mean. It is odd, when you're used to being a soft little human with blunt fingernails and tiny teeth and hide made out of flowers and rainbows.'

Iya giggled. 'Right! And then suddenly you've the hide of a drauk and a muumuk put together, and you're the size of a few houses. I'm terrified I'll squash someone, and that's just the least of it.'

Teyo nodded. 'You've got to get used to all the senses you don't have as a human. Draykoni can be effortlessly graceful, despite their size, and they are extremely sensitive to their surroundings. It just takes a little while to figure out where all those things are.' He lifted the light-globe until he could see Iya's face, and peered at her. 'You didn't track me down to talk about shapeshifting. What can I do for you?'

'Nothing,' said Iya cheerfully, and probably mendaciously. She had seated herself cross-legged atop a large bucket and perched there, grinning, like an overgrown sprite. 'I just came to catch up.'

Teyo let the silence stretch.

'Fine, fine. It's Serena.'

Teyo was immediately alert. 'What? Is she all right?'

'Ohh, yes. She's fine. At least, I think so. How am I to know what goes on in her head? But you barely spoke to her yet.'

'Hasn't been a whole lot of time,' Teyo pointed out. 'Anyway, we spoke.'

'Yeah, but only as part of the whole group-chat thing. Weren't you anxious to see her?'

'She's a much better leader than I am,' Teyo said. 'It's good for the team when she's around.'

Iya nodded slowly. 'So it's just about the team?'

Teyo mustered his most severe frown, which probably wasn't very scary, and aimed it in Iyamar's direction. 'Just what are you driving at, young lady?'

Iyamar gave him an appallingly innocent smile. 'Nothing.'

Teyo put away his knitting. He disturbed Jisp in the process, who responded with disgruntled muttering until she realised that Iyamar was nearby. Then she leapt at the girl with unbecoming eagerness and swarmed up Iya's shirt to her shoulder, taking up residence there with her tail curled around Iyamar's neck. Teyo tried not to feel hurt at this enthusiastic desertion.

Teyo caught the drift of Iya's questions easily enough, and cursed himself for any unguarded comments he might have made about Serena. By now, he'd had ample opportunity to witness how appallingly observant Iyamar was. Time to head off any speculations she might have been making.

'Serena,' Teyo said after a moment, 'Would probably like me a lot more if I was a woman.' He waited to see what Iyamar's reaction to that might be.

197

Raised eyebrows, to begin with, and lips parted on a soundless *oh*. 'I see,' she said.

Teyo nodded. 'So whatever might be in your head, you'd best get it out again.' He'd spoken with uncharacteristic severity, but he really didn't want Iyamar poking around in any of *that*.

'Sorry,' said Iya, and she did sound genuinely contrite. 'Um… she and Egg…?'

'Not to my knowledge. Why are you so interested in everyone's private lives all of a sudden?'

Iyamar shrugged. 'Maybe I'm bored. Everyone's gone off to plot and plan, but they didn't seem to want or need the likes of me. Egg stomped off somewhere to sulk by herself, and Bron's strutting about trying to lord it over everyone else and generally failing. That was amusing to watch for a while, but it got old.'

Teyo's frown reappeared, which Iyamar, with her cursed perceptiveness, didn't fail to spot.

'What did I say? Bron?' She rolled her eyes. 'Yeah, he's a pain. I think he's driving Serena nuts.'

'Oh?'

Iya shrugged. 'Following her about, showing off all the time. I think he likes her, but he doesn't seem to get that undermining her authority and trying to look cleverer all the time is just irritating her.'

Teyo blinked. 'Bron likes Serena? Surely not. He's horrible to her.'

Iya nodded wisely. 'You know how there are some people who are really clever about a lot of things, but completely stupid about people? I think he's one of those.' She paused, considering. 'Also he's too happy with himself. Not sure it's occurred to him that Serena might *not* like him, considering how he's obviously soooo much better than everyone else.'

Teyo shrugged. 'Well, he's out of luck either way.'

Iyamar giggled again. 'Yeah! I wonder if he realises?'

'Probably not.'

Iyamar hopped down off her bucket and went to the door. 'Hang on, I hear something.'

Teyo listened, and discerned the faint, distant sounds of running feet. Damnit, did the girl have to have infinitely superior hearing as well? Getting older hurt.

Iyamar flung open the door to the cupboard and bounced through it, returning a few moments later. 'Something's up!' she said with glee. 'Fabian and Egg are coming.'

Teyo hauled himself out of his nest of cloths, ignoring the way his back creaked and cracked as he straightened up. 'Something exciting, or something catastrophic?' he enquired.

'The former, I think,' Iya said. 'Nobody looks like someone died.'

They both emerged from the cupboard and met Fabian and Egg in the process of dashing past.

'Oh,' said Fabian with a puzzled frown. 'There you are. What were you doing in there?'

'Knitting,' said Teyo.

Fabian blinked. 'Okay. Well, we're needed. The Glour site's been found, and Mae wants every warm body she can get her grimy little hands on to go. She reckons it might get messy, this being the last key.'

Teyo nodded. 'Iya, stay with me.'

'Boss.' Iya saluted and fell in with Teyo as he dashed up to the main deck. Lady Glostrum and her husband were up there, together with Mae, Ayra, Wrob, Serena and Bron. The latter was standing a little too close to Serena, Teyo noted, and appeared to be paying more attention to her than to Mae, who was attempting to hold court in the middle. *Iya's right again,* thought Teyo. The girl really had remarkable discernment; he ought to listen to her hunches.

'We're in two groups,' Mae shouted over the bustle and chatter. 'Half with me, half with my charming descendent. It's going to be a long hop, so you might be a bit disoriented at the other end. Don't worry about it! It will soon go away.' She paused to direct a beaming smile at her little audience. 'When we get there, it's — what is it that you say? — *all hands on deck* to find the key. I don't care what it takes, and I don't care about the site either, because you can be sure Ylona won't. Whatever you have to do, *get me that key.*'

There was a fair amount of nodding and a quiet chorus of agreements. The response struck Teyo as a tiny bit lacklustre, but Mae seemed satisfied. 'All right. Wrob, Ayra, Bron, Iyamar and Egg with me. Serena, Fabian, Teyo and Tren, with Eva. Off we go!'

Her allotted passengers all joined hands — Bron with a reluctant glance cast in Serena's direction — and they soon blinked out of sight.

'All ready?' said Eva, with a reassuring smile. 'It won't be too bad, I promise.'

Teyo doubted that, but he gamely took the hand she held out to him. Serena took his other hand. He barely had time to brace himself before the world dissolved around him and he hurtled into blackness.

'It's a tree.' Fabian said it flatly, in the tone of a person both confused and wholly unimpressed.

Their group stood huddled together in some distant corner of the realm of Glour. Teyo wasn't sure exactly where. Tren had said "far north", which meant they were somewhere in the midst of the largely uninhabited areas of the realm. It was Darklander territory, of course, and these parts of Glour were darker than most; the valleys and mountains of the north, largely uninterrupted by human settlements, were extensively farmed for a variety of plants (and some animals) which only thrived in darkness.

It made no difference to Teyo. Though not a Daylander himself, he was used to the daylight, and he had spent the last few years of his life living primarily in Irbel where night never fell. He stood in silence, struggling with a persistent feeling of nausea courtesy of the abrupt and disconcerting journey, and an equally unpleasant sense of disorientation. He couldn't see a thing, and it was taking his eyes a damned long time to adjust.

'It's not just a tree,' Tren said from somewhere ahead of Teyo. His nocturnal eyes revealed a great deal more of the terrain than most of his companions were ever going to be able to discern for themselves; they were collectively relying on the Glostrums to orient them. 'It's about the size of several ancient trees put together, as far as I can judge from down here. And it's varied. The part we're standing in front of right now? It looks like a glostrel tree, all silvery bark and white leaves. But if I walk a bit this way...' There was a pause, and the sounds of footsteps. 'Round this side, the bark is much darker and the leaves are a different shape. And also purple. And higher up, they turn green, and then red and rounder, and the bark turns gold. In short, it's like at least five different types of tree all in one, and that's just the part I can see from the ground.'

'That's more or less inkeeping with the other Dreams,' said Serena. 'Although... it's a tree. Not an underground cave, or a bubble in the air, or something. Is there a way in? Is it a site or an object?'

'How do we know this is the place?' added Mae. Teyo was slightly reassured to hear a note of doubt and confusion in her tone; even the lofty Lokants could be befuddled, sometimes.

'Not sure,' admitted Tren. 'The report didn't say. Have to assume, though, that Ylona has something to do with it. She probably knew that one of the Dreams was a tree, even if she didn't know where it was.'

Teyo's eyes began to adjust a tiny bit. He received the impression of something pale and towering perhaps ten feet in front of him, which must be the tree. Other than that, he could hear, feel and sense a great many other people around, but he could see little of them. It was unnerving. He inched a little closer to Serena, anxious not to lose her in the confusion. The scent of her hair reached him, and he felt a tiny bit better.

'I had word on that,' Lady Glostrum put in. 'Some scholar in Glour City found an obscure passage in an ancient, half-rotten book. You know the routine. Apparently it didn't make any sense until now.' She paused, and added, 'As I recall, people have noted this tree before, but nobody could figure out what it is, why it's here or how it works.'

'Is there a way in?' said Mae.

'Not that I can see,' said Tren, but he was interrupted by the faint, distant sound of bells. Eerie and mournful, it wasn't a pleasant sound, and it gave Teyo the shivers.

'What just happened?' he said.

'A ladder came down,' replied Tren.

Teyo blinked. 'What?'

'More than one. They're dropping all around the tree.' Tren's voice became more distant. He was probably walking around the trunk, and if it was as vast as he'd said, that would take him a minute or two. 'I've no idea how,' he called back, 'but they seem sound.'

'I called them,' said a new voice: female, powerful and pitched a little low. 'The tree is part of the Dream, but what I want is at the top.'

'Ylona,' said Mae, flatly.

She was answered with a soft laugh. 'I remember this one, a little bit,' said Ylona. 'My sister Treah's work. She had a more vivid imagination than some of us. Dear father never *would* tell me where he put it. Wasn't that disobliging of him?'

Her voice faded steadily as she spoke; Teyo thought that it was disappearing in an upwards direction. She was climbing.

Everyone else reached much the same realisation at the same time, and activity exploded around Teyo. 'Up, up!' yelled Mae, in the kind of hearty shout which could rally armies. Teyo was moving before the command had even registered with his brain. He was still largely in the dark, but his eyesight served him well enough to identify a ladder not far from him. He swarmed up it, aware every second that he was far too handicapped by his lack of night vision to be of much use. Mae had said *all hands on deck,* however, and their employer, Lady Glostrum, seemed to be in support of this venture. As such, it was his job to obey.

Someone swung onto the ladder directly behind him. 'Serena?' he called.

'It's me,' she confirmed. 'Up, up! Keep going!'

Teyo climbed. He didn't need to see very far in order to stay on the ladder, especially since, a little way up the tree, some kind of moss or lichen clinging to the strange tree's branches began to exude a soft, silvery glow. The scene enlarged. He could see colours: spiky, pointed leaves in pale, sky blue, and then fat, juicy round ones coloured rich jade; frondy foliage painted crimson-red; leaves as large as his head, sunny coloured and spotted with blue. Some of the leaves began to glow, too, as he ascended, until he felt adrift in the midst of an endless sea of branches twinkling and gleaming in every imaginable colour. So much beauty met his wondering gaze that he began to forget the urgency of his mission, lingering longer and longer on his way up the vast, endless trunk.

'Tey?' Serena called at last. He was holding her up, he realised with a faint blush and a hurried apology.

'Why don't you fly?' she added, and he blushed even harder. Why hadn't that occurred to him before? Hastily he transformed into a bird — some bird, any bird, he wasn't even sure if the slight, sleek, nocturnal form he'd adopted was any kind of recognised species at all — and soared upwards. His progress was much faster this way, but the sense that the tree would go on for ever didn't lessen one bit.

He saw nothing that hinted at any end at all. The branches kept on going and going, turning ethereal and glassy and then richly painted by turns. Tiny light-globes, or something of the kind, hovered in the air higher up, drifting there like dreaming glowflies, and Teyo began to feel distracted again. Their gentle, swaying motions were mesmerising, truly dream-ridden...

He flew into a branch. The impact broke the peculiar spell of the tree, and he snapped back to himself. Was this all part of the Dream? A defence of some kind, designed to divert all but the most determined before they reached the top? Or perhaps he was just being a dreaming idiot, and letting down the team. He flew on, trying not to focus too hard on the lights, until the branches abruptly ended and the sky filled his vision.

He'd reached the top. The ladder ended just above a large, circular platform of woven branches. Teyo landed carefully upon it, horribly aware of how far away the ground was, and shifted back into his human form.

He stood, panting a little after his exertions, and waited while his human-again eyes adjusted a little to the gloom. A nebulous haze of colour and light hung in the air on the other side of the platform, rosy pink and then sun-gold and then seawater-blue and on and on through an endless array of colours. The form it took was vaguely door-shaped, but it looked too insubstantial to be opened.

There was no sign of Ylona, though somebody Teyo didn't recognise hauled himself onto the platform moments later and made straight for the door, or whatever it was. She'd brought associates.

Teyo paused in brief indecision. Should he follow the man immediately, or wait for Serena? This dilemma was resolved moments later when Serena herself appeared, swinging up onto the platform with enviable grace. She paused a moment to examine the strange doorway, then set off at a near run.

'Come on!' she called, and Teyo followed. She reached the coloured haze ahead of him; as soon as her body came into contact with the ethereal substance, she vanished.

Teyo didn't hesitate. He ran straight into the stuff, and with a sickening lurch he found himself elsewhere.

Compared to the splendour and magnificence of the tree, the Dream itself was a little underwhelming. It was a bubble of some kind, or so it seemed. The walls were the same misty swirl of colour as the door they had stepped through, if it was a door? Teyo had the odd feeling that they were actually standing *inside* the thing; that it had become a great deal larger as they had entered, or they had become a great deal smaller. Or, even more disconcertingly, that relative size was somehow irrelevant in here. The patterns of rainbow light threatened to mesmerise him once more, and he hurriedly averted his gaze.

Ylona stood in the centre of a knot of people on the other side of the bubble. Teyo recognised none of them. A group began to form around himself and Serena, too, as Egg and Ayra appeared, and then Wrob and Bron and Iyamar. No one had any idea how to proceed, not even Ylona. They stood in an awkward face-off with a palpable air of confusion.

The floor was obscured by a thick golden mist. Teyo couldn't tell what they were standing on, if anything. He tried not to think too hard about that, either. The air was filled with white, softly glowing motes, which cast just enough light for Teyo to see a little. The light was too much for Tren and Eva, who appeared soon afterwards. They each took their characteristic shadowed glasses out of their pockets and hurriedly donned them, mouths twisting in annoyance.

Teyo crouched down and felt the ground beneath the mist. It was glassy and smooth. He walked about a bit, and found nothing secreted there. Where could the key be? The bubble was uncluttered with objects of any kind; there was nothing but light and colour and mist. Perhaps it was like the Orlind bubble: someone would trip over the thing, sooner or later, and perhaps another vision of Rhoun Torinth would appear.

'I don't see—' began Mae, but the bells sounded once more and all conversation ceased. The two groups waited, spellbound, for the next occurrence.

A key appeared in the air, two inches from Teyo's nose. It bore the characteristic spiral shape of the others, and it was the same size. This one was marked with a marbled pattern of yellow and cream. Teyo grabbed at it, and caught — nothing. The thing was insubstantial; he couldn't grip it.

More appeared, all identical in size and myriad in colour and pattern, filling the air all around him with ghost-keys. He watched, arms folded, as half of his group and most of Ylona's went into a frenzy of eagerness, clutching and grabbing at every key they could reach. The logic seemed clear enough: one of these floating temptations was the real key, and the rest were decoys. It merely fell to a matter of chance, as to who would get their hands on the prize.

Teyo wasn't sure. Neither were Serena and Fabian, for they, too, abstained from the chaos. Fabian stood with his hands in his pockets, frowning, and Serena chewed absently on her lip.

'I recognise this trick,' she said at last.

'Yep,' said Fabian. 'Classic.'

Teyo nodded. It was a kind of double-bluff. Keep the target distracted with supposed decoys in some clearly apparent place, and they would never question the "obvious" assumption that one of the decoys was real. You could do it with anything: jewels, gold, people. They'd pulled that very trick on Bron, essentially, and even he had swallowed it.

The real key was somewhere else entirely, tucked away where no one would think to look for it.

'Where would I put it, if I'd built this thing?' mused Serena.

Ylona hadn't fallen for the decoys either. She was prowling around, ignoring the ghost-keys that filled the air. She didn't know where to look, then, but she might guess sooner than they would. Teyo stopped watching her. She was a distraction.

'Somewhere innocuous,' murmured Fabian.

'You know what,' Teyo said softly. 'I wouldn't put it in here at all.'

The siblings gazed at him with almost identically thoughtful expressions. They looked eerily alike, when they did that. 'Genius, Tey,' whispered Serena. 'It's outside, isn't it? We all ran straight past it, distracted to a man by that shiny, lovely door-thing.'

'However,' said Fabian, 'how do we get out again?'

Good question, though Teyo. There was no apparent means of exit, now that he thought to look.

'Where did we come in?' he murmured. He'd got himself turned around a bit in his search of the floor, but he headed back in roughly the direction he thought he had travelled in.

There was a place where the colours faded slightly, the lights dimmed, and no keys floated in the air. Teyo headed straight for it —

— and he was outside again in the blink of an eye. The platform of branches was empty and silent, until Serena and Fabian followed him through. And then Egg, who announced herself with a characteristic curse.

'Damned riddles and games,' she muttered. '*So* glad we are

nearly finished with this rubbish.'

'I thought you said it would be fun,' Teyo murmured.

'It isn't.'

Teyo couldn't help smiling. Egg so often said what he was secretly thinking, but wouldn't speak aloud.

The four of them divided up the circular platform between them, and each took one quarter to search. It wasn't long before Fabian gave a cry of discovery. Teyo turned to see him holding up something small. his triumph palpable.

'Got it!' He handed the thing to Serena, who showed it to Teyo. This key was unlike the others. Instead of stone it appeared to be made from glass, and was perfectly clear and untouched by any trace of colour. Its appearance was oddly simple and subtle, given the extraordinary vividness of its surroundings.

'Right,' said Serena. 'We need to get this thing out of here before —'

'Ah!' came a strong female voice from behind them. 'Very good work. Mae was right to hire you, wasn't she?'

Ylona approached at speed, flanked by three of her hirelings. Teyo couldn't tell if they were Yllandu, or scholars, or something else entirely, as they were dressed in bland uniforms and bore no identifying characteristics. Whatever they were, they did not look very friendly.

'I'll buy it from you,' Ylona said, stopping before them with a winning smile. 'You're for hire, aren't you? I'll double whatever Mae is paying you.'

'That's not how it works,' Serena said coolly. 'The agency gets paid; we just do as we're told. And what we've been told is to support Lady Glostrum, not Mae.'

This wasn't quite true. They chose most of their assignments, and if the fees were increased for whatever reason, they all received a share. But it was a solid enough rebuff. Teyo folded his arms, and waited for Ylona's response.

'Then I'm bribing you,' she said with a shrug. 'Nobody needs to know that you found it first. We can just say that I did, and you will all become significantly richer. *Without* having to share your fee with the agency.'

This cunning proposal was met with complete silence.

Ylona sighed. 'I'll get them one way or another, you know. All four of the keys you're currently withholding. You can have no notion how important this is to me, and I will stop at nothing.'

'Is it about your father?' said Serena, in a tone of mild curiosity.

Ylona went still. 'Who told you about my father? Mae?'

Serena nodded once.

'You can know nothing of him,' she said coldly. 'Not truly. Mae is an ignorant fool, and I will brook no meddling in my personal affairs.'

'We have been obliged to brook a great deal of meddling in our world,' Fabian pointed out. 'You've set the Seven buzzing with this riddle business of yours, and you've shown no regard for the impact it might have on everything *we* care about. We aren't puppets. We can choose to assist you, or choose not to.'

Teyo expected another cold response to this sally, but Ylona merely gazed at Fabian thoughtfully, and finally nodded. 'A fair point,' she said. 'I have been ruthless, but it was the only way. Who better to find the lost Dreams of the Seven Realms than the people who live here?'

'It's all perfectly logical, certainly,' said Fabian. 'But the people who've done all the work for you will gain nothing by it. They won't even learn what it was all about. The promise of secret doors and mysterious prizes will never be fulfilled.'

Ylona raised her brows. 'Won't they? Mae intends to seal up the repository, yes, but I do not. Its contents will be released to the people of the Seven Realms, as you call this world. You will all be the richer for it, I assure you.'

That silenced them. Teyo's mind reeled, remembering the visions of untold knowledge Mae had shown them and trying to guess at what it might include. If even travel through time was possible, what else might they gain by it?

He could feel Fabian's uncertainty, and Serena's too. Could they be responsible for denying their world so much knowledge? The lives of everyone in the realms could be immeasurably improved. Lives could be saved.

On the other hand... some knowledge was dangerous. Mae was right about that. Did they want everything that the repository contained? Ylona could be offering a poisoned fruit; the contents of Teoricq could transform their societies for the worse, not for the better.

It was an insoluble problem. Teyo felt hopelessly ill-equipped to make such a momentous decision, and so did Serena; the glance she cast at him was despairing. Even Fabian, forthright before, was silent now.

Ylona's voice broke the silence. 'How about an incentive? I'm willing to bet that Mae didn't tell you where to find the door. Did she?'

'No,' Serena admitted.

'As proof of my sincerity, I will tell you immediately. There is a tiny island off the coast of the place you call Nimdre. South-easterly in direction. It is so small that it would not appear on any of your maps, but there you will find the door to the repository.'

A clever move, Teyo thought. Mae had explained a lot, but grudgingly and only under duress. The information she had given was mere background data, interesting but not vital. She hadn't advanced anything that might give them an advantage, or allow them to oppose her goals. But Ylona just had. What was her motive? Had she done it purely in hopes of securing the outstanding keys, knowing all the while that they would never be able to use the information? Or was she indeed bargaining in good faith? They only had Mae's word for it that Ylona wasn't to be trusted.

'Ah, Ylona,' said Mae from about three feet away. Teyo jumped, startled; he hadn't noticed her approach. 'Trying to subvert my excellent team, are you? They are far too sensible and far too loyal to be tempted by your offers.'

Ylona smiled faintly. 'I think they were tempted, in fact. Shall I hire them away from you? I could convince their Oliver Tullen, I'm sure.'

'I doubt it. Lady Glostrum's contract is secure.'

Ylona shrugged, and turned back to Serena. 'Is it to be?' she said.

Serena hesitated, and finally shook her head.

Ylona sighed. 'I *will* get those keys. You can be enriched by it, or you can suffer by it. Final choice, now.'

'Choice made,' said Serena.

Ylona nodded once. 'So be it.' She vanished.

Mae gave one of her alarmingly bright smiles. 'Good girl!' she said. 'Very well done, all of you. I take it you've secured the key?'

Serena held it out. It looked tiny in the palm of her hand, its transparency rendering it almost invisible.

Mae put out her hand to take it, but Serena closed her fingers around the stone, hiding it from sight. 'We've trusted you. I want a mark of trust in return,' she said firmly. 'This one stays with me.'

Annoyance flashed briefly across Mae's face. 'Fine, fine,' she said, waving a hand. 'When you have secured the other keys, I will receive them all at once.'

Serena said nothing. Teyo couldn't guess at her reasoning, but he applauded her tactics. If they couldn't trust either Lokant, then it helped to retain an advantage, and in keeping one of the keys, Serena had just secured one.

20

Two days later, Serena and her team were ensconced, more or less comfortably, in a tiny inn just outside of Draetre, in northern Nimdre. The inn was owned by the Torwyne Agency. It operated as a fully functional waystation, but its agents had priority, and it always kept rooms free for them.

Their conversation with Oliver himself had been interesting. Typically, he had shared none of his thoughts regarding the competing interference of Mae and Ylona. But he had not chosen to throw in his lot with either side, either. Lady Glostrum's contract was considered to be complete, and had been closed. He had declined Mae's and Ylona's subsequent attempts to hire them.

Instead, their new assignment was to acquire the two keys Ylona held and deliver them to Oliver himself. This was an arrangement which appealed to Serena, and the whole of her team. The prospect of having to decide which side to support, purely on the basis of the stories they each told, was unpleasant in the extreme. Used as she was to making difficult decisions quickly, she had balked at that one. Let Oliver deal with it. He was older, wiser and infinitely sensible, and he probably had more information than they did, to boot.

Serena had been less delighted to discover that Bron was to be temporarily assigned to their team.

'I'm sorry,' Oliver had said in response to Serena's indignant protests. 'G.A.9 have informed me that they would like one of their people along, and I can't refuse them.'

Serena had been forced to fume over it in impotent silence. Even *Oliver* couldn't refuse G.A.9! What an interfering, power-tripping bunch of busybodies they were. Worse, Bron had behaved as though he expected her to be delighted. It didn't seem to have occurred to him that she might feel anything else. On beholding her evident lack of rapture, he had simply put it down to resentment.

'I know it's hard, having to work with someone who's better equipped, better trained and more experienced than your people, but it's for the best. I can help you.' He'd given what he apparently thought was an encouraging smile. 'I won't rub your faces in it, I promise.'

Too late, thought Serena sourly. She didn't think he was more experienced than her team (excepting Iyamar), but that G.A.9 gave more comprehensive training and offered superior equipment could hardly be denied. He hadn't lost any time throwing *that* in her face.

Oliver had given her private instructions, too: On no account whatsoever was she to permit Bron access to the keys, once they were secured. The glass one from Glour was hidden, and she was confident that Bron knew nothing of it; she had allowed him to think that Mae had taken it. The Orlind key was safe with it. Eva still held three, so that left two in Ylona's possession.

Or in the possession of the Unspeakables. Teyo didn't think that the Yllandu would consent to be used as errand boys. If they were involved, they'd expect to be treated like equal partners, and that meant they'd be holding at least one of the two outstanding keys.

Bron agreed. More than that, he asserted that G.A.9 had received positive intelligence to that effect. In this one respect, Serena begrudgingly allowed him some leeway. With all their superior resources, G.A.9 probably held more information about the Yllandu than anyone else, even the Torwyne. Galling, but true.

And so, to the Unspeakables they must go. The organisation had long since spread itself across the Seven, and possessed headquarters in every Realm. The chief of them all was in Nimdre, for in Nimdre alone could they receive both Daylanders and Darklanders with tolerable ease.

211

Halavere Morann was based in the Yllandu's Nimdren offices, and Ylona was known to frequent the place, too. Not that it could rightly be called an office; only the street-level entrance, a law office, could be so named. The rest lay underground. It spread beneath several streets in the port city of Tinudren.

The assignment would be hard on Teyo, Serena knew, but they were relying on his connections for entrance. Trying to masquerade their way inside would be futile; the Yllandu knew their members all too well for that. Teyo had contacted a former associate within the organisation, and she had consented to get them inside.

What they did after that was up to them. Serena was heartily glad that they now had *two* draykoni among the team, for she expected to rely heavily upon their shapeshifting talents.

In the hours before their departure, tensions ran high. Iyamar was not ready. Serena knew it, and so did Iyamar herself. Their youngest member veered back and forth between towering over-confidence and crippling self-doubt. At present she was wallowing in the latter phase, and her nerves were infecting the whole team. Egg repeatedly threatened to bang her head against some obligingly solid object, but only because her own nerves (which she would never admit to feeling) were frayed to shreds by Iyamar's pacing and fretting. Teyo, meanwhile, walked about with his usual calm, but Serena could see the signs of strain. He was facing a much harder task than the rest of them, and Serena was proud of him for his composure — and more than a little bit worried about him.

Only Fabian was untouched by the doubts and fears which assailed the rest of his team. The prospect of infiltrating the closely-guarded headquarters of the most ruthless criminal organisation in the Realms caused him no qualms whatsoever; on the contrary, he was delighted, and looking forward to it with alarming fervour.

He cherished hopes of finding the elusive Valore Trebel somewhere down there. Serena had the extra task of keeping him on track, his mind on the job at hand. She wasn't at all sure that she could do it. Fabian had detached himself almost completely from the matter of the keys; he'd stopped even pretending to care about it, or even to pay any attention to it. All his thoughts were for Thomaso Carterett and the woman who'd caused his suicide.

As the time finally arrived to depart for Tinudren, Serena felt a headache approaching. She loved her team, and felt the greatest confidence in their abilities, but they had never felt so disparate, so little *together*. She'd lost Fabian completely; Teyo was inflexibly lost in his own thoughts; and Egg and Iya bickered all the long way to Tinudren, stopping only when Teyo (surprisingly) threatened to throw them into the road. And there was Bron, an intruder in their midst, wholly unwelcome and offensively critical. His presence only added to the general discomfort, Serena's most of all.

She had wanted to take only two with her on this assignment, but that hadn't worked out. She would need Iya and Teyo's shapeshifting abilities, and possibly Egg's talent for lock-picking and thieving. Bron simply refused to be left out, and her orders were to include him in all possible respects anyway. As for Fabian, she didn't dare leave him unattended. There was no telling what he might get up to if left alone for too long, and she didn't want to have to worry about him while she was supposed to be focusing on the job. Not that he would consent to be left behind, not when their destination was the one place he could hope to find news of Valore Trebel.

She could have left herself behind, of course, but that didn't work either. Teyo absolutely declined the job of leading the team on this mission, and she couldn't trust Fabian to do it with his current abstraction from reality. And so, all of them must go, and she must merely hope to providence that they could keep it together long enough to complete the job.

All she could do was ensure that *her* discomfort didn't show. She found herself play-acting as the calmly unruffled and effortlessly competent Serena she knew they needed. It was a shame that the act didn't work nearly so well on herself as it appeared to on the rest of her team.

Nightfall over Tinudren. Having arrived early, they had passed the time in a nearby eatery. A more cheerless gathering Serena had rarely endured, for Teyo and Fabian were still engrossed by their own thoughts, Egg and Iya were not speaking to each other (or to anybody else, much), and Bron's nose was too high in the air to allow for conversation.

'Time to go,' Serena said at last, gratefully abandoning the remains of the cake she hadn't really eaten.

Darkness blanketed the city like a comforting cloak as they regained the street. Serena checked her timepiece: ninth hour of the afternoon and a quarter. Perfect. Teyo lead them past the front entrance to the law offices which masked the Yllandu's lair, and around to the back. He had arranged for significant help getting inside. If all had gone well, one of the rear exits ought to be occupied only by Teyo's contact.

They hung back and waited while Teyo went up to the door and knocked. Serena couldn't see what followed, for the darkness was too complete. In half a minute, though, Teyo was back.

'All's clear,' he whispered.

Moments later, they were inside and the door was closed behind them by Teyo's erstwhile friend. She was about Teyo's age, Serena judged, or perhaps a little younger. Full-figured and stately, she was undeniably attractive, with long black hair and dark eyes. She greeted Teyo with a degree of intimacy which left Serena wondering about the precise nature of their shared history.

Something else caught her eye. The woman had closed the door with every appearance of complacency, but something was slightly off. Perhaps it was the hard lines of tension about her mouth, or the way her eyes darted to the door and back to Teyo. Serena caught his eye, her own asking a question, but she could read nothing useful in the glance he gave her.

'This way,' he said softly. Pausing only to clasp the woman's hand in thanks, he led them down a flight of stairs and farther into the heart of the Yllandu's domain. The way was clear, as promised, but still they took the precaution of sending Iyamar ahead as scout. She shapeshifted into a tiny furred meerel, camouflaged in black, and scampered away.

'Go,' Teyo said a few moments later, apparently on signal from Iyamar.

They proceeded in this fashion through several winding corridors and down two long flights of stairs. After entry, the next challenge was to discover where the keys might be hidden, but Teyo had waved away this question. In the heart of the Warren, as it was sometimes known, there was a room — the "Heart" — devoted to the use of the Yllandu leader and his or her closest associates. Anything of particular value would be stored there. Getting in was no small task, of course, but Teyo had sought help there too. The extent of his knowledge and his connections surprised Serena a little, and she began to wonder just how deeply involved in the organisation Teyo had been.

Their path wound down and down, and still no one was to be seen. This seemed far too much to hope for, even if Teyo's allies were extensive indeed, and Serena's misgivings grew.

She stopped. 'Tey…' she began.

'I know,' he said grimly. 'This is too much.'

They had spread out somewhat on the way down. Bron had insisted on taking the lead, citing "combat training" as his reasons, and Egg had taken up a position at the rear. Serena waved them back.

'Something's amiss,' she said. 'Teyo's good, but even he couldn't get us a free ride right into the heart of the Warren.'

'Haven't seen hide nor hair of anyone, ahead or behind,' said Egg. 'It's not right.'

Bron shrugged. 'So maybe it's a trap. It's too late to worry about that. We must be close to the Heart by now?'

He directed the question at Teyo, who nodded. 'Almost on top of it. But there's a big job on tonight, that's why we picked the timing. It might just be that.' He sounded doubtful, but Bron was already nodding enthusiastically.

'Then we go on,' said Bron decisively. 'Whatever's waiting up ahead, we can deal with it.'

Serena frowned. Her instincts told her to withdraw, but was that option still open to them? And, much as she hated to admit it, perhaps Bron was right. If most of the Yllandu were out, and Teyo's friends had decoyed the rest, a quiet walk is exactly what they'd get. They should at least *try* to secure the keys; time was running short, and they didn't have the leisure to be indecisive.

'All right,' she said curtly, gratified to note that her team waited for her approval before they moved. They proceeded down one last, shadowy flight of stairs and around a long, winding, echoing corridor, its walls featureless. A pronounced chill hung in the air.

'Here,' Teyo said then, and stopped before a nondescript door. It was identical to the others that lined the walls, and she could see no possible way for Teyo to identify it as special.

He took out a key. Not a Seven Dreams key, but a normal door key. To Serena's astonishment, he inserted it into the lock.

It was no ordinary lock, of course. It bore some of the same security features as the LHB's offices, but the technology was a little different. The key Teyo held *looked* ordinary, but when he turned it, lights flashed and a buzzing noise sounded, brief and sharp.

'You have a *key*?' Serena hissed.

Teyo nodded. His face was impassive, but she detected a hint of pain, and shame, lurking in his eyes. 'Don't ask,' he said softly.

Serena very badly wanted to ask; she began to suspect it might be her duty to do so, in fact. How could Teyo possibly have a key to the Heart of the Warren? A valid, functioning key? His involvement with the organisation had ended years ago... hadn't it?

Now was not the time. An instant's lurking suspicion entered her heart, only to be immediately dismissed. Teyo's loyalty was above question; she couldn't seriously doubt him, not for more than a moment. Whatever his explanation might be, she trusted that it would be sound.

He paused before the door, head slightly tilted as though listening. Serena heard nothing, but she detected a brisk movement at the floor as Iyamar-the-meerel whisked underneath.

A moment later, the door swung open. Teyo stepped back, astonished and alarmed, but there was no time to retreat. A woman stood in the doorway, beaming.

'Come in!' she said, with a grand sweep of her arm. 'We've been expecting you!'

A curse from Egg split the air, and Serena whirled. Egg had resumed guarding their rear, to no particular avail; behind her had appeared a quartet of grim-looking men, two of whom had seized her by the arms. Egg twisted and struggled furiously in their grip, but uselessly.

Teyo swore. 'Denaya—'

'Is loyal to the Yllandu,' said the woman with another smile. 'Reluctantly, perhaps, but she knows which side her bread is buttered.'

Denaya, presumably, was the woman who had admitted them. Serena watched with pain as Teyo's face crumpled, and his shoulders dropped. He sighed and stepped into the Heart, and Serena had no choice but to follow.

The room beyond was a surprise. Compared to the

featureless corridor outside, its decoration was positively sumptuous. Expensive rugs covered the floor, tapestries hung from the walls, and a full complement of furniture built from silvery glostrel and bronze silner wood was arrayed around the room. But the chamber bore no formality whatsoever. The chairs were well-stuffed and comfortable, and there wasn't a hint of stateliness about the place.

'Have a seat, do,' said their self-appointed hostess. Her words were friendly, but an edge of steel in her voice advised against arguing with her. Serena, Fabian, Bron and Egg sat, the latter with some less-than-gentle assistance from her captors. Teyo didn't so much sit as fold into a chair, as limp as a ragdoll.

There was no sign of Iyamar, which gave Serena a moment's hope.

'And the other one?' said their hostess, and accepted a small, dark, furry shape from one of her henchmen. She held the tiny creature up to her face, eyes narrowed. 'I suggest you change back,' she said, patting Iyamar ungently upon the head. 'It would be so easy to squash you by accident, and wouldn't that be a shame?' She set the meerel down upon the floor, and a moment later Iyamar-as-human appeared, glowering.

'Have a seat,' said the woman pleasantly, and after a moment's futile glaring and pouting, Iya obeyed.

Something about the woman was familiar. There was a distinctive curve to her lips when she spoke, and she had a way of holding her head slightly to one side that jogged Serena's memory. Her hair was curly and blonde, rather than white, and her posture and demeanour were different, but Serena felt certain of who she was talking to.

Before she could speak, Fabian shot to his feet. He had maintained a stony silence up until now, or perhaps he had merely been absorbed in his own reflections. His sudden energy startled Serena, and she stared at him in mingled dismay and alarm.

He stared intently at their captor, studying her face with feverish eagerness. His excitement grew, together with his disgust, and in another instant he spat upon the floor.

'Valore Trebel,' he announced in tones of withering contempt. 'It's you, isn't it? I have a sketch. I know that it's you.' He advanced on the woman he'd called Valore, ignoring her henchmen completely. 'I hoped we'd be seeing you. Second-in-command down here, aren't you? You've done well for yourself since you *killed my father.*'

Valore, if it was she, had taken an involuntary step back as Fabian advanced upon her, but she took no more. She straightened her shoulders and laughed into Fabian's face. 'What, me? Many of us are murdering bastards, it's true, but I am not one of them. Killing is so *messy.* I do not think I am this person you seek.'

'Fabe,' said Serena warningly. 'That's not— that's Halavere Morann.'

Fabian blinked. 'So it is,' he said after a moment. 'Then they are one and the same.'

'They are, as it happens,' said Halavere, with a slight bow and a mischievous smile. She waved away her henchmen with a cool smile which irritated Serena and incensed Fabian.

'You may not have killed him directly,' he spat, 'but you were responsible. He killed himself after *you* took everything he had! You and your friend.'

Halavere's head tilted. 'Which friend?'

'Bironn Astre.'

Teyo stirred. He caught Serena's eye and shook his head, his eyes wide. *Yes,* she thought. *I'd love to stop him, but it's too late.* She had seen Fabian like this once or twice before, and when he worked himself into this state he was unstoppable.

Halavere's smile broadened. 'Bironn, Bironn,' she repeated. 'Poor sap. He really wasn't up to much, was he? But I still can't recall…'

'*Thomaso Carterett,*' bellowed Fabian. 'A respectable landowner! A good man, with a wife and children — you cheated him out of every penny he owned—' He was working himself into a frenzy of rage, but he was brought up short as Halavere — or Valore — began to laugh, heartily and helplessly.

'You poor, foolish boy,' she said at last, when her unseemly mirth had ceased. 'Thomaso Carterett, a respectable landowner? A merry tale!'

Fabian blinked, opened his mouth, and closed it again. 'What?' he finally croaked.

Serena's breath stopped. Instinctively, she looked at Teyo.

He gazed back at her, eyes full of sorrow.

Serena closed her eyes, her hands balling into fists. Her heart knew what was coming. When she looked up, all traces of mirth had faded from Halavere's face, and her eyes were hard.

'Thomaso Carterett wasn't a *mark*,' she spat. 'He was a *partner*. A double-crossing, faithless worm who tried to cheat his *friends* out of their share of the profits! That card game was a goldmine, and he tried to take the lot.' She shrugged. 'He got what he deserved.'

Fabian tried to hurl himself at her, but he was instantly caught and restrained by two of Halavere's brawny henchmen. He struggled and kicked, cursing. 'It's not true!' he bellowed. 'Lies, all lies! He was a good man!'

'Oh, I know it's hard to hear,' said Halavere. 'You should be grateful. He was a friend, once. At least we granted him the dignity of an apparent suicide.' Her eyebrows went up as Fabian tried again, futilely, to hurl himself upon her. 'Don't,' she said coldly. 'The deed was not mine. Bironn's is the hand that did for your noble *father.*'

Bironn's may have been the hand, but Halavere's had been the mind; Serena felt no doubt on that score. Nor could she seriously doubt Halavere's story, as desperately as she might wish to. Her anger was too intense, too ferocious, too *real.* Here was an old story that still rankled.

Besides, she was not wholly surprised. Thomaso had been a changeable man. At times he had been hearty, congenial and affectionate, and at others cold, secretive and judgemental. He had spoken of "business" arrangements without explaining what they were, even as his children — his beloved son and heir, in particular — had grown to adulthood. And some of the associates he invited to the house… they had left Serena alarmed, Fabian cold and their mother anxious. Thomaso had treated Fabian with clear favour throughout their childhood, and they had been very close, but even he couldn't explain the mysteries of their father's behaviour.

Her heart hurt. For herself, for her mother, but mostly for Fabian. He had idolised their father growing up, and had never truly got over his death. But worst of all, Serena knew that the same thoughts that were passing through her mind were also passing through his; that as desperately as he wanted to deny it, he couldn't, any more than she could.

He had the look of a man whose world had come crashing down, and who was fighting violently to deny it. Serena found herself on her feet — she didn't remember standing up. She fought her way to his side, flailing blindly at the men who still restrained him, and wrapped her arms around him.

'Fabe,' she said against his chest. 'Fabe. You've got to calm down.'

He didn't hear her. It didn't matter. Halavere ignored his cursing, her own anger vanishing beneath her earlier veneer of cool unconcern.

'We're wasting time,' she said. 'I can't let you have the keys.' She checked her timepiece, and nodded once. 'By now, my associates have finished ransacking your rooms. It was obliging of you to leave your bolthole unguarded. I'm sure my colleagues are grateful.' She flashed a humourless smile at Serena as she spoke.

She had nothing further to add, apparently, for she swept out of the room without another word, or even a glance for her captive audience.

With a burst of desperate strength, Fabian tore himself free of his captors and ran after her. Serena stood, frozen in surprise and dismay, for a few agonisingly long seconds; then, shaking herself, she ran to the door.

There was no sign of Fabian, or Halavere.

'Tey,' she gasped.

She heard the sound of something heavy hitting the floor behind her, and whirled just in time to see Teyo flooring the second of Halavere's guards. This was a vision of Teyo she'd never seen before, or even dreamed of. All his mildness was gone. He bristled with fury, and wielded his height and his bulk with unsuspected skill. He left two inert bodies sprawled upon the floor, and turned to Serena.

'I'll find him,' he promised.

In an instant, he was gone, leaving the wreck of their team in shocked silence behind him.

21

Teyo felt for Fabian, but it was the look on Serena's face that broke his heart. Fabian thought only of his own pain, but Serena's eyes had gone straight to her brother; the look in them proclaimed that for every ounce of her own pain, she felt Fabian's tenfold.

Worse, the appalling shock of such a revelation could have been averted, if only Teyo had been braver. He'd known the truth about Thomaso, for he had met the older man once or twice during his later years as Yllandu. He'd never been able to find a way to tell Serena, let alone Fabian. If the vision they'd held of their father's character comforted them, who was he to tear that away? He had put it off indefinitely, hoping that the truth would never reach them. How foolish that now seemed.

Well, if he couldn't be brave before, he could be brave now. He left Serena to the dubious care of Egg, Iyamar and Bron and tore off after Fabian. He and Halavere could be anywhere in the Warren. Teyo began a methodical search room-by-room, his eyes and ears straining for any signs of activity.

It didn't take long. As he neared a staircase leading up towards the surface, he heard sounds of a confrontation: shouts, blows, and something falling. Heart pounding, Teyo raced around the corner.

Fabian had caught up with Halavere, or Valore, as she was halfway up the stairs. Fabe probably hadn't got anywhere near

221

his quarry; her two guards had intercepted him, and they weren't holding back. Neither was Fabian. His dark eyes burned with an emotion far beyond mere rage, and he laid about himself with his fists, oblivious to how wholly outmatched he was.

Teyo couldn't reach him in time. Fabian took a hard blow to the head, and fell. His skull cracked, harshly and audibly, against a stair, and he lay still.

'Idiot boy,' muttered Halavere. She continued on her way without a backward glance for Fabian — and therefore, she didn't notice Teyo. Her guards followed, leaving Fabian alone.

Teyo ran to Fabian. It didn't look good. He was slumped with the boneless, helpless posture of a broken doll, and blood poured into his eyes from a dark, violent gash on his head. His eyes were rapidly developing a glazed look.

'Fabe,' Teyo said urgently, snapping his fingers in front of his friend's face. 'Come on, focus.'

Fabian's eyes focused briefly, and he tried to sit up. 'Tey... I...'

'Hey, now. Take it easy.' Teyo pushed him gently back down. 'We're getting you out of here just as soon...'

He trailed off as Fabian sagged limply back to the ground. All expression faded from his eyes and he stopped trying to speak. In a few seconds, he stopped breathing as well.

Running feet sounded from the floor below, and an instant later Serena stood beside him, Egg and Iya and Bron not far behind her.

'Serena—' said Teyo warningly, but he couldn't prevent her from pushing past him. She fell to her knees beside her brother and began a desperate attempt to wake him — too late, and far too little.

At last, she stopped, and sat back on her heels. An awful hush descended.

'Serena?' Teyo said at last.

She didn't look at him. Her eyes were fixed on nothing, her face blank. She was far too quiet for Teyo's comfort. Bron approached, words of pointless comfort dropping from his lips. Teyo ruthlessly shoved him away before he could so much as touch her.

'Don't,' he growled.

Serena ignored it all. 'Tey,' she said slowly. 'Egg, Iya. I'm going to need you.' She touched her brother once, lightly, on the forehead, and stood up.

'Anything I can do…' Teyo said wretchedly. His shock was fading, leaving him vulnerable to a slew of unwelcome emotions. Crippling guilt warred with sick despair, leaving him feeling weak and nauseous. If he'd done something sooner — if he hadn't uselessly kept secrets — Fabian wouldn't have died.

Serena smiled at him, but it was an odd, distant smile without warmth. 'It isn't your fault,' she said, touching his arm.

How like her to guess at his thoughts, and to take a moment to reassure him, even at such a time. It should have comforted him, but it only deepened his pain: she didn't deserve this.

He opened his mouth, but Serena placed a hand over it, silencing him. 'Hush,' she said. 'There's no time. Get us out of here, Tey?'

Teyo nodded, and glanced, painfully, down at Fabian's sprawled corpse. 'What about—'

'Leave him,' said Serena, turning her back on her brother. 'It doesn't matter.'

Teyo blanched at that. 'It doesn't—'

'No,' Serena interrupted. 'We're going to fix this.'

A feeling of grave foreboding knotted in Teyo's gut. 'What are we—'

'I need the keys,' she said.

Teyo saw the whole of her plan in an instant. It was probably impossible, but he didn't care; if she needed to try it, he could only support her.

Egg and Iya needed no prompting, either. 'The keys are all taken,' Egg pointed out. 'How can we get them back?'

'We don't need to,' said Serena. 'Once Ylona's got all seven, what will she do? She'll go straight to the gate, and to the repository. That's where we'll go.'

'Wait just a minute,' said Bron, slower to catch on. 'You can't go to the repository. You can't access such a dangerous technology just to revive one man!'

Four pairs of eyes turned upon him with identical expressions of furious contempt. Bron stepped back a fraction, and held up his hands. 'I'm sorry for your loss, truly,' he said, with a passable attempt at sincerity. 'But you must see that this is ridiculous. I can't possibly permit it.'

'And who,' said Serena, with dangerous calm, 'appointed you leader of this team?'

Bron bristled. 'Damnit, if it comes to that, I did!' he said, his voice rising. 'I seem to be the only sane person around here. It's what my bosses would expect.'

Serena turned her back on him, and headed up the stairs. 'I care nothing for your bosses,' she said.

Bron spat something else, but what it was supposed to be no-one would ever know. Before he had uttered more than two syllables, Teyo planted a fist in his mouth. Bron dropped with a satisfying thud, and lay inert.

Egg clapped him on the back. 'There might be something to this violence thing after all,' she observed.

'Shouldn't we...?' Iya said, gesturing helplessly at Bron's sprawled form.

'Leave him,' Serena called back. 'He's the greatest agent in all of the Seven, after all! He can get himself out of this.'

'Serena, love,' Teyo called to her retreating back. 'Wait just a moment.'

She turned, and raised an enquiring brow at him. Her skin was horribly pale, but she looked resolute and calm. Teyo felt proud of her. 'Yes?'

Teyo smiled up at her, and shifted. His legs and arms contracted, his back lengthened; dark fur sprouted from every pore, and his teeth transformed into horrific fangs. Where the man had stood moments before there now stood a whurthag, one of the most fearsome beasts living. The stuff of legends only a year or two before, the whurthag had been recalled from its home in the Lower Realms and unleashed upon the Middles to catastrophic effect. It was wholly illegal to take the whurthag's shape, of course; every realm of the Seven had unanimously agreed upon that. Teyo didn't care. His only concern was to escort his team safely out of the Warren.

Iyamar grinned and shifted. Seconds later, two whurthags stood, fur bristling, at the bottom of the stairs.

You know you could get into serious trouble for this? Teyo enquired.

Iyamar's heavy jaws dropped open in a canine grin. *Oh, noooo,* she replied. *Say it isn't true!*

Teyo snickered. *Very well, then. Off we go.* The two whurthags surged up the stairs, barrelling past Serena, and headed into the upper corridors at a run. *Try not to kill anyone,* Teyo added as an afterthought.

Yessir!

Six hours later, a vast, crimson-scaled draykon landed on the shores of a tiny, uncharted island off the south-east coast of Nimdre and instantly collapsed in exhaustion. A human passenger, miniaturised in comparison with the draykon's size, slithered down off the recumbent beast's back and folded to the ground.

A second, smaller draykon landed beside the first, its scales dark amber. Another human passenger descended, and for a few minutes all four members of the unusual party lay inert and exhausted on the stony, pebbled beach.

Then the crimson draykon vanished, and Teyo returned to himself.

Draykoni, he thought fuzzily, *really aren't made for long-distance flying.* He was lying with his face in the wet sand, but it took him a while to realise it.

'Tey?' said Serena. 'Are you all right?'

'Mmpf,' uttered Teyo. Every bone in his body felt like soup, and he couldn't stop trembling.

'I'm sorry,' Serena whispered, touching his hair. 'I shouldn't do this to you.'

That was more than enough. Teyo got his hands underneath himself and managed to achieve a sitting position, albeit a shaky one. He smiled at Serena, and shook his head. 'It's okay. I can do it.'

She nodded, but doubtfully. 'Iya?'

Iyamar had by this time resumed her human shape. Her condition was no way near as bad as Teyo's, which mortified him. It took him a moment to remember that she was twenty-six years his junior.

'I'm fine,' she said breezily, although she said it from a recumbent posture. At least she had managed to land face up rather than face down. She wasn't shaking, either.

Egg was on her feet and prowling around. 'This place is rubbish,' she pronounced irrelevantly as she rejoined the group.

Teyo glanced around, blinking. He hadn't even bothered to look. The island was truly tiny, so small he could clearly see the opposite coast. It was largely featureless, nothing but bare rock fading to sand at the edges. Its only discernible point of interest was a collection of tall stones gathered at the centre, each one coloured a slightly different shade of honey-brown.

'That's where they'll be,' Serena said, following Teyo's gaze. 'Say when ready.'

'Ready!' called Iyamar, bouncing up from the sand with appalling energy.

'Ready,' said Egg. She had picked up a dagger from somewhere and had taken great pleasure in wielding it ever since. Teyo wasn't sure whether she knew how to use it, but probably she did. She just hadn't employed that particular ability in a while.

Teyo levered himself to his feet, unable to suppress a groan. 'Ready,' he croaked. Everything hurt, but he was rewarded with a warm smile of gratitude from Serena, and he felt fractionally better.

'Let's go,' she said, and strode away in the direction of the stones.

Teyo hurried to keep pace with her, alert for any signs of danger. There were none, at least for a while; the island was bare of all life save for an occasional winged creature soaring somewhere above, or settling briefly upon the sands. He was braced for that to change as they neared the standing stones, but the island remained shrouded in a stillness he might have found peaceful, in different circumstances.

At the heart of the circle of stones there stood an archway of smooth rock, unmarked and undecorated. This place had probably been the subject of numerous archaeological pamphlets, Teyo thought, but he doubted anyone had ever guessed at any part of the truth.

Serena walked around the archway, inspecting it closely. 'Aha,' she said softly, and beckoned.

Teyo joined her. She was standing directly under the archway, looking up. Arrayed around the inside of the smooth curve were seven alcoves, perfectly sized and shaped to contain one small stone key.

All seven were in place, each one pulsing with a soft light.

'She's already gone through,' Serena murmured.

Teyo nodded. 'It might be too late.'

'I know. We still have to try.'

Teyo had no opposition to make, but he did have a question. How did they *use* the gate? Here it was, apparently active; all the keys were present and doing *something,* and there was no sign of Ylona, Halavere or any of their people. But despite all this, nothing was happening.

Serena put out a hand. The instant her fingertips touched the honey-brown stone of the gate, she vanished.

'Oh,' said Teyo, and stretched out a hand.

The world dissolved.

If the repository had been impressive as a vision, it was far more so in reality. After a moment's dark disorientation, Teyo's eyes focused upon a chamber so toweringly vast he could barely comprehend its proportions. The ceiling soared up and up and up, leaving him dwarfed and feeling wholly insignificant far below. Every inch of the walls and much of the floor was fitted with shelves of all conceivable shapes and sizes, containing everything from traditional books to stacked, crystalline boxes and... well, Teyo had no idea what half of the things were, except that they probably stored information by some means or another.

All of this passed through his thoughts in an instant. He had no more time to muse on the contents of those boxes and books, or the mysteries and secrets that might be resolved were he to explore even a single shelf. The moment he became aware of his surroundings, a curious scene revealed itself.

Ylona and Halavere had indeed entered the repository ahead of them, for they stood near the centre of the room, only a few feet away from Teyo. They had brought two others with them, two men whom Teyo did not recognise. All four were peculiarly still. After a moment, Teyo realised they were frozen in place, for he detected not the smallest movement from any of them. They did not even appear to be breathing. They had stopped in the midst of talking, apparently all at once, for their mouths were open and their faces alight with expressions of eagerness (Halavere), wariness (the unfamiliar two), and dismay (Ylona).

Standing not far away was a fifth person, so still and quiet that Teyo didn't notice him at first. *He* was not frozen. He stood leaning against one of the bookcases, his arms folded and his brows lowered. He appeared to be deep in thought, so much so that he did not immediately notice the entrance of Teyo's party either. When he did, his head turned slightly and he regarded the newcomers with a blink of surprise.

The man looked to be about Teyo's own age, or a year or two older, though his hair was white. His eyes were dark green and thoughtful, his skin Darklander pale. He was dressed in a pair of loose trousers and a soft blue shirt, the sleeves rolled up to his elbows. His feet were bare.

'Rhoun Torinth,' blurted Teyo.

The man nodded once.

'Aren't you supposed to be dead?' said Iyamar, her tone accusing.

'Hush,' muttered Egg. 'You can be so rude sometimes.'

Teyo smothered a sudden, surprising desire to laugh. *Egg* lecturing Iyamar on manners? He loved his teammates so much sometimes, it made his heart hurt.

Rhoun Torinth's brows shot up at Iya's words, and he blinked. 'Hmm. I don't think I will answer any questions on my state of health until I know the identity of my... visitors.' The language he spoke wasn't quite Nimdren, but it was close; he was matching the words of his uninvited guests with the nearest dialect he knew. That realisation intrigued Teyo. Was it a forerunner of the Nimdren tongue, whatever he was speaking? He wished he could ask, but the moment was far from appropriate.

Serena stepped forward. 'We're here for a good reason,' she offered. 'We apologise for the intrusion, but it's very important. Besides, Iyamar's phrasing might have been a little abrupt but she raises a good point: we didn't expect to find anybody here.' She paused, and added with a smile, 'Least of all you.'

Rhoun Torinth considered her, unspeaking. '*Nimoruen* has developed a little differently than I might have expected,' he mused in a thoughtful tone. 'How did that come about, I wonder?'

Serena blinked.

'Your language,' he said, with a faint smile. 'You are not a native speaker, I think?'

Serena shook her head, nonplussed by the sudden change of direction. 'Teyo is,' she said, gesturing. 'And Iya.'

Rhoun Torinth's gaze flicked past Iyamar and settled on Teyo. 'Ah, the topic interests you,' he said. 'I can see that clearly enough. Perhaps we will discuss it.'

Teyo opened his mouth, hesitated, and closed it again.

'Very well,' said Torinth, unfolding himself from the bookcase. 'This "important matter" you spoke of. I suppose you had better tell me about it.'

Serena glanced at Ylona, standing frozen with one arm half-raised and her mouth open. 'Ah... should we expect to end up like them, in the near future?'

'Possibly not.' This unreassuring assertion was all they were to receive, for Torinth said nothing more.

Serena swallowed visibly. 'It's my brother,' she said, a little shakily. 'He... he died, and I cannot—'

'Ah,' interrupted the Lokant. His gaze, fixed upon Serena, sharpened. 'It was not curiosity that led you here, then, but self-interest.'

Serena's shoulders slumped slightly. 'Um, no,' she faltered. 'It's for Fabian that I—'

'Let us not deceive ourselves,' Rhoun Torinth interrupted. 'It is sad for your brother, yes, but he is gone. He feels nothing. It is for yourself that you wish him restored.'

Serena glanced uncertainly at Teyo. He had never seen her so much at a loss, and he was obliged to smother a brief desire to do the supercilious Torinth a minor injury. Or perhaps a major one.

'He didn't deserve it,' she said softly.

'Few people deserve to die,' Torinth said, with chilling indifference. 'We cannot reverse every death. Why this one?'

Serena had nothing to say. She sighed, and all the hope seemed to go out of her with the exhalation. If Torinth would not help them, how were they ever to find the information they sought? And if he was inclined to actively oppose them, the task swiftly grew from *extremely difficult* to *impossible.*

But Serena rallied. She gestured at Ylona, and said in a firmer voice: 'Your daughter, I gather?'

Rhoun Torinth's brows rose again. 'I would be so interested to hear where this information is coming from.'

Serena ignored that. 'Ylona believes you to be dead,' she said. 'She came here with the same purpose as mine: to find the secret of travelling back through time, in order to restore *you* to life. Can you so easily dismiss her intentions?'

'She believes no such thing.'

Serena blinked. 'What?'

'She knows I did not die. She has always known it. Whatever her purpose here might be, it is not as you suppose. And so, I'll ask you again: where is this information coming from?'

'Mae,' said Serena warily.

Torinth's surprise grew. '*Orintha* Mae?'

'I don't know. She wouldn't tell us the rest of her name. Or anything else.'

Torinth was silent for some time. 'Orintha Mae sent you here,' he said, flatly, as though the notion displeased him.

'No,' Serena replied coolly. 'On the contrary, she was eager to prevent anyone's coming here. It was Ylona who started the search for the keys.'

'Tell me everything,' Torinth ordered, and Serena did. Teyo stood in silence, only interrupting once when Serena neglected a detail in her tale. Rhoun Torinth heard it all without speaking a word, and when she had finished he remained silent for some time.

'Ylona offered you the contents of the repository?' he said at last.

Serena nodded. 'If we handed over the keys we had secured. I imagine she has offered the same prize to everyone she's worked with. Even the Yllandu.' She frowned. 'But now I think that she had no need to make any such deal. I suspect she let us gather up several of the keys without interference, knowing that she could take them back any time she wanted. But she made us *think* that she opposed us, because it lulled our suspicions and kept us going.' Her mouth twisted in disgust. 'We pulled the very same trick ourselves on an unwelcome colleague, yet we failed to recognise it being wielded against us.'

Torinth's gaze drifted to his daughter's inert face, his own expression puzzled. 'I suspect,' he said at last, 'that this is about Orlind. She regretted its passing, more deeply than her siblings. If she felt there was a way to undo its destruction and restore the great Library to the world, perhaps she would take it. Though I do not know why she would do so only now, after so many years.' He shook himself, blinking, and said: 'But this is no concern of yours. To return to your stated purpose: though I sympathise, most sincerely, with your plight, the matter is not so simple as you imagine. Consider: were you to wander back some hours in time, and prevent the demise of your brother, what then? It may seem as though you have merely rectified a wrong, righted an injustice. In fact, you have interfered with the order of things at a fundamental level; you cannot know what the impact of your actions will be, nor their eventual effect.'

'But—'

Torinth held up a hand. 'Why do you imagine I locked all of this away?' he said, softly. 'Why do I persist in guarding it? For I *am* its guard. You asked me how I am alive: in truth, I am not, precisely. One might more accurately say that I am *preserved*. It is a sacrifice I made for precisely this reason. The contents of this repository are both deeply important and extremely dangerous. They cannot be freely given away, and I do not for a second believe that my daughter had any such intention.' He paused, frowning. 'When I created the Dreams, it was not for any such purpose as *this*. If ever some future denizens of the Seven were to come crashing through my doors, I thought that it would be a matter of grave emergency; of life and death on a grand scale. I have preserved myself against just such an eventuality: great need. *This* was not what I had in mind.'

Serena lifted her chin. 'It is a matter of grave emergency to us.'

'Yes,' he said, with a trace of irritation, 'but you have merely landed here by accident, because of my daughter's actions. Ah, the irony! That I should lock this away because of Orlind, and because of Orlind my daughter has opened my repository to the world...' He sighed, shaking his head. 'One death is inconsequential,' he said, recalling himself once more to the topic at hand. In a gentler tone, he added: 'I know it doesn't seem so to you, but when you have lived as long as I—'

'I don't *care* how long you've lived!' Serena burst out. 'I hope I never live as long as you, if I should end so *cold*! NO death is inconsequential! Every single one matters!'

Torinth blinked at her, momentarily silenced. 'Well—'

'Save it,' Serena hissed. 'I care nothing for your distant judgements and your heartless pronouncements. Who are you to decide whether my brother lives or dies? You hold here the secret to his resurrection and *I will find it.*'

Teyo was intrigued to notice signs of real strain in Torinth's face. He appeared visibly shaken, and for a long moment he had nothing to say. 'Have I come to that?' he said, so softly Teyo barely heard him.

Serena merely glared at him. She was magnificent, Teyo thought: drawn up to her full height, her shoulders back, chin up, her eyes blazing determination and contempt and passion as she stared Torinth down. He may be a Lokant of impossible age and unthinkable powers, but next to Serena he suddenly looked pale, fragile and very old.

Torinth gathered himself. 'If,' he began, 'I permit you to restore *one* soul, where does it end? I must permit it again, and again; every single one of you who comes crashing through the gate will have some other request, some other desire. If I allow yours, I must allow them all. This you can surely see.'

'I don't care,' Serena said bluntly. 'My thoughts are for Fabian only.'

Egg cleared her throat. 'Ah… if it helps, I don't think you'll be getting any more visitors for the next while.' She held up both of her hands. Clutched in her tightly-curled fingers were seven keystones, three in one hand and four in the other.

Serena stared. 'Egg! How did you —?'

'Palmed them on the way through,' she shrugged. 'Wasn't easy, I grant you. I got stuck halfway between, for a while. Thought I'd torn it for good.' She smiled.

Serena threw her arms around Egg and squeezed her tightly. Such a display of affection was uncharacteristic of Serena, and it was even more uncharacteristic of Egg to permit it, but Teyo thought she looked rather pleased.

Torinth's jubilation was not such as to equal Serena's. He observed Egg with an air of mingled approval and chagrin, and finally sighed. 'I don't think you understand what you are asking,' he said. 'Do you imagine that it will be as simple as stepping back a few paces in time, correcting one mistake and that will be the end of it? It cannot be. Consider all the myriad of events that led you up to this moment in your lives. A mere few seconds of reflection ought to bring several events to mind which, if they had turned out differently, might have sent you in any number of alternative directions. These may be big events, or the smallest of occurrences, but the impact they have had upon you is profound. Every single happening in your life, no matter how small, can have an extraordinary degree of influence over your future. Consider what that *means*.'

Torinth paused, and nobody spoke. Teyo's own thoughts were whirling, for he grasped the Lokant's meaning in an instant. How had he come to be standing here? Because he was a part of Serena's team. And why was that? Because he had erred so far as to involve himself with the Yllandu, and amends must be made. Why had he joined the Yllandu? Because on one appalling day far in the past, his parents, his brother and his entire family

232

livelihood had been wiped out by a robbery gone wrong. Had that not happened, he might be a stonemason today, like his father. Or better yet, a farmer. At this moment he might be out in his orchards, harvesting the year's crop. The thought left him with a familiar pang of regret.

On the other hand, he might never have left the Yllandu; that choice had come about as a result of the things he'd chosen, or been obliged, to do during his time as an Unspeakable. Had that turned out differently, perhaps he might never have left; he might still be crooked and thieving, a stain upon the world.

The others were engaged in similar reflections, he judged, for the repository was quiet, and their faces were thoughtful. Without Serena, of course, his team wouldn't even exist, and she was here because of the actions of Thomaso Carterett. Her team was a refuge, for Teyo and Egg and Iya. Even for Fabian, whether he realised it or not. A new idea entered Teyo's brain at that thought: deplorable as Carterett Senior's actions may have been, were the consequences wholly bad? If he could somehow have been prevented from behaving as he had — if his death could be reversed — then all of the many good things that had grown out of it would be lost.

And the same applied to his own life.

He realised slowly that Torinth was looking directly at him, a shrewd look upon his face. 'The reflections are interesting, are they not? Difficult, but interesting.'

Teyo nodded, feeling obscurely uncomfortable as his team-mates all turned to look at him. 'Um, yes,' he said, wittily.

Torinth smiled faintly. 'The point I wish to make is simply this: we all believe we wield some degree of control over the things that happen to us, and around us. We are deluded. Suppose I permit you to try to save your brother. What do you think will happen?'

Silence. At last Serena said: 'He fell, and cracked his head. We just need to prevent that fall, that's all—'

'And the conditions that led to the fall? Can you control all of that?'

'No,' Serena admitted.

'Everything could turn out differently the second time. *Everything*. And you have no control over any of it. Do you, then, still wish to proceed? Whatever the consequences might be, they are yours to live with.'

Teyo began to feel that sick foreboding in his gut again, but Serena said without hesitation, 'Yes.'

Torinth said nothing, only raised a brow.

'I understand everything you've said,' Serena continued. 'Truly, I do. But I have no choice. He's my brother, and I have to try.'

'There are always choices,' said Rhoun Torinth coolly.

'Not in this case. What if it were one of your children who—'

'*Stop.*' Rhoun Torinth barked the word with a vehemence which took them all by surprise. He was angry: his hands had balled into fists, and his eyes blazed. 'I would not proceed any further with that line of thinking,' he said after a moment, and more calmly. 'I have lost more than you can imagine, and yet I *cannot* permit myself to feel as you do. I thought, once upon a time, that my discovery was a gift; a blessing. What a fool. The constant temptation — the *compulsion* — to change every little thing in my life that displeased me; to fix every problem that assailed my friends, my children; to strive, in short, for a perfect world where nothing could ever go lastingly wrong. It was *intolerable,* and dangerous beyond words.' He passed a hand over his face, suddenly weary. 'As long as I am here, I am safe from it,' he said dully. 'Or I was, until now.'

'For that, I am sorry,' said Serena. 'But my mind is unchanged.'

Torinth scowled at her. 'Some people refuse to be helped,' he muttered, and then straightened. 'Very well. On this *one* occasion, I will make an exception. I have made mistakes, in the past. Perhaps your venture will be more successful than mine, and I will have atoned for some part of them. *However,* I will never do so again. Whatever happens next is your affair, and yours to live with. Is that clear?'

Serena nodded vigorously, a broad, relieved smile gracing her face. 'Yes! Completely!'

She began to utter ecstatic thanks, but Rhoun Torinth cut her off with an upheld hand. 'Don't thank me,' he said. 'You could be walking into total disaster, every last one of you.'

This pronouncement was met with nothing but silence, and he sighed. 'I was hoping your colleagues might have a little more sense,' he said to Serena, 'but apparently they stand with you. Very well: let us go.' He held out both of his hands.

His audience stared at him in confusion. 'What do we need to do?' said Serena.

Torinth laughed. 'You were expecting something more impressive, perhaps. A machine of some kind, with flashing lights and exciting buttons and levers? Or a magical gate, swollen with mystic power. I must be a disappointment indeed, compared to such lofty ideas, but the truth is that *I* am the key to time travel.'

'Oh,' said Serena.

'It's related to the Map, you see. I discovered that it is possible to step over *time* as well as *distance,* and thus to move about freely in all directions. Remarkable, no? Someday, some other of my people will come to the same realisation, but I am relieved to hear that it has not happened yet.' He smiled briefly. 'Some would say that my mind works in unusual ways. Perhaps I will prove to be altogether unique.'

Oh, no. Teyo hated the way the Lokants whisked people about all over the Seven. It was like being picked up none-too-gently and hurled, at bone-rattling speed, across unthinkable distances. And Torinth proposed to cart them through time as well as space? Teyo swallowed, and tried to brace himself.

'I need you to tell me precisely where you were when your brother died,' Torinth said, as Serena gripped his hand. 'And when.'

Serena described both in as much detail as she could muster, and Torinth nodded. 'We will make the attempt.'

And they did, with no further preparation or even warning. Iyamar went forward to take Torinth's other hand, and forcibly grabbed Teyo's as well. The next instant, the repository was gone and Teyo was hurtling through a dark expanse of something, or nothing. The experience lasted for barely a second, but it felt much longer. Teyo was left shaking, dizzy, nauseous and deeply confused.

He had no time to recover. He, Serena, Egg and Iyamar stood once again in the strong room at the bottom of the Warren, but Torinth had vanished somewhere along the way. Two guards lay on the floor nearby; they were the ones Teyo himself had clubbed senseless, and apparently this event had only just happened. Teyo suffered a moment's surprise upon seeing Bron, for he had forgotten his existence completely. Halavere Morann and Fabian were already gone.

They were barely in time. Teyo exchanged one brief, startled, panicked glance with Serena, and they both ran for the door, Egg and Iya barely a step behind.

22

The hallway was full of people. Teyo stopped dead in surprise. It had been empty before; where had these people come from? Their attire was more casual than protective, so they were not guards. They produced weapons rapidly enough, though, when they saw Teyo. One of those random happenstances Torinth had hinted at, Teyo thought with an inward groan. A group of Yllandu had business down here, and they'd chosen this precise moment to conduct it. Teyo must have missed these people by seconds, last time.

He eyed the sudden sprouting of deadly weapons with a mixture of panic and dismay. These assailants looked eerily familiar. Nimdren citizens for the most part, they looked like younger versions of himself. He'd worn the same kinds of clothes, carried the same kinds of weapons, once upon a time. And he'd known how to use them, too.

Many years had passed since those days, and he'd most willingly avoided all weapons and violence ever since. His body remembered some of the moves; he dodged and struck with his fists, bringing the first man down. But he couldn't hold his own against all of them, and he had his team to protect. He needed to shapeshift, but his rattled brain couldn't focus long enough to effect the change — not while he was simultaneously fending off attacks from three directions at once.

Then Bron was there, bellowing something

incomprehensible. He wielded a long dagger in one hand and some type of firearm in the other, both of which he utilised against the Yllandu with all speed. Slashing at the nearest foe with his right hand, he fired with his left. The man dropped, bleeding from two places at once.

'Don't kill them!' Teyo shouted, furious. Their attackers may be criminals, but how could they justify saving Fabian's life at the expense of other people's? Bron cast him an annoyed look and shook his head, even as he fired again. 'No choice,' he returned and fired once more. Two more Yllandu went down.

Teyo had no time to argue with him, or to regret his actions, for these people were blocking his path to Fabian. Desperate, he took advantage of the cover Bron provided and shifted whurthag once more. He was hoping that the mere sight of his horrific claws and teeth would clear a path for him, and it worked, to a certain extent; some of the Yllandu backed away, though whether it was out of surprise or fear he couldn't tell. He didn't care. He barrelled through, using his body weight to shove obstacles aside. A horrible growling from behind him told him that Iyamar had followed his example; good. He could trust her to shield the others. Breaking free of the pack of assailants, he ran full-tilt for the stairs where Fabian had died.

They were empty. He charged all the way up them and around the corner, and found no one at the top. No one was in sight, anywhere.

He stood, heart pounding with full-blown panic. What had happened? Had Halavere taken a different route from before? Had she stayed downstairs, disappeared into some other room? Or had Fabian caught up with her somewhere else?

Teyo's great lungs heaved in a deep breath as he forced himself to calm down. It wasn't all bad, he reminded himself: Fabian couldn't die again on this staircase if he wasn't *on* this staircase. But any number of other appalling things could happen to him, or to his team downstairs.

They had the priority, he decided. Fabian's earlier fate was averted, one way or another. Meanwhile, the rest of his team were in danger. He charged back down the stairs and came to a sudden halt at the bottom.

Serena, Iyamar, Egg and Bron were just starting up them, Iya still wearing whurthag shape. Serena's face was thunderous, and Egg and Iya had their backs turned firmly upon Bron, who was trailing behind them covered in blood. Teyo eyed the quantity of blood uneasily.

What happened? he asked Iyamar, silently.

He killed every one of them, Iya told him. *He wouldn't stop. Said it was a matter of security, and he was the best judge.*

Teyo smothered a surge of rage. How many of them had there been? Five, six? Bron had undoubtedly protected the team, but at such cost! It gave him no comfort to think that all six of the dead Yllandu would have slaughtered every one of his team without a second thought, had they been given the chance. The kinds of firearms Bron wielded weren't readily available to all. They were new technology, expensive and rare. Some Yllandu carried them, but not all. Apparently, these hadn't.

Or had they? Bron was trailing because he was weakened, and he wore a strip of torn cloth bound tightly around one arm. Wounded by knife or gun?

Where's Fabe? said Iyamar.

No idea.

'Fabian's missing,' Teyo announced out loud.

Serena turned frightened eyes upon Teyo. 'Right,' she said, visibly pulling herself together. 'We're splitting up. Iya, you're protecting Egg. Tey, Bron and I are with you. Notify each other the instant you find something. Egg, do you have your voice-box?'

Egg dug hers out of a pocket and waved it.

'All right, we're all in communication. Iya, Egg, this floor please. Tey, Bron; we're going up. Go.'

They advanced up the stairs in a tight knot. Bron insisted on going first, despite Teyo's whurthag form. The hallway above was empty as they reached it, but a moment later a door opened and a man stepped out. He stopped on the threshold, blinking in surprise at the sight of three strangers ascending the stairs before him.

He wasn't a young man. His brownish hair was liberally laced through with grey, and his face displayed the wrinkles and lines of long experience. But he had the posture of a man well able to handle himself, and his surprise was brief. A split second, and he launched himself at Bron.

Teyo realised, with a sickening lurch in his stomach, that he knew the man. Distracted, he struggled to shift human in time — his mouth worked — "LEVAN!" he bellowed. "Stop!"

239

Levan stopped indeed, his face swivelling towards Teyo etched with an expression of extreme surprise.

Bron shot him. The sound of the gun firing was swiftly followed by a curse from Bron, who dropped to his knees beside the fallen man.

'Friend of yours?' Bron said tersely.

Teyo fell in beside him with a nod, staring in dismay at the blossoming stain of blood spreading over Levan's shoulder. He had been something of a mentor to Teyo during his early days as Yllandu. The man was crooked to the core, but he'd been good to Teyo when he'd desperately needed a friend.

'I'm so sorry,' he gasped. 'This wasn't supposed to happen.' He was no medic; he couldn't tell whether the wound was fatal or not, and there was *nothing* he could do for Levan now.

His former mentor stared up at him in silence, confusion warring with some other, unrecognisable emotions in his face. 'Tey?' he said at last. 'What are you—'

'VALORE TREBEL!' It was Fabian's voice, raised in a bellow of pure rage. Shouting followed, but softer and too confused. Teyo couldn't make sense of it.

'Fabian,' gasped Serena, and bolted away in the direction of the noise, Bron right behind her. Teyo stared after them both and then back at Levan, torn between the conflicting needs of his friends.

Levan looked at him, his lips twisting in a sardonic smile. 'Go,' he croaked. 'There's sod all you can do for me anyway.'

Teyo went after Bron. The two of them tore away in the direction of Fabian's voice, but they couldn't catch Serena. She ran with desperate speed, rounding a corner in the corridor ahead of them and vanishing from sight.

Teyo caught up three seconds later. Three seconds too late? Fabian had found Halavere, but her guards hadn't accosted him this time. He had acquired a firearm from somewhere and was pointing it at Halavere Morann's head. She, too, had drawn a gun, as had both of her guards, but the fact that three other weapons were trained upon him did nothing to daunt Fabian. Teyo suffered a jolt upon seeing Fabe, alive and well; the image of his dead and bloodied body was fresh in his mind. It took a moment for him to realise that the gun in Fabian's hand very closely resembled Bron's.

Bron realised it at the same instant. 'Hey,' he blurted, 'That's where — Fabian, you need to put that down. It's not — you can't just grab it and—'

'Shut up,' muttered Fabian. 'Does it look like I can drop it right now?'

Bron trained his own weapon upon Halavere. 'I'll shoot you before you can hurt him,' he said.

Halavere sighed in annoyance. 'I don't want to hurt him, imbecile. I just want you all to *go away*, so I may move on with my life.'

It took Teyo a moment to process this. Of course: at this stage, the keys were still at large, some of them still in Serena's possession. They were being stolen by the Yllandu at this very moment, probably, and soon afterwards their new owners would take all seven to the tiny island and the gate.

'Take it back,' snarled Fabian. 'Everything you said about my father. Take it all back!'

Halavere rolled her eyes. 'I can't, can I? It's all the truth.'

'It is NOT true,' bellowed Fabian.

'Fabe,' said Serena. 'This isn't the way to pursue this. We need to go home, and talk it over.' Her voice was calm and reassuring, and Teyo hoped for a second that it might suffice to bring Fabian back to rationality.

Instead, he swung towards Serena, gun still extended, until it was pointing at *her*. She stepped back, appalled. Fabian realised a horrified instant later what he was doing, and swung back. He was losing it entirely, Teyo realised. Confusion, dismay and rage warred in his face, and he was obviously far beyond his own control. Teyo saw, in a brief flash of insight, that there was only one way Fabian could relieve his overwrought feelings. Teyo knew it, because he'd been there himself.

He didn't have time to think. He leapt, shapeshifting in mid-air into his draykoni shape. The hallway was far too small; he barely had time to adjust his size before he came crashing down in between Fabian and Valore Trebel. Somebody's weapon cracked off a shot as he landed, and a bullet pierced his hide with a flash of sharp, intense pain. He fell heavily, a blaze of agony spreading rapidly outwards from his shoulder — the one turned towards Fabian.

He heard Serena shriek his name in shock and panic, but he couldn't understand anything else that was happening. People were shouting, another shot fired, and then there were running feet and a door banged. Halavere's voice rose above the rest. 'Damn you, what a horrible mess.' Her voice receded as she spoke; had she left the room? What had happened to the rest of his team?

He couldn't maintain his shape an instant longer; the pain in his shoulder and the confusion in his mind were too intense. He collapsed rather than shifted back into his human shape, and bit back a groan as the pain intensified.

Serena fell to her knees beside him, her face a mask of fear. 'Tey?' she gasped. 'Are you alive?'

23

Serena knew her words weren't reaching Fabian, even as she spoke. She'd seen this mood of his twice before: once when they were children, and their father had fired a farmhand for stealing. The man had been a favourite playmate of Fabian's, and indeed — whether he was guilty of stealing or not — he'd been good to the child. But stately, dictatorial Thomaso Carterett had refused to listen to eleven-year-old Fabian. Fabe had displayed such a powerful rage, everyone had been shocked by it. By the time he'd finished, he had broken every single toy in their shared playroom, along with every article of furniture in that room and his bedroom. When he had finally calmed down Fabian had been shocked by the destruction himself, as though he had committed such violent acts in some other state of mind, so far removed from his normal self that he didn't recognise it.

The second time had been when their father had died. Fabian had discovered Thomaso's body, hanging from the long wooden beam in the ceiling of his study. That time, Fabian hadn't been rational again for two days.

Serena recognised the look in her brother's eyes, and quailed. This fit of rage was, if anything, worse than ever, and she was genuinely helpless to call him back. What would he do? What *wouldn't* he do?

A shot sounded, appallingly loud in the confined space. It

pierced Serena's eardrums and her heart with equal impact. Her head turned towards Fabian, expecting any instant to see him clutch some vital part of himself and fall, bloodied and dying yet again — but something large and crimson blurred before her vision and fell heavily to the ground instead. *Teyo.*

She couldn't move, because suddenly Halavere was standing in front of her and the cold barrel of a firearm was set against her head. 'You people are boring me *excessively,*' Halavere said with a pleasant smile. 'I'm tempted to break my usual rules. I mean, I don't *want* a trio of corpses littering my hallway, but you'd be *quieter,* wouldn't you?'

Serena barely had time to process this before a door banged somewhere behind her and the sounds of many pairs of feet informed her that a lot of people had entered the hallway.

'Here!' barked Bron, and suddenly her vision was swarming with young, tough-looking men and women wearing identical dark, unobtrusive uniforms and waving firearms exactly like Bron's. Some shouting ensued, and somebody fired another — horrifically loud — shot which thudded into the wall not far from Serena's head. Serena could only stare, hopelessly confused. Who were these people? Associates of Bron's? Had he brought half of G.A.9 in here without even *telling* her?

Halavere stepped back, allowing her gun to hang slack in her grip. Her guards backed off, too. Serena didn't wait to question it; she ran to Teyo's inert form. He had shifted human again at some point and lay frighteningly still, his arm and torso covered in blood.

'Tey?' she gasped. 'Are you alive?'

His eyes were open, slightly, and he peered blurrily at her. 'I think so,' he croaked.

A little of Serena's panic eased, though the rate at which he was bleeding alarmed her. Teyo tried to clutch at her hand; she gave it to him.

'Fabian shot me,' he whispered. 'He didn't mean to, but he'll hurt over it.'

Serena started, and stared wildly around. For an instant, she'd allowed her concern for Teyo to wipe all thoughts of Fabe from her mind! She spotted him not far away, surrounded by some of Bron's — were they Bron's? — associates. His firearm was gone, to her relief, and he looked more poleaxed than enraged. Teyo was right: Fabian was staring at his fallen friend with an expression of appalled self-loathing upon his face.

'Blazes,' she spat. 'If I'd *known*. I didn't think it could get *worse*.'

'It's not worse,' Teyo whispered. 'We're all alive.'

Serena looked sadly at him. 'At what cost, though?' she said, and then shook herself. 'Now isn't the time. We need to get you out of here.'

The words were barely out of her mouth before she was pushed aside, firmly if not roughly, by some of those grim-faced uniformed G.A.9 operatives. One of them bent to tend to Teyo, showing signs of skill and experience as a medic. Serena fell back with a sense of relief, and let them get on with it.

Only then did it occur to her to wonder what had become of Egg and Iyamar. She grabbed her voice-box from her pocket and switched it on, pressing the buttons to call its partnered device. It beeped and flashed, but there was no answer. Serena waited, her stomach dropping with renewed anxiety.

Finally, Egg's voice. 'That better be Serena.'

Serena almost laughed with relief. 'Who else were you expecting?'

'The evil queen, after she'd stolen your device. Fabian?'

'Fabian's all right, but Tey's been shot.'

Silence for a second. 'And the bitch queen? Is she dead?' Egg's words were mildly flippant, but her voice held a degree of grimness Serena hadn't heard before.

'What? No, she isn't dead. She's—' Serena, looking around, broke off. Where *was* Halavere? A few moments ago she'd been secure in the grip of several of Bron's colleagues; now there was no sign of her. 'I don't know where she is right now.'

'When you find her, I get to kill her.'

'No one's killing her.'

'But—'

'Never mind. Get yourselves upstairs at once, if you please. We're up one and a couple of turns left from where we left you.'

The voice-box deadened without any answer from Egg, and Serena was left to wonder whether she intended to follow instructions at all.

But a few minutes later, Serena caught a flash of Egg's red hair as she elbowed her way unceremoniously through the cluster of uniformed people still thronging the hallway.

'Who are these people?' Egg said, panting a little.

'G.A.9, I think? Apparently they're saving our rears.'

Egg's eyebrows rose. 'Did we know about this?'

Serena shook her head. 'No. They'd better get Teyo out of here, that's all I'm saying.'

'They're my people,' said Bron, appearing behind Serena. 'And we just saved your man's life.' His hair was wildly dishevelled, and his shirt had developed a tear in the fabric at some point. 'Teyo's going to be fine, but he'll be out of action for a while. Might want to look to your brother, though.'

Serena nodded, already moving towards Fabian before Bron had finished speaking. 'Egg, can—'

'I'll stay with Teyo,' Egg interrupted.

'Me too,' said Iyamar.

Serena didn't stay to reply. In an instant she was at Fabian's side, wrapping an arm tentatively around his shoulders. 'Fabe? We're going home.'

Fabian stared sightlessly at her, and the look of anguish in his dark eyes broke her heart. 'I killed Teyo,' he whispered.

'No,' said Serena firmly. 'Tey's going to be all right.'

'I killed Teyo,' repeated Fabian, as though he hadn't heard her. 'And Valore *escaped*.'

Serena took his face in both of her hands. 'Look at me,' she ordered, and waited until his eyes focused upon her. 'Teyo is going to be *fine*. You killed no one.'

Fabian blinked twice, and then his gaze sharpened; at last he seemed to be truly seeing her. 'Thank goodness,' he whispered. 'But still, I almost—'

'Don't think about it now,' Serena said, and stood on tiptoe to place a kiss upon his forehead. 'Come home.'

'Valore—'

'Never mind her. She doesn't matter anymore.'

Fabian allowed himself to be led away. With the assistance and escort of Bron's colleagues, they made their escape from the Warren with a minimum of complications. Teyo was taken to Tinudren Sanatorium for treatment. Serena, Fabian, Egg and Iyamar returned home and retired, exhausted, to bed.

When Serena woke some hours later, befuddled but rested, she found Egg and Iyamar seated at the kitchen table, clutching identical mugs of something that steamed and smelled of cayluch.

246

'Serena...' said Egg. 'Um.'

Her tone gave it away. 'Fabian?' Serena whispered.

'He's gone. We don't know where.'

Panic spasmed, once again. 'Why didn't you wake me?!'

Egg set down her mug. 'His bed hasn't been slept in. He probably didn't stay much above half an hour, if that, and we discovered his absence all of twenty minutes ago.'

Serena whirled around, her head full of confused notions of following her brother. How large a head start did he truly have? Where might he have gone?'

'*Serena*,' Egg barked, with uncharacteristic authority. 'You can't follow him. He's long gone.'

'But I must,' Serena replied, heedless, her head full of one thought only: *find Fabian.*

'You can't,' said Egg brutally. 'He could be anywhere. Besides, has it not occurred to you that maybe he needs some time alone? Have you two ever been apart for more than a day or two?'

Serena turned slowly back around. 'I... well, no, but we've always been better together.'

'Maybe,' said Egg, her mouth twisting sceptically. 'Maybe not.'

'He's chasing Valore again,' said Serena desperately. 'I need to stop him, you don't know what he might do—'

'I know pretty well what he *might* do,' Egg interrupted. 'I don't know that he *will* do any of it. Neither do you. You don't know that he's chasing Valore. He could be lying on a beach somewhere right now.'

Serena shook her head. 'I doubt it.'

Egg grinned. 'I doubt it, too, but you never know. He was pretty shaken up, with what happened to Tey. I don't think he'll be in a hurry to rush out and try it again.'

Serena sighed, drew out a chair and sat down heavily upon it. 'I need a holiday.'

'Don't we all,' said Egg. She picked up her mug once more, drained the dregs of her cayluch and set it back down with a satisfied sigh. 'You did good, mother Serena. But it's time to stop flapping and clucking and settle down a bit.'

Serena fixed her with a steely glare. 'You're on *very* thin ice, Miss Rutherby.'

Egg grinned. 'Aren't I always?'

Serena opened her mouth to reply, but Iyamar thrust a steaming mug at her. 'Cayluch?'

Serena looked at Iya. The girl looked relaxed, she realised. So did Egg. The two of them seemed pretty comfortable together, sitting here drinking cayluch and chatting. Almost like they were friends. And Tey? Dear, good-hearted Tey, fiercely loved by every member of his team. He would be all right, and he would come home, and... and maybe Fabian would find his way home.

She had her team. They hadn't emerged unscathed, but they had emerged. They were okay. And maybe Fabian would be okay, too.

'Cayluch,' said Serena, accepting the mug with a smile. 'Cayluch would be just *fine.*'

EPILOGUE

Teyo arrived at their Draetre hideaway a few days later, escorted by two G.A.9 operatives and, to Serena's dismay, Bron. Tey was immediately put to bed in the room Serena had prepared for him. He looked thinner and drawn and somehow *smaller* than before, as if he had collapsed in upon himself. It wasn't a wholly physical complaint, Serena guessed, looking at the dark shadows under his eyes and the deepened lines around his mouth. He mustered only a tired smile for her as he was helped into bed, and then closed his eyes and fell swiftly into a deep sleep.

Serena presided over the two agents as they settled Teyo, ruthlessly ignoring Bron. The moment Teyo was asleep, she ushered everyone out of his room — her team, the G.A.9 agents and especially Bron — and shut the door carefully upon his slumber.

'Thank you for your care of Teyo,' she said to Bron in a wintry tone, and turned away. She had no desire for any further conversation with him.

Bron caught at her arm, stopping her. 'Can we talk?' he said in a low voice. He cast a glance around at his two colleagues and at Egg and Iya standing nearby, and added, 'In private?'

Serena sighed inwardly. She didn't want to grant his request, but Bron was impervious to hints. He would keep coming back until she dealt with him.

She took him into the parlour and shut the door on everyone else. 'What is it?' she said crisply.

Bron tried on one of his charming smiles, and took a step closer to Serena. 'I was hoping for a little gratitude,' he said.

Serena's brows shot up. 'What?'

'We saved your skin back there! Not to mention patching up your man. Come on, aren't you just a little bit grateful?'

Serena glared. 'Is that why you did it? To make me grateful?'

'No, of course not. I did it because it was the thing to do, you know? I knew your plan couldn't work. Just the few of you, to infiltrate the Warren and come out alive? You needed major backup, and you couldn't see it. This kind of job just isn't suited to small agencies like Torwyne.'

Serena's stare grew frostier than ever. 'So you just arranged it all, without telling me.'

'If I'd told you, would you have permitted it?' Bron folded his arms, unabashed.

'Whether I permitted it or not doesn't seem to have troubled you at all,' Serena said coldly. 'At least I would have been forewarned. If I couldn't have stopped you from bringing in your friends, at least I could have planned for it. As it was, you turned a shambles into total chaos.'

'Hey!' blurted Bron. 'That isn't fair. Can you deny that we got you out?'

'No,' Serena said, keeping hold of her temper with an effort. 'I can't. I *am* grateful to you for Teyo. But that's all. Who's to say that we couldn't have handled it, and handled it *better*, without your assistance? You killed several people. Your friends probably killed more.'

Bron shrugged. 'Just crooks.'

Serena's mouth dropped open in shock, and it took a few moments for her to muster her thoughts sufficiently to compose a sentence. 'You've treated me and my agency throughout as — as just — *amateurs*,' she spat. 'Small fish, wholly inconsequential. You've patronised us since the beginning. But if you were wondering why I chose to work with Torwyne instead of G.A.9, you've just demonstrated exactly why. *Just crooks?* No one is *ever* disposable. Teyo was "just a crook", once. So was Egg. With the right help, they've turned themselves around. They're some of the best people I know, and they're making a difference every day with what we're doing.' She drew herself up to her fullest height and stared at Bron with poisonous contempt. 'And you and yours would've cut them down without a thought.'

Bron blinked. 'Well… well, yes, once in a while there's an exception, and it's good that you got to those people.'

Serena's mouth twisted. 'The people you killed? Maybe they could've been "exceptions", too. There are reasons why we don't kill. But G.A9 just doesn't care.'

'If I hadn't killed those people, they would've killed you,' Bron said, his face darkening. 'Or your team. Doesn't that matter to you?'

'They might have,' Serena corrected him. 'They might not. There might have been something else we could've done, but you gave us no chance. You went straight for killing.'

'Oh, like *what*?' Bron said scornfully. 'What else do you propose to do when faced with armed assailants?'

'You could've aimed to wound and disarm,' Serena said. 'You could at least have *tried*.' Bron began to say something else, but she held up a hand. 'Enough, please. I don't wish to hear any more. Thank you for bringing Teyo home, and have a safe journey to wherever you're going.'

Bron eyed her. 'And that's it?'

'That's it.'

'I was hoping maybe we could get together some time. Have a meal somewhere. There's a great place I know not far away, they've got the best ice cream for miles —'

'Stop!' Serena all but shouted the word. 'Gracious, is there truly no end to your effrontery? After everything I just said?'

Bron just blinked at her, hopelessly befuddled. 'What? I like you, you've got spunk. We could be good together.'

Serena marched to the door and yanked it open. 'Out,' she hissed. 'I'm going to hope very hard that I never see you again, though I imagine that's too much to ask.'

Bron sighed and crossed to the door. 'If you change your mind —' he began.

'OUT!'

Bron left, his face set. Probably he was more displeased by her rejection than her contemptuous words of before; his was that kind of ego. Serena watched Bron and his two associates out of the house, then firmly shut the door upon them all.

Egg and Iya showed up moments later. 'We heard all that,' Egg said.

'Tosspot,' said Iya concisely.

'Pisseater,' added Egg.

'Clotpole.'

Egg blinked at her. 'Clotpole?'

'It's an insult,' Iya explained. 'It means...' she frowned, and thought. 'Actually, I don't know what it means.'

'Did you make that up?' Egg eyed her young friend suspiciously.

'Yeah.' Iya grinned. 'Might have, at that.'

Serena threw an arm around each of them and squeezed. 'You two are a delight,' she said. 'I'm grateful for *you*.'

Teyo slept, almost uninterruptedly, for the next two days. Serena hovered outside his room, anxious to learn how he went on but afraid to disturb him. When he finally showed signs of waking, she almost had to physically restrain Egg and Iyamar from leaping upon him at once. Between them, they plied poor Teyo so liberally with food and drink — everything he could possibly desire, all at once, and without delay — that he was obliged to beg for mercy.

They gathered in his room late one afternoon, when his strength was returning and colour once more graced his drawn cheeks. Everyone wanted to sit near Teyo; Serena was obliged to cede the bed to Egg and Iyamar, who perched one on either side of him. She herself settled in an armchair nearby. Tey's eyes followed her, but he didn't say anything.

The conversation was frivolous, for a time. Egg and Iya took turns ribbing Tey about all manner of things, each trying their hardest to draw a smile from him. It wasn't an easy task. Teyo had been quiet and withdrawn ever since his return; his characteristic, easy-going charm had subsided into silence, and his ready smile had vanished.

'Look,' said Teyo after a while, 'I know what you're trying to do, but I wish you wouldn't. I...' He tailed off, his hands plucking restlessly at the coverlet. 'I'm going to be... that is, I... I can't.' He paused, his face anguished. 'I can't do it anymore. I'm sorry. I'm off the team.'

Nobody spoke.

'I know I'm disappointing you,' Teyo said sadly, 'and I'm so sorry.' Serena thought she saw a sheen of tears in his eyes, before he turned his face away.

Egg laid a hand over his. 'Tey,' she murmured. 'How did you know Fabe was going to shoot Halavere?'

Teyo blinked at her, nonplussed by the sudden conversational diversion. 'Uh? Oh, I. Well. That place Fabian was, at that moment? I've been there before.' He sighed, and seemed to shrivel a little into himself. 'Years ago. Back when I was Yllandu. I, um. I found some of the people who'd… there was a robbery at my father's business. He and my mother and brother were killed, and the place was burned down. Nobody knew how or why the fire started, but it didn't matter. I was burned, but I got out alive. And, years later I… I found one of them again. And I almost killed him. With a knife.' Teyo stopped speaking, his eyes unfocused as he stared into the past. 'That look on Fabe's face? I knew it instantly, and I knew he couldn't hold back. I also knew… he'd regret it. If he carried it through. He's not the type to kill without regrets; he's got too much conscience.'

'You regret it, then?' Egg said, gently.

Teyo nodded. 'You can't repay death with death, it only spreads the misery. Do you see? I satisfied my rage, but I almost took a life. I could've made a family husbandless, fatherless. He might have been *scum*, but who was I to decide he deserved to die?' He passed a shaking hand over his face. 'That's why I'm here. I had to do *something* good, something constructive. I needed to combat the bad in this messed up world, but without adding to it. Do you see?'

'Totally,' Egg said.

'But I don't know if I made the right choice. Have I done enough good, or have I inadvertently made everything worse? A few days ago, I almost died. A lot of Yllandu *did* die, including my oldest friend. And Fabian… Fabian's broken and gone, partly because I kept secrets from him. And from you.' He almost, but didn't quite, look at Serena. 'It's time I finished this.'

Egg nodded once with satisfaction, and looked to Serena. 'Do you want to tell him, or shall I?'

Teyo blinked. 'What?'

Serena stood up, gently shoved Egg aside, and perched carefully on the edge of Teyo's bed. 'First, your friend — Levan? — isn't dead. He's pulled through. And he tells us that the casualties in the Warren weren't as bad as they might have appeared. Only three died.'

'Three,' repeated Teyo, dully.

'Three,' said Serena. 'And according to Levan, they were rotten to the core and the bastards deserved it.' She paused. 'Those were his words.'

Teyo stared at her in confusion. 'You've spoken to Levan?'

'Yes, and so will you, quite soon. The other thing is—'

'Levan is *here*?' Teyo moved as though he intended to get out of bed. Serena restrained him with a hand to his torso.

'Peace, Tey,' she said softly. 'Rest first. Levan's not here, but you'll see him soon.'

Teyo subsided, collapsing back into his pillows. The look of pain in his eyes had eased a little, and Serena smiled. 'Now, the next bit: you'll like this. We've seen Oliver, and—'

'Oh, blazes.' Teyo covered his face with his good hand. 'How bad is it?'

'Not at all bad, in any conceivable way,' Serena reassured him. 'Look.' She put a piece of paper into his good hand, but Teyo merely stared at it, unseeing. Serena took it back, opened it out and held it before his face. 'See what that is?'

Teyo blinked, and frowned. 'No.'

'What?' Serena stared hard at Teyo, alarmed. Had something happened to his eyesight, some unforeseen consequence of his injuries? 'Why?'

'Because you're holding it too close to my face.'

'Oh.' She pulled it back a few inches, but Teyo grabbed it from her.

'It's a deed,' he said after a moment. 'I don't understand. What is this?'

'It's the deed to a piece of land,' said Serena. She was so excited she could barely contain it, but she forced herself to speak calmly. 'It's a farm in southern Nimdre. Not too close to Tinudren, don't worry.'

'My name is on this,' said Teyo, blankly.

'That's because it's yours.'

'Huh?'

'Oliver's idea. It's waiting for you. We're travelling there as soon as you're feeling lively enough.'

Teyo blinked. 'We?'

Serena nodded. 'Oliver felt you'd earned a peaceful retirement. He said he's expecting some especially good gloren cider in a couple of years, when you've had time to get set up. As for the rest of us, apparently we need a holiday.' She grinned at him, her excitement overflowing.

'A holiday?' Teyo repeated numbly. Serena fully understood his feelings: Oliver Tullen, head of the Torwyne Agency, hadn't previously appeared to be *aware* of the concept of a holiday.

'He was pretty firm about it,' she said. 'Told us we could consider it suspension from duty, if that would help.'

'Oh.' Teyo stared at Serena for a second, then back at the paper in his hand. He didn't look delighted; more… lost. 'I, um. Hope you have a good holiday.'

Oh, foolish man. 'Tey,' Serena said gently. 'This farm of yours. It's been empty for a while, and it's not in great shape. It needs a lot of work to make it habitable, and productive. You're going to need some help.'

Teyo's brows rose. 'Oh? How much help?'

'Three able-bodied women have volunteered, for a start.' Serena smiled. 'Winter's in the air. That gives us two or three months to sort out the house, I'd think? Then in the spring, it's time to get started on your orchards.'

'Orchards,' Teyo repeated in a whisper.

'Acres of them,' Serena said. 'Gloren fruit, nara, rylanes, even pippeens. Some of the trees are a bit sickly, not best suited to the climate perhaps, or the light. You might want to rethink the crop distribution, but there's time for all that.'

'Serena.' Teyo dropped the deed and gripped her hand, a little painfully. 'You've seen it?'

Serena nodded.

'What…' Teyo's words dried up; he moistened his lips and tried again. 'What's it like?'

Serena beamed at him, and squeezed his hand. 'It's perfect, Tey. Perfect for you.'

'And it's really mine?'

'Every last inch of it.'

Teyo pondered that for a while, his gaze straying from Egg to Iya and back to Serena. 'That must have cost a bob or two,' he said.

'Well, yes.'

His eyes narrowed. 'You surely aren't expecting me to believe that Oliver just gave this to me.'

'No,' Serena admitted. 'He only paid for, um. Some of it.'

Teyo nodded. 'Uh huh. And the rest came from…?'

Serena coughed. 'Um, we might have rustled up a little between us. But that's beside the point, Tey! Don't ask these questions! Just enjoy it.' She smiled, but Teyo wasn't having it.

'Serena.' He shook her her arm insistently. 'Tell me you didn't bankrupt yourselves over this.'

'Noooo,' she smiled. 'Not in the least. I *did* say it was empty for a while! The owner was delighted to finally get rid of it.'

Teyo looked at Egg, his face full of suspicion.

'It's true,' Egg drawled. 'No one's bankrupted. Miss Carterett here has at *least* three Nimdren pennies left to her name. It might even be four.'

Serena glared at Egg, who looked wholly unrepentant.

'I can't...' croaked Teyo. 'I can't accept that.' He tried to give the deed back to Serena, but she waved it away.

'Pshaw, of course you can. Besides, it's too late now! We can't hand the farm back.'

'Not that we *would*,' interjected Iyamar. 'Serena's right, Tey! It's so perfect for you. You'll love it so much, when you get there.'

Teyo shook his head. 'But *why*,' he said in confusion, 'Why would Oliver? Why would *you*...?'

'Because we love you,' said Egg, and smiled.

Teyo blinked. 'Oh.' His eyes strayed to Serena's face. She detected a sheen of tears in them, for definite, and felt moved to lay a kiss on his forehead.

'It's true,' she said. 'We do. And we are *raring* to get going on that gorgeous house, so I hope you plan to get better quickly.'

A tear dropped, and Teyo hastily wiped it off his cheek. 'Thank you,' he whispered. 'I don't... know how to...'

'Then stop talking,' Serena recommended, 'and sleep some more. You'll need your strength.'

'But if we're all going, and for months, what about Fabe?'

Serena's ebullience faded a little. 'If... *when* Fabe comes back, he'll go to Oliver. And Oliver will tell him where to find us.'

Teyo nodded. 'We'll keep a room for him.'

Serena smiled. 'He'll appreciate that.'

The following morning, there came a knock upon the door of their little hideaway. Serena was not surprised, upon opening it, to find Orintha Mae standing there. She was only surprised that the Lokant woman hadn't paid them a call sooner.

'Come in,' said Serena graciously, opening the door wide. 'May I say how flattered I am that you used the door, rather than simply appearing in my bedroom?'

Mae's lips twitched sardonically as she stepped into the house, dusting a speck of mud off the long, sky-coloured coat that she wore. 'You credit me with powers I don't possess, I assure you.'

'Oh?' Serena shut the door behind her somewhat unwelcome visitor, and led her to the parlour. Egg and Iya had gone out to the market and Teyo was still asleep, so they were, to all intents and purposes, alone. 'Seems to me that various of your associates have appeared in some mighty strange places, of late.'

'It's not as impressive as it looks,' said Mae. 'Nor as flexible. There was preparation involved. Anyway, that's not what I came to discuss.'

Serena acknowledged that with a nod, and gestured Mae to a seat. 'Something to do with Ylona, I imagine?'

'Where are the keys?' said Mae, without preamble.

Serena shrugged. 'The ones I had are gone. I know nothing more.'

Mae sipped from the glass of water Serena handed to her, then set it carefully down upon the table. Flashing Serena one of her charming smiles, she said: 'Let us not waste time dissembling, Miss Carterett. I am acquainted with the adventure you and your team enjoyed by way of our keys. I would like to know what you did with them afterwards.'

Serena blinked. 'But if you know about that, then you know that we *reversed* the event of Fabian's death, and everything that happened afterwards. So, in effect we never had anything to do with the keys after they were taken from us.'

Mae raised a single, speaking brow. 'So it never happened, did it?'

'Not anymore,' Serena said. 'We unmade it, I suppose?'

Mae nodded wisely. 'And yet, you remember it.'

'Uh,' Serena said.

'How is it that you recall every detail of it, if it never happened?'

'So it *did* happen, even if we changed it afterwards?'

'Apparently.' Cool as a mountain stream, Mae sipped her water.

An appalling thought occurred to Serena. 'But then... that

means... does *Fabian* remember everything?'

'I imagine so.'

If he did, he must remember his own death. Blazes. No wonder he had bolted.

Serena shook off these reflections. 'Even if all of this is true,' she said, 'I don't know what became of the keys. None of us cared about them, after we'd gained access to the repository.'

'Oh? None of you?'

'No. Why should we? Fabian was our concern, and we didn't need the keys after that. Our assignment was over, there was nothing more for us to do.'

'Tell me everything that happened,' said Mae, and Serena complied. When she'd finished, Mae sat in thoughtful silence for some time, tapping her long fingernails against the table.

'If Ylona went through to the repository and remained there, then the keys should still be in the gate. But, they are not.'

Serena blinked. When she had returned to her quarters after their disastrous second attempt at the Warren, the keys had been gone, just like the first time. As far as she could figure, then, Ylona's people had still taken them, and they had, presumably, still gone through to the repository. But since, the second time around, Serena and her team had *not* followed them and taken the keys, then the seven stones should still be in the gate. If they weren't, whyever not? How could that be possible?

Mae smiled faintly. 'The way I see it,' she said at last, 'there are a few possibilities regarding the fate of those keys. One: you're correct in thinking that you diverted the course of events. Perhaps Ylona and her people never went through the gate, or perhaps they travelled to the repository, accomplished whatever it was they set out to do, and came back — taking the keys with them. But if that were the case, I'd expect to see some big changes around the Seven Realms right now. Such as, for example, the mysterious reappearance of the long-lost Library of Orlind. Since that hasn't happened, I do not think that Ylona made it back from the repository. Perhaps she never set foot in there in the first place.

'Two: perhaps the actions of your colleague, Miss Rutherby, hold true in spite of your subsequent jaunting about in time. In which case, the keys may still be in the repository. If that's so, I shall be glad of it, as it effectively seals the door forever. That would also explain where Ylona and her followers are;

presumably they remain with Rhoun Torinth.'

She shifted in her seat, fixing Serena with an iron stare. 'The third possibility is that the keys did *not* remain in the repository. The same person who transported them there may have transported them away again.' She raised her brows at Serena, and sipped.

'If Egg had them, she would have told me,' Serena said.

'Would she indeed.'

'Undoubtedly. We have no secrets among my team.'

Mae nodded slowly. 'No doubt you are right, only I find the mystery curiously impenetrable. Ylona has vanished, along with her little riddles in the sky. Rhoun Torinth is not only alive, he was also persuaded to leave his precious repository for the first time in I-don't-know-*how*-long. But there is no sign of him either. And the keys are missing, but there is surprisingly little furore about it — if one overlooks the crushing disappointment, outrage and general confusion suffered by the fine people of the Seven, now that their treasure hunt is over without the discovery of any apparent prize. And I find that you and your excellent fellows have considerably muddied the waters with your meddling.'

Serena's brows shot up. 'I'm sorry if we complicated your life,' she said with a touch of asperity. 'Meanwhile, I have my brother back.'

Mae inclined her head. 'And I am glad of it, though I could wish you had handled things a little more professionally *before*, and therefore spared yourselves the necessity of bumbling about fixing your mistakes *afterwards*.' Serena opened her mouth, but Mae held up a hand. 'Save yourself the trouble, dear. I am a crotchety old woman, and I won't hear a word that you try to tell me.'

Serena simmered inwardly, and said nothing.

Mae got up, patting a stray wisp of her coifed white hair back into place. 'I will go, but I won't be far away,' she said. 'If you should happen to discover what became of those keys, I hope you'll inform me.'

'I'll consider it,' said Serena coolly.

Mae smiled graciously. 'Lovely. And now, if you'll excuse me, I have a dinner appointment with my delightful great-grand-daughter and her charming husband. Do wish your colleague a speedy recovery, on my behalf.'

259

Serena was given no time to respond, for Mae vanished in a blink, leaving her standing alone in the parlour.

Egg sauntered in a moment later. 'I wasn't eavesdropping,' she said.

Serena snorted. 'So, you may as well tell me.'

Egg's head tilted curiously to one side. 'Tell you what?'

'Do you have the keys?'

'What keys?' Egg grinned, her eyes twinkling at Serena's discomfort.

'Egg! Come on. This is important.'

'I might do,' said Egg.

'You do have them!'

'Then again,' Egg continued, 'I might not.'

Serena glowered.

Egg swung a chair out from the table and threw herself into it. 'Come on,' she said. 'Seriously. Those keys are a nightmare. If I did have them, would you really want to know?'

'Yes,' said Serena without hesitation.

'Why?'

'It's my job.'

Egg shook her head. 'Nuh-huh. It *was* your job, when we were hired to participate in the whole weird, treasure-hunt adventure thing. It's not part of our assignment anymore. Our *assignment*, in case you'd forgotten, is to muck about on Teyo's farm and get our shoes very muddy indeed.'

'Egg—'

'You don't want to know what became of the keys,' said Egg bluntly, all trace of humour gone from her face and voice. 'Think about it. Rhoun Torinth was right. Imagine if you knew you could always change things, no matter what went wrong. What would that do to your life? You'd grow careless, thinking there would always be some recourse. You'd stop caring about things, knowing you could always fix everything so you could get what you want. And you wouldn't be able to ever relax and *enjoy* anything, because you'd feel like it was your responsibility to fix everything that might go wrong in the lives of those around you. You'd be eaten up by guilt every time you didn't. What's that but a perfect nightmare? What I recommend is: put those keys out of your mind and pretend none of it ever happened. That's what I'm planning to do.'

Serena stared narrowly at her friend, but neither Egg's words nor her demeanour revealed any clue as to whether she had the keys or not. 'Just tell me one thing,' she said. 'Fabian. Does he have them?'

Egg's eyes narrowed. She appeared to consider this question for a little while, and finally, infinitesimally, shook her head.

Serena sagged with relief. No fear that Fabian was out there trying to change their shared history. 'Very well,' she said. 'We can leave the topic alone for now, but we'll talk about this again, someday.'

'Deal,' said Egg, and jumped up. 'Right, anyway. Are you packed? Teyo says he's feeling much better. I reckon we could leave the day after tomorrow, even.'

All of Serena's worries vanished in an instant, and a broad smile crossed her face. 'Really? That's wonderful! I can't wait to show him the farm. I'm not packed, are you?'

Egg shook her head, and gave an exaggerated bow, gesturing towards the doorway with a grand sweep of her arm. 'After you, boss.'

Upon reaching her room, Serena discovered a new addition to her narrow, cosy bed. Laid with utmost care across the end was a gorgeously sunset-coloured blanket, knitted in a delicate lace pattern. Touching it, Serena found it to be deliciously soft as well.

Smiling, she folded it up and placed it reverently inside her travel bag.

MORE STORIES BY CHARLOTTE E. ENGLISH:

THE DRAYKON SERIES:

Draykon
Lokant
Orlind
Llandry
Evastany

Seven Dreams

THE DRIFTING ISLE CHRONICLES:

Black Mercury

www.charlotteenglish.com

Made in the USA
Las Vegas, NV
13 September 2021

30208417R10148